THE Lonely Hearts TRAVEL CLUB

DESTINATION: INDIA

Praise for
KATY COLINS

'Brilliant, life-affirming story of a jilted bride who heads off to explore Thailand. Perfect escapism.'

– Heat

'Katy writes with humour and heart. *The Lonely Hearts Travel Club* is like Bridget Jones goes backpacking.'

– Holly Martin, author of *The White Cliff Bay* series

'It is a really enthralling page turner and a brilliant start to a new series. I can't wait to read the sequels, *Destination India* and *Destination Chile*!'

– Splashes into Books

'I cannot recommend this book enough. It is beautifully written with a brilliant plot and fantastic characters. READ IT!!'

– Blabbering About Books

'If you're looking for an escape from the cold, winter nights, the drudgery of day-to-day life and love to read about exotic locations then Katy Colins' debut novel is the book for you.'

– Ellen Faith

'*Destination Thailand* had me hooked from the very first page and kept me up til 2:30am as I was dying to know what happened next. I'm thrilled to have found Katy's books and cannot wait to see what is in store in the next instalment of the series, *Destination India*. I want to read it now!'

– Books and Boardies

'I loved this book.'

– For the Love of Books

Katy Colins

CARINA™

First Published in Great Britain 2016
By Carina, an imprint of HarperCollins*Pubishers*
1 London Bridge Street, London, SE1 9GF

ISBN 978-0-263-92369-8

98-0616

Our policy is to use papers that are natural, renewable and recyclable products and made from wood grown in sustainable forests.
The logging and manufacturing processes conform to the legal environmental regulations of the country of origin.

Printed and bound by
CPI Group (UK) Ltd, Croydon, CR0 4YY

KATY COLINS

Katy completed her first novel *A Dogs Tale* at the age of 11 which received rave reviews . . . from her Grandad and English teacher. This was just the encouragement she needed to carry on writing.

As a qualified journalist with articles published in *Company* Magazine and *The Daily Star*, Katy Colins crossed sides to work in public relations before selling all she owned to back-pack solo around South East Asia and finally put her thoughts into words, writing as she travelled. This experience inspired her debut novel *Destination Thailand*, the first in the Lonely Hearts Travel Club series which is out now.

When she is not writing about romance, travel and adventure, she loves travelling, catching up with family and friends, and convincing herself that her Mr Kipling cake addiction isn't out of control – just yet.

You can find out more about Katy, her writing and her travels on her blog www.notwedordead.com or via twitter @notwedordead

Available from
KATY COLINS

The Lonely Hearts Travel Club

Destination Thailand

Destination India

Destination Chile

Darling, I won't let you fall when
I know that you can fly.

Isobel, this is for you.

CHAPTER 1

Turbid (adj.) Confused; muddled

The first thing I heard were the keys at the door, scratching and jangling against each other as the lock slowly turned.

Bollocks. I'd done it again.

I whipped my head off my laptop, QWERTY imprinted on my left cheek as I rubbed my tired eyes, probably wiping the residue of clumped, black mascara everywhere. I heard the clanging of the metal bell as the door opened, and quickly hid under my desk, wincing at the pain of cracking my funny bone on my metal chair leg – not so bloody funny at all. Pulling my knees up to my chin I tried to tuck myself in the corner, hoping that he wouldn't notice my shoes forlornly left at the edge of my desk.

I heard his heavy footsteps slowly clump across the tiled floor, tiles that had been imported from Morocco by the previous owner, once dusted with desert sand but now forever ingrained with Manchester mud and dirt in the narrow cracks. They were beautiful but a bugger to keep clean. He was whistling to himself; I could just make out the tune from that TV series that everyone was talking about but I'd never got around to watching. I mentally slapped myself for being in this position again but there was no way I would let him find me here. No way.

Suddenly his footsteps stopped. My breath caught in my throat. I could make out his smart chestnut-brown shoes from here, the ones that I'd seen in the shop window down the road when they were in the January sales and mentioned how much they would suit him.

The shoes were now facing in my direction. I tried to stay as still as I could. A deep sigh replaced the whistling. *Why is he not moving?* I could feel my heartbeat hammering through my chest. Why had I done it again? Put myself in this ridiculous situation with only myself to blame. As his feet picked up and started to edge closer to my desk, I heard the door being flung open once more.

'All right?' Kelli's croaky morning voice filled the silent room.

'Morning, Kel, did you leave the lights on last night before you left?' he asked.

I heard Kelli groan. I could imagine her rolling her heavily kohled eyes, throwing him her best sarky look, the one she had down to a tee.

'What? Nah, weren't me. I left before Georgia did.' She yawned loudly. I could now see her dirty, battered Converse trainers edge into my view, her once-white laces caked in what looked like brown sludge. I really did need to give this floor a proper going over, something else to add to my forever growing to-do list. Maybe I'd hire one of those super-duper carpet vacs or steam cleaners. I was sure my mum had one that she'd won at the bingo a while back. *Focus, Georgia. Focus on staying out of view.* I tensed my body once more. My shoulders ached from being hunched over my laptop all night and now pins and needles started tickling my legs.

'Oh, right,' Ben said. His feet were out of my eye line now. I heard the wooden sign clang against the pane of glass in the door, turning us from closed to open. 'Can you just turn Georgia's lamp off then? I'll have a word with her when she gets in. Maybe it's some new security measure she's put in place,' he called out.

Shit. I'd forgotten that I'd left that on.

'Yeah, fine,' Kelli mumbled, sloping over towards me. Her feet were just next to my chair. I could see her pale white legs through the rips in her faded denim jeans. 'Can't she turn her own bloody lights off?' I heard her grumble under her breath as she reached across my desk. I scrunched my eyes shut. How was I going to get myself out of here without either of them seeing me?

'Damn. We're out of milk. Could you go and grab us some coffees? You can take some change from the kitty tin,' Ben called over from the small kitchen at the back of the room.

'Fine,' Kelli huffed, knocking one of my pens to the floor.

'Careful,' Ben warned. 'Don't mess up her desk.'

'Yeah, we both know how OCD she is,' Kelli replied, sniggering.

'Organised, Kelli. The word you're looking for is organised,' Ben said. I could sense a smile in his voice.

'Hmm, more like psycho control freak if you ask me,' Kelli muttered quietly.

'What was that?'

'Nothing. I just said I won't make a mess.'

I wasn't a psycho control freak nor did I have OCD. I just liked order. I liked to keep tabs on things, to have a plan, to know that everything was going as it should – so yeah, I did need to have some level of organisation, something Kelli could do well with learning, I silently seethed.

Kelli's skinny arm dipped down to pick the pen up, her hand fumbling on the floor inches from my feet followed by her blue-streaked hair and anaemically pale face. Her bloodshot eyes clocked mine. 'Oh!'

I pressed my finger to my lips, wincing.

'What?' Ben called out.

I shook my head and pointed to the roof of the desk. A slow smirk broke out on Kelli's face and she straightened herself up.

'Nothing. I just, erm, just found that stapler I've been looking for.' Her feet backed out of view. 'Erm, actually I think you should get the coffees. I've got lady problems and shouldn't be out in the cold air for too long.'

I stifled a laugh. Nicely done, Kelli; every woman knows if you want to get out of doing something then talking about your period is the number one way to spook a man out.

I could sense Ben's face turning a lovely shade of crimson as I heard him stutter. 'Right, OK. Not a problem. You just, erm, get to work and I'll grab us some coffee.'

Kelli dramatically slunked onto the office chair opposite. 'Thanks, Ben. *Really* appreciate it. I promise I'll go when I'm off the blob.'

I heard a rustle of fabric and the bell tingling as the door opened and quickly closed again. Nervously I peeked around my filing cabinet to check the coast was clear.

'S'all right. He's gone,' Kelli said, swinging her feet up. I crawled out from under my desk and picked off large pieces of fluff from my creased skirt. 'You slept here again then?'

'I don't know how it happened. I was working on the European trips and the next thing Ben's coming through the door waking me up. He really can't find me like this, not after what happened last time.' Kelli and I both winced at that memory.

A few weeks ago I'd been burning the candle at both ends to get a pitch presentation finished for a new tour operator we were hoping to partner with when I'd fallen asleep at my desk. Ben had found me drooling on one of the slides and when he'd woken me so abruptly I'd accidently spilt a whole mug of cold tea over my laptop. The laptop where I'd collated all our hard work and hadn't saved a copy, meaning all that effort was for nothing. The technicians hadn't been able to save anything as brown drips puddled around my keyboard. Ben had shrugged that it was just one of those things, a lesson in the importance of backing up our work, but I knew he was pissed off.

When we first started this business I had visions of us spending our days working hard but having fun with it, and our evenings wrapped around each other in bed. I hadn't realised how much this company had pushed us away from each other. The come-to-bed eyes had been replaced with looks of disappointment.

I glanced at the clock; it was gone nine a.m. I wouldn't have time to get home and change without Ben wondering why I was so late. I'd just have to hand iron the crumples in my skirt and hope he wouldn't notice I was wearing the same blouse as the day before. I pulled on my black, scuffed heels and scurried to the bathroom to try and sort out the bird's nest masquerading as my hair.

'I've got some make-up you can borrow if you want?' Kelli called out behind me. Glancing at the purple bags under my bloodshot brown eyes, my sallow, almost greyish skin and the furry coating on my teeth, I accepted. Moments later I resembled less the night of the walking dead and more the morning of the walking dead. Heavy powder caked my cheeks, a smear of maroon lipstick and a flick of thick kohl completed the look. I wasn't sure if it was an improvement but at least I'd got the crusty sleep from my eyes and rubbed the creases from my face. My hair was another matter – in desperate need of some TLC

I couldn't even remember the last time I'd managed to visit a hairdresser, let alone had some home hair care. Wiry, dull and sticking up in tufts, it looked a mess.

''Ere, just try and pin it back.' Kelli handed me some grips.

'Thanks, Kel, I really appreciate this.' I took them and smiled at her, hurriedly pulling strands of hair from my face and prising a hairgrip in.

'No probs, boss. I, erm, didn't mean what I said about you being a psycho control freak either.' She scuffed her shoes on the floor.

'I don't know what you're talking about,' I said with a half-smile. The dinging of the bell caught us both.

'Kel?' Ben called out. 'They didn't have your half-fat, extra-tall, two-shot latte so I got you a normal filter coffee that's apparently for someone called Heyli.'

Kelli left me to continue sorting myself out. 'Right, fine, thanks.'

'Is Georgia here? Why is her coat on the floor?' I heard his trousers rustle as he bent down to pick up my jacket that I'd dropped in the hurry to make myself presentable.

'Erm, well, er…' Kelli mumbled.

'I'm here!' I walked out smiling, trying to look as fresh and well slept as I could. 'Sorry, I must have knocked my jacket over as I nipped to the loo.'

'Hey, morning,' Ben said looking slightly bemused by the new look I was rocking on my face. 'You…erm…look nice today. Here, they didn't mess up on your order.'

'Thanks.' I blushed and quickly sat at my desk, acting as normal as I could. I gratefully took the steaming coffee from Ben, trying to ignore his furrowed brow that suggested he was trying to work out what was different about me. 'So, you ready for our staff meeting?'

'Yep.' He pulled himself together and headed over to his desk.

Staff meetings were in all the business management books I'd been trying to read; OK, well, I'd downloaded the audio books onto my iPhone as they helped drown out the noise of rowdy school kids getting the same bus as me to town every morning. Apparently staff meetings were vital in ensuring that all tasks are evenly distributed, targeted and have measurable results, as well as checking in with your colleagues in a bid to strengthen team relations… or something like that. I never could concentrate on the droning voice on *1001 ways to improve your business* when some spotty teen was playing Justin Bieber out of their tinny phone speakers.

When I'd suggested we hold weekly staff meetings both Kelli and Ben had tried not to laugh at me. With just the three of us working here, plus the occasional visit from Ben's godmother and previous owner Trisha, they'd scoffed that we didn't need them but I'd insisted. Mostly because I needed to make sure that every ball we were juggling wasn't being dropped.

'Kel? You ready?' I called out.

'Yeah.' She grabbed a notepad, mostly full of her angst-ridden scribbles, and sat on the edge of the sofa, ignoring my pursed look when she flipped her feet onto one of the chenille cushions.

'Great, so…' I scanned my tired eyes down my to-do list, mentally reminding myself to add steam clean the floor and bring in a spare change of clothes that I could leave under my desk, in case I pulled an all-nighter again. Just in case. 'We've got the visuals back for the summer campaign that I sent both of you. I didn't have time for your feedback so signed it off but trust me it looks really good. Then coming up this week we've got the tour going to Iceland; Kelli, will you make sure that you email the tour guide with everyone's passport details?' She nodded.

'Actually, I can just do that; it'll only take two minutes. We also need to send the updated itinerary out. I've started that so may as well finish it,' I said, crossing a line through it.

I ignored Ben's quizzical look and continued to scan down my list.

'OK, so next on the agenda is the Indian tour leaving in a couple of weeks. As you know this is proving to be one of our bestsellers and definitely where we need to be focusing our energy, so although the demand is there I really think we need to question our relationship with the visa company that we've been using.'

'What's wrong with them?' Ben asked.

'Well, nothing. I just think we could do a better job if it was all in-house. Apparently streamlining a business's services only adds value.' I ignored them both raising an eyebrow at me. 'I'll look into that –'

'Georgia,' Ben cut me off.

'Yep?' I looked up from my list.

'Is there anything you want Kelli and me to do?'

'Oh yep, sorry,' I replied sheepishly. 'Kel, if you could sort out getting a steam cleaner as these tiles need a good going over?' She wouldn't be able to mess that task up. 'And, Ben, you've got enough to worry about with preparing for the Travel Trade Convention and getting the copy finalised for the website. You said you'd have the new "what's happening" page live by last week…and well…it's still not gone up.'

'It was yesterday that you asked me to do that. Not last week,' he said with a slight frown.

'Oh really?' God had it only been yesterday? 'Well, either way it needs to be sorted, please.'

'Consider it done,' he replied with a wink that made my lady parts do a funny wiggle.

I cleared my throat, forcing myself back on track. 'Thanks, and finally I was also thinking that we should look into each learning a new language? Take a class over lunch or something like that? It would really help with attracting new clients and in building relationships with foreign guides if we can speak their language.'

Looking expectantly at their faces I could tell my new idea had fallen on deaf ears.

'I think that might be one for the future maybe?' Ben said softly, trying not to laugh as Kelli yawned dramatically.

'Yeah, maybe we can re-visit that soon, although I've read that Mandarin is the most widely spoken language in the world, so we really should be hitting that market. Oh and then last but not least, I've managed to get a meeting with Hostel Planners later this week to see if we could tie in some of our tours with them.'

'You didn't say.' Ben's deep brown eyes caught mine. A flash of confusion and hurt flickered across his face.

'I only found out this morning, I-I mean last night,' I stuttered.

'You want me to come with you to that? You know your list is sounding pretty heavy – it might be best to share the load a little, Georgia?' He tilted his head at me.

'It's all under control. Trust me.' I smiled weakly, not wanting to look at Kelli who I could feel was giving me a look that said she knew things weren't under control.

'If you're sure.' Ben wasn't letting this go.

'Ben, I'm sure,' I said, a little more forthrightly than I'd meant to. I softened my tone. 'Sorry, I think you've got enough to look after with preparing for the convention. How's your speech coming on? Do you want to practise it with us? Maybe you could send it over so I can check it before you go?' I tried to say it as lightly as I could, hoping to sound like a caring colleague, not a control freak who needed to keep tabs on exactly what it was he would be saying.

'It's all under control.' He grinned, tapping a finger to the side of his head.

'But you *have* written it down?'

Ben smiled and waved his hands around. 'Yeah, it'll be fine.'

He hadn't written it down. He always said that he preferred to speak off the cuff, but just the thought of that made me physically shiver. I nodded and added *write Ben's speech* onto my notepad. I'd just try and sneak it into his pocket so it would be there if, sorry *when* he needed it and he'd come back thanking me for helping him.

'Right, so, anyone else got anything to add?'

Ben shook his head but Kelli raised a skinny arm. 'It's not really work-related but my band are playing at the Academy tomorrow night.'

'Wow, that's amazing!' Ben said.

Kelli blushed. 'Nah, it ain't the real Academy, it's the one in Rusholme above a curry house but still it's a gig. I guess.' She paused collecting her thoughts. 'So, I wondered if you both wanted to come? I'll put you on the guest list if you fancy it. You know, if you weren't too busy or anythin'?' She nibbled her thin bottom lip.

'Course we'll be there. Won't we, Georgia?' Ben said, interrupting me from scrolling through the calendar on my phone.

'It might not be your kinda vibe but the booze is cheap and you get ten per cent off any curry *and* free poppadums if you come.'

'Georgia? You in?' Ben persisted.

'Yeah, yeah sounds good,' I said distractedly giving them both a tight smile. 'Right, let's get down to work.'

It had turned out to be a good day actually, minus the dramatic, unprofessional start. We'd had four walk-ins who booked tours on the spot and another six who took brochures away, making all the positive noises of coming back to pay a deposit. I was just in the middle of my emails when my phone buzzed: Mother calling.

'Hi, Mum, I haven't got long. I'm pretty snowed under,' I answered quickly.

'You always say that,' she tutted, and I rolled my eyes. 'Well, I won't keep you, it was just to check that you haven't forgotten about tonight.'

Tonight? Tonight? My mind raced through my mental to-do list. What was tonight?

'Erm… Yep. It's all under control,' I lied.

She breathed a sigh of relief. 'Great. Your dad is so excited to see you. We'll let the rush-hour traffic die down before we head out. You know he doesn't like to drive when all the maniacs fill the roads,' she babbled. 'What time is the restaurant booked for again?'

I paused. Then suddenly it all came rushing back. I quickly glanced at my calendar to check I was right. Yup. Shit. Today was my dad's birthday and weeks ago I'd promised my mum I'd get us a table at Chez Laurent's, the fancy French bistro that the Manchester glitterati raved about, the place where you needed to reserve stupidly far in advance.

'Erm, nine p.m.,' I lied.

'Perfect. Right, well I'll let you get on. See you later, love.'

I said goodbye and hung up, my stomach in knots. I forgot what I was doing and hurriedly found the phone number for the restaurant, crossing everything that there would be by some miracle a last-minute cancellation for tonight.

No such luck.

The snooty receptionist, talking in a blatantly fake French accent, told me that 'eet just wasn't posseeeble'.

I told her to leave it and focused my attention on scouring the net for other possible options, my workload suddenly seeming less important. I'd set alarms on both my phone and email reminding me to buy my dad a gift and book this place but every time they'd pinged I'd cancelled them as I was always in the middle of doing something else. I could kick myself now. After the stressful end of last year, I'd planned to really treat him for his birthday, to celebrate in style that he was still here with us when we had so nearly lost him. I sighed, mentally slapping myself in the face for being such a terrible daughter.

All the finest five-star restaurants were either fully booked, didn't answer the phone, or only had tables at five p.m. in two weeks' time. Now I was really behind. By this rate I'd be pulling another all-nighter just to catch up on what I'd not got done today.

I sighed loudly, which caught Ben's attention. 'You OK, Georgia?'

'You don't happen to know any Michelin-starred chefs who could come and cook dinner tonight, do you?' I asked, with my head in my hands.

'Sorry?'

'It's my dad's birthday and I promised him a fancy dinner but completely forgot all about it,' I half moaned.

Kelli looked up from her paper-strewn desk. 'My mate Sticky Shaun works at TGI Fridays. I could try and bag you a table there? Nah, scrap that – he got his name for a reason.'

Ben grimaced and turned to face me. 'Why don't you have a change of plan and cook for them at yours?'

I laughed. 'I want to treat him, not kill him. Do you not remember how bad I was at cooking when we were in Thailand?'

Memories of being in the spicy, steamy kitchen in Koh Lanta flooded my mind. I blushed slightly thinking back to how close we'd been then, how I was convinced something would have happened between us by now other than swapping secret-Santa gifts and sharing business ideas in a friendly yet professional manner.

Ben smiled at the memory. 'Yeah, maybe stick with the restaurant idea.'

I went back to my laptop, wanting to focus on work instead of what could have been between us when Ben called out. 'Wait, didn't you go to some networking event or something at Verde, that new Italian place? You could call whoever organised it and see if they could fit you in.'

'Genius idea! Thanks.' I flipped through the stack of business cards on my desk; note to self, must get round to organising these one day. I thought back to that utterly boring evening where my restless mind had wandered away from death by PowerPoint to the fresh flowers and walnut fittings in the restaurant. I'd spent the rest of the dull meeting wondering whether we should redecorate the shop in similar hues.

I found the business card for Luigi, the restaurant manager, a no-nonsense Italian man with gelled-back hair and heavy musky aftershave who'd been very keen on sharing his advice on the best places to visit in Rome when I'd told him about our Italian tours. Five minutes later and I'd bagged us a table for three at nine p.m. tonight. Bingo. Maybe I could pull this back after all.

CHAPTER 2

Disillusion (n.) A freeing or a being freed from illusion

'It's very fancy, isn't it?' my mum exclaimed, picking up the creamy porcelain salt and pepper pots from the starched linen tablecloth. 'But, weren't we meant to be at that French place? Viv always goes on about it since her son Adam took her when he visited from London that one time. I swear I've heard more about the bloody crème brûlée they serve than I have about Viv's sciatic nerves, and trust me, she never shuts up about them.'

'It did sound pretty good though. The pudding, not Viv's backache,' my dad chimed in before clocking my face.

'I tried to get us in there, but it was fully booked,' I apologised, ignoring my mum pursing her lips that Adam had managed to get *his* mum in. 'This place is meant to be really good though. It's the number one Italian in Manchester, or something like that.'

'Hmmm,' my mum said. 'It's a little on the poky side.'

'Or you could say cosy?' I tried putting a positive spin on the large faux-marble pillar that we were tucked away behind. Luigi had come true on offering us a table; he just hadn't specified that we would be sardined behind the Roman coliseum next to the toilets. The comforting garlic and rosemary smell of the busy restaurant was sliced by regular wafts of strong bleach every time the door opened.

'Well I think it's great and makes a change from watching the evening news as I tuck into your mum's famous corned-beef hash.' My dad chuckled. After ordering from a harassed-looking waitress, who'd obviously forgotten about us judging by the look on her shiny red face, we tucked into the free, salty breadsticks.

'So, you've come straight from work, Georgia?' My mum nodded at what I was wearing: my creased work skirt, two-day-old blouse that now had both an ink stain and a coffee stain on the cuff and my Kelli-inspired, emo make-up.

'Yeah, sorry. I'd planned to go home first but I –'

'You were running late,' she butted in, and then sighed. 'Well it's so nice to finally get to have a proper catch-up with you. Although, I have to say, you are looking a little peaky, love.'

'I, erm, tried out a new make-up look today; don't think I'll be doing it again,' I said, brushing crumbs from my lap. 'So anyway, happy birthday, Dad.' I raised my glass of Chianti and pecked him on the cheek, smelling his familiar scent of clean linen and tomato plants. 'Your present's in the post,' I lied. Well, half lied. As soon as I got home I'd order something super-duper online to be delivered as soon as possible.

'Seeing you is the only gift I need.' He ruffled my hair. 'Now tell us everything. It's been ages since we've seen you, pet; how's it all going? You're not working too hard I hope?'

'Well, you know the first year of any new business is always a little tough, but we're fighting our corner of the travel market and even making a small profit.' I winked, feeling a warm glow inside of me. This was why I worked my bloody socks off: to get results.

'That's excellent news.' My dad grinned and chinked his glass to mine.

'What about outside of work? Any men on the scene we should know about? I always thought you and Ben would make such a lovely couple. With your intelligence and his dark brown eyes the children would be like genius supermodels.'

'Mum!' I hurriedly wiped the dribble of crimson wine from my chin.

'What?' She innocently shrugged. 'Don't be so busy working that you forget to have fun, Georgia.'

'I do have fun.' I half pouted, ignoring her as well as trying not to gag at the smell trailing an overweight man who'd just squeezed past us coming out of the toilets. 'I'm having fun right now.'

'Coming out tonight for your dad's birthday doesn't count. It's not like you're going to meet the man of your dreams in here,' my mum tutted.

'I have to say I agree, pet.' My dad jerked his head to the male bogs before laughing.

'I haven't got time for all that at the moment.' I wafted my hands around, wishing the waitress would hurry up with our mains and take the attention away from what a failure I was in every area other than my career. No way did I want my feelings about Ben bubbling to the surface, not when I'd tried so hard over the last few months to keep them neatly locked in a box marked *do not open*.

'Hmm, well we're worried about you, that's all,' my mum said, gently placing a hand on mine. 'When you came back from your travels you were so fired up about this business idea and it is great it's working so well. Really it is.' She sighed. 'But, Georgia, you need to be careful it isn't taking up *all* of your time.'

I pulled my hand away, took a big gulp of wine, and smiled at her. 'I told you I'm fine.'

My mum kept her eye on me and raised an eyebrow before slowly nodding. 'So, how's Marie? And little Cole? It's been ages since we've seen him; I bet he's growing up so fast.'

'They're fine…' I said, thinking about my best friend and her son. 'I've not seen them for a while but you know how it is, she's doing her thing and I'm doing mine. I'll give her a call soon.'

'Well when you do please say that your dad and I said hi.'

'I will, I promise. So how have you spent the rest of your birthday? Get any nice presents?' I asked my dad, wanting to change the conversation and quickly. There was something about being around my parents that made me revert to being a sulky teenager, not wanting to talk about boys – or at least this one boy in particular.

'Well yes. Your mother here outdid herself this year with this top-of-the-range digital radio.' The laughter lines around my dad's eyes crinkled as he spoke. 'You should see it, Georgie. I can tune into radio shows I never even knew existed before. I mean, what will they think of next?'

I was listening to him tell me about how he was listening to a gardening talk show hosted by a man called Wayne in Dorset, when my phone buzzed. 'Sorry, I need to take this. Hold that thought; I'll only be a minute.' I got up, trying not to bang my head on the eaves we were sat under to answer it.

'Oh right, OK.' My dad nodded sadly.

I quickly headed outside, walking out of the warm cosy restaurant into the chill of the spring wind so I could hear the caller better. I had completely forgotten I'd scheduled a late call with Dan Milligan, head of sales for the leading travel magazine *Itchy Feet*. I'd been working on trying to secure some advertising space with them as I'd noticed all our competitors had super-snazzy, full-paged ads and whatever they could do we could do better.

‘Evening. Georgia Green speaking,’ I said in my poshest phone voice, hoping the fading sound of sirens wouldn’t be too noticeable.

‘Hey, Georgia, Dan here. I wanted to give you a call ’cause, as you know, today’s the last day for advertisers to bag space in the next issue. I’ve got a cracking deal that I may be able to sort out for you.’

He then launched into a rehearsed sales pitch covering readership numbers and other figures I didn’t fully understand but that sounded impressive before taking a dramatic pause.

‘So…as we’re really keen to include up-and-coming tour operators in the mag, keep it fresh and bang up to date you know, we could do you a half- or full-page ad for…’ he paused again ‘…forty per cent less than the usual price.’

‘Wow, that’s a lot less than I’d expected.’ I coughed in surprise.

He let out a cheesy, game-show-host-style laugh. ‘The thing is, I can offer it to you at this price as we are literally down to the wire, meaning I will need that information, like, pronto. It has to get off to the printers ASAP, if you know what I mean?’

‘Tonight? It can’t wait until tomorrow?’ I glanced at my watch. I’d have to leave my dad’s birthday dinner to rush back and quickly knock something up. Plus it would mean not running this past Ben first. Surely they could wait until tomorrow morning?

‘No can do. I’m already stalling things ’cause I wanted to offer this heavily discounted rate to you. We’re basically giving this away!’

I stayed silent thinking it through; even with the cheaper price it was still a huge chunk of our advertising budget.

Dan must have sensed my apprehension. 'You know, I do have Totally Awesome Adventours waiting to hear from me too. I wanted to offer you first refusal but I know as soon as I get off the phone to you they'll snap this offer up.'

Usually Ben was in charge of the advertising budget but this was too good a deal to resist; I'd have to apologise to my dad but I was sure he'd understand. I took a deep breath.

'Yeah, great, let's go for it. Count us in.'

'Excellent. Let me make some calls and I'll bell you back to confirm. Once that's done then I'll need your copy in the next hour.'

'You have my word.' I smiled to myself and hung up.

I'd lost track of time. My arms were covered in goosebumps and my teeth were chattering, but I'd managed to bag us a full-page coloured ad in the next issue. I couldn't wait to tell Ben. OK, so he may go a little mental at how much of the advertising budget I'd just blown in the space of five minutes, but I was convinced it was the right thing to do.

Things were really taking off with Lonely Hearts Travels, our bespoke travel tours designed to help broken-hearted singles go from lost to wanderlust with like-minded people. Since we launched back in November I'd lived, eaten and slept the business, desperate for it to become a success and amazingly it seemed to be working. I rubbed my arms and headed back into the restaurant.

'I'm so sorry. That took longer than I thought…' I faded out once I took in my mum's pissed-off, tight face and my dad's disappointed, creased forehead. Their dinner plates were empty whilst my spaghetti carbonara had congealed into a disgusting buttercup-yellow sticky mound.

'We couldn't wait any longer.' My mum pursed her lips.

'Oh, right – course. Sorry,' I mumbled, trying to get my fork into the dried-out sauce, after scraping a layer of skin off the top. I couldn't stomach it so pushed the plate away. 'So, tell me what else you got for your birthday,' I said to my dad who was struggling to make eye contact with me.

'Well, the lads down the local clubbed together and bought me a new –'

The sound of my ringtone cut him off. 'Sorry.' I winced. 'I won't be long.' I picked up my mobile and headed back outside once more.

'Georgia!' Dan said cheerfully on the other end. 'You've got yourself a deal!'

'Wow, erm, great.' Was it strange that a slight nugget of worry was dancing in my stomach? No, this was too good to let pass, especially not to those Totally Awesome Adventours bastards.

'The only thing is I'll need your copy in, like, the next hour or so. That going to be a problem?'

I shook my head. 'Nope. I'll get onto it right away.'

I hung up and was just about to go back inside, working out how quickly I could get away and back to my office, when the main door of the restaurant opened and out came my parents, wrapped up in their winter coats.

'Mum, Dad? Where are you going?' I called out and jogged over to them. 'We've not had dessert yet,' I said, rubbing my arms for warmth.

'Georgia. We're going home. We came here to see you, not to sit staring at an empty third chair and being gassed by strange men's farts,' my mum snapped. 'Have you forgotten it's your dad's birthday? That all he wanted was to see you and spend some family time together?'

Even though I did need to be making a move myself I didn't want tonight to end like this. My stomach dropped and my cheeks grew flushed. 'I told you I was sorry; I'm just caught up in the middle of something that I needed to get sorted. But it's done now. I've managed to get us into

Itchy Feet; you know that magazine I mentioned a few weeks ago?'

My dad cleared his throat before giving me a weak smile. 'That's nice, love. Sorry to be a party pooper but I'm just feeling a little tired – you know how it is getting older and all that. Another time?'

I nodded and bit my lip. 'Are you sure you're OK?'

'Georgia, it's late. Let's just call it a night. You can get back to your work and we'll see you soon,' my mum said, fastening up her coat before giving me a peck on the cheek.

'Well call me soon! Oh and happy birthday, Dad,' I called out behind them.

I was about to head back inside the restaurant to grab my jacket and pay the bill when I heard my mum talking to my dad in a not very hushed whisper. 'Also, have you seen how tired she looks? I swear owning this business is getting too much for her.'

'I think she just needs a good sleep and a little TLC, Sheila,' my dad replied.

'Hmm, I hope you're right. It's not normal how hard she is pushing herself, trying to prove something that doesn't need to be proved. I'm worried about her – that's all, Len.'

'I know you are, we both are but she'll be OK. She'll figure it out. She's a Green after all.'

I trudged into the restaurant. Did *everyone* think I was a complete failure? I was doing fine. More than fine.

CHAPTER 3

Workaholic (n.) A person who works compulsively at the expense of other pursuits

'I heard that you help people like me? I just came in on a whim really as I don't know if anyone can really help me.' The woman sat opposite me spoke in a whisper of barely audible breath that seemed to come in bursts from her rattling chest.

She was slowly shredding a Kleenex apart between her long thin fingers, not realising what she was doing as she spoke. She was getting ripped bits of tissue everywhere, all over the floor and her knee-length, plum-coloured cord skirt. I noticed her fingernails were impeccably painted, a deep red that shone against her pale trembling hands. I remembered doing that when I was in her position, thinking that if my nails were perfect then everything else in my jumbled-up life would follow suit, that somehow a lick of nail lacquer would make it all OK. It was only when the tiny flecks started to chip away that you were brought back to reality.

I looked down at my own hands as she sipped her cup of tea. My fingernails were bare, my cuticles ravaged and the thinnest line of white kept trying to break through before I bit it off again, not through sadness this time but through stress. Going for a manicure was on my to-do list, one of many I had on the go. Go to the gym, join a gym, learn how to use the smoothie maker my mum bought me at Christmas, be home enough to have time to use the smoothie maker, make a date with my best friend, call my parents more; all these things including go and get a manicure had been long forgotten. Tomorrow, I always seemed to tell myself. Tomorrow.

'So he packed everything whilst I was away at a work team-building weekend and just left. I came back to find our flat half empty and a note explaining what he'd done,' Nice-Nails Lady whispered.

I winced. 'God, I'm sorry.'

I tilted my head and passed her a fresh tissue, whilst at the same time trying to keep an eye on Kelli who was chatting to an equally unsure-looking man in the corner of the shop.

I hadn't realised how much of my time would be spent acting as a counsellor to customers. Fresh from messy break-ups they would wobble in here looking for a calming place to talk to people who understood that love doesn't always go to plan. My experience of being a jilted bride had kick-started the idea of the business as I had been in the exact same position as they were now – feeling unsure, scared, but desperate to make changes to my life – when I first donned a backpack and went off to travel. These customers today were still coming to terms with what had happened in their lives but I knew that booking into one of our travel tours would soon cure them of pining for their exes.

'He had been having an affair with our neighbour.' Nice-Nails Lady sniffed loudly, grabbing another tissue to wipe her chapped nose. My heart ached for her. I knew this pain. And not to seem too heartless I also knew it did get better. I wanted to shake her thin shoulders, to rattle the plastic beads across her neck and sing out loud that it would get easier, that he had probably done her a favour, that she would look back at this in a few years' time shaking her head at how upset she'd been over something that now seemed so insignificant. For me, going travelling – having that time and space away from everything I knew back home – fixed so many of my problems, gave me the confidence to believe in myself once more and inspired me to create this business. Plus, I met Ben and reignited the hope and desire to love again. If only I could move us past this *flirtationship* stage we had found ourselves in, where we were surely out of the friend zone but nowhere near to being in a proper relationship.

'This was all six months ago and since then I've just been in some awful nightmare, hoping I'll feel happy and like my old self again. I visited Spain on a foreign exchange programme when I was younger and I just remember having such a carefree, happy time. That girl, that version of me feels like she has died but I'm desperate to get her back, which is why I'm here today.' She blew her nose and gave me a sad smile, before telling me about her hazy student days in a small Spanish village teaching English to adorable children, drinking cold sangria outside on heady evenings, longing for the neighbour of the homestay she was staying in to notice her.

'Juan.' She smiled. 'Funny how the neighbour seems to have such an impact on my life.' Well at least she could see the ironic side. It was the first time in the twenty minutes since she'd been sitting opposite me that she'd smiled, the worry lines on her pale thin face receding as she was instantly taken back to her youth. 'I saw an advert about the tours you organise, with people like me I guess, and just hoped you would have something for me?' She looked so lost I wanted to give her a hug, but I noticed the guy talking to Kelli kept staring over at us – breaking the intimate moment with a strange cold glance.

I nodded and patted her hand. 'We will do our best to get you back to that happy young woman. I'm positive about that.'

I started to tap on my keyboard, looking for tours that would suit her. We had had an amazing success rate of matching people with countries and challenges that seemed to pull them out of their comfort zone and fix them back together again. The wall of the office behind me was tacked with so many thank-you cards and postcards from other customers who had once been sitting in the exact same chair as her. This was why I loved my job. The satisfaction from helping people get back on their feet was immeasurable – so what if it meant other things in my life may have been slipping?

Not long later, Nice-Nails Lady was booked to go to Barcelona, looking to reignite her Spanish youth. She would be in a small group dusting off her language skills, joining fun nights out and soaking up the architecture all around her. She left the shop clutching the information to her bony chest, beaming. I couldn't help but smile too.

I noticed that the strange man Kelli had been talking to had also left. 'What was he after?' I asked her, picking up shreds of tissue from the floor.

Kelli shrugged. 'Was a right weirdo. I asked him what he was looking for but all he was bothered about were boring facts about the business.' She popped a piece of gum in her mouth and chewed it loudly.

'Did you speak to him like how we told you?' I shuddered thinking back to when we'd first hired her, a favour to Trisha who was friends with Kelli's aunt. A few weeks after she'd started, a new customer had walked in, someone in a similar position to the lady I'd just helped:

red ringed eyes and chapped nose from the constant wiping of tears and snot. Ben and I were both on the phone at the time so Kelli had bounded over to her, thrusting our brochures into this poor woman's sad face. She had started crying almost immediately seeing the faded band T-shirt that Kelli was wearing and explained mid-sobs how her ex loved that band. Instead of consoling her, offering her a cup of tea and a seat in a comfy chair, Kelli burst out laughing, exclaiming that she wore that T-shirt ironically as their music was utter shite. A true believer in tough love was our Kelli; let's just say the client made a quick exit and never returned.

She always used to rock up late with pillow creases down her pale cheeks and no apology, she never wore suitable clothes and barely brushed her hair but Ben was adamant we keep her on to please her aunt and said that with a little encouragement she would blossom. He was right. Ben had spent a lot of time patiently explaining to Kelli how she needed to listen to the customers before judging them on the music their ex liked or chucking our tours down their throats. Some customers were just not ready to go off and explore the world; they were still grieving their relationship and not yet ready to turn the page and start a new life.

Kelli's hunched-up shoulders had gradually softened, her timekeeping had improved and that sulky teen attitude that she'd had when she first walked in here had evolved into a sort of vulnerable confidence. She wasn't the perfect employee but she had a heart of gold and got what we were trying to achieve here, even if she did still have as much tact as a heavy-handed butcher at times.

'Err yeah.' Kelli rolled her kohl-heavy eyes at me. 'Even if he was acting shifty I still offered him a brew. He said no though.'

I chucked the tissue in the bin and looked at her. 'What do you mean shifty?'

'I dunno. Just asking about how the shop was doing… something about turning?'

'Turnover? Money?'

She shrugged, bored with this conversation. 'Maybe. I said you were doin' all right, although you could pay me a little more.' She said this so matter-of-factly I wanted to laugh.

'If I could, you know I would.' I smiled at her as she rolled her eyes. 'Did he look like he was going to book a tour?'

'Er, he was asking about that India one, you know the one that's going tits up.' She yawned.

'It's not going tits up.' I pursed my lips at her. 'It's just had a few not so great reviews, that's all.' Getting to the bottom of why was high on my to-do list. We had been lucky to receive almost five stars for every other trip we offered, and the India trip had initially received similar reviews, but now it just felt like the black sheep of the family.

She nodded slowly. 'Well anyway, I gave him the brochure.'

'OK, good,' I mumbled distractedly. There was another Indian tour leaving in a few weeks and I was determined to make sure this one was the best ever.

'Hey, what's with that face?' Ben asked as he put his phone down and got up to flick on the kettle.

'Nothing. Just thinking about those Indian reviews again.' I sighed. 'Kelli was just with a customer asking about going to India with us. I can't face another set of one stars.'

Ben got the milk out of the fridge. 'Don't worry, Georgia. Our winning streak was bound to come to an end one day. I'm amazed we've managed to notch up so many five stars already. It's only normal that we're not going to please everyone.'

'But we should! We work hard in picking the best tour guides, the nicest hotels, the funnest activities,' I half cried. 'Every tour should go without a hitch.'

'Yeah and My Chemical Romance should get back together and tour again, but not everything we want works out,' Kelli piped up.

'Thanks for that, Kel, really helpful,' I said sarcastically.

'She's right, you know,' Ben said, passing me a full-to-the-brim cup of tea. I took the mug and smiled gratefully. On the front was a photo of us from the local paper when we opened our business just last year. We looked so happy, unaware of what we were getting ourselves into and the adventures that lay ahead. I still cherished this mug even if the dishwasher had smeared off most of the colour and my smile had faded half away.

'Cheers,' I said and he winked back. 'What do you mean she's right?'

'Well, I know we want to offer the best tours to our customers and make everyone who comes in this shop or travels with us happier than they were before they met us, but it doesn't always work like that, Georgia. We can't fix everyone's problems. Getting some duff reviews is just part and parcel of this business, especially when we're working with some very heartbroken people. It's just the way it is.' He shrugged and sat back at his desk.

I sighed. Maybe he was right. Maybe the perfectionist in me needed to just chill out. 'But don't you think it's weird that a lot of these reviews are coming from the Indian tour?'

'I've been to India a few times. That is one crazy place.' Ben shook his head, lost in some memory. 'I bet those people struggled with the country rather than our tour. It's a whole other world over there, far removed from the life we live here and for some that culture shock is too much to take. Come on, please don't get stressed about it. Like you say, we have the best guides, the best trips planned and we give it one hundred per cent, but we can't control everything.'

I nodded slowly. 'I guess.'

'So, how was your dad's birthday meal? Did they like the restaurant?' Ben asked, changing the subject.

I tapped my forehead. 'Oh my God, I completely forgot to tell you.'

'Tell me what?'

'OK, well you know that sales guy Dan at *Itchy Feet*?' Ben nodded slowly. 'Well, I managed to negotiate a very good rate on us getting some advertising space with them. Forty per cent off!'

He raised his eyebrows. 'Wow, how did you manage that?'

'My womanly charms.' I grinned. 'I sent the copy over last night and we should be in the next issue coming out in a few weeks.'

Ben's smile faded in a second. 'What?'

'I needed to act quickly on this offer as Dan had others waiting and there was no way I was going to let Totally Awesome Adventours take it.'

'Wait – so you signed off on this and sent over copy without speaking to me first?'

I nodded, my bubble of excitement popping. 'Yeah, 'cause if I didn't we would have lost it,' I said quietly, feeling the atmosphere close in around me. Kelli sensed the mood and nipped to the loo, mumbling something on her way past.

'Georgia,' Ben snapped. 'You promised me that big decisions like this, decisions that cost money, would always be made together. Even with the discount this has probably wiped out our advertising budget.'

'I'm sorry; I just didn't want us to lose out.'

'That's the oldest trick in the book: say you've got others interested to make the first shmuck agree to the sale before thinking it over.'

'Oh.'

'Yep, oh.' He rubbed his face. He seemed a lot more tired these days. 'I thought we had an agreement that we didn't make any big decisions without checking with each other first.'

My cheeks felt flushed. 'I'm sorry. I thought I was doing the right thing; you'll see, this will bring in loads of business.' I laughed weakly, hoping that I would be proved right.

The afternoon flew by and before I knew it Kelli had clocked off in a whirlwind of nerves for her gig tonight, leaving just Ben and me finally alone.

'I am sorry about the advert thing,' I said as I emptied my waste-paper bin.

'It's fine. I'm sorry for flying off the handle.' Ben flashed a genuine smile. 'I just want you to know that I'm here to help. I want this business to work just as much as you do.' He placed a warm hand on my shoulder that gave me a tingle of excitement. My body just seemed to melt at his touch, no matter how small or infrequently it happened.

'I know.' I smiled at him, hoping I didn't have any poppy seeds stuck in my teeth after inhaling a bagel at my desk earlier.

'Right, well I'd better be making a move; I said I'd go and get changed and then help Kel set up,' he said, taking his hand away and breaking the moment. 'Did you know Jimmy and Shelley are coming too?'

'Yeah, she sent me an email about it earlier. Something about how there was no way she would refuse the offer of curry no matter how bad Kelli's band might be.' I hadn't seen Ben's best mate Jimmy and his girlfriend, my backpacker friend Shelley, for ages, even though we lived in the same city now. As much as the sound of Kel's emo band wasn't getting me excited I did have to admit it would be nice to actually be out in the real world with real friends and to be hanging out with Ben away from work. This had been the first 'date' that Ben had asked me on. OK, so officially it wasn't a date when I'd be stood in a sea of faces in close proximity to Ben, cringing as Jimmy did his best Bez impression but still it was a chance to socialise outside of this place.

'Cool, well. I'll see you later then, Georgia. You sure you're OK to lock up by yourself?'

I shooed him away. 'Tsk. Course I am. I'll see you all soon; save me a spot in the crowd.'

Ben looked as if he was going to say something else but stopped himself and gave me a quick wave as he left the shop. I was going to tie up some loose ends and be on my way. I was definitely going to be out of here at a reasonable hour, proving to my parents that I had more going on in my life than just work.

Only sending one email became ten and now I was late. Very late. I'd planned to go home, take a soak in the bath, maybe even paint my nails and leisurely get ready. I used to love the whole prep part of a night out. Me and Marie would crank up the stereo, pour huge glugs of cold white wine and dance around as we preened ourselves before falling into a taxi in a fit of giggles and excitement at what the night could hold. Most of the time getting ready was the best part. I'd never really got into the whole clubbing scene and hated feeling like I was on show as nameless strangers wandered past unsteadily holding a pint of lager and looking us up and down. We'd eventually return home with our purses lighter and feet heavy, telling ourselves we were too old for this until the next time when the ritual would start all over again. I really did need to get in touch with Marie; how long had it been since I'd seen her? My mobile phone buzzed on my messy desk, breaking my thoughts.

'Hey, I'm on my way!' I said quickly to Ben.

'Georgia. Are you still in the office?' he asked. I could sense a sharpness in his tone.

'Yep but I swear I was just heading out the door then I realised that we hadn't sent out the itineraries for the Iceland trip, which I know was my job to do but it completely slipped my mind. Anyway I'm leaving right now…' I babbled.

Ben cut me off; I could hear the disappointment in his voice. 'Georgia, you promised Kel that you wouldn't be late.' His voice grew quieter, smaller against the thrum from the room he was in. 'She's counting on us to be there to support her; you know, put this teamwork theory into practice. Also, Jimmy and Shell have been asking where you are.'

'I know. I'm so sorry. I didn't mean to get caught up in work. I'll be there before you know it –' My stomach sank. I honestly hadn't meant to let work get in the way of this evening.

'Just try your best, please. Listen I need to go. The warm-up act have nearly finished.' With that he hung up.

Double shit. I kicked the leg of my desk, causing my ticket to the event to flutter gently onto the floor. Picking it up, I glanced at the clock. If I could grab a taxi right now I'd still make it. Yeah, so I'd be the only one dressed for the office but at least I'd be there. I put on my jacket and turned off my laptop, hoping there would be a long queue of black cabs waiting patiently at the side of the main street. I plonked my handbag on my desk to find my keys and accidentally pushed a pile of papers that I hadn't had time to sort through onto the floor.

'Bugger.' I leant down to pick up the loose sheets of paper, scribbled notes and brochures. I scooped them up and dumped them on my desk, trying not to freak out at how disorganised my work space looked when I noticed a pale grey sheet of paper sticking out. This was from Kelli's pad when she passed us messages.

'Another one star review. For India tour. Seriously tits up!!' she'd scrawled.

I hurriedly read the text she'd printed off the internet and felt a little bubble of sick rise up. All the other reviews we had received had been slightly negative but this took it to a whole other level. Personal, vitriolic, scathing and full of detail with not one spelling mistake to be seen. I flicked open my laptop and waited for it to come back to life before quickly typing in the web address where this review was posted; it linked to a travel blog that I'd never read before. This one post had received hundreds of likes and comments and been shared a stupid amount of times. It even came with its own hashtag. This was serious. With our next Indian tour taking place soon *and* it being one of our biggest earners, I had to do something right now.

I grabbed my phone, jabbing in Kelli's mobile number to see if she'd seen any more reviews like this without telling us. Her answerphone rang on a few seconds later, reminding me that she would be warming up for her gig. I sighed and went to call Ben when I stopped. If I told him about it now he'd know I was still in the office and would tell me to leave it, that it could wait until tomorrow, but I knew that it couldn't. I needed to sort this out myself. Right now.

I quickly jabbed a text message to Shelley telling her I was running late but would be with them all soon, shrugged my jacket off and flicked the lights back on. Work had to come first. There would be other gigs; surely Kelli and Ben would understand. Wouldn't they?

CHAPTER 4

Spontaneous (adj.) Arising from a momentary impulse

I turned my phone off after it started beeping constantly with texts from Shelley asking where I was, telling me how great Kelli's band actually were, and how there was still enough curry left for me to join them. I needed to concentrate. I couldn't let my business go the same way that my social life was – down the shitter.

Christmas and new year had been a whirlwind of activity as we wanted to attract the resolution crowds, fired up to make this year the one in which they followed their dreams and travelled. Then Valentine's Day came and went with a silly amount of bookings for single people determined not to sit at home and sob. It was also the time when I lost the courage I had been building up to ask Ben out for a coffee or maybe even a dinner date as we were both at different networking events. So what if my love life was non-existent? At least our business was going from strength to strength, all because of hard work, determination and sacrifice; tonight was just one of those sacrifices.

The Indian tour guide, Nihal, wasn't answering any of the numbers we had for him. I let out a deep sigh as I realised that it was silly o'clock in the morning over there so no wonder my emails went unanswered and he wasn't online on Skype. I was about to draft a firmly worded email to the author of the awful blog post asking them to take it down when the door to the shop was flung open. I must have forgotten to lock it after Ben left.

'We're closed,' I called out, as I tried to work out the best way to start a conversation with an internet troll.

'Hey! You never close; *that's* the problem.' Shelley beamed at me, holding two bottles of wine in her outstretched arms, her pretty doll-like face looking slightly squiffy.

'What are you doing here?' I got up and hugged her; she smelt like a curry house, and my stomach gurgled loudly. 'Thought you were all at Kelli's gig?'

'Well when you said you were running late I figured I'd have to come here and drag you out with the incentive of wine. But the gig finished, the curry ran out and still there was no sign of you. Anyway how are you doing? You look like shit by the way,' she said in her throaty Australian accent, peering at me through glassy eyes. The gig must have been good.

'Thanks, Shell, always a pleasure to see you too.' I half smiled and took the wine from her, locking the shop door behind her. 'I look like shit because I've just found yet *another* bad review for one of our tours, the nastiest one we've ever had. Made worse by the fact it seems to have gone viral and the bloody tour guide has gone AWOL so I can't get to the bottom of what's happened.'

'Ah. Right.' She nodded along as she rummaged in the kitchen for two clean mugs. 'What's that mean?'

I sighed and ran my fingers through my knotted hair. 'It means that I couldn't make it to Kelli's gig, that I couldn't stomach eating a curry as the only Indian thing my brain is processing is how stressed out I am at trying to track Nihal down. It means we have paying customers planning to head to Delhi in two weeks for a Lonely Hearts Indian Tour with an apparently absent tour guide. And it also means that both Ben and Kel are probably really pissed off with me for not making it tonight, especially as I go on so much about the value of teamwork.' I sighed and massaged my temples.

'Ah, yup, that is a kick in the balls,' Shelley said filling up the mugs with wine and passing me one. I took it gratefully. 'Well, if we're not going to be leaving here anytime soon then the least I can do is help you figure this out. Sit down and tell me *everything*.'

So I did, in between filling up our mugs and cracking open bottle number two I told her how important it was that this tour still took place, how hard we had worked to secure Nihal, who had come highly recommended, as well as the other suppliers that I'd personally hand-picked, spent ages interviewing via Skype and God knows how much cash on promoting this route. 'Crap!' I slapped my hand to my head, leaving wine residue on my forehead. 'I've just forked out a shit ton of money to *Itchy Feet*.'

'Itchy what?' Shelley laughed.

'*Itchy Feet* – it's, like, the number one travel magazine, and I paid for us to advertise the sodding Indian tour.' I pounded my fist on my desk. What an idiot. 'Ben doesn't know about this yet. I thought I'd try and fix it without bothering him about it.'

'Hmm, so about Ben. What's going on with you two?' She tucked her legs under herself.

'Nothing,' I said forcefully before downing the rest of my drink. 'Pass that wine, would you?'

'Here, top me up too.' She leant over and grabbed the bottle, knocking off a stack of brochures to the floor but I felt too stressed even to flinch at the mess. 'Well here's the thing, Georgia, and I'm going to tell it to you straight.' Her eyes had gone even more squiffy as she tried to focus on me, pointing her finger out. 'You're a workaholic.'

'What? No I'm not.' I pushed her accusing finger away and filled my mug to the brim, spilling some on my trousers.

'You are. You're a workaholic who is SO determined to make this business a success that you've forgotten everything else in your life, including finding the courage to actually make a move with Ben.' She sat back with a smug look on her alcohol-flushed cheeks.

I huffed. 'Shell, I appreciate your opinion but I'm not a workaholic. I've just invested a lot of time and cash into the business and I need for it to go well, that's all. I'm just like any other business owner.'

She raised an eyebrow. 'Right. So where's Ben then? Your business partner? If you were running this together why isn't he here working all hours?'

I gave her a look. 'He works hard.'

'Yes, but he also knows when to take a break and, you know, live a little. He really missed you tonight,' she said, making my heart flutter.

'Really? He said that?'

'Well, not in so many words.' The butterflies that had been prancing in my empty stomach stopped doing the conga and played dead. 'But I know he *felt* it. You two are made for each other. Everyone can see that apart from the bloody pair of you.'

'You really think that?' I asked, feeling the warming glow of the cheap wine kicking in.

She nodded her head. 'Tsk, course, we *all* do. But you know, Romeo would never have gone all lovey-dovey for Juliet if he thought she wasn't interested in him. Instead he'd probably have copped off with some distant Capulet cousin or some shit, got married and had loads of Leo lookalike children whilst Juliet just grew old and shrivelled up, kicking herself that she hadn't been brave enough to tell him how she felt.'

I laughed. 'I bet old Shakespeare would be turning in his grave hearing your version of the greatest love story of all time.'

'I'm serious, Georgia. How do you expect Ben to make a move if he doesn't even know you have the world's biggest crush on him? Ain't no way he'd risk asking you out on a date and be knocked back *then* have to work together, dying of wounded pride as the business collapsed due to the stale atmosphere that would cause.'

I was beginning to feel like this was the Spanish Inquisition with both Shelley and my parents questioning me about my non-existent love life. 'I think he knows.'

She let out a throaty laugh. 'He's a guy, Georgia. They *never* know, unless you're stood butt naked waving a condom in the air.'

'Well, he comments on my appearance, says I look nice.' I cringed thinking about the unplanned makeover that Kelli had given me the other day. That wasn't quite the glamorous look I was going for. 'I always make sure I put the radiator near him up higher than mine so he stays nice and warm and he notices that.'

She scratched her head, humouring me. 'Oh wow, and what else?'

'Well he, erm, he always makes me tea in my favourite mug – the one with our picture on. Oh yeah, and we have this little shared joke…well, we did…where each of us would try to drop random words in on phone calls with suppliers; we haven't done that for a while actually, but it was really funny,' I said thinking out loud. I was struggling now. Maybe I wasn't putting out any please-take-me-to-bed subliminal messages, but then again, neither was he. And I needed to act like I didn't care. I just wished I could stop my heart whispering that I blatantly did. *Shut up and just do your job pumping blood*, my brain growled back.

'Hmm.' She rolled her eyes, looking majorly unimpressed with my seduction skills. 'Well if you want my opinion…'

'Do I want your opinion?'

'Yes. If you want my opinion, the girl he was crazy for back in Thailand seems to have stayed on that beach.'

'What?'

'I'm just saying the fun, carefree, live-for-the-moment Georgia that he first met isn't here any more.' She gulped her wine, ignoring my look of surprise. 'When did you last do something just for fun? And I don't mean playing lame word bingo on the phone, I mean *really* fun?'

I took a long sip thinking about it. 'Drinking wine in the office is fun, risqué even.' I winked as she tutted.

'I'm serious, Georgia. Where's the girl I met who would go skinny-dipping in the Thai ocean, who had the balls to travel solo after being left jilted, who would say only yes to new things, not check if she could fit them into her busy schedule first?'

I mumbled a response. 'I can do fun…'

'When did you last do something spontaneous? Really let your hair down?'

'Shelley, there is no spontaneity in running a business.' Just then an email pinged through to my inbox. Ignoring her rolling her eyes I leant over to see if it was Nihal explaining the scathing review.

'Is it that Nihal fella you're waiting to hear from?' Shelley asked.

I shook my head. 'Nope. Just an automatic email saying the Indian visas for the tour group are ready to collect,' I said sadly. How ironic.

'That's it!' Shelley exclaimed sloshing some wine on her legs as she pointed a finger in the air.

'What? Visas?'

'No, you daft sod. *This* is the answer to your problems.' She grinned and then took a dramatic pause. 'We should go to India.'

'Ha ha very funny,' I said sarcastically.

'No. Georgia, I'm serious. We should go together to meet this Nihal bloke in person, see what's really going on, put an end to these bad reviews once and for all. Why not? I love samosas and I even came first in a vindaloo-eating competition at home,' she boasted. 'Plus I've always wanted to go to India. And you can go and track down this tour guide. Wait – we can go undercover! Yes, that would be perfect. Get the real scoop on what's happening. This is the perfect spontaneous thing for you to do!' She looked like she could burst with excitement.

'I think you need to start drinking some water,' I said, shaking my head at the absurdity of the idea. Pfft, I couldn't just take two weeks off work to jet off to India. How would the business survive without me?

'I'm not drunk; this is the best idea I've ever had. Trust me, it's a win-win. I mean, you never take any holidays, or days off for that matter. Plus you get to show Ben how you can be fun and daring Georgia again. I get to take a trip with my best friend *and* your business problem will be all smoothed over.'

'Really, you think it could work?' I tilted my head, thinking about what she was suggesting. The alcohol was making my head feel fuzzy and I couldn't concentrate properly. *Maybe* it could be a good idea. It was just two little weeks.

'Yes! Getting that email from the visa agency is a sign. See, the world wants you to go!' She started to do a little jig. 'That is, unless you're too boring to say yes. The old Georgia would have booked her flight straight away…'

I shut my eyes. 'I'm not too boring. Yes. Fuck it. Let's do it. Right now!'

'Yay!' She began whipping a wet tea towel over her head in excitement then hesitated. 'Wait, you don't want to talk to Ben first? Check it's OK that you're gone for a few weeks?'

I shook my head – probably a little too dramatically – as spots appeared in front of my eyes. 'No, we need to seize the moment. He'll think it's a great idea being proactive and courageous, trust me!'

'OMG we're going to India, baby! Let's book it!' Shelley beamed at me.

I looked at my smiling reflection in my black laptop screen. *Yes this will help everything. We are a pair of geniuses. Wait, what is the plural of genius? Genii? Whatever it is, that's what we are.*

CHAPTER 5

Repercussion (n.) An effect or result, often indirect or remote, of some event or action

The sound of the bin lorries rumbling down the street woke me with a start. I opened my eyes and immediately felt like I was being stabbed in the corneas with all the sunlight beaming through the office windows. I groggily turned over and nearly chucked up. The room was a complete state. I carefully sat up holding my throbbing head. My mouth was as dry as sandpaper and I reeked of booze. I'd slept in the office again, only this time I had Shelley and her melodic snores for company.

I combed my fingers through my hair and winced as a piece of gristly kebab meat fell onto the sofa that I was spreadeagled over – the sofa that we used as a waiting area for customers to sit and browse our brochures, which was now wet in patches from spilt wine and drool. Easing my weary bones to stand up I grabbed a cloth and half-arsedly wiped the stains before turning my phone back on and giving Shelley a shove to wake up. Missed calls, a drunken voicemail from Jimmy and three texts from Ben beeped through, each of his worried messages growing more disappointed in their tone that I didn't make Kelli's gig and hadn't even bothered to apologise.

'Shel, Shel, wake up!' I nudged her.

'Mdnasudhu' came from her as she turned and got comfier on the floor cushions.

'No, I'm serious, Shelley; you need to get up now. Ben and Kelli will be here soon.'

'What?' She leant up, rubbed her eyes and let out a dry chesty cough. 'What time is it?'

'Time to get up and sort this disaster zone out. Man, what time did we even go to bed? I feel like ass.'

'Eurgh, I dunno. Maybe about three or could have been four. Whenever we finished that third or was it fourth bottle of wine?' She unsteadily got to her feet.

'What? I thought you only brought two with you,' I said, puffing the sofa cushions back to life and staggering to the bathroom.

'Yeah I did but then you said we could open this other bottle that someone had bought you.'

I blinked, trying to remember, then suddenly it hit me. 'Shelley, that wasn't wine that was rum one of the customers bought us as a thank-you present. No wonder I feel so rough. I hate rum!'

She clapped a hand to her pale face as if burping down vomit threatening to escape. 'Eurgh, me too. I need sleep, a shower and greasy food, pronto. Do you need me to tidy up first?'

I glanced at the room that smelt like a brewery but judging by her clammy almost-green cheeks it was probably better that she made a speedy exit. 'Nah, I'll open all the windows and Febreze the shit out of this place. I'll call you later.'

She gratefully stumbled out as I collected the empty bottles and greasy kebab boxes and tried to make the room look presentable before Ben and Kelli turned up. I sprayed air freshener everywhere including over my crumpled clothes and quickly washed my face, rubbing the mascara smudges from under my itchy eyes, hoping to wake myself up.

Once I looked as decent as possible, given zero sleep and yesterday's clothes as I still hadn't remembered to leave a fresh change under my desk, I sighed and flicked on the kettle; may as well make a start with work. I hadn't drunk like that in a long time. Why the hell had I opened that bottle of rum? Why had I been guzzling it down like a fish? What had we even been chatting about till four a.m. this morning? Where had the kebabs appeared from? My tired brain refused to wake up and give me the answers I needed. Bastard.

'Kelli, you do know we have chairs?' Ben tilted his head and comically raised his eyebrow at our office junior who was sat cross-legged on the floor surrounded by plastic wallets, sticky labels and, worryingly, a glue gun. He'd been out at a meeting for most of the morning so thankfully the smell of kebab meat and stale alcohol had faded by the time he returned.

'Nah, I like it better down here.' She flicked her multi-coloured hair back and carried on.

'You know you really did miss out on a good night last night, Georgia,' Ben said, sitting at his desk and turning his laptop on. 'Who knew our Kel had so many hidden talents.' Kelli beamed back at him and avoided my gaze like she had done all morning. She'd barely acknowledged me since she'd arrived. I'd tried to apologise for missing her gig and asked her how her night went but had so far been met with polite but short answers.

'I promise I'll be there for the next one; I just got caught up with things here.' I apologised again. 'Right, it's my turn to do the coffee run. The usual, everyone?' Ben nodded gratefully whilst Kelli just shrugged. 'OK, I'll be back in a tick.' I pulled my jacket on and walked out into the chill of the street. The icy spring wind was just what I needed to help blow away this raging hangover that I was trying to keep hidden from the two of them.

As I came back from Starbucks wobbling a latte, a hot chocolate and a cappuccino in a flimsy cardboard holder I felt the atmosphere in the small room buzz with electric tension. Kelli was sat on the comfy, thankfully stain-free sofa nervously twiddling her thumbs as I breezed in.

'OK, here's yours.' I passed her an extra-large hot chocolate with all the trimmings. She took the cup and gave me a tight smile by way of thanks; I noticed she looked even paler than usual. Maybe I wasn't the only one suffering in silence.

'I got the one with the extra small marshmallows you like and, Ben, they asked if you wanted syrup but I took it without as I said you were sweet enough,' I said cheesily and walked over to Ben who was sat rigidly in his seat glaring at me. 'Everything OK, guys?' I tried to keep my tone light whilst placing his steaming cup of coffee on his desk.

'Kelli, will you give us a moment, please?' Ben muttered to Kelli, ignoring my question; this seemed to be what she was waiting for as she jumped up like a rat out of a trap, grabbed her creased leather jacket and sprinted out of the shop, leaving her hot chocolate untouched.

'Ben? Is everything OK?' I asked, sinking into my seat. A strange prickly sensation rose up my neck.

'Georgia.' Ben sighed. 'You promised me there wouldn't be any more secrets between us.'

I shook my head, my eyes wide open and hands outstretched. 'I know. There aren't.'

He rolled his eyes skywards. His jaw was clenched as he spoke. 'So now you're lying to my face?'

'I'm not lying. What's going on, Ben?'

He stood up and placed his arms behind his head, closing his eyes and trying to calm down. 'Whilst you were out getting coffee, Kelli took a phone call from Indian Airways asking if you and Shelley would like an upgrade on your upcoming trip.'

My mind was as blank as my face must have been. 'What trip?'

'The trip in two weeks to New Delhi,' he said sharply, unable to keep his cool any longer.

I sat back, stunned. 'India? There must be some mistake; I don't know what you're talking about.'

'Well that's what we thought, so Kelli asked them to email me your itinerary and, bingo, you and Shelley are booked on a flight to New Delhi. Apparently the booking was made at one a.m. this morning.'

Oh my holy everything. It was starting to filter back now. Me telling her about the awful reviews of the India tour and Nihal going AWOL and then us…us deciding to go undercover and find him in India. Shit. 'Oh.'

'Yep. Do you know how stupid I look as a business partner? Finding out that you're jetting off when Kelli brings it up? Let alone that you were too busy to go to her gig as you had *far* more important things to do, like book a girly holiday with Shelley.'

'I don't remember doing this! It happened late last night; we'd had a few drinks.' I paused to try and assemble my thoughts. 'You know the India tour isn't doing very well –'

Ben cut me off. 'Yes and we spoke about this. You can't control everything, Georgia.'

'I know that. But then I found this blog that had posted the worst review about the trip, like really bad, and I just got caught up in the moment. You know what Shelley's like…' I paused. 'I wanted to do something spontaneous.'

Ben took a deep breath. 'Georgia, I don't mind you going on holiday; that isn't the point. The point is you didn't think to tell me this before Kelli found out and you didn't even check that it might be convenient at such short notice. Why didn't you tell me about this review?'

'I didn't want to worry you about it,' I said quietly.

'But that's the thing – I'm your partner; if you worry, I worry.' Ben's expression softened slightly.

'I swear I don't remember booking this trip. It was a silly spur-of-the-moment idea, but I'll call up and cancel straight away,' I said picking up my phone.

He sighed loudly. 'No.'

'What?' I stopped dialling and stared at him.

'No, don't cancel it. You deserve a holiday to let your hair down and not get so stressed about the business. You've always wanted to go to India plus it will cost nearly as much to cancel. Maybe this is what you need, what we need. To have a little break from the office and each other.'

'A break f-from us?' I stuttered. I felt as though someone had pressed an icy palm to the back of my neck.

'No, you know what I mean. Just a break from here.' He waved his arms around the room. 'Go, Georgia. I think actually this might be a good thing, a bloody shock, but a good thing.' He gave me a weak smile and picked up the phone that had started to ring next to him.

This wasn't how it was supposed to be. So much for Shelley's bright idea at making Ben more interested in me. I had imagined him giving me a look of admiration for being so ballsy and taking control, not being unable to look at me at all as I'd let him down – again.

I opened my emails and typed furiously to check with Shelley that she knew we were actually going to India. We *had* to make this work.

CHAPTER 6

Tremulous (adj.) Exceedingly sensitive; easily shaken or disordered

I hadn't really had time to let the rash decision that I was going to India on one of my own tours sink in. I was too busy making sure that my handover would be as simple as possible for Ben and Kelli. I'd cleared my diary, rearranged meetings that I was meant to have and politely declined networking events, asking to be emailed the presentation notes instead.

The most urgent thing of all was to get our visas sorted, as without those the whole trip wouldn't take place. I'd put a call in to Sanjay, who worked for Visa Express, to see if he could take care of it like he did for our customers. However, word had got round that I was planning on breaking ties with his company as I wanted to bring it all in-house so he politely but firmly told me to bugger off.

So, here I was one wet morning waiting for the visa office to open, huddled under a shop front as I'd forgotten to bring an umbrella in my rush to leave my flat and be the first one here when the doors opened. Only, it was like the whole of Manchester had had the same idea. At least thirty other tired-looking people were patiently waiting in the queue ahead of me, and Shelley being Shelley was running late. The minutes ticked past and the doors still weren't opening; I was cold, miserable and really didn't have time for this. Where the hell was Shelley?

'This your first time?' the tall Indian man in front of me asked as I strained my neck past his shoulder for the umpteenth time to see what the hold-up was. It was now two minutes past nine and there was no sign of the rusty shutters being raised.

'Oh, erm, yep,' I replied not wanting to get into conversation with anyone.

His pale, hazel-coloured eyes circled with a ring of olive green creased as he laughed. 'I could tell. You know they say that this is the first step in your preparation for going to India.' He paused, half smiling at me.

'What's that then?' I stared at him, taking in how good-looking he was. His brooding eyes seemed to pop from his light brown skin and designer stubble; his thick mane of black hair screamed *tug me* and his crooked smile was bashful but playful at the same time.

'Patience.' He laughed.

Despite how absolutely gorgeous this guy was, I was in no mood to fall under his spell; I had far too much I needed to be getting on with to even think about what his body looked like under his classic, well-fitted suit.

I huffed. 'We're not in India; we're in Manchester where things open at the time they're supposed to.'

He just shook his head in mirth. 'If you think this is testing, wait till you get over there. You will learn things about yourself that you never would have discovered in a million years. Oh, and you're going to love it.'

I knew his type: fit but he knew it, full of condescending arrogance thinking because he fell from heaven he was somehow better than you.

'I think I know myself pretty well, thank you,' I retorted with a tight smile, wishing this queue would hurry up and move so I didn't have to look at his annoying, smug face. I was going to be fine in India. Fine.

'Georgia! I'm here!' Shelley called out, running over red-faced and waving at me. 'Excuse me; my friend's saved me a place.' She pushed her way down the line, pretending not to see the looks of disgust and hear the irritated huffs and puffs from the queue. 'Sorry I'm late, hon,' she said breathlessly, fanning her flushed cheeks with her phone. 'God look at this queue. Could you not have got one of your contacts to sort this out for us?'

'If I could have I would have, trust me.'

She nodded, seemingly picking up on my pissed-off tones. I had so much I needed to be doing thanks to our spontaneous holiday; waiting in line to get a stamp in my passport was not one of them. After realising that our rash, drunken decision didn't just affect the two of us I'd been trying to make my unplanned leave as seamless as possible, including looking into getting an extra pair of hands to help Ben and Kelli out whilst I was gone. Ben had said that they would be fine but I wasn't a hundred per cent convinced so thought it would be better if I hired a temp just in case. Ben would thank me; I was sure of it.

The only problem was that out of the many applicants the local temp agency had emailed over, hardly any seemed suitable. I had made two piles – one of potentials and one of absolute no-nos but I needed to get someone lined up soonish.

'Ah, I see. Well hopefully we'll be in and out before you know it.' She smiled. 'So, how are things? No regrets?'

'No regrets. Apart from I'm never drinking rum again.' I noticed that buff Bollywood guy had suddenly become engrossed in his phone, thankfully.

Shelley pulled a face. 'Me neither. So, how was Ben? Did he mind that you've booked this trip? He must be pleased that you're taking the initiative in sorting out these negative reviews?'

I hadn't had time to call her properly since he'd found out. 'Let's just say he wasn't super impressed with my spontaneous decision to go all undercover boss in India. He was more disappointed that I hadn't mentioned this idea to him first.'

'Oh. Bugger.' I nodded in agreement. 'Hey, don't worry. Absence makes the heart grow fonder and all that. Plus, when he realises that this idea was brilliant and we are a pair of masterminds I'm sure he'll change his mind.'

'I hope so.' I smiled sadly.

Suddenly a small pathetic cheer broke out as the doors were finally opened and the throng of people gently pushed forward and filed in. The visa office was as drab on the inside as it was on the outside. A table propped up with a wedge of yellowing newspaper under one wonky leg held leaflets and biro pens tied on with scratty pieces of string to stop anyone from stealing them. Three musky pink coloured counters stood at the back of the cold room and tired-looking employees plodded around putting out plastic chairs for customers to sit on.

I took a ticket, like at the delicatessen counter in Tesco, and waited our turn, far away from smug Mr India know-it-all, tapping my feet impatiently and hoping they would hurry up and call our number.

'I still can't believe we're going to India,' I said nodding at the large, albeit tatty, poster of the Taj Mahal on the wall opposite.

'I know! It's going to be amazing.' Shelley grinned.

'How was Jimmy about it? Not going to be pining for you for too long?' I teased.

'Probably.' She let out a throaty laugh. 'Like I said, absence makes the heart grow fonder.'

'Number thirty-two,' a robotic voice buzzed over the intercom.

'That's us!' I jumped up out of my seat and we rushed over to the booth where a middle-aged woman with thick glasses looked at us expectantly. 'Hi, we need to get visas for India, please.' I slid our passports under the grubby glass screen and checked my watch.

'You got your forms?' Glasses Lady asked in a bored, nasally tone.

I jerked my head up to face hers. 'Forms?'

She rolled her eyes. 'Your forms – we need them to process your application.' She sighed. 'All this information *was* on our website.'

Bloody hell.

With our customers we simply put them in touch with Sanjay's visa services and he got on with sorting that aspect out. I didn't know that there were forms involved.

'Erm, no, we don't have any forms.'

The woman sighed and looked at the queue of people behind me. I could feel Mr Smug India's eyes on me; bet he had bloody forms.

'What's the matter?' Shelley piped up.

'We were meant to bring some forms,' I grumbled.

'Forms? I thought we just got a stamp in our passports and we were on our way?'

'Me too.' I let out a deep breath and turned to Glasses Lady. 'Do you have any forms here we could fill in?'

'All the forms are online.' She was loving the power; you could tell.

I tried to stay calm. 'So we need to go home, download the forms, fill them in and print them off then come back here? To join that queue again?' I was so behind I just didn't have the time for this.

'Well, they're the rules.'

'Seriously?' I gave her my best begging look but she just continued to stare blankly at us.

'Come back with the forms and your passport-sized photos. You do have your passport-sized photos, don't you?' I bit my lip and shook my head. 'Well then, I'd be getting a move on if I was you. We shut in two hours.'

I flashed her an insincere smile. 'Great, well thanks for your help. Come on, Shell.' I turned on my heel and walked to the front door.

'Wait? She can't be serious?' Shelley gasped. 'Seems a bit over the top if you ask me. What did she say about passport photos?'

'We need some, pronto.'

Shelley nodded, then added quietly, 'Thought you knew about this sort of stuff.'

'Please don't start.'

'You ladies OK?' Smug, gorgeous Mr India know-it-all sidled up to us as I shoved my passport back in my bag.

'Fine,' I muttered.

'You don't know where there's a photo booth near here, do you? Or an Internet café? We need to download some forms.' Shelley flashed him her most dazzling smile.

'It's fine. We'll find somewhere.' I placed my hand on her shoulder, trying to steer her past this irritating guy.

'I've got some spare forms here that you can use.' He rustled in his black leather man-bag. Course he did.

'Wow, that's really nice. Isn't it, Georgia?' Shelley beamed.

'Hmm. Got a mini camera in there too to take our photos?' I said sarkily. Why was I being so obtuse with this man? There was just something about him that got on my nerves.

Mr India laughed. 'Nope, but there's an ASDA not too far from here where you can get some printed. If you want, I'll save you a place in the queue.'

I was just about to tell him that we didn't need his help when Shelley clapped her hands and thanked him profusely before tugging me out of the doors to the supermarket.

'He was so nice!' she mused as we trudged over the slippery pavements. 'And bloody gorgeous.'

'You're too trusting,' I said, narrowly avoiding stepping into a pile of fresh dog turd.

'Pffft. And you're too cautious. You can trust people, even strangers; sometimes they really do just want to help a girl out.'

'We'll see about that,' I muttered. I wanted to add that I spoke from experience of misreading people who I thought I could trust, but I stayed quiet, as in a weird way I wanted to be proved wrong.

True to his word, Mr India was indeed waiting patiently for our return holding out forms and even a stick of glue to attach our admittedly awful-looking passport photos.

'Here you go, ladies.' He handed them over, stifling a laugh at my photo. 'So, Georgia Green and Shelley Robinson,' he said, reading our names off the forms. 'I hope you have an excellent time in India. Right, I'd better be off. Oh, my name's Rahul, by the way.'

'Thank you so much, Rahul!' Shelley called out behind him just as our number was called. 'God, what a nice guy. Shame we're both taken; well your heart is taken, as otherwise this trip could be getting a lot hotter – and I don't mean the spicy curries.' She laughed, pretending to fan her face as Rahul walked off.

I mumbled a response. 'Come on, let's get this sorted.'

'That was quick,' Glasses Lady murmured as she took our forms. 'OK, these look all right.' I let out a sigh of relief. 'I'll get them processed and let you know if you've been successful.'

'Wait – *if* we've been successful? So even after wasting our whole morning here it still isn't guaranteed that we'll be granted a visa?' She shook her head, making her dangly earrings jangle loudly. 'Well how long is that decision going to take?'

'If you've been approved then you'll receive your passport back with visa in ten business days.'

'Ten days!' I screeched. 'I thought you just gave us a stamp in our passports? We're leaving in ten days!'

She gave me a look that screamed *not my problem* and pointed to a small notice taped to her booth that said verbal abuse towards staff would not be tolerated. I tried to calm down. 'You'd better hope it arrives in time then.' She glared at me and hollered for the next customer. 'Number fifty-nine.'

'So much for being spontaneous,' I grumbled as we walked out of the soulless visa office into a torrential rainstorm. The heavens had opened and the wind whipped our cheeks as we trudged to the bus stop. Shelley stayed silent during the whole bus journey to the other side of town.

I walked through the door of our shop, dripping wet and covered in goosebumps, which did not improve my mood. It felt like this trip was doomed before it had even started. Although, I did cheer up drastically when I realised that we had a visitor. Sat in my chair cradling a cup of tea was Trisha, Ben's godmother and my friend; I couldn't stop the grin taking over my wet face.

'What are you doing here?' I said as I pulled her in for a hug.

'Hello, dear, got caught up in that storm did you?' She nodded at my soaked trousers. 'Well, I hear the weather in Delhi is much nicer this time of year.' She winked.

'Ah, so Ben told you.'

'Yes, oh how exciting! You are going to love India. Every time I've been I swear I've ended up leaving feeling like a changed woman,' she gushed. 'It is the birthplace of spirituality after all and just has this aura about it. India inspires, thrills and frustrates like no other country.'

'You can say frustrates again,' I grumbled, hanging up my jacket that was dripping on the floor. 'I've spent all morning waiting in line at the visa office and still might not get it in time before we fly.' I sighed, trying not to panic about what would be the alternative if my passport didn't arrive back before our flight. I could picture smug Rahul shaking his head at how late we had left it to sort out.

'Ah yes, I know it is a pain but it will be worth it once you step off that plane in such a wonderful land. It's an enigma; nowhere stirs the soul like India does. You'll see.'

'Hmm, I'm not sure I want my soul stirring.' I winced.

'Oh but you don't get a say in the matter.' Trisha chuckled. 'Mother India will do what she wants.'

I nodded as if I knew what the hell she was going on about. 'Anyway, how are you?'

'Fine fine, getting used to this retired life has been a bit of an adjustment.' She flashed a bright smile that didn't quite meet her eyes.

'You know you could have stayed working here?' I said.

When we first decided to launch Lonely Hearts Travels, Trisha had still been running her Making Memories tours but we quickly overtook her loyal base of clients and merged the two together to create Young At Heart. Pitched as small groups to European destinations where solo mature men and women could experience one of our less lively but still as wonderful tours that Kelli liked to call Randy Retirees. So far it had really taken off with retired over sixties looking to spend their children's inheritance on treating themselves to travel. Trisha still popped in every so often but her visits were a rare and delightful surprise rather than routine.

She patted my hand; I was taken aback by how translucent her wrinkled hands were next to mine. 'I know, but this is yours and Ben's baby now.' I blushed. 'You know what I mean!' She laughed. 'It is looking so good in here; Kelli was just telling me how busy you have all been. I think she was hoping for a pay rise.' Trisha winked.

'Wouldn't we all.' I rolled my eyes. 'So have you started any new hobbies then? When my dad retired it seemed like he suddenly sprouted green fingers.'

Trisha shook her head. 'Not me, I can barely keep cacti alive. I have been reading a lot more and catching up with friends now that I have more time on my hands.' The way she said this was as if it was more a chore than a freedom. 'I'm sure I'll find my feet soon.'

She smiled brightly and began flicking through one of our brochures when a thought suddenly came to me.

'Trisha, what are you doing on the twenty-seventh?'

She looked up. 'Nothing. Why?'

'How about coming out of retirement for a while?'

CHAPTER 7

Nescience (n.) Lack of knowledge; ignorance

'So, did you say a fond farewell to lover boy?' Shelley pretended to smooch a cushion as she watched me repack my backpack in my small lounge.

'Hmm, more of a see-you-in-a-few-weeks-oh-colleague,' I replied, thinking how tense the past two weeks of work had been. I'd purposely tried to avoid any conversations about India, knowing I'd overstepped some invisible line between us. 'I don't get it. OK so yeah, I did spring this whole travelling to India idea on him, thanks to you.' I shot Shelley a look. 'But *he* was the one who said he thought I should go. That it was for the best *we* had a break from each other.' My stomach skipped remembering the look in his eyes as he'd told me that, disappointment etched on his tired features.

'Well, he's probably feeling slightly jealous.' Shelley shrugged.

I looked up at her. 'What do you mean?'

'He loves to travel; you knew that from the moment you met him.' I thought back to the collection of postcards sent from exotic destinations all around the world when I first stepped foot in Trisha's travel agency. I'd nosily read these postcards written by a guy called Stevie, Trisha's godson, without knowing Stevie was Ben Stevens. 'He's probably just sulking that he can't go to India with you,' she offered.

'Maybe,' I said slowly. It was true he probably did feel like his wings had been clipped since taking on the business. There were times when I'd spot him looking through our brochures and gazing at pictures of idyllic beaches and remote jungles, but whenever I asked him about it he would snap his head up, plaster on a smile and tell me he didn't regret a thing about starting the business. I just wished that he'd added 'with you' on the end of that sentence.

'Right, I reckon we finish up here and head to the pub,' Shelley said jumping to her feet.

'I dunno, I've still not checked I've got everything I need.' I nodded at my half-filled bag.

'Pfft, we're going for two weeks. All you need is a couple of pairs of knickers, a toothbrush and your passport.' Our passports had been returned just this morning, complete with Indian tourist visas; I could have cried with happiness when Kelli signed for them. 'Come on, Miss Spontaneous, let's go and have a drink – get us in the mood for tomorrow's journey!'

Walking into the dim light of my local pub, hearing the jingly tones of the fruit machine and breathing in stale cigarette air masked by bleach, I remembered why I hardly ever came here. But it was cheap, close to home and the locals were friendly enough. With Shelley putting our order in at the bar, I sat down on one of the grubby seats and got my phone out. Trisha had been thrilled to be back working in the shop whilst I was away, and Ben had seemed pretty happy too. It solved the problem of finding a temp and meant I knew everything would be looked after in Trisha's very capable hands. I know I was only going to be away for two weeks, but a lot could change in that time. I was just scrolling through my emails, making sure I'd forwarded everything I needed over to the pair of them, when someone called my name.

'Georgia?' I looked up to see Mike, Marie's boyfriend, grinning down at me.

'Oh hi! How are you?' I said, smiling at his paint-splattered overalls. 'You just finished work?'

'Yep, nothing gets past you, does it!' He smiled as Shelley walked over holding two pints of cider. 'Oh hiya, Shelley, how are you?'

'Ah, it's Mike right?' Shelley asked, carefully placing the pints on the rickety table. Mike nodded. 'It's great to see you again; God, the last time was at Georgia's launch party, wasn't it?'

'Time flies hey?' Mike laughed.

'You can say that again; so how's little Cole doing?'

'Great, thanks. He's slowly learning the joys of using a potty.' Mike grimaced and sat down sloshing some of his pint on the floor as we moved our chairs around the table. 'Anyway, what are you both up to? Georgia, you never come in here!'

'Well we're off to India tomorrow so thought we'd get in the mood and have a quick drink,' Shelley said proudly. I still hadn't told anyone; it wasn't like when I jetted off backpacking round Thailand last year. This trip was purely business. Get in, find Nihal, sort out the problem and get out again.

Mike's eyes widened. 'Whoa, Marie never told me that. How exciting!'

'Yeah, it was kind of a spur-of-the-moment thing,' I said, not adding the fact that we'd been pissed on expensive, super-strength rum at the time. 'Is she about?' I craned my neck around the empty pub to try and track down my best friend.

'She's just dropping Cole at her mum's; we're having a night off from scooping up poo and wiping wet patches from the floor, thank God.' Mike laughed and glanced at his watch. 'She should be here any sec –'

Right on cue, Marie walked in – her green eyes darted around the gloom of the pub until they found us. 'Oh my God, Georgia!' A huge grin broke on her face as she ran over and squeezed me tight. 'You never come out; what are you doing here? I haven't heard from you in ages.'

I winced. 'I'm so sorry I've just been…'

'Busy, yeah, yeah, I know. Well the odd text back would be nice,' she said before shaking her head. 'Anyway, how are things?'

'Marie!' Shelley's voice boomed making Marie jump. 'How you doing, chick?'

Marie almost stumbled back in surprise. 'Shelley, what are you doing here? I thought you were going round Europe?'

'Yeah, I was. Managed to Interrail round a few places but then Manchester sort of stole my heart.'

'Yeah, Manchester and Jimmy,' I teased.

'Ben's best mate? The beefcake?' Marie asked.

'Yep, that's the one.' I laughed.

'So what are you up to? Having a girly night in the pub together?' The question was light enough but I could sense Marie bristling slightly.

'Yeah kinda. We decided to sod the packing and come and get a few drinks in us in preparation for tomorrow.' Shelley grinned.

'Packing? Tomorrow?' Marie repeated.

'Did Georgia not tell you? We're off to India!' Shelley wrapped her arm around my shoulder and squeezed me.

'India?' Marie echoed. I nodded. 'Ah, great,' she said in a tone that sounded very un-great. 'No, erm, she didn't say.'

Shelley didn't pick up on the faux-friendly tones and continued to babble on. 'Yeah, flying into Delhi and then maybe have a little trip around, take in the sights, head over to Bollywood before catching some sun on a beach in Goa.

Lord knows this Aussie bird needs a good dose of vitamin D.' She laughed, rubbing her freckled forearms.

Mike stood up to give Marie a peck on the cheek and a small glass of wine, which she almost necked in one.

'You…you're going to Bollywood?' Marie faced me.

'Pretty cool, huh?' Mike chipped in.

Marie turned to him. 'So you knew about this?'

'Only just heard before you got here, babe,' Mike said, putting his hands up defensively and making a speedy exit back to the bar, mumbling something about buying a bag of pork scratchings.

'Right, great, well I hope you have a fantastic time,' Marie said through gritted teeth. Shelley must have picked up on the tension between us and hurried off to the fruit machines.

'I'm sorry for not calling you before now. I've been meaning to call you for ages,' I said quietly.

'Mmmm.' Marie gulped her drink and avoided eye contact. 'Well my number's not changed.'

An old man hacking up a load of phlegm and the repetitive tinny music from the fruit machines were the only sounds breaking this awkward silence that had settled around us.

'So, Bollywood, huh?'

'Marie, it's not like that.'

'Oh really?' She whipped her flaming red hair towards me, put a hand on her hip and narrowed her eyes. 'Tell me, Georgia, what *is* it like?'

'Well, you'd actually laugh about it,' I said, rolling my eyes at how the trip to India had even come about.

'You think this is funny?' I stopped smiling and looked to the floor. 'You want to know something funny?' By the look of her pinched mouth I wasn't sure that I did. 'I encourage my best friend to go off backpacking after being a jilted bride; I was there fully supporting her, helping her to get over the really shitty thing that had happened to her. And what do I get in return?'

'Wait I –'

'No you wait. If I don't say this now when will I get the chance again?' I nodded and swallowed the lump in my throat that had suddenly risen.

'I understand that you're busy with work but I *never* hear from you; you never return my calls or answer my texts. Then I randomly walk in here for a drink with my boyfriend and see you and your cool backpacking friend sitting here laughing. Only to find out that you and her are jetting off to India tomorrow, to a place I've always wanted to go. I mean, fucking Bollywood! Did it not occur to you that maybe, just maybe, your actress friend would want to experience that with you? Or are you too busy being backpacker businesswoman Georgia to notice?' Her eyes filled with tears but she blinked them back.

'Marie, I'm sorry. I understand that it might look like this from your perspective, but trust me, it's nothing like that.' I placed my hand on my chest feeling like I wanted to cry too.

'Is this because I've got a kid? Or because I'm just working as a mobile hairdresser? Not cultured enough or fancy enough for you now?'

'No!! Of course it's nothing to do with that. I'm sorry for being a crap friend; I've just had a lot going on but as soon as I get back I'll make this up to you, I promise.'

She continued to glare at me. 'It might be too late then.' With that she turned on her heel and got lost in the pub.

I should have raced after her, apologising to her for being a shitty friend recently, but the truth was I was tired. Tired of messing things up, tired of having people tell me they were worried about me, tired of letting people down and feeling their disappointment.

I was tired of it all.

CHAPTER 8

Drawn (adj.) Tense; fatigued

We'd overslept. I must have cancelled the three alarms I'd set on my phone as the sound of the pre-booked taxi impatiently beeping its horn woke me with a start.

'Shit! Shell, get up; we are really fucking late!' I jumped from my bed and flung on some clothes before hopping into my shoes.

'What?! Ah man,' Shelley cried, tumbling from the sofa to her unsteady feet.

After the bust-up with Marie we'd stayed in the pub until closing time, nursing a bottle of wine as I'd resolved that this trip would be the solution to all my problems. I'd be like Trisha and come back a changed woman. That plan had seemed possible at eleven o'clock last night but wasn't going quite so well this morning.

My small flat turned into a hive of activity as I raced from room to room chucking last-minute bits and bobs into my bag. I triple checked I'd turned off the heating, locked the windows and hadn't left the oven on. Not that I could even remember the last time I'd used it but you never could be too careful.

'We have to go; this taxi fella's not happy,' Shelley called from the front door as I did a final scan that I'd unplugged everything. 'Georgia, come on!'

'Coming!' I called back, lugging my backpack onto my back. I had to admit that it did feel nice having it back on.

In the taxi to the airport, driven by the world's most pissed-off driver, my empty stomach fizzed with anticipation and excitement. Working in tourism I thought I'd always be jetting away to exotic places but I had just been too busy to take any time off. Even though the circumstances weren't ideal for this trip, at least I got to add another stamp to my passport.

We paid the driver and raced through the packed departures hall, scanning the large boards for our flight. We were so behind schedule it wasn't even funny.

'There!' I pointed. 'New Delhi – desk twenty-nine to forty-one. Shit, it says the desks are closing in like five minutes! Hurry!' I raced off as fast as I could with a lumpy, heavy backpack on, leaving a tufted-haired yawning Shelley staggering after me.

'Good morning. Can I have your passports and tickets please,' the overly made-up woman at check-in asked. We looked like bedraggled rats compared to her. 'You're leaving it a little late, ladies.' She pursed her glossy, plump lips.

'Here and here.' I wheezed and smiled apologetically before passing over my documents as Shelley rustled in her bag for hers.

'OK, my ticket is here –' Shelley slapped the piece of A4 paper on the desk '– and my passport is…' Her thin hand rummaged around her slouchy hobo bag. 'Wait, it's in here somewhere…'

'Shelley?' Watching her arm frantically searching amongst the folds of multi-coloured cotton I felt my stomach clench.

'It's in here somewhere. God these bloody bags. Jimmy is always calling me Mary Poppins for the amount of crap that gets swallowed up in here.' She smiled tightly and continued to force her hand deep into the inside pockets.

The check-in lady raised a thick, painted-on eyebrow at us – they were painfully *on fleek* – before peering at Shelley's ticket. 'Everything OK, Miss Robinson?'

'Fine,' Shelley said more breezily than she looked.

'Shell? You packed it, right?' A taste of bile caught at the back of my throat watching her grow more panicked with every second that passed without finding it.

'Miss Robinson, I'm afraid if you do not have your passport you will be unable to travel today,' the check-in lady unhelpfully reminded us before glancing at a silver watch on her tanned wrist.

'I understand that.' Shelley flashed a tight, fake smile at the woman whilst looking as if she was desperately trying to restrain herself from lurching across the desk and punching her.

'We overslept,' I said, wanting to fill this tense wait. She nodded and looked us up and down as if that explained everything.

A few moments later Shelley glanced up. The colour had completely faded from her face. 'It's…it's…not here.'

My stomach lurched. 'No!' I gasped. I stared at her, desperate for her to break into a huge grin and pull it out of her bag, waving it around saying: 'Ha gotcha!' But instead Shelley looked like she was about to cry or pass out or both.

'Shell? You're a hundred per cent sure you haven't got it?' I started rooting around my own bag in case I had picked it up by mistake. 'Empty everything out and let's check again,' I ordered, much to the disgust of the check-in lady. It had to be here. We simply didn't have time to head home to search for it *and* make our flight.

'Ladies. Please hurry. I should have closed check-in five minutes ago,' Check-in lady hissed, trying to ignore the mess we were making on the cold, hard floor of the departures hall.

'It must be here!' I cried, shaking my bag out as pens and spare socks tumbled to the floor. It was becoming very obvious that Shelley's passport wasn't in either of our bags. 'Check your pockets. Wait – maybe we left it in the taxi? Are you sure you even had it?'

Shelley turned her empty pockets inside out and roughly wiped her eyes. 'Positive. I put it in the inside pocket of my bag before we went to the pub. I even took this bag with me last night as I was paranoid I'd lose it…' She trailed off as if thinking about something before jerking her head up. 'Marie.'

'What?' I stopped scrambling on my knees and stared at her. 'What do you mean Marie?'

'I mean, I left my bag at the table when you two were talking, well, arguing – remember? Then you both left it unattended after your fight,' she whispered, biting her bottom lip.

'What? Well then it could have been anyone in there, couldn't it?' I said, feeling faint with the worry bubbling up inside of me. Marie wouldn't sabotage this trip, would she? Would she?

'Excuse me, Miss Green?' Check-in lady barked, pulling me back to the immediate crisis we were dealing with. 'I need you to go through security right now; your flight will be boarding imminently. Miss Robinson, if you don't have your passport then you will be unable to fly today.'

I held up a hand to stall for time. 'Maybe it's still at the flat? Maybe it fell out of your bag in the pub? Maybe someone's handed it in? Maybe it's in the taxi?' I was clutching at straws and I knew it.

Shelley shook her head sadly. 'I had it last night and now I don't.'

'And you *didn't* think to check you still had it this morning?' I was half screeching now as waves of hysteria washed over me. Shelley had to come with me; I couldn't do this trip alone.

'I'm so sorry, Georgia. You're going to have to go without me.'

'Miss Green, please, if you do not go straight to security I will have to let them know to close the flight without you, without either of you.'

'OK!' I snapped. 'Sorry. I'm sorry. It's just I can't believe Marie would do something like that.'

Shelley sniffed loudly. 'I can. She was so pissed off with you. Maybe this way you would finally remember her and not leave her out in the future.'

I shook my head violently. 'No, Marie would never do something so crazy and spiteful as this. No way.'

'Excuse me, Miss Green.' The check-in lady seethed. 'Are you travelling today or not?'

'Is there another flight, maybe a later one that we could get booked onto?' The woman huffed but looked down at her screen and started angrily tapping at her keyboard.

Shelley turned to me. 'I really hope you're right about Marie. At least this way I can go back to yours, do a proper search for it, head to the pub and ask them, call the taxi firm and…' She trailed off listing all the options we had for her to make this trip and for my best friend not to be responsible for this fuck-up.

'Yes, good idea. Retrace your steps, find your passport, then fly out later to join me.'

'Sorry,' the check in lady interrupted, not looking sorry in the slightest. 'The later flight is all booked up. The next available flight I could get you on would be next Thursday but it's coming up at almost double the cost of the flight you had booked today. That is, if you find your passport by then.'

My heart sank.

Shelley's face drained of colour. 'Well that's that then.' She sighed, blinking away tears. 'We'll have to leave it. I'm so sorry. Will you be OK going by yourself?'

I didn't have time to answer as the check-in lady had now stood up and logged off her computer. 'Miss Green, please follow me or neither of you will be heading to India.'

'I'm going to have to be.' I sniffed and quickly pulled Shelley into a hug. 'Call me as soon as you find your passport.'

She nodded. 'Be safe, Georgia, and good luck!' she called behind me as I raced to keep up with the woman striding ahead in her shiny black court shoes.

This would be fine. Fine. I swallowed back the bile that burned my throat. Wouldn't it?

I was rushed through security, raced down the never-ending bright corridors and half tumbled into my seat, wheezing and out of breath. I nervously stared out of the small aircraft window as they ran through the safety announcement, hoping beyond hope that Shelley would miraculously turn up and take the seat next to me. However, once the doors were pulled shut there was no chance. I was now on my own. There was no turning back.

All the other passengers around me were excitedly chatting about their travels, the friends and family they were meeting or the places they were going, but all I could think was how I was going to survive. I let myself cry thinking of what lay ahead of me, ignoring the strange looks I was receiving. How was I going to face travelling round this enormous country by myself? Being spontaneous comes with its downsides. This was all Shelley's idea and now she wasn't even here to help me.

I thought back to the way Marie had looked at me last night, how hurt and angry she was. She couldn't have hidden Shelley's passport; she would never do something so spiteful and stupid, would she? A small voice piped up in my head: *She would if she wanted to teach you a lesson, let you be this fearless backpacker that she thinks you are.*

But the truth is, I'm not fearless at all.

CHAPTER 9

Trepid (adj.) Timorous; fearful

Fifteen hours later I landed at New Delhi airport. *You can do this*, I repeated in my head, giving myself a pep talk as I traipsed through immigration and headed to the baggage carousel. Steeling myself I grabbed my backpack, wiped my red-rimmed, teary eyes and followed the large crowd to the arrival doors. *Come on, get a grip; you're in India, not on Mars. It will be fine. You can do this.*

However, if I thought arriving into Bangkok airport was overwhelming it was *nothing* compared to here. I stepped foot from the safety of the air-conditioned terminal building into what felt like a wall of noise. People were shouting, smells of spicy, fried food and cow poo mixed in the stuffy, oven-like heat and intimidating stares from strange men made me want to flee back onto the next flight home.

There are more than a billion people living in India and it felt like they had all congregated in this small space to welcome my flight. A pulsating energy was constrained by a weak wire fence just in front of me. Thin brown arms poked through holes, swiping at the air. Voices yelled out 'taxi', each competing for the best fare. The knackered-looking railings seemed to surge forward as other passengers walked past. 'Taxi?' 'Madam, good price, taxi?'

My tired eyes stung from the sunlight. I felt like I was in the middle of the stock exchange with people bartering all around me, pushing and shoving for business. I jumped, feeling something touch my arm and looked down to see a small street boy grinning at me with half his teeth missing. He placed his tiny, dirty palm out – wanting cash – but all my money was safely stored away in my unsexy, beige travel belt, which was currently sweating against my stomach.

'Oh, sorry, erm, no money,' I apologised and pulled out a handful of boiled sweets from my pocket that I'd been given on the plane. 'Here, take these.'

'Bitch,' he said, chucking the sweets on the floor and spitting at my dusty feet. I gawped back in shock as I watched him scurry off to find someone else to ask.

My head was spinning with all the people milling around me, relentlessly pushing and shoving me. I tried to focus on the many handwritten signs bobbing up and down in front of me, looking for my name or Shelley's, but they were nowhere to be seen. We expected all the guides on our Lonely Hearts tours to be at the airport meeting and greeting guests as they arrive in their country, to provide safe and preferably air-conditioned transport that takes them to the hotel where they meet the other guests and get their adventure started. I couldn't even find my way to get from this cattle market section of arrivals over to where an official taxi stand might be. Looking at the chaos before me I was reminded of a quote from one of the awful reviews: *I was left stranded at the airport like an unwanted sales phone call when you're just about to eat dinner. After a long-haul flight and already feeling emotional it was not the welcome I had expected or paid for. Little did I know that this was a taste of things to come…*

Suddenly someone grabbed my bag, almost toppling me over with the force.

'Madam, I am very sorry but your hotel has burnt down. They sent me here to take you to other hotel,' a gangly Indian man with surprising strength said, bobbing his head as fast as he was tugging my bag straps.

'What? Wait. Can you just let go of my bag, please?' I replied in shock. My hotel had burnt down? Oh my God! I needed him to let go of me so I could breathe and think, impossible to do with the ceaseless caterwauling noise around me.

'Miss, we need to go now – come, come.' He had a firm grip on one of my straps and started to lead me away like a dog on a leash when I heard someone else shout out.

'Miss Green?' I spun my head to face where I thought the voice had come from.

An old man with peppered grey hair holding a scratty piece of paper with my name scrawled on was waving a thick arm to get my attention. The guy pulling my bag straps instantly let go and scampered off. *What the…?* I elbowed my way over to the tired-looking man with the sign.

'Miss Green?' he asked again.

I nodded. 'Yes, that's me. Are you Nihal?' Things must be bad as I was positive the guy I'd spoken to briefly on Skype a few months ago was a lot younger and fresh-faced.

The old man chuckled. 'No, I'm Deepak; Nihal is much uglier than I am. So, welcome to Delhi!' His wrinkled face broke into a warm grin, flashing his blackened gums.

I smiled back, wiping a layer of sweat and grime from my flustered face. 'Thank you. Erm, I've heard that the hotel has burnt down?' I asked, wide-eyed.

Deepak huffed and muttered something under his breath. 'No, Miss Green, that is a scam. They tell you that so they

to be sharing this with me, to give me someone to talk to about it all. I wasn't strong enough to cope with this by myself.

'Do you know if we're nearly at the hotel?' I asked Deepak as we headed back onto what looked like another motorway, suddenly desperate to be tucked up in bed, to wake up and find out that this was all a nightmare.

CHAPTER 10

Invidious (adj.) Unpleasant and causing bad feelings

Standing in the small but clean reception of the hotel it was as if the volume had been muted on the chaotic, busy street outside. Now I was here I needed to toughen up and get things sorted, starting with my new persona. I'd been thinking on the journey over here about using my middle name, Louise, and telling everyone I was a hairdresser from Manchester. I figured that Green was a common enough surname; no one would put two and two together if who the CEO of the tour group company was ever came up in conversation.

After a smooth check-in and only tearing up once more at the fact I wouldn't be sharing my room with Shelley I was feeling slightly more together, although I still hadn't seen any trace of Nihal or the rest of the tour group. The friendly receptionist with slicked black hair told me that the tour guide preferred to let the guests arrive separately so they didn't feel too overwhelmed and that the welcome meeting would take place later. I'd nodded as if I understood but surely there was safety and security in numbers, especially battling through the bedlam of the New Delhi airport arrivals hall?

After a refreshing shower and a little nap I was as ready as I would ever be to take on my challenge. I'd changed into a light and floaty cream-coloured dress that I hoped would be both cool and smart for the restaurant. I'd wrapped a Primark scarf around my shoulders and headed back to reception to finally meet this elusive Nihal and the other guests.

I knew we had five guests booked on this tour: Oliver Chalmers, Christopher Kennings, Rebecca Jackson, Liz Lowes and Felicity Black (Flic). I'd met Liz before when she came into the shop – a willowy pale thing – but the others had reserved the tour either online or over the phone so I didn't have much to go by. I was hoping that Liz wouldn't remember who I was; Ben had been the one who'd booked her trip after all.

I was the first one to arrive so awkwardly sat on a beige leather sofa near the front door. Ten long minutes later a guy with short, messy strawberry-blond hair, freckles scattered over his chiselled cheeks and toned, pale arms straining under his T-shirt strode into reception. He caught my eye; relief spread over his handsome face as he briskly walked over to me.

'Alreet! You on the tour too? I'm Ollie by the way,' he said in a friendly Geordie accent. The cute Ed Sheeran lookalike stuck out his hand and grinned, revealing perfect straight white teeth.

'Hi, yep I sure am. My name's, erm, Louise. Nice to meet you Ollie.' I shook his hand.

'So, you know what the plan is?' he asked sitting on the sofa opposite me and rubbing the back of his neck. 'First time I've ever been on a tour and wasn't sure what to expect to be honest.' His voice was deep and friendly. His light green eyes creased as he smiled and he had two adorable dimples in his unshaved cheeks.

'Yeah it's a little nerve-wracking isn't it? The first day always feels a little awkward.'

'Oh, so you've done this before?'

'Erm no, well I travelled with a tour to Thailand last year but not this kind of tour,' I blustered.

He nodded. 'Ah, I think here are some more of us now.'

I turned to follow where he was staring; three women had walked into reception looking as apprehensive as we did. They headed over to Ollie and me.

'Hey, I'm Bex. You on this sad and solo tour too?' the shortest and roundest one of the trio called out before laughing. The other two sort of hid behind her ample frame.

'Yep, I'm Louise and this is Ollie.' I smiled and shuffled up the sofa for them all to sit down.

'Blindin''. Well this is Liz and Flic.' Bex did the introductions and waved a chubby arm at the two women behind her. Liz nodded hello, holding a crumpled tissue in her hands. Her watery eyes grew wide at seeing Ollie. With her high cheekbones and willowy frame she could have stepped off a catwalk in Milan, but judging by the way her shoulders hunched and her hands trembled she had as much confidence as a kitten at Crufts.

'Hey, welcome to the club. Shit I hope I'm not the only bloke.' Ollie laughed.

'You scared about being in touch with your feminine side?' the other woman, Flic, said sharply before slumping on the sofa next to me. I suddenly got a strong whiff of ylang-ylang; it smelt like the stuff my mum used to slap on her feet after a hard day at work.

'No, no. I'm fine around women, very happy in fact,' Ollie replied sheepishly under Flic's stare.

She was what you would call a typical hippy backpacker. Sun-lightened dreads were piled on her head and her tanned arms were covered in bangles and tatty threaded bracelets. The brown sack she was wearing just nailed the whole boho chic look she was aiming for. I suddenly felt very clean and overdressed next to her.

'I was only joking with you,' Flic said before stifling a yawn and titling her head back so her nose piercing glinted in the light. Ollie mumbled that he knew that. 'So, any of you know what we're doing tonight?'

Liz – who was perched on the arm of the sofa and fidgeting with the hem on her sleeve – shook her head. Her long, light brown hair danced with the movement. 'I forgot to print off the itinerary we were sent,' she half whispered, staring at the polished floor.

'I think we're meeting everyone before going out for dinner,' I said.

Where the hell was Nihal? I really hoped he wouldn't be late as by my count there was one more tour goer left to join us. I tried to catch the receptionist's eye to see if he was sorting out a welcome drink for everyone, as we expected on all of our tours, but he was staring intently at his computer screen.

'Good, I'm starvin'. That stuff they serve on the plane weren't food. I wouldn't even give me dog that,' Bex said. 'And Barking Brenda eats everythin'! I once found her chewing on a box of tampons, happy as Larry she were. Don't worry, they weren't used ones,' she added catching Ollie's shocked and awkward expression.

Flic frowned. 'You know you shouldn't be so dismissive of the time, effort and cost that went into preparing that *dog food*. People starving in Africa wouldn't turn their noses up at it.' She shook her head and lightened her tone; her plummy English accent seemed so alien compared to her hippy dress sense. 'This is just another example of the western world brainwashing us through our stomachs. Just because it doesn't adhere to our prescribed cultural norms or look like it does in a supermarket doesn't mean it tastes any worse.'

'Right…' Bex humoured her. 'Here I was thinking it was just high-altitude mush.'

Ollie stifled a laugh as Flic rolled her eyes. 'Is that like those weird-shaped carrots that get chucked away 'cause no one wants them?' he asked faux innocently.

Bex laughed. 'To be fair I do love a knobbly parsnip.'

Flic tutted and mumbled under her breath that she doubted Bex would even know what a parsnip looked like. Liz, who didn't seem to know where to put herself, smiled gratefully at a man I hadn't noticed before who emerged from behind a tall white pillar.

He was wearing khaki shorts that flashed his hairy pink legs and was looking down at his phone with his tight face creased in a frown.

'You all right, mate? You on this tour too?' Ollie called out, pleased to have a break from the politics of airline food and not to be the only male.

The guy – although he looked only a few years older than me – was completely grey, which added to his severe look. He spun his head up and looked at Ollie, put his hand up as if telling him to wait then went back to his phone and tapped out a short message.

'Oh, right then.' Ollie shrugged, looking embarrassed, and quickly sat back down.

Fifty-shades-of-grey man finished his text before slowly walking over to us with a painful smile on his drawn face. I could see deep purple bags under his light, almost grey, eyes; his sallow face was such a contrast to Ollie's cheeky grin. Ollie had bounded over full of excitement. This man looked like he wanted to be anywhere but here, as if this was some sort of huge inconvenience. I tried to shake this out of my head. Maybe he was just tired; he'd had a long journey and was probably feeling overwhelmed like the rest of us after landing here. But for some reason I had to shush a prickling feeling that I was forcing myself to believe this.

'This the tour group meeting place?' he asked, his voice as monotone and grey as the rest of him.

'Well if it's not then we're in the wrong place.' Bex grinned, flashing crooked front teeth. 'I'm Bex, this is Ollie, Liz, Louise and sorry I've forgotten your name…' She gestured to Flic who seemed highly unimpressed.

'Flic,' she replied tartly.

'Right. I won't remember any of that. I'm Chris,' the new recruit said curtly, giving us all an intense look before checking his watch. 'Where's the tour guide then?'

'Erm, he should be here soon. Sit down if you like,' I said, trying to see if these bloody welcome drinks would ever materialise. I'd never needed the social lubricant of alcohol more. Chris muttered something under his breath about timekeeping and stayed standing up. Something clawed at my brain; he looked familiar but I could swear I'd never seen him before.

I was just about to go over to see the receptionist when an Indian man rushed through the entrance doors, sweating and wheezing. He raced over to the reception desk but stopped when he noticed all of us waiting on the sofas. Taking a deep breath and wiping a sheen of sweat from his forehead he pulled himself up straight and wandered over to the group.

'Hello. Lonely Hearts Travel Club, yes?' We all nodded. Chris rolled his eyes at the state of this flustered, red-cheeked man and I took a sharp intake of breath. This couldn't be…

'Nihal?' I boldly asked, ignoring looks from the others that I knew his name; Nihal didn't seem to register this.

'Yes, I am Nihal, your tour guide.' He stretched his clammy palm out to shake everyone's hands before unsubtly wiping them on his trouser legs. 'Fantastic, erm, welcome to India.' He cleared his throat as if remembering what to say next, although judging by the state of him he may have just rolled out of bed to be here so probably hadn't woken up properly yet. 'If you want to follow me we'll be walking the short distance to the restaurant. Let's get going.'

I got to my feet as uncertainly as the rest of the group. A quote from the travel review flashed in my mind. *The tour guide, not that you could call this waste of space that, was late, lazy and had the social skills of a drunken sloth. For the first-timer in India he was not the man you wanted to be in control of your safety and enjoyment. Seriously.*

I gulped and steeled myself for what this evening would hold.

CHAPTER 11

Galvanise (v.) To startle into sudden activity; stimulate

I know you shouldn't judge someone on first impressions but it was quite hard not to feel both disappointed and angry with this man. It wasn't just Nihal's unkempt appearance – even his creased shirt wasn't done up correctly – it was that he showed so little interest in the tour goers and was walking at such a quick speed I almost had to break into a jog to keep up with him. He was like the crap Pied Piper of India leading the way down the noisy, busy streets not even checking we were all together.

Ollie bounded over to join me at the back. 'Hey, Louise right? I'm crap with names,' he said with his hands in his pockets, distracting me from glaring at Nihal.

'Yep, that's me – Louise,' I said, the name sounding weird even on my own lips.

'So how come you chose to come to India then?'

'Just, erm, just always fancied coming here, you know?' *Cool story, bro.*

Ollie nodded then quickly sidestepped over a large dollop of cow manure on the pavement.

'What about you?'

He sighed and ran a hand through his ginger hair. His muscular right arm was covered in an intricate sleeve tattoo. 'I'm the same, always dreamt about visiting this country but just never had the time or money to do it. I, erm, I split up with my girlfriend about a year ago now and just thought if I didn't go now then I never would, like.' He smiled bashfully.

'Well that's as good an excuse as any.'

He laughed. 'Yeah, every cloud and all that. Don't get me wrong, I was crushed when it happened.' He scratched his freckled nose. 'Then as time went on I just realised that I'd changed too. Maybe my mam was right; my ex was the right girl at the right time but we had an expiry date. So after that deep epiphany I booked myself here.' His mouth broke into a pearly white grin as he stretched out his arms over the chaotic street we were half jogging half walking down to keep up with the others. 'Sorry, is that TMI? Feel like a reet girl now.'

I shook my head and smiled. 'Don't let Flic hear you say that. Hey if it makes you feel any better I sometimes forget to brush my teeth at the weekends,' I said.

'Now that is too much information.' Ollie let out a booming laugh. 'I wondered what the smell was.'

I nudged him playfully, flirtatiously in fact, before realising that the others had stopped walking and I barely knew this cute guy in front of me. *Must be the jet lag*, I told myself. The rest of the group had congregated outside the doors of a large restaurant; you could smell the spicy food cooking from out here. I noticed Flic was staring disdainfully at Bex who was panting loudly, half bent over her knees from the hike here.

'Wait here,' Nihal ordered and went inside, leaving us stood on a badly lit street corner. Liz, who looked like she needed a lie-down, quickly jumped out of the way of a speeding motorbike that almost careered into her.

'He's the silent type then.' Flic snorted and nodded her head after Nihal.

I smiled weakly, trying to hide the irritation I felt. 'Yeah, looks that way.'

Five awkward minutes later Nihal was back with us. 'Change of plan.' He rubbed his hands together, looked over our shoulders down the dusty street and lit up a fag. 'Follow me.'

'Is there a problem?' I called out ignoring both Chris who was sighing loudly and the knotted feeling in my stomach.

'No, follow me,' Nihal replied after exhaling a deep lungful of smoke.

'I don't reckon he's booked us anywhere,' Ollie whispered.

'I have a feeling you might be right.' I winced.

Another thirty minutes of walking on crumbling pavements, sidestepping cow poo and dodging wild rickshaws and we stopped again. Nihal nipped inside another restaurant. Only this one wasn't anywhere near as bright or welcoming as the last place, but I was so tired and hungry I had gone past the point of caring.

'Bet you wish you'd had that plane food now,' Flic said in a sing-song voice, looking at Bex who was still panting after power walking here.

'I'll eat *you* in a minute,' Bex muttered under her breath.

'OK, guys, come in,' Nihal interrupted Flic's sarky reply and propped open the low door, acting as if this had been part of the plan all along.

We ducked under the door and entered a large restaurant. In the dim light it looked much better than it had from the outside. I breathed a sigh of relief that this night would be OK after all. White linen tablecloths that were topped with gleaming silver cutlery and tea lights shone against the deep maroon walls. Smiling, smartly dressed waiters milled around the busy room, which was full of people of a mixture of ages, all tucking into mouth-watering food. There was a stage set to the right with unusual-looking instruments, some of which I'd never seen before, propped up waiting for the band to arrive.

'Thank God we can finally sit down,' Bex said, wiping beads of sweat from her clammy forehead with a napkin.

'I dunno about you lot but I cannae wait to get stuck into my first real curry. I bet the local Indian near me ain't a patch on this place.' Ollie grinned.

'Well I don't eat meat, carbs, farmed eggs, anything mass-produced…' Flic was ticking things off on her piano-playing, thin fingers. That caused a loud groan from Bex at the other end of the table. 'Seriously if you knew how much the food industry controls what we eat, it'd make you think twice about stuffing your face with anything and everything.' Ollie raised an eyebrow, trying to understand what she was going on about. 'There's SO much that the government lies to us about regarding where our food comes from. I mean, if you think about it, this industry is as big as tobacco companies *and* weapons manufacturers but no one ever questions the politics that go on behind closed doors. It's truly fascinating and scary that more people don't know this,' Flic said before Nihal interrupted her.

'The menu has already been decided,' he said sharply. 'We're having a taste of India so you can pick and choose what you do and don't eat.'

Flic dipped her eyes to the ruby red placemat in front of her, muttering under her breath that what she chose to eat was a basic human right.

'Right, what we drinking, guys?' Bex rubbed her hands together ignoring Flic's pout. 'I wonder if they do pints of Guinness in here?'

I called for a waiter to take our drinks order as Nihal was talking on his phone. He'd pretty much ignored the group since we'd sat down and, feeling responsible, I tried to take charge. 'Erm can we get a bottle of red and a bottle of white, some mineral water and, oh, do you do Guinness?'

'No. Sorry, miss,' the young fresh-faced waiter apologised.

'Ah no worries, make it two bottles of red and two bottles of white wine,' Bex shouted out. 'After a few glasses I'll be on my way.' She roared with laughter.

Once the drinks had finally arrived followed by a bazillion silver dishes filled with rice, curry and brightly coloured sauces, Nihal hung up his phone and seemed to perk up slightly. He barked at the waiter to lay out the dishes in order of strength starting from the mildest, yoghurt-based korma to the super spicy Phall, hotter than a vindaloo, right at the end. I could see Ollie eyeing that one up.

'You up for it, Chris? Being the only men on the tour, we better show these ladies we can handle the heat,' Ollie joked, ignoring Flic's scowl.

Chris gave him the sneery look that seemed permanently etched on his face. 'I don't think so.'

'Ah, OK. Well, no worries,' Ollie mumbled, tearing off a huge hunk of naan bread. 'More for me then hey!'

With our plates piled high with a selection of curries and our glasses full, the lights in the restaurant suddenly dimmed even more. A band headed up to the stage followed by a loud round of applause, and soon the mesmerising and melodic sound of a sitar was the only sound in the busy room.

I glanced around at the faces of the other tour goers to see if they felt as entranced as I did. Nihal had nipped out for a cigarette; Chris was poking around a few grains of boiled rice on his empty plate using the light of his phone to pick out pieces of carrot from one of the less spicy sauces; Ollie gave me the thumbs up and both Liz and Flic were swaying to the calming beat.

Bex caught my eye and gently squeezed my arm. 'Welcome to India,' she whispered excitedly before shoving a forkful of lentil dal in her mouth then wiping off a splodge that had landed on her T-shirt.

I smiled back, feeling a rush of happiness at being sat in an Indian restaurant with a group of strangers eating real Indian curry and listening to three bearded men who were now singing what sounded like a slow, romantic love song in ruddy India.

As the emotion of the song intensified I couldn't help but think about Ben. I wondered what he was doing, if he missed me or was glad that I was out of his hair for a while. He was one of very few people who got me; he knew when to let things pass and when to stand up and tell me I was being a dick. I loved that about him. I loved a lot of things about him.

You could hear the passion in the lead singer's voice as the lilting harmonies effortlessly combined and it gave me a fluttery feeling in my stomach but also a pang of disappointment in myself. I'd had the courage to walk away from my cheating ex-fiancé, to travel to Thailand and to start my own business, but I couldn't find an ounce of bravery to tell this one person that he meant the world to me.

I took a deep breath and tried to put it out of my mind; it wasn't like I could change anything from all the way in India, so instead I sat back in my chair to watch the rest of the musicians' set. When the music finished, the whole restaurant, including my tour group, broke into loud, appreciative applause for the talented stars. As the lights rose slightly I turned back round in my seat and noticed that we were a man down; Nihal was missing.

'Anyone see where Nihal's gone?' I asked, feeling a prickling sensation down my spine. He couldn't still be smoking, surely? Everyone else shrugged. I scanned my eyes around the restaurant, which had emptied slightly now that the band had finished. Nihal was nowhere to be seen.

'Maybe he's gone to the loo?' Bex suggested licking her fingers. 'Or another fag?'

'Yeah, maybe,' I replied. Although I slowly realised as time ticked on that our tour guide hadn't nipped to the bathroom but had done a runner. As the restaurant emptied out it felt like the mood of the group had bombed too. Liz was fiddling with the straw in her glass of Coke, Chris was back checking his phone, Flic was yawning and Ollie and Bex looked like they were in a food coma, gazing off into space. I needed to liven this group up and quickly. So what if Nihal had abandoned us? He had hardly been Mr Partay Animal anyway. I had to take control and make this tour memorable for the right reasons. I felt responsible for them now that Nihal had left and, yeah, we could have slunk off back to the hotel but it was still early and I wanted them to enjoy every minute that they had paid for.

The depressing mood wasn't helped by the brilliant band being replaced with what must have been the worst sitar player in all of Delhi. Sat cross-legged on the single spot-lit stage was an old man with long, straggly grey hair hanging limply over his hunched shoulders. He was drawling out some incomprehensible lyrics with his eyes shut, completely unaware that no one was paying any attention to him.

'Has everyone eaten enough?' I asked. We still had so much food on the table but they all murmured that they were full. I necked my glass of white wine and tried to top up the glasses around me. Alcohol was always the way through deadly awkward silences.

'Doesn't look like our awesome leader is coming back,' Chris said, stifling a yawn.

'What is with him? I mean I thought we would be with the best travel guide in all of India from the way the Lonely Hearts Travels website goes on about it,' Flic commented. I felt a stab in my chest. 'I mean, this dude could not give two shits about us. He probably only brought us here so he could get some sort of commission, a back-handed payment from the restaurant owner or something.'

'Did you see that review?' Bex leant forward and asked in a hushed whisper as if Nihal would suddenly spring out from behind her.

'What review?' I asked feeling flushed but hoping my face remained blank.

I knew the review they were talking about. The whole reason I was sat here now.

'You didn't read it?' Bex asked sucking air through her teeth as if about to give the bill for a clapped-out car's MOT. 'Everyone else did, right?' she asked the others who nodded and winced.

'I nearly cancelled my trip because of it,' Liz said quietly.

'So, erm, what did this review say?' I asked, pouring a big glass of water for my dry mouth.

'Just that it was a complete shambles, the tour guide was useless, the activities were crap and it was really disorganised,' Ollie said.

'Oh right, God that's…erm…bad, awful,' I said inhaling sharply. 'But it didn't put you off coming then?'

'Nah, I mean you can't believe all you read online,' Ollie said shrugging. 'Yeah so whoever wrote it was right about Nihal being a wazzock but even if he is getting a little extra in his pocket at least he brought us to a nice place. This scran was probably the best I've ever had, like.'

'You're such a man, thinking through your stomach; what about the ethics of the whole thing?' Flic pursed her lips. 'I'm serious. If this Nihal fella doesn't sort his shit out then I will not hesitate to demand a refund, or at the very least leave an equally crap review.'

I felt my heart rate quicken; I noticed Chris's beady eyes look up from his phone screen as Flic finished and took a gulp of her water.

'I think I'm going to call it a night,' Chris said letting out an over-the-top yawn.

'No!' I yelled.

Chris stared at me. I had made my decision. Stuff the bad review and stuff Nihal; they had all come here to have fun and I was going to make sure that they did.

'Let me just see if maybe they can sort this music out and then why don't we get another round of drinks in?' I blustered and scraped my chair back. 'It's our first night here; we need to celebrate!'

I walked over to the old sitar player and knelt down next to him. Sensing movement around him he flashed open his wrinkled eyes and looked at me.

'Erm, excuse me, I don't suppose you have anything a bit, I don't know, a bit jazzier?' I asked making jazz hands.

He just stared at me.

Worried that he couldn't understand I asked again but louder and slower.

He nodded slightly and pointed to the mic that the lead singer had been using earlier.

'You…you want me to sing?' I asked.

He nodded; he looked like he was enjoying this. The rest of the restaurant including the tour group were focusing not on their dinner but on the woman interrupting the awful music.

'Oh no, I really *really* don't think anyone in here wants to hear that,' I said feeling my cheeks heat up.

'Go on, Louise!' I heard Ollie call out; he was punching his fist in the air and looking at me.

'Yeah, Louise!' Bex shouted followed by Liz, although slightly quieter.

Oh balls.

The sitar player fidgeted on his cushion and nodded towards me. I was still half-crouched, half-stood up at this point, hoping that the ground would suddenly swallow me up. I nervously looked back at our table; all these new faces were smiling at me encouragingly. I *had* promised them a good time and I *did* need to do something so they would forget the stupid awful review. Taking a deep breath I stood up and forced my trembling legs to slowly step onto the stage.

The sitar player strummed a few notes and nodded his head over to the microphone. I didn't know any Indian songs; what on earth was I going to sing? Then as his arthritic fingers danced away I realised that I actually did know this song! It was an unusual bhangra version of 'Let it Go' from *Frozen*. I could have burst into laughter that this gummy-mouthed old man had even heard of this film, let alone could play the notes.

Then I realised that the restaurant, including the staff and our tour group, were poised ready for me to burst into song. My stomach dropped, my hands went sweaty and my mouth was suddenly stupidly dry.

'Woo, Louise!' Bex called out. 'You can do it!'

The sitar player had made the first note last as long as possible. It was now my turn to jump in.

'Let it go, let it go, can't hold it back any mooooorrrreeee!' I warbled.

I was surprised glasses didn't suddenly start shattering as I murdered the high notes. As I continued channelling my inner Elsa with some awkward hand movements and random hip shimmying I noticed that people had started to clap. And cheer. Oh wow, maybe I was better than I thought I was?

'Let the storm rage onnnnnnnnnnnnn, the cold never bothered me anyway.' I ended with a dramatic flourish almost kicking the amps off the stage as I stamped my feet.

'Wooo hooo!' 'Encore!' 'More more more!' people were calling out, not just from my table but groups of locals who were probably quite enjoying this impromptu performance. Who knew I had such finesse in entertaining the crowd. They seriously loved me! I couldn't wait to tell Shelley and Marie about this; they would not believe it! I bashfully bowed and curtseyed hearing even more rapturous cheering from the audience, from my fans, my people.

'OK, one more?' I asked as people banged their fists on the table. I could hardly see any of their faces because the halogen spotlights were blinding me, but if they wanted it I was going to give it.

'Do you know any other songs like that?' I asked the sitar player who nodded and placed his fingers on the strings. I was just about to burst into my best Whitney impression when I noticed that Liz had crept up to the stage. Maybe she wanted to make a request, I thought excitedly, quickly running through my best karaoke performances in my mind. It had been ages since I had been given a microphone and free rein; usually my ex, Alex, would wrestle it off me telling me his ears were bleeding as Marie ignored him and carried on throwing some serious shapes as my backing dancer. Maybe that was what Liz wanted? To join me! I could get the three girls up here and teach them the 'Single Ladies' routine! I wondered if the restaurant had napkin holders that we could use as rings.

Liz was chewing on her bottom lip. 'Louise,' she whispered loudly, indicating something with her wide eyes.

I couldn't work out what it was she was trying to tell me. I shimmied over to her, getting even more cheers as I did and crouched down out of the spotlight. The sitar player had given up waiting for me to start singing and had carried on playing another Indian song, badly.

'You OK?' I asked, fanning my hands at my flushed cheeks, strands of hair sticking to my neck.

'You…erm… I don't know how to tell you this but…' She trailed off nervously, twitching her fingers, pointing at me.

'What? Do you want to join me? We could do a duet!' I said brightly.

Liz's porcelain skin visibly paled even more at the thought of it. 'No. But you probably need to stop.'

'Why?' I tilted my head wondering if she knew the lyrics to 'Breaking My Heart'. I could be Elton if she wanted.

'Because. You…erm…' Her eyes grew even wider. 'We can see everything!'

I looked down slowly. My dress, my cream, floaty dress was in fact blindingly see-through under the bright spotlight. They didn't love my voice – they loved my bits!

'Oh my God!' I screeched, jumping off the stage ungracefully.

People started to boo at the back of the room. Once I was out of the glaring light and my eyes adjusted, I realised that the crowds of people who I thought were loving my work turned out to be a table of five or six workers and the kitchen staff who had clocked off for the night. I shuffled over to our table feeling mortified.

Bex was cackling with laughter. 'You're a dark horse, Louise! You really did *let it go*!' she slurred.

She'd already finished the whole bottle of wine that I'd left next to her on the table before I thought it was wise to jump on the stage and literally give everyone a show. Ollie didn't appear to know where to look so focused on a tiny speck of vibrant red curry sauce that had splodged on the tablecloth in front of him. Liz and Flic both looked humiliated for me, and Chris just sat back in his chair, his arms crossed behind his head, a strange, slow smile playing on his thin lips.

'Ha, ha, yes, erm. Right, erm, OK, everyone ready to get back?' I asked, wishing I had a jacket to wrap around me and protect what shred of decency I had left.

I felt utterly humiliated. What a brilliant start to the tour: the boss got her bits out as the form of entertainment. I winced. Well thank God they didn't know who I really was. In a country where women were expected to cover up and dress conservatively, I'd broken a hundred cultural rules in the space of one badly screeched song.

'You not going to perform an encore then?' Chris asked, faux innocently.

'No. I'll wait for you by the front.'

This was all Nihal's fault; if he hadn't done a runner I'd never have been so bold as to practically perform a striptease in front of this group of strangers. Speaking of whom, where the hell was he? I half fled from the stunned-into-silence table, knocking into a few chairs in my rush to get the hell out of there.

CHAPTER 12

Petulant (adj.) Insolent or rude in speech or behaviour

I dreamt I was walking through Manchester high street wearing nothing but a blue silk turban on my head, trying to run away from jeering strangers who were cat-calling me as I streaked through town, desperate to hide my modesty. I'd woken up with a start, gasping for breath and sweating, trying to calm myself down and thankful that it was all just a dream. Until it slowly dawned on me that nope, I had exposed myself to the other tour goers last night. Great.

To be fair, I'd fallen asleep like a baby, completely knocked out with exhaustion from travelling here and the evening's hectic revelations. In more ways than one. It was only on waking up and throwing back the curtains in my small bedroom that I realised Delhi never sleeps. Through the double-glazed windows I could see the busy road outside was already heaving with traffic, noise and people milling everywhere in various states of shabbiness. Horses pulled carts with men sat up loosely holding the reins, cows ambled around groups of women who carried heavy sacks of rice on their heads and dogs chased everything that moved.

It was still slowly sinking in that I was here in India and without Shelley; she would never have let last night's striptease happen if she were by my side. Feeling a pang of homesickness I eventually managed to connect to the pretty dodgy Wi-Fi and quickly sent her a WhatsApp message to see if she'd found her passport or if her allegations were true about Marie before the connection dropped. I hadn't heard anything from Ben since I'd left Manchester and felt that sick knot in the pit of my tummy when I read that he'd been online just a few minutes ago. That was the problem with time stamps on iPhones; it turned you into a maniac and forced you to ride the wave of emotions that came with it. I thought back to what Shelley had told me a few months ago when I'd gone through an obsessional message-checking phase to see if Ben would ever send me anything non-work-related or reply to my sort-of flirty texts.

'Stop torturing yourself to see if he's messaged you,' she'd said for the umpteenth time.

'But on WhatsApp it says he was online one minute ago, so why has he not replied?' I'd wailed.

'Control. This is all about control,' she told me matter-of-factly. 'You're like everyone else in the fact that you want to be wanted, desired and loved, so if the person you like isn't doing that then…'

'Then they're just not that into you?' I said sarkily.

Shelley had rolled her eyes. 'No, if they don't message you then you work yourself up convincing yourself that you're a worthless, undesirable, fat slug when in fact he just probably hasn't realised that because you added an extra kiss at the end of your previous message you basically want to shag his brains out. I told you, men don't get subliminal messages.'

My rumbling stomach forced me to stop thinking about it and head downstairs for breakfast – after a refreshing shower and making sure that today's outfit would not be so revealing.

'Good morning, Miss Green, how did you sleep?' An employee with neatly gelled-to-the-side, petrol-coloured hair and kind eyes asked cheerfully as I wandered into the bright and airy breakfast room that was completely empty. 'My name is Rashid. Please come and take a seat.'

I wondered briefly if I was late, as according to the plan I had we were meant to be spending the day visiting the old part of Delhi, starting at 8.30 a.m., but glancing at the gleaming silver wall clock it was already twenty past. The other guests must still be fast asleep, and I hadn't heard a peep from Nihal.

'Oh, yep, fantastic, thanks.' I smiled and sat down at a table next to a large gilded picture of Ganesh, the elephant-headed Hindu god.

'Ah, that is very good to hear.' His eyes brightened. 'What would you like to drink?'

'I could murder a cup of tea; you don't have Tetley's do you?' I laughed.

'Oh.' His face fell. 'I'm very sorry but we only have coffee or chai tea. I can send someone out to get you a tea from one of the restaurants down the street if you would like?'

I blushed. 'Oh no, please don't go to any trouble. A cup of coffee will be fine.'

'So, is there anything I can help you with today? We can arrange cars to take you around the most famous sites in the city or I can advise where to find the best cake in all of India?'

'Well that's quite the promise.' I laughed. 'But I think I will be meeting the others soon, including Nihal, to spend the day in the old quarter.'

Rashid's face fell; he would make a lousy poker player. 'I don't think there are any plans for today, Miss Green – not according to what Nihal told me.' He added quietly, 'A day of rest, as it were.'

No plans. The second day of the trip and nothing had been organised, added to the fact our tour guide had rocked up late to the welcome meeting and then bailed during dinner… I didn't like the sound of this. Well I guess I'd found the answer to why all these reviews had been so bad – all thanks to Nihal. I let out a deep sigh. When we'd hired him he'd come so highly recommended. What the hell had happened?

'Oh right,' I mumbled, trying to hide my annoyance and confusion as I popped a slice of bread in the toaster. Rashid gave me an apologetic smile and started polishing a stainless-steel water jug. 'Erm, is Nihal about? I don't know if you knew but he skipped out on dinner last night and I could really do with talking to him.'

After a long pause Rashid cleared his throat. 'He's not here but I could try contacting him. Nihal's not in good shape at the moment.'

Yeah, I gathered as much.

'What do you mean? Is everything OK, Rashid?' I asked raising an eyebrow.

He bobbed his head in a way that seemed to indicate both yes and no.

'Rashid, is there something you're not telling me? About Nihal or the tour?' I paused. 'I really *really* would like to know.'

Rashid carried on polishing the jug but increased in speed.

'Rashid?' I pressed.

A deep crimson flush coloured his cheeks. He stopped manically cleaning and turned to face me, biting his bottom lip. 'I know who you are.'

I jolted back in my seat and let out a small laugh. 'Sorry?'

'I know who you are,' he repeated. 'Georgia Green. CEO of Lonely Hearts Travels. It's true isn't it?'

I dipped my head and didn't say a word. Rashid edged closer to me and dropped his voice to a hushed whisper.

'Once we had a member of the royal family staying here – well he was a third-removed duke or something but still very important – and I only found that out after he'd left. I could have kicked myself for being so unprofessional by not addressing him in the correct manner.' He shook his head lost in some uncomfortable memory. 'So, since then I try to Google all our guests to ensure I never make that social faux pas again. I Googled you and discovered that you own the company that runs these tours.'

I nodded slowly. 'Wow, you do take your job seriously.'

'I am wrong?'

I sighed. 'No, you're right. It's true.' I peered around the empty room in case someone had suddenly snuck in. 'Does Nihal know?'

Rashid shook his head. 'No, not yet. I wanted to talk to you first to see if he or indeed I am in some sort of trouble; surely that is the reason you have come all this way – to check up on us?'

'I'm not checking up on you, Rashid.' I was grateful that there was no one around to hear us. 'The thing is we've had a few bad reviews about this tour.' A look of horror crossed his face. 'Don't worry, not about your hotel, more about the, let's say, *disorganised itinerary*.' Rashid nodded slowly. 'So I thought I'd come undercover to experience it for myself, see if I can find the problems and fix them. I'm guessing, from last night's example at least, that the main cause of this is Nihal.'

Rashid slammed down the jug causing small silver bowls to shake on the long breakfast table. 'I told him! I told him he needed to sort himself out or else he and everyone else who works with him would be paying for it.' He caught my shocked expression and calmed down slightly. 'Sorry, Georgia, Louise, Miss Green… Oh should I call you Boss?' His bottom lip quivered.

'No, Rashid, Louise is fine, especially in front of the other guests – it's my middle name.' He nodded and I took a deep breath. 'So what's going on with him?' Suddenly the toast I was chewing tasted extremely dry.

He shook his head. 'I'm sorry, Louise. I really am in no position to be the one to tell you; it has to come from Nihal himself. As a friend I'm worried about him, especially finding out that he's being secretly watched by the big boss.'

'Please, Rashid, you're making me really anxious now.'

He sighed and peered through the glass of the door, checking the coast was clear. 'As you have the day with no itinerary how about I arrange a car for you to go and find out for yourself?'

'What? Go and see Nihal?' I stared at him. 'But what about the other guests?'

'I can arrange cars to take them around the old district; I know one of the kitchen staff who speaks excellent English would be able to step in as a tour guide. It may not be as wonderful as if you had organised it but it will be better than nothing.'

'Can you not just tell me what's going on?'

He thought for a moment then leant forward, words forming on his lips, when the door was flung open and in walked Bex and Ollie laughing about something. Rashid instantly straightened up and smiled at the guests. 'Welcome! Please sit down and I'll get you a cup of coffee.'

'Cheers, mate. Oh, morning, Louise, how you doing?' Ollie asked brightly.

'Oh here she is: Princess Elsa.' Bex winked as I rolled my eyes. 'Just kidding; you were great last night. I'm paying for it today though. I feel as rough as a badger's arse.' She rubbed her face and groaned.

'Blame the jet lag.' I smiled distractedly as I tried to catch Rashid's eye.

'Or the two bottles of wine she had?' Ollie teased as Bex visibly paled.

'Do not mention the W word. Otherwise it will all be coming back up over you.'

Ollie and I both grimaced as Bex struggled to keep a loud belch down.

'You already eaten, Louise?' Ollie asked, pointing to my half-chewed, now cold slice of toast.

I was about to answer when I spotted Rashid out of the corner of my eye looking like he was trying to make a swift exit before I bombarded him with questions about Nihal.

'Erm yep. All done. Listen, I'll see you guys in a bit. Enjoy your breakfast!' I quickly stepped round them to grab Rashid before he scuttled into the kitchen.

'Rashid,' I hissed before he wandered off. 'OK, I'll go and talk to Nihal.'

Thirty minutes later I was sat in a knackered-looking, silver car driven by a scowling nineteen-year-old man who didn't speak a word of English. Being in a car that was barely fit for purpose in a chaotic foreign city *and* not being able to communicate with the young driver en route to have it out with an incompetent tour guide in God knows where set my anxiety levels high.

This angst was not helped by the fact the roads were as chaotic as when Deepak had driven me here. I thought Bangkok was busy and frenzied, well, that was like a leisurely Sunday country drive compared to this. With no road markings or apparent Highway Code to follow my driver swerved and braked and shouted, gesturing wildly at other cars he'd amazingly managed not to hit, though he got as close as possible without crashing into them.

I suddenly realised why so many drivers here had figurines and bobbing heads of gods and goddesses tacked to their dashboards: so passengers could pray to these tiny deities as their life flashed before their eyes on these frenzied streets. I glanced at the small ornament of a blue-coloured man. I think it was Krishna, a Hindu god that Flic had been trying to teach us about last night. I said a silent prayer that everything would be OK.

We had been driving for around twenty minutes or so when we pulled off the main street and drove down a cramped, unpaved side street full of tilting shops that seemed to be holding the one next to them upright. Crowds of men stood on the corners, chatting and smoking rolled-up cigarettes next to piles of rubbish that had been swept to one side of the dusty street. We suddenly stopped.

With no cars in front or behind us I nervously peered out of the window, wondering what the holdup was. The driver still had the engine running but took his hands off the steering wheel and folded them on his lap. What the hell was happening? I leant forward, my seat belt pulled taut against my beating heart.

'Everything OK?' I asked him.

He turned to face me, his baby face completely blank, not understanding a word of what I was asking. He gave me a confusing head shake, which didn't clear up whether it was a yes or a no, and turned back round to intently watch two men who were unloading huge, stonking sacks of potatoes from a tatty blue cart.

'Is there a problem? Why are we not moving?' I pushed. My voice sounded strangled as I desperately tried to control a bubble of panic rising up inside me. The teen driver didn't bother turning his head; he just nodded like he had before.

Some of the men who were on the corner had stopped chatting and were throwing obvious glances at our stationary car, peering round one another to look through the window. I shrank back into my seat. I'd heard so many stories of solo female travellers in risky situations in this country I felt stupid for putting myself in such a vulnerable position, all for the sake of clearing up some bad reviews. My poor parents would be beside themselves if they knew.

I suddenly wanted to be anywhere but here, in this small alley in a foreign country with a driver who couldn't understand me surrounded by intimidating, staring men. Why wasn't he moving? Was this a trap? A set-up? What if Rashid had told him to take me here for one of the many men to drag me out by my hair? A way of getting me back for thinking I could spy on my employees?

'Please, take me back to the hotel,' I said forcefully, my bottom lip trembling. 'Hotel. No stop here.' I jabbed my finger, pointing up the street, and moved my hands together to hopefully show driving a car.

The driver wobbled his head once more.

The group of men had dropped their sacks and started slowly inching their way closer to the car.

Oh my God, what am I going to do? OK, breathe. You're locked in. It is the middle of the day. You have ID and money on you. I was running through my escape options when I heard the spluttering noise of a clapped-out motorbike. A red bike pulled up just next to the driver's window. The teen driver acted as if he'd been expecting the mysterious biker and wound down his window.

What was going on?!

A pudgy arm stretched through the half-open window and passed over a package that the driver took and nodded his thanks. Oh bloody hell, he was a drug dealer. He was planting drugs in the car…and on me?! The motorbike spluttered off up the street and my driver put the car in gear and followed him.

'Can you let me out? I want to walk,' I said banging on the door. He didn't turn round but instead passed the package over his head to me as he swerved past a couple of scrawny chickens pecking the ground.

'What is it? I don't want it.' I folded my arms but he kept shaking the package at me to take it off him. Nervous about us crashing, seeing as he was steering with only one hand and only one eye on the road, I reluctantly took the small box. I was too scared to look at it. Was I an accomplice if I willingly took it off the drug dealer? Now he had my fingerprints all over the box. Oh shit, this was bad.

With one eye closed and the other half open I nervously peered down and then started to laugh.

In my trembling hands I saw not a box of narcotics but instead a box of Tetley teabags! Rashid must have told the driver to swing by here to pick some up for me after I mentioned I wanted a brew. I let out a deep sigh that I didn't realise I'd been holding and giggled to myself at the ridiculousness of it all. What a bloody drama queen.

I thought back to what Trisha had told me about her trips to India. 'It's a place that makes your heart swell with both happiness and humbleness at the kindness of complete strangers,' she'd explained, smiling before following that statement with, 'But it also infuriates you, tests you to your limits and develops your patience levels. It really is a country of two halves, but that's what keeps it so enchanting and never boring,' she'd chuckled.

I leant forward in my seat. 'Thank you,' I said softly.

The teenage driver just bobbed his head in a forwards and sideways motion. Probably for the best he didn't have a clue how paranoid I'd just been.

CHAPTER 13

Wretched (adj.) Characterised by or attended with misery and sorrow

Thankfully the drugs/tea drama had taken my mind off what I was actually going to say when I saw Nihal. Should I go in all guns blazing, demanding he quit? Should I try the good cop approach of encouraging him to talk whilst I sympathetically listened to his problems? I didn't have long to decide as we had pulled to a stop down a tightly packed street full of small, brightly painted houses. The young, silent driver opened my door and nodded at me to follow him down the maze of rabbit-warren alleyways that he was striding down purposefully, leaving me to ungracefully trot behind him to keep up.

Children smiled and waved as we went past; some ran up to get a better look at this sweaty western woman practically glistening in the bright sunlight whilst others hung back staring out of the corners of their eyes. The kids looked so well cared for here, their hair and eyes bright and their clothes clean and colourful, not like those poor children begging for coins on the streets. I could hear pans being bashed together, smells of spices carried on the warm air and the sound of women laughing rang out as small groups huddled around wide blue basins that they were washing clothes in and gossiping over.

I picked up my pace, determined not to lose my driver who waved to the children and nodded politely at the women who blushed and giggled. He eventually stopped and pushed open a creaky wooden door that led to a tiny backyard cluttered with growing vegetables and pieces of scrap metal. He pointed at a turquoise-blue door just up the stone steps in front of me.

'Nihal.' It was the first thing he'd uttered since I'd met him and I was taken aback at how young and soft his voice was.

'Oh, OK.' I dipped my head to say thanks and gingerly stepped forward to rap at the door, hoping this would give me the answers that I needed. A few seconds later a short and squat Indian woman wearing a navy blue sari flung open the door and eyed me suspiciously. She had a long, thin plait snaking down her curved back. Greys peppered her crown and a bright red bindi took centre stage on her wrinkled, frowning forehead.

'Oh hi, my name's Louise. I mean Georgia. Georgia Green. Rashid sent me. I'm looking for Nihal?' I said politely.

The middle-aged woman looked me up and down quickly and tutted before calling out to the driver, not moving her light brown eyes off me. She had one long white hair standing proudly from a large mole on her chin and what looked like flour dusted on her sallow cheeks. I felt like I was being judged by a bouncer at a trendy nightclub in Manchester, high on the power trip of deciding who they did and didn't let in. I gave her a toothy smile, which may or may not have helped my cause. I think the mole hair waved back in the breeze.

The driver who had hung back at the wooden door shouted something. The old woman grunted, looked me up and down again and slowly shut the door in my face. Your name's not down; you're not coming in.

What the…?

I swung round to the driver hoping he would understand from my outstretched arms that I had no idea what had just happened. He just bobbed his head in an unhelpful yes/no motion. Oh Jeezus. I was feeling hot and unsettled. Irritating flies were buzzing round me and I just wanted this trip to be over already. I couldn't decide whether to stomp all the way back to the car or rap hard on the door, demanding to be seen, when the decision was made for me.

The door was flung open once more.

Thankfully the old hairy woman had gone and in her place stood Nihal wearing a baggy, stained T-shirt and tatty shorts. He looked utterly desperate, drawn out and exhausted.

'Hey, you're on my tour, aren't you?' he asked, his inky eyes wide in shock seeing my flustered face on his doorstep. 'There isn't a trip planned for today. What are you doing here?' He seemed to trip over his words in surprise and self-consciously moved a skinny arm over his chest to hide the worst of the stains. The disinterested and rude Nihal I'd met yesterday had been replaced with a vulnerable shell of a man.

'Rashid sent me,' I said bluntly, looking him up and down, mirroring what the old woman had done to me.

No wonder there wasn't anything planned for today as this guy looked like he'd just rolled out of bed. I wondered when he had last had a proper night's sleep.

'I think you and I need to have a little chat,' I said, more softly this time, peering round behind him into the house.

'I don't understand.' He jolted his head back. 'What do you mean Rashid sent you here?'

'My name is Georgia Green; I'm the CEO of Lonely Hearts Travels.' Slowly it seemed to dawn on him why I was awkwardly hovering on his doorstep. 'Do you remember me from the Skype interview we did a few months ago?' Nihal's face was a picture as he put two and two together. 'I hoped we could talk about a few things.'

Something crossed his tired eyes. I couldn't tell if it was worry, fear or a mixture of them both. He bit his lower lip and slowly nodded. 'Of course, of course. Please come in.' He called something in Hindi behind me to my driver who nodded and walked out towards where he had left the battered car.

'Oh, no…he's supposed to take me to my hotel later,' I fretted, not wanting to be left alone to figure out my own way back.

'It's OK, I told him to come back here later. I'm not sure how long we might be so I didn't want him to wait,' Nihal explained and held the door open for me. 'Please, come in.'

As I crossed over the stone step into his home, my nose was flooded with smells of spiced curry leaves, saffron and coriander. A large silver pot was bubbling on a small, unwatched stove in the room on the right. Calling it the kitchen would be an overstatement. The roughly painted room held the stove, a single wonky cupboard and a large sink precariously leaning against the back brick wall.

I followed Nihal as he headed deeper into the house, being careful to duck when he told me to. 'Please, take a seat. I'm sorry; we weren't expecting visitors today,' he said blushing slightly as he waved an arm across the small cosy room opposite.

'Thanks. I think your house is charming.' I smiled, wanting to ease this embarrassed and exposed air that was clouding him as he straightened up a small cushion.

I walked around soft squidgy beanbags that were scattered on faded, patterned rugs; in the centre was an ornate, low table covered in teacups next to a gleaming teapot and tiny jars filled with goodness knows what as a centre piece. All that bravado I'd felt earlier imagining I was coming here for a fight had puddled out of me now seeing him in such a state in his own home.

'Would you like a drink?' he asked rubbing his hands together nervously.

'Yes, that would be lovely, thanks.' I smiled softly.

He nodded and called out something in Hindi through the doorway. Within seconds the old woman who had previously opened the door to me wandered into the lounge. She still had her eyes tracked on me but didn't seem as surprised to see me sitting on her sofa.

She said something back to Nihal in a croaky voice, which made him blush, and then swatted away his hands from the tea service, tutting loudly, and began to carefully pour out hot milky water, mixing it with handfuls of herbs and cinnamon sticks from the small pots.

'Wow, this seems quite complicated,' I said to her, wanting to fill the silence. 'I'm used to just dunking a teabag in a mug of hot water.' I indicated the box of Tetley teabags that were poking out of my bag and let out a shrill laugh that didn't sound like my own.

She ignored me and carried on stirring the spiced water.

'That's my mother. She doesn't speak any English,' Nihal politely explained. I nodded and stayed silent as his mum filled up two cups and left them side by side on the coffee table before scuttling out, giving me one last glance as she did before leaving us alone in the dimly lit room.

'Please take this; it's chai tea. An Indian speciality,' he offered, passing me a steaming cup and finally sitting down himself. He cleared his throat. 'So, Georgia, how can, erm, how can I be of service?' I noticed his hands trembling slightly as he passed me my tea.

I put the hot drink on the coffee table and sat up straighter. 'Well, firstly, I don't want the other guests to find out who I am. To them my name's Louise and that is how it will remain for the rest of the trip. Their experience of this tour needs to be one hundred per cent positive, and having my identity exposed –' I blushed slightly as my mind was flooded with embarrassment after the karaoke incident last night '– could affect how they view our service and enjoy the trip.'

Nihal took a long sip of his tea and then leant forward. 'So you really *are* the boss of Lonely Hearts Travels?'

'Yup.' I nodded.

'Ah, OK.' He scratched the dark stubble that peppered his sallow cheeks, looking like he didn't know what to say next.

I cleared my throat, desperate to fill this awkward silence. 'Nihal, when we hired you, we heard only glowing reviews about your service as a tour guide.' He blushed and bashfully dipped his eyes to the stone floor. 'So it came as quite a surprise when recently we've been receiving a few negative reviews of your tours, including one in particular…' I paused to rummage in my bag and pull out the creased copy of *that* review and passed it to him. 'I came here to find out what was going on as I want, no, I *need* to put things right.'

I could see his Adam's apple visibly bob up and down as he took deep breaths, scanning through the colourful way his tour had been described by this anonymous blogger. I watched him read and clasped my hands together, not really sure where to put myself. He eventually laid the paper on his lap and slowly looked up at me.

'I am so sorry.'

I was just about to question him further when he began to cry. His chest started trembling with big, heavy gulps of tears. Shit.

'Nihal. Nihal, what's happened?' I leant across my cushion, unsure of whether it was acceptable or professional of me to reach out and comfort him, but from the way he was sobbing so forcefully he just seemed like a lost little child. I thought back to those ravaged street children and suddenly wanted to scoop him up into a big hug and tell him everything would be OK. This was such a contrast to the surly, vacant man I had met yesterday.

'I…I…' He gulped at air as tears streamed down his unshaven cheeks and plopped onto the printout of the review.

'Nihal?'

'I thought I was doing such a good job to hide what has been going on. I thought no one would notice…'

My stomach lurched that something truly awful had happened to him; why hadn't Rashid warned me about this? I was about to say something when I heard a female voice call through the house, echoing off the exposed stone walls. Nihal roughly dried his eyes and straightened up at the sound. Within seconds a teenage girl raced into the lounge. She had long, thin, black plaits dangling past her shoulders and tied with fluffy hair bobbles at the bottom. She was wearing baggy, patterned trousers and a white T-shirt that had a large pink and purple flower in the centre.

'Oh.' She stopped as she saw me.

'Hello,' I said softly, unsure if she would even understand me.

'Hi,' she replied eyeing me cautiously just like Nihal's mother had done. Nihal turned to face her and as she took one look at his tear-stained face she burst into a fit of laughter.

'Oh God, what's happened now?' She rolled her large eyes skywards, flecks of glittery eyeshadow rested on her young cheeks. 'Wait – who are you?' she asked me bluntly.

'My name's Georgia. I'm just visiting Nihal, and you are?'

Nihal just blew his nose noisily, obviously not interested in doing the introductions.

'I'm Priya, the sister of this sad sack.' Priya nodded her head towards her brother.

'I'm not some sad sack,' Nihal half protested before slumping back onto his beanbag; his sobs had now calmed down to intermittent snuffles.

'Priya, do you know what's happened?' I asked slowly as she plopped onto the cushion opposite and helped herself to a cup of chai tea before tucking her slim legs underneath her. Nihal grumbled that we were trying to have a serious business meeting and that she needed to leave us alone; at this she burst into laughter again.

'Oh come off it! You, the businessman? You couldn't even sell cocoa to a chocoholic ever since Ameera left you.'

'Don't talk about her like that,' Nihal responded gruffly.

'Wait, who's Ameera?'

'She's –' Nihal started to speak.

Priya jumped in before he could finish. 'He's moping around, getting under my mum's feet and annoying me, all because of Ameera. That's the name of his *now* ex-girlfriend.' She lay back on a cushion and shut her eyes. 'Ridiculous if you ask me.'

'Wait, Nihal, have things with work been going wrong all because of a girl?' I asked.

Nihal ignored my question and glared at his young sister. 'Just because no boy has ever shown an interest in *you*. Keep out of things that you don't understand.'

Priya stuck her tongue out.

'Wait, Nihal. So you're telling me all these bad reviews are because you've been dumped?' I asked incredulously.

Priya piped up. 'Yeah, ironic isn't it? Broken-hearted backpackers being led around India by a broken-hearted tour guide.' She giggled. 'You couldn't make that up.'

Nihal looked like he wanted to throw a cushion at her but was caught by my shocked face and realised that a brother-and-sister play-fight was probably not the most professional way to conduct himself in front of his boss.

'That's the only reason?' I repeated.

Nihal nodded sadly.

Thank God for that! I wanted to laugh with Priya at the ridiculousness of it all. I thought back to that review now sopping wet under the weight of his tears.

'I thought for one moment that something more serious had happened.'

'It *is* serious,' he half barked then dipped his head. 'I'm sorry. I mean, I love working with the tour groups and I take pride in making sure all the guests have a great time and leave happier than when they arrived, but it's just recently, since Ameera and I broke up, it's been very hard to feel motivated enough to provide this kind of service.'

'But we can fix this, surely. You're very good at what you do, Nihal.' He blinked proudly and rubbed his face. 'You can't let this break-up ruin what good work you've done so far, work that I know you're capable of. What about the tour group waiting in the hotel now? Relying on you?' He didn't need to know that they were all being given a tour of the old city thanks to Rashid stepping in and picking up the pieces.

Priya started laughing. 'I'd cancel the rest of this trip if I were you.'

I was expecting Nihal to stand up and fight back, to use reverse psychology on his sister and make sure that didn't happen. But instead he visibly slumped forward and nodded dejectedly. 'For once, she's right. You saw me last night in the restaurant; as soon as I heard that love song I just had to get out of there. I can't function without Ameera.'

'No,' I said, firmly ignoring Priya making sick noises. 'These people have also been through a bad time and they haven't come all this way to be let down once more.' I decided I needed to change tactics to the tough-love approach.

Nihal just sat there playing with one of the burnt-orange tassels hanging off the cushion he was sat on. 'I'm sorry, but I can't do it. I can't eat, I can't sleep, Ameera is all I can think about,' he admitted quietly. His sister just scoffed in the corner. I didn't want to laugh; I understood that being dumped hurt, a lot.

'But maybe work would take your mind off that. They say the best remedy is to keep busy,' I counterbalanced, before realising that hanging around a bunch of other heartbroken people was probably not a good mix for anyone.

Nihal shook his head. 'No. I am so sorry you have come all this way to see me but I really think it would be better if I quit. I would prefer not to work at all than to ruin the tour.'

For the love of…! He couldn't quit.

My heart felt for him, it really did. But then the other rational side of my brain politely tapped my conscience. I had a business to run here. I'd come all this way, causing problems with Ben and Marie in the process, specifically to sort this problem out. I was not ready to let this go.

'Right, why don't you tell me what happened between you and Ameera,' I said, thinking that if I had all the information then maybe I could come up with some sort of plan of attack.

He sat up, wiped his eyes and told me how they'd been together for two years; everything had been perfect until he'd started working for the Lonely Hearts. Suddenly he was spending longer away from home then returning with all these incredible, inspirational stories of the men and women whom he had helped and Ameera had started to get jealous.

'Jealous of the other women on the tour?' I asked.

He shook his head. 'No. Jealous of the things I was doing. She works in a small travel agency as she hopes to see the world one day but so far has never left this city.'

'So, there was no cheating involved?'

'No!' He looked horrified at the thought.

'And she hasn't specifically said she wanted to end it with you because she doesn't love you any more?' Again he shook his head. 'Well, then we can fix this!' I said brightly.

He eyed me sceptically. Priya scoffed and I ignored her.

'It's simple; we just need to go and find Ameera and ask her to join one of the tours. Once she's taken part she'll know what it is you get up to and, who knows, maybe we can train her up to be a tour guide too?'

There had been so much demand for this Indian tour, if we had two tour groups going we could help even more people. The business side of my brain high-fived itself.

'I don't know,' Nihal said, slowly running his fingers over the rim of his cup.

'Please, Nihal, you said yourself you enjoy your work. Well, it shouldn't come between you and Ameera, but sitting around here crying about the end of your relationship isn't going to help you either.' *Plus if you don't pull yourself together then where am I supposed to find another tour guide at such short notice?* I tried not to sound desperate.

Priya sighed and chucked a small cushion over at her brother. 'Oi, you need to at least try, Nihal – even just to get you out of Mum's house and out of my way. It's not like you're some rich prince who can turn down the cash, is it? Just suck it up and sort it out.'

Nihal sniffed loudly.

'So, we're on?' I pushed.

He sighed. 'OK but just please don't be upset if your idea doesn't work. Ameera can be very stubborn when she wants to be.'

I put three fingers together in a Girl Guide salute. 'I promise.'

'Well if it fails then just think, you could book yourself on the tour as a guest this time,' Priya added before falling into a fit of giggles.

'Don't listen to her; we're going to get this fixed,' I said, crossing my fingers behind my back.

CHAPTER 14

Shilly-shally (n.) Vacillation; indecisive behaviour

Fifteen minutes later we were walking up the street to the travel agency where Ameera worked, nestled in between a higgledy-piggledy electric store and a boarded-up laundrette. I told Nihal to wait outside as I went to scope it out, hoping I could use my womanly charms on Ameera to help her get back with the love-sick puppy pining for her in the street. I was actually feeling quite smug that this would all work out just fine.

A small bell tinkled my arrival like it did in Lonely Hearts Travels back in Manchester, taking me right back to thinking about work. Ben's handsome face flooded my mind, making my tummy do a strange, silly flip. I wondered how he, Kelli and Trisha were getting on without me and how they were managing the workload. As I stepped into this travel agency a world away from home it dawned on me that since leaving Shelley at the airport my mind hadn't been swimming with things I needed to do or emails I needed to send. It felt strange and I wasn't sure I liked it.

I shook my head to focus on the task at hand: once I had match-made Nihal and Ameera I could confidently leave the tour group in their hands and be back where I belonged, catching up with my own business. I stepped into a small room that held two large desks with empty chairs opposite and a battered-looking filing cabinet squished into the small gap in between; it made my shop seem like a palace. The whitewashed walls were covered in beautiful prints of exotic beaches and palm trees, which added bursts of colour to the unloved room. A plump woman was sitting behind one of the desks hunched over a clunky laptop that was wheezing as she typed. Beads of sweat dripped down her cheeks and she wiped them away with the back of her chunky wrist.

'Hello, how can I help you today?' she asked in a soft Indian lilt, looking up at me as I entered the shop.

'Hi.' I walked the three strides it took to stand in front of her. 'Erm, are you Ameera?'

The fat woman pursed her lips. 'No I'm not! But if you see that girl you tell her she will not be receiving *any* references from me after just running out on the shop like that.'

'What? So Ameera's not here any more?'

The chubby lady shook her head, spraying drops of sweat as she did.

Oh no.

'No. She just upped and left with no warning or even working out her notice period. It's left me in a right mess. Had to miss my nephew's birthday party to be here to open up today and let me tell you that did not go down well,' she huffed before her squinty eyes flicked to the window and she huffed again. I followed her gaze and saw Nihal peering through the glass, his face pressed against it trying to see how our mission was going.

'Is that Nihal? You can tell him to get away from my shop before I come out there and make him. I know that Ameera leaving has something to do with him.' She awkwardly tried to get up from the battered chair she was wedged in.

'OK, we'll go. Sorry for taking up your time,' I said edging quickly to the door while she muttered under her breath as she heaved herself up.

Nihal almost pounced on me the moment I went outside. 'So? I couldn't see her. Was she in the back? Is she OK? How did she look? What did Fatso say? Why is she glaring at me like that?' His words tumbled out as I steered him away from the shop.

I shook my head and took a deep breath. 'It didn't work. I'm sorry, Nihal.'

'What?' His shoulders slumped and his face visibly drooped. I panicked that he might start howling with tears again.

'Ameera wasn't there.'

'What? Well where is she?' A look of worry danced on his tear-splattered cheeks.

'She's quit. Her boss said she hasn't turned up for work. She's pretty annoyed to be honest; we really should start walking away.' I looked over my shoulder, expecting the sweaty woman to waddle out of the shop after us.

Nihal cleared his throat and stayed planted in the same position letting what I'd said wash over him. 'She's gone?'

I nodded. 'That's what she told me.'

He looked like he was totally alone with his thoughts, as if the noise and mayhem of this Delhi street literally didn't exist. I kept glancing at the shop nervously. After the world's longest pause, he spoke. His voice sounded measured as if he had spent the never-ending silence choosing exactly the right words.

'Well this changes everything. I have to go and find her.'

'What?' I coughed, ignoring a man tugging a rickety cart who spat red paan at my feet. Nihal turned to face me and gave a sharp nod.

'No, you *have* to lead our tour group. You *have* to act like everything is normal. If she's moved on then you need to do the same,' I pleaded.

Nihal let out a deep sigh. 'Georgia, I don't know if I can.'

My stomach dropped; just moments ago I was preparing myself to get this all sorted out and head back to Manchester. Now I was standing on a baking hot street corner with some stranger's chewed tobacco dripping on my toes and a maverick tour guide on a mission. I couldn't have come all this way for nothing. 'Nihal, everyone has been dumped at one time in their life and yeah it's crap but that doesn't mean staying at home sulking. You can't lose your job over this. You need to show Ameera that you're doing totally fine without her.'

Nihal turned to face me. 'I can't live without her. I love that woman with all my heart. We Indian men are not like the men you know. We don't have that stiff upper lip, as you say. For us, the heart rules the head. I'm sorry, but I need to go and find her.'

'No, you can't leave the tour group without a tour guide! Wait – what if I join you?' I suddenly blurted out to Nihal, without fully thinking it through.

He did a double take and scratched his stubbly chin. 'What?'

'I know you want to find Ameera but you have responsibilities to finish here first.'

'Georgia, I told you I could hardly focus when Ameera dumped me. You saw me at the restaurant last night, but now I know she has left her job I definitely won't be able to do anything until I find her. I can ask around to find another tour guide to stand in?'

My mouth filled with saliva and my stomach tightened. I was not losing him now, especially when I knew what potential he had. I silently waved goodbye to my speedy exit to Manchester.

'Nihal, just finish this tour and then I promise we can try and find Ameera together. I'm on the tour already, maybe I can just, you know, step up a bit more to support you. Without the others noticing of course.' I cleared my throat. 'This way you get out of your mum's house and away from Priya's teasing, keep yourself busy and do what you love, but you have me to cheer you on if things get too tough. Please.'

He looked like he might cry again.

'Nihal?'

He sighed deeply. 'OK. You're on.'

I got back to the hotel feeling exhausted. Nihal had given me his word that he would be here tomorrow to lead the tour group and he would put off trying to find Ameera until the guests had left. I'd thanked Rashid for the box of tea without explaining how freaked out I was by the way it had been delivered. His face had dropped when I mentioned that Ameera had gone AWOL but then broken into a wide toothy grin at hearing the news that Nihal was back on board. I was suddenly aware that it wasn't just the tour goers or our bank balance that suffered if we cancelled these tours. All the hand-picked suppliers we worked with would also lose out. He told me that the other guests had had a great day sightseeing and that he'd explained I wasn't feeling so well, hence my bailing.

I flopped on my bed and allowed my body to relax and my mind to catch up on everything that had happened today. I eventually managed to pick up a half decent Wi-Fi signal and turned onto my side as a message buzzed through from my parents asking if I'd arrived safely and one from Shelley telling me that her passport had been handed into the pub by one of the cleaners. I breathed a sigh of relief. Thank goodness we were wrong about Marie; it must have just slipped out of her bag without us noticing. I quickly typed back that this undercover boss mission was harder than I'd imagined but I was starting to find answers to the questions I had.

I tapped out a message to my parents letting them know I was OK and WhatsApped Ben asking him to call me. I needed to fill him in on today's revelations plus I remembered that I'd forgotten to give him my log-in details for my emails, and judging by how sketchy the Wi-Fi was it would be worth him asking Kelli to check that nothing urgent had slipped through the net if I couldn't access my messages. Especially now I was going to be staying here for longer than I had thought.

After a few minutes, FaceTime chirruped to life; I patted down my frizzy hair, hoped the bright lighting wouldn't highlight my under-eye bags and pressed the green button. Ben's face filled my small phone screen and I felt my stomach flip and my lips curl into a smile.

'Hey.' Ben's bloody handsome face smiled back. 'You're alive,' he said, sounding as relieved to see me as I did to see him. 'I was worried about you,' he half mumbled, causing my smile to grow even bigger.

'Hey, I'm here.'

God he looked cute. His hair had this adorable natural wave that framed his features and only made his almond-shaped eyes more inviting. He was wearing the checked shirt that always made me gawp at his strong arms. I felt my vagina do a funny squeeze and forced myself to concentrate.

'Shelley called me and told me that she'd lost her passport and that you'd carried on and travelled without her?' A worried expression creased his forehead.

I nodded. 'Yep. That was pretty scary but I'm here safe and sound.' That seemed like it had been weeks ago. 'God, Delhi is one crazy busy city.' I laughed lightly as he nodded gently then distractedly glanced out of the shot to a phone that was ringing. 'I won't keep you but I realised that I'd forgotten to send you my email log-in details. I'll send you a message with them so you can keep an eye on things.' I paused, taking a breath as he nodded. I was sure I noticed him roll his eyes but that may have been a time delay. 'So, how's everything going?'

The phone stopped ringing and Ben sighed deeply. Suddenly I realised that his eyes had red rims around them and his stubble was almost at Nihal levels. 'Not good.'

My stomach dropped. 'What? Why?'

Balls. I'd only been gone a few days and already things were falling apart.

He ran his hand through his messy curls and briefly closed his eyes. 'Trisha's had a fall.'

'What? Oh my God! Is she OK?'

Ben cleared his throat and nodded slowly. 'Yeah, she tripped up in the middle of Boots; she said the shame of it was more painful than anything else. Thankfully she's only sprained her ankle so the doctors have ordered bed rest.'

'Oh, thank God she's OK. Well of course she needs to take things easy for a while.'

'Yeah.' He sighed. 'Not to sound callous but it has left us in the lurch a little. I'd banked on her being here so took on extra work whilst you're away and I doubt Kelli and I will be able to cope with it being just the two of us.' He paused. 'I've just been thinking about maybe hiring a temp whilst you're not here. What do you reckon?'

I answered without hesitation. 'Poor Trisha, she was really looking forward to being back in the shop, but yep, I think you should get an extra pair of hands to help you out. I actually have a list of possible temps on my desk, in the green or maybe orange folder. I can't remember.'

Ben smiled and nodded. 'So you planned for this then?' he said, not giving me the chance to answer. 'Course you did.'

'No not like that.' I bit my bottom lip. 'I just started looking into maybe hiring a temp way before Trisha offered to help out, just as a back-up plan.' He nodded but stayed silent. 'Anyway I divided the list into suitable and, let's say, not suitable in a million years. I thought it might be helpful.'

'I know.' He rubbed his face with his hand. Was this how exhausted I had been looking? I heard someone chattering in the background that grabbed his attention. 'OK well thanks. I'll check it out and try and get someone soonish. Listen, I'm sorry, Georgia, but I'm going to have to go. It's getting pretty chocka in here.'

'Oh, all right, well…'

I was cut off from saying goodbye as Ben's screen turned black. He'd hung up. I hadn't even had the chance to tell him about Nihal. I turned onto my back and stared up at the ceiling. Maybe I should have just cancelled the tour, given the guests their money back and flown home to help Ben in the office. It did feel like this whole trip was cursed. I let a single tear roll down my cheek and closed my eyes, hoping a good night's sleep would fix everything. For the first time I felt helpless and completely out of control. Of everything.

CHAPTER 15

Rigmarole (n.) Confused or meaningless talk

Everyone was still half asleep owing to the fact that we were sardined in a stuffy minibus on the long drive to Agra to spend the day at the Taj Mahal, and all before the sun had completely risen. The navy sky was just beginning to be lit up with wisps of hazy golden sunlight but even at this godforsaken hour the roads were ridiculously jam-packed, full of people setting up their stalls and shops for the day, men in suits racing to get to the office and children scampering across the street picking up plastic water bottles. Nihal had arrived as promised, on time and dressed in smart, clean clothes, looking a lot fresher than when I'd last seen him. He had also remembered all the guests' names and even handed out small bottles of orange juice and pastries as we tumbled into the minibus half asleep.

See, this is going to be fine. The start of the tour was just a blip but we are getting back on track. Ben will get a helpful temp in and get a hold of things back home and as soon as these fantastic reviews start flooding in from the guests here then this will have all been worth it.

I smiled proudly at the clean-shaven Nihal before nestling into my seat, trying to catch some more shut-eye on the lumpy bumpy roads. Ollie and Chris were already in the land of nod, Liz and Flic were leaning against the window using bunched-up scarfs as makeshift pillows and Bex's head kept lolling forward, startling her awake for long enough to wipe the dribble of spit from her mouth before she drifted off again.

Everyone had been too dozy to question where I'd been yesterday. As we waited to board the bus Liz had stifled a yawn while asking me if I felt any better, and in my still fuggy sleepy state it had taken me a few seconds to remember that was the lie I had to follow. My mumbled and delayed response hadn't raised any alarm bells as she'd gone on to tell me in a croaky morning voice that they'd spent the day sightseeing but I hadn't missed much as the old market smelt of urine and cabbages as some old dude persistently trailed after them trying to sell his mouldy veg. I vowed to myself that this tour was going to get the excitement and wow factor it needed.

A few hours and unusual sleeping positions later we pulled up to Agra, a much smaller city than Delhi and shrouded in rich history. Cows leisurely trundled past red brick shops that had faded hand-painted adverts on their crumbling walls, unfazed by the many motorbikes that had whole families piled haphazardly on top and that nipped around them leaving a cloud of soot in their wake. Children were cradled in the arms of relaxed-looking mothers who had huddled up next to their husbands, some even sitting side-saddle on skinny bikes. I was so engrossed with looking out of the window I was only half listening to Nihal who had turned round to face the other passengers who were all just waking up.

'OK, when we pull up to the Taj Mahal, it is going to be very, very busy, guys. So please take care of your bags and keep an eye out for each other. I will go and get your tickets so you don't have to join the queues and will meet you back here in fifteen minutes,' he yelled before jumping out and racing off.

'What's up with him?' Bex yawned widely, revealing a couple of silver fillings.

'What do you mean?' I asked nervously, wiping the sleep from my eyes.

'Well it's like he's had a shot of energy or something. I'm not complaining, like; it's just a bit weird isn't it?'

'Maybe he was just having a bad day the other day?' I suggested, feeling my cheeks flush with the half lie.

Bex shrugged, looking more interested in what was going on outside of her window than our conversation.

Once our patient driver had found a parking space and pulled open the heavy door to the van we all piled out, relieved to be able to stretch our legs. Despite it still being relatively early the heat was already stifling and swarms of people had started patiently queuing to be let in to see this wonder of the world.

'Whoa, this place is crazy!' Ollie looked around in awe. 'Are we in the right place though 'cause I can't see the Taj?'

Flic tutted and rolled her eyes. 'You have to go inside before you see it.'

'You been here before then?' Ollie replied.

'No, but I already know it's my spiritual home,' Flic said, her voice as floaty as the strange, bright purple dress she was wearing. 'Although, it's such a con that we're totally ripped off just to enter. Did you know that Indian residents can go inside for, like, pennies?' She huffed and folded her arms. 'So unfair.'

'But it's through tourism that sites like this are preserved and not left to crumble away to nothing,' Chris added before taking a large gulp of water, ignoring Flic's scowl for disagreeing with her that everyone on this planet should be equal.

'Has everyone put on sun cream?' I said changing the subject and realising that as Nihal was getting our tickets I needed to step in as tour guide. 'I also read that women need to dress conservatively.' I nodded to Bex's blotchy pink shoulders that were on show in her tank top. 'Did you bring a scarf or something?'

'Crap! I left it at the hotel.'

'I've got one you can borrow,' Liz piped up and rummaged in her small backpack before pulling out a baby-pink, chiffon shawl and handing it to a grimacing Bex.

'Cheers…I think.' She held the fabric in her hands as if it was a sack of steaming cow poo before sighing. 'My mam will *never* believe I'm wearing pink.'

'You look gorgeous,' Flic said, blowing an air kiss that Bex shrugged away.

'I've also got some sun cream,' Liz said quietly and passed a bottle of factor 50 to Ollie who had the fairest skin of us all. She almost dropped it when their hands touched.

'Oh, erm, thanks,' he stuttered looking up at her under his long lashes.

'Guys! Over here!' Nihal shouted out, breaking off this moment of affection between Liz and Ollie. We walked over to him, dodging leering men who were offering camel rides to take us right to the front door; I noticed Chris jump when a long, blackened tongue slipped out too close to his face.

'Think you've found a friend there.' I smiled.

Chris grimaced and strode on ahead.

'OK, guys, so here we are at the famous gates to the Taj Mahal.' Nihal handed out our entrance tickets and made sure there was enough water for everyone. 'Now, follow me, stay close together and let's go through to see the wonder that is the Taj Mahal.' He grinned excitedly and gave me a small wink. I noticed Chris give me a look as I shrugged it off and started to try and push through the hordes of people slowly dawdling in front.

I could feel the heat bouncing off the caramel-coloured stone as we inched forward into an open-air courtyard. The atmosphere was electric. Everyone around me from all walks of life seemed to be pulled by some invisible magnet through the heavy, dark brown gates opposite.

'Wow, I can't believe that I'm here, about to see the Taj Mahal with my own eyes,' Bex said pretending to wipe away a tear with the edge of Liz's scarf.

'I know, me too!' I replied in a hushed whisper. I felt a frisson of excitement course through me, and was immediately taken back to that stressed-out girl waiting in the dreary visa office in Manchester and seeing the large poster of the creamy, domed site tacked onto the wall. Now I was just inches away from seeing it in real life; I felt like someone should pinch me.

Then suddenly someone did pinch me.

'Oww!' I called out.

I turned around, difficult to do with this many hot bodies pressed up against each other, to face my attacker. A warm-faced Indian woman with large hooped earrings and bright pink lipstick smiled at me.

'Sorry! I was just hoping we could take a photo of you and your friend?'

'Oh, right, erm, yeah, OK,' I said, nudging Bex to turn round and smile. This was odd. 'I think she thinks we're celebs!' I whispered.

As the woman smiled gratefully and rummaged around her bag for her phone, Bex nodded sagely. 'Ah, I've read about this. Apparently it's, like, *the thing* for locals to want to get photos with westerners. It'd be like us if Jeremy Kyle wandered past – I would be on a selfie-taking mission.' She shrugged. 'Wait, let me take my scarf off first; there ain't no way anyone's taking a photo of me wearing this girly thing,' she said, tugging at the delicate fabric.

I stopped her. 'You can't, remember. It's really rude to be exposing yourself, especially in a sacred place like this.' Bex tutted and left the scarf where it was. 'Anyway, it really suits you.'

'Here we go!' The Indian woman smiled at us and held up her phone. 'OK, say cheese.'

'Chee… What the…?'

Suddenly everyone around us huddled closer and turned round, flashing big, toothy grins at the camera; a small baby was placed in my arms and a little girl with curly black hair was hoisted up for Bex to hold. The baby I was awkwardly cradling had started wailing and a few men who were proudly stood to my right were doing the peace sign. Bex and I looked at each other and burst into a fit of giggles. I watched Bex uncomfortably hold up this toddler who was more interested in poking her eyeballs than smiling for the camera.

'So much for that serene entrance.' I laughed, carefully handing the baby back.

'Oh God, it's this scarf, isn't it?' Bex moaned as the little girl finally let go of a clump of hair she was gripping and went back to her parents. 'I told you pink was a bad colour; it gives people ideas.'

We were still laughing about the impromptu photo shoot and the thought that Bex and I would be in photo frames in houses all over India as the crowd started to slowly inch forward. The doors were flung open and there it was. The Taj Mahal, just metres away from us.

Our laughter stopped, the crowd grew silent and everyone shared this moment of respect and adoration for the stunning structure that seemed to glisten in the sunlight.

We slowly tiptoed forward, gazing up at the building that shimmered at the end of the impeccable, rectangular lakes. Opulent and elegant, it was a thousand times more impressive than I had ever imagined it to be.

'Fuck me, that's beautiful and I don't even like *Grand Designs*,' Bex breathed.

I nodded, unable to speak. I suddenly had this sense of calm settle around me. Marie had once dragged me to a yoga class at her gym but that state of relaxation was nothing compared to the peace I felt here. It was as if the rest of the world had been turned to mute and all that mattered in this very moment was me and this true labour-of-love building.

'You OK, Louise? You're freaking me out with your spaced-out face.'

'Yeah fine, no, better than fine. I mean, you hear people go on about these places you need to visit before you die but, whoa, I never expected a reaction like this at one of them.'

'Come on, you daft sod, let's go and try and find the others.' Bex laughed and led the way down a set of crumbling steps, ducking past selfie sticks and iPads thrust in the air as everyone tried to get a photo, admittedly breaking the magic spell instantly.

We wandered down a gravel path lined with lush green grass, neatly tended shrubs and exotic, flowering bushes to where Nihal had gathered the troops and was in full tour-guide mode.

'Hey, guys! Thought we'd lost you for a minute then.' He smiled at us. 'Pretty impressive huh? I never get bored of looking at it.' He gazed at the milky white domes, ducking his head in a sign of respect, and turned to face us. 'As I was saying, the Taj Mahal is the perfect balance of symmetry and design. If you look you can see the four white minarets on each corner that are designed to lean outwards in case of an earthquake, to save falling and crushing the Taj. I think we can all agree that love seeps from the building that was created by the emperor Shah Jahan in adoration of his beloved wife Mumtaz Mahal…' Nihal trailed off.

He was too busy gawping at an Indian woman with jet-black, glossy hair and shining emerald eyes who was leading a small group of tourists behind her to finish his sentence. She had one slim, bangled arm raised high in the air as if giving the group behind her some sort of marker to follow. Wait, were they wearing matching T-shirts with a picture of a broken heart on them?

'Erm, so as I was saying…' Nihal tried to pull his attention back to us but stalled again. The beautiful Indian woman had walked over and stood directly next to our group.

The other tour goers started glancing at each other wondering why our guide had momentarily lost the power of speech. I shrugged along with them hoping to catch Nihal's eye that was instead trained on this beautiful woman and her crowd in matching tops. As the glamorous new guide glanced over at Nihal under thick black lashes and flicked her hair back, I felt a chill rise up my spine.

No. This couldn't be…

'A-Ameera?' Nihal stuttered.

CHAPTER 16

Scupper (v.) To defeat or put an end to

Shit. This stunner was Ameera? She hadn't quit the travel agent's to have some duvet days; she'd quit to become a tour guide! Obviously anything her ex could do she could do better.

Nihal had gone really pale and was trembling slightly. I noticed Flic and Bex pass a look between them trying to work out what was going on. Ameera gave Nihal a loaded smile, flashing pearly white, straight teeth, and continued talking to her group. She was obviously lapping up the effect she was having on him.

'The Taj Mahal is one of the most recognisable buildings in the world. It took twenty-two years to build and was commissioned to house the tomb of the emperor's wife, who tragically died during childbirth. Who would have thought the act of a grief-stricken man could create such beauty?' She paused as we all listened to her soft, Indian lilt that had sent Nihal mute. 'Most men don't even act like they appreciate their girlfriends, let alone build something so grand to celebrate their love,' she added cattily.

Hearing this it was as if something twigged and Nihal cleared his throat. He seemed to pull himself up straighter and turned back to face us, avoiding making eye contact with me.

'So, where was I? Ah yes, people have believed for years that this is the greatest love story in India; however, it was not all romance and happiness. The emperor ordered the hands of the artists who had helped design the tomb to be cut off so they would never recreate something so magnificent again.' He half spat on the pebbles at his feet.

Ameera raised her voice even louder, competing with Nihal. 'You should never listen to these folklore tales though. I mean people tell you lies all the time. It can be very difficult to decide whether what people tell you is the truth or complete rubbish.'

Bex and Ollie turned round to face me. I tried to look as confused as they did rather than actually wanting the ground to swallow me up. This could not be happening. The only one who looked like he was enjoying this tour-guide-off was Chris. He had taken his camera phone out and shoved it in Nihal's face.

By now Ameera's tour group, which consisted of three men and a woman, had caught on that there was *something* going on but they didn't have the faintest idea why their pretty Indian tour guide was explaining the history of the Taj Mahal in such an unusual manner. An overweight Chinese man in Ameera's group put his hand up to ask a question but was cut off by Nihal clearing his throat to speak.

'I personally think it's unfair that throughout history people have always sided with the women, agreeing that it's so wonderful for a man to put on such a large display of affection. But some would say that it's actually completely over the top, showing off, if you will. The sort of women who expect such excessive declarations of affection are probably the sort of women to be avoided. Aren't I right, men?' Nihal nodded to Ollie and Chris. The Chinese man started clapping in agreement but stopped when Ameera glared at him.

Ollie scrunched up his face under his Ray-Bans; bless him, he looked like he didn't have the foggiest what was going on. 'Err, yeah, I guess?'

That only caused Flic to huff loudly and mutter that she knew he was a macho tool all along.

Ameera ignored her and increased in volume. 'The beautiful and heartfelt gift of the Taj Mahal is seen by many as one of the Seven Wonders of the World, due to its grace, beauty and symmetrical form. Emperor Shah Jahan obviously loved his wife so much that he put his heart and soul into the structure to show her what she meant to him. I know not *all* women expect huge declarations of love like this but actually if men showed women *how* they felt rather than expecting women to *know* then women would probably understand a lot better.' Ameera paused and glared at Nihal. 'Actions speak louder than words.'

'When are we going inside?' a lanky man with a heavy German accent piped up from Ameera's group, snapping her back from this competitive tour-off she was having with Nihal.

'Oh, right,' Ameera blustered and shook her cascade of hair from her face that had turned pink with the emotion. 'Well you now have some free time to explore the grounds and then meet back here in around thirty minutes so we can all go inside and see the wonderful mausoleum.' Her group looked relieved and wandered off, muttering that she was a bit strange.

Nihal watched Ameera walk off and quickly called out to our group. 'OK, guys, quick break. Meet us back here in thirty minutes.'

I shrugged at the others as if I hadn't the faintest idea what was going on and then moved to grab Nihal before he raced off behind Ameera.

'What the hell was that?' I asked through gritted teeth. 'What is *she* doing here?'

Nihal looked flustered; his eyes were flicking across the emerald lawns and trying to find Ameera through the crowds. 'I don't know! Although didn't you say you thought she could join us and become a tour guide too?'

'That was just an idea, a suggestion of how I could help you through your break-up. She can't just become a tour guide overnight!'

I knew I was half screeching but I was so confused. I'd tried to get Nihal back on his feet, and having his ex-girlfriend ruin it all for us with her own broken-hearted tour group complete with snazzy matching T-shirts simply wasn't an option.

'OK.' I pressed my fingers against the bridge of my nose. 'OK, so here is what we do. You go and find her, apologise for whatever it is you've done. Get back together, tell her we can find a job for her with you – maybe we could make you a double act?' I suggested before debating whether our guests would even want to be surrounded by a couple or not.

He shook his head and growled, 'No.'

'What do you mean no?!'

'I mean I haven't heard from her in ages, since our fight. I was so worried about her but actually she doesn't seem at all bothered about me. She's come here today *knowing* that I would be here working. She's come purposely to try and sabotage my job to get back at me somehow. She doesn't want to make up; she wants to get revenge!' He looked like he might burst in anger; a purple vein was suddenly very prominent on the right side of his temple. I noticed that his fists were balled up at his sides. So long Mr Heartbroken and enter Mr Taking No Shit.

'Nihal, we need to fix this!' I screeched, still not able to believe what I'd seen with my own eyes. Although maybe we should get matching T-shirts, or hats, or both? They did look kind of cool. 'If you're not going to fix this like adults then at least make the effort to give our tour group the best day out they've ever had. I want them to leave here buzzing with adrenalin, not feeling depressed and reminded about their problems back home by being surrounded with bickering couples. They have paid good money to get away from all of that!'

'Oh my God, it all makes sense!' Nihal slapped his hand to his forehead; he'd obviously not listened to a word I'd just said.

'What? What makes sense?'

'We'd been bickering for a while, always over my job and then, about a month or so ago, I came back from a really good tour full of excitement at how it went. The strange thing was though, instead of ignoring me when I spoke about what I'd been up to, she seemed really interested. Asking questions, even writing things down, I think.' He scrunched up his nose as if trying to remember, and then his face dropped.

'Nihal?'

He visibly gulped and inhaled sharply. 'You know that bad review you showed me about one of my tours?'

I nodded.

'I reread it yesterday after you left and something didn't add up. There were details in there that were slightly off. I put it down to my memory but now I think I know who may have written it.'

He didn't have to say her name for me to know whom he was referring to. It was now my turn to morph into the incredible hulk. *That business-wrecking bitch!*

'Really! You think Ameera wrote it? But why?' I gasped.

Nihal nodded slowly. 'I think she wanted to show me that anything I could do she could do better.'

'Oh my God!' So it had all been lies. The tour wasn't going tits up; everything was fine apart from some psycho ex-girlfriend wanting to get revenge.

'I'm serious, Georgia. She's lost any chance of ever getting back with me by playing this dirty trick.' Nihal spat on the gravel before stomping off and leaving me alone.

I threw my head heavenwards, giving the Taj Mahal the evil eye. *I thought you were supposed to be all about love, not sabotage?* I turned to try and find the others, nervous to hear what their interpretation of this drama would be when I walked slap bang into someone.

'Oh, sorry,' I said in shock, looking up to see Chris standing there.

How long had he been there? He had his phone out, but instead of snapping shots of the Taj Mahal I swear it was pointed in our direction. He must have heard everything.

'You OK, Chris?' I said brightly. He almost dropped his phone.

'Yeah, it's something else here, isn't it,' he said quickly. 'Very, erm, interesting.'

I mumbled a response and plastered a smile on my face, trying to spot Bex and her pink scarf or Ollie's ginger locks amongst all the people milling around.

'Oh, there they are!' I waved and hot-footed it away from Chris who I was sure was smirking at me as I left.

'Hey, so you should hear Flic's theory,' Ollie said with a laugh as I walked over to them.

'Oh yeah, what's that then?' I asked, wanting some light relief as my brain computed everything I'd just learnt in the last five minutes.

Flic rolled her eyes, throwing a look to Ollie for landing her in it. 'I was just saying to the group that I've worked out why Nihal is so strange.'

'Strange?' I squeaked.

'Yeah, you know, moody and distant then over-the-top helpful and informative but with very limited attention skills…' Flic said building the tension. I took a deep breath, wondering whether I should just come clean with what had gone on, when she continued. 'He's on drugs,' she finished, proudly crossing her arms as Liz gasped.

'What? No…' I said, laughing weakly.

'Come on, Louise, think about it. Highs and lows, mixed emotions. I'm telling you he's a crack head,' Flic added.

'That's ridiculous. He's not a crack head.' I lowered my voice, noticing a group of Swedish tourists staring at us. Oh God, I couldn't let the tour group believe Nihal was a druggie. Imagine their reviews. 'He's…he's…' I stalled not knowing what to say. If I told them about Ameera they would wonder how I knew, but if I stayed quiet they would believe Flic and her zany ideas.

'He's diabetic,' Chris said matter-of-factly as he walked up to the group. 'Quite common in Indian men of his age, meaning his mood depends on his insulin levels.'

'He is?' I gawped. 'Oh, I mean, yes, he is. He told us earlier.'

'Aww poor guy. I could never imagine shoving a needle in my arm every single day,' Bex sympathised and tutted at Flic. Ollie rolled his eyes and Liz let out a deep breath she'd been holding.

'Oh, right,' Flic mumbled. 'Well the signs were there that he *could* have been a druggie.'

'Yeah, but he's not,' Chris said before walking off to take a photo of Princess Diana's bench. I had to stop myself from shaking my head in disbelief as I watched him leave. He had got me out of a hole just then; maybe he wasn't such a weirdo after all.

'Well that solves that then!' I said brightly, hoping my heart wasn't hammering loudly enough for them to hear.

I'd been preoccupied looking around for Ameera and her tour group amongst the crowds rather than looking around the marble mausoleum. I was fired up to find this cow and have it out with her for writing that fake travel review but she was nowhere to be seen. As we snaked our way past sweet-smelling plants lining the perfectly still pools, the white domes reflected in the tranquil blue waters, I forced myself to calm down and breathed a sigh of relief that finally things were going to get easier. Surely. We would all go and have some lunch and everything would be OK.

'Here, this looks all right,' Nihal said when we arrived at a nearby snack bar away from the tourist site.

A few taxi drivers were sat on plastic chairs in the shade of tamarind trees drinking masala chai tea next to large, gurning camels that were loosely tied up to tree trunks and whose mouths were dripping long strands of spit on the dusty ground as they ate. My stomach audibly grumbled as Nihal placed our order. I needed to eat something soon, if only to stop the gnawing feeling in my empty tummy that Nihal was obviously working through the stages of a break-up, starting with denial that would eventually lead to anger, which could mean him making some rash decisions. So far he seemed to be coping by jutting out his lower lip and taking control of the group. I just hoped it would last.

'Right, I've got a mixture of things,' he said, passing over full plastic bags, paper serviettes and plastic cutlery.

'Did you go for the mild curry?' I asked nervously.

He nodded. 'Got a fiery one for me but everything else is bland, sorry, mild.' He winked. 'Here you go, guys, tuck in.' He passed out foil dishes to the group who hungrily grabbed the food and got stuck in.

'It's bloody awesome here,' Bex said, peeling the lid off what looked like lentil curry.

Liz agreed with her. 'What a romantic husband.'

'My ex never did anything like this for me,' Flic said grumpily, poking a fork around her foil dish.

'Yeah, well, I doubt most men would,' added Ollie. 'You know, those of us who aren't shahs sat on millions of rupees who can afford to do something as grand as this.' He laughed.

Flic pursed her lips. 'No, but you men could think outside of the box when it comes to romance a little more. Netflix and chill is not the way to a woman's heart, trust me.'

Liz blushed. 'I agree that this is a little excessive but it would still be nice if men, I mean if my ex, had at least tried to make some sort of gesture.' She paused. 'He forgot my birthday last year.'

This elicited matching gasps from the women in the group, me included.

'Mine remembered my birthday but got me a paper shredder,' Bex grumbled. I winced. 'Nothing says romance like office supplies.'

'Well maybe if women didn't nag so much you would have gotten something a little nicer,' Chris jumped in. The way he spoke was as if Bex had hit a nerve; maybe he had bought an ungrateful woman a shredder before.

'I…I didn't nag.' Liz blushed. To be fair she looked like she wouldn't say boo to a goose so I doubted she would have been wearing the trousers in any of her past relationships.

'Guys, it's going cold,' I said, pointing to the food and wanting to move the conversation on before Chris lectured Bex on having an attitude of gratitude even when receiving naff stationery.

As if to demonstrate, I plunged my spoon into the curry nearest to me, a bright orange, oily sauce with what looked like mushrooms bobbing about. Swallowing it down I thought my mouth was going to explode. Chillies scratched at my throat, clawing at my epiglottis. I coughed up and grabbed the nearest plastic cup of lassi, swiped a fly away from it and took a big glug, hoping the smooth yoghurt would cool the inferno in my mouth.

'You OK, Louise?' Bex asked opening a bottle of mineral water to pass to me. I nodded, my eyes streaming and face flushed. 'I think that was Nihal's,' she added apologetically.

Ollie chuckled to himself but stopped when he saw Liz frowning at him. Finally, after drinking the whole of Bex's water, the pain subsided.

'Watch out for that one; it's a little spicy,' I added lamely.

'So, Chris, what's your story then?' Bex asked as I wiped my mouth, my lips stinging at the oily residue still clinging to them.

He put down his cutlery; I noticed that he ate like a little bird, picking out the dishes with vegetables and snacking at the bright pilau rice. 'What do you want to know?'

'Well, where are you from?' Bex asked. She seemed to be the only one not put off by his boring stare.

'London.'

'How old are you?'

'Thirty-four.'

'What's your job?'

'IT consultant.'

God this was painful, but Bex didn't seem ready to let it drop.

'Why did you come on this tour?'

At this Chris straightened up slightly and tore off a piece of naan bread to slowly chew over before he answered. Bex looked at him; her chestnut-coloured eyes narrowed, sizing him up, waiting for an answer.

'I…I broke up with my girlfriend at Christmas and wanted to get away,' he stuttered. A slight blush danced on his angular, grey cheeks.

'What's that you were saying about getting crap presents? Getting dumped at Christmas has to be one of the worst times,' Ollie sympathised. Chris nodded quickly and carried on eating. 'Dumped on your birthday would be pretty shite too,' Ollie added.

'Or during winter, as no one wants to go out looking for a new date when it's so cold outside,' Bex reasoned.

'Yeah but summer's crap too as everyone is at festivals or on holiday with their boyfriend,' Flic added.

I laughed. 'So basically getting dumped anytime sucks!'

'So, Nihal, are you seeing anyone?' Liz asked. I almost choked on a torn-off piece of chapatti as she continued. 'I bet it's quite hard finding someone here as even with so many people around I assume you don't get the chance to strike up conversations that often.'

'No, I…' Nihal faded out, looking like we were deadly close to regressing back to the grief stage as tears pricked his eyes and his chin trembled slightly.

'He's too much of a ladies' man to worry about that,' Ollie jumped in and patted Nihal on the shoulder, saving him from explaining the truth.

Nihal dipped his head and then clapped his hands together. 'Ha ha, something like that. OK, so if you've finished eating we need to be making a move,' he said after clearing his throat.

I thought the sudden decision to finish lunch was because of the awkward conversation but when I looked up to where he'd fixed his steely gaze I spotted Ameera and her group dawdling over to us.

I overheard Ameera call out, 'Come on, guys, a change of plan. The restaurant we were going to eat at is actually filthy. We'll find a much better place.' She turned her neat nose in the air and stalked past us. Some of her tour members, in their matching broken heart T-shirts, smiled at us apologetically.

'It's not dirty here, is it?' Liz turned to face me; she had her small bottle of hand sanitiser out already.

'No, it's perfectly fine. All the locals were sat here and they always say if you want the most authentic food then you have to follow the locals.' I smiled, hoping that Nihal had checked it out before we came here. OK, so there were a few flies around and the overweight guy serving was hardly a picture of good health but I was sure it would be fine.

Just to piss me off, my stomach gurgled loudly.

Oh no.

CHAPTER 17

Ailing (adj.) Sickly; unwell

The rest of the afternoon was a disaster. After leaving the Taj Mahal and pushing our way through sellers and touts all desperate to take our group off to their cousin's/brother's/friend's gem shop for a *nice price, nice price,* we made it over to the Red Fort. It was actually more of an imposing, walled city made of dusty red sandstone that stood out against the piercing blue sky. However, I couldn't tell you a thing about this striking building as I was forced to rush to the nearest public bathroom, a stinking hole in the ground guarded by swarms of flies and mozzies, doubled up in pain whilst trying to keep my balance over the squat toilet.

I eventually emerged, scuffing my sturdy but ugly travel sandals on the ground, trying to wipe off what had been left by other toilet visitors that I'd accidently stood in. Clutching my stomach and almost limping outside, I managed to track down a shaded place to sit under a nearby tree. Everyone else had traipsed into the fort so I had some time to kill and try to rehydrate before they would be finished. I flopped on the stone bench and slowly sipped on a bottle of mineral water, cursing Nihal for leaving his super spicy curry near me, and for Ameera's prissy look that had encouraged my stomach to experience the souvenir no one wants: Delhi belly.

I'd already tried to ignore the advances of two skinny, well-dressed Indian men wanting to show me some tatty carpet samples and a gaggle of children who'd run up to me with their hands outstretched asking for cash; but with only notes tucked away in my travel wallet, and too doubled up to access them from my money belt, I waved them away. Beads of sweat collected at my forehead. I hoped Nihal's tour wouldn't take too long, although thinking about the long taxi journey home made me want to rush back to the stinking loo to throw up.

About ten minutes later I heard footsteps make their way over to the bench where I was lying. I was almost passed out. I looked up pathetically to see Nihal striding over to me, pale-faced and knotting his hands with worry.

'We need to go now,' he said quickly.

My heart sank that I'd left them alone for no longer than thirty minutes and something else had kicked off with him and Ameera's group. I was about to ask him why but I was saved from using what little energy I had left by taking one look at the grey, drawn faces of the tour group slowly staggering behind him. They looked as bad as I felt.

'Oh no. It's not just me, is it?' I asked.

Bex's normally wide grin was now contorted into a grimace, Ollie was holding his stomach, and both Liz and Flic were taking slow deep breaths. They looked like zombies with some life-threatening parasite had attacked them – well, everyone apart from Chris.

'I think it was that food; that Indian woman with the other tour group did say it was dirty in there.' Bex grabbed her chubby waist as it gurgled loudly in agreement.

'We've all been sick,' Liz replied. Strands of slicked-down hair were clinging to her sweating forehead.

'Not all of us,' Chris said. I couldn't tell if he was being sympathetic or loving every second of watching the others writhe around in pain. 'I told you not to eat any meat or dairy here.'

I could have punched his smarmy face but the energy involved in swinging my arm would have wiped me out completely.

'Oh, right. Yeah, I'm not feeling so great either,' I answered.

Nihal looked fine health wise. His gut was probably used to the local strains of food poisoning; he looked partly pitying and partly embarrassed. 'We have a tour of the nearby market planned but…' He trailed off seeing the washed-out faces of the group. 'We could go back early.'

Everyone nodded fervently apart from Chris who acted like he was really annoyed, even though I imagined looking round a hot and stuffy market hall was not exactly high on his list of things to see and do. Our minibus pulled up moments later and with fresh bottles of mineral water, plenty of tissues and taking a deep breath we boarded the van to go back to Delhi.

Every rock, hole and bump we juddered over on the road back was met with yelps of pain from the rest of the passengers. I had willed myself to try and sleep but kept getting the urge to go to the toilet. With five of us out of action the minibus stopped almost every twenty minutes for one or all of us to rush off into the prickly bushes on the side of the road, clutching handfuls of loo roll and staggering back on board. The journey home felt like it took for ever. And it wasn't helped by Chris opening up packets of nuts and seeds that he had brought with him. The smell of food, no matter how bland, made my stomach turn even more.

Back at the hotel the group swiftly disappeared off into their own rooms, Rashid watching on horrified as we staggered past. We may not have had the chance to sit and get to know the guests as well as I had hoped yet but I certainly felt like we all knew each other a little better after vomming and shitting in such rough, raw conditions. I had never been so grateful for a clean bathroom and a western-style toilet before.

After another painful trip to the loo, I felt convinced I had nothing left in my system. Thankfully Nihal had left us all bananas and more bottles of water outside our doors, along with tiny rehydration sachets. I just hoped I could keep it all down long enough for it to work.

Flopping on my soft bed I instinctively curled into the foetal position. I had the urge to call Ben; I needed to hear his soothing tones. I needed him to tell me I was going to get better, that this was just an Indian rite of passage. I needed comforting from someone who knew me. I also wanted to know what was going on back at the office and if he had managed to find a suitable temp worker. And I needed to take my mind off running to the bathroom and sinking down on the cool hard tiles.

But as much as I tried with the limited movement I could muster, I couldn't get onto the Wi-Fi in my room and there was no way I could crawl to reception to get a good signal. I slumped back onto my pillow, feeling as limp and disgusting as a wilted lettuce leaf at a summer barbecue. I stayed like this, cradling my stomach with my eyes closed, until a loud hollow gurgle made me bolt from my comfy position.

Why on earth did I agree to do this tour again?!

CHAPTER 18

Green-eyed (adj.) Jealous; envious; distrustful

We'd been given a free day to rest and recover as everyone, apart from Chris, was still feeling slightly tender and empty. I spent most of the day with the air con turned up, curled up in bed eating dry toast and drinking mineral water that Rashid brought me, worrying about how bad this tour was turning out to be and crossing everything I could that surely things had to start looking up soon.

I still couldn't face leaving my room and the hotel's Wi-Fi seemed to hate me as much as Indian curry did, but I desperately wanted to hear Ben's voice so I ignored how much it would cost me and called his office phone.

'Hello?' a woman said distractedly on the fourth ring.

'Hiya, Kel,' I said warmly despite the fact that no matter how many times we told her she needed to answer the phone 'Hello, Lonely Hearts Travels, Kelli speaking, how may I help you?' she always seemed to forget.

There was a pause down the line.

'Who's that?' the woman said, in a plummy accent and sarky tone. The woman most definitely wasn't Kelli. I suddenly panicked that I'd called the wrong number. Maybe this food poisoning had sent me delirious.

'Oh, sorry, is this Lonely Hearts Travels?' I asked.

'Yeah,' she replied, sounding bored at the very effort of speaking to me.

'Who am I talking to, please?' I felt my patience wane as my confusion rose.

'What's it any of your business?' she replied followed by a loud yawn.

'Well, as a matter of fact, it *is* my business. I'm the co-owner, Georgia Green. Who the hell is this?' I asked gritting my teeth.

There was a long pause. After what felt like for ever the rude woman changed her tone to an almost purr. 'Oh, I am sorry, Miss Green. I think there were a few problems with the line just then,' she said calmly and blatantly lying through her teeth. 'My name's Serena DeVere. How may I help you today?'

'Erm, is Ben there?' Who the hell was Serena DeVere and why was she picking up my work phone?

'Ben!' she called out in the same way she would if she had just climaxed with him. 'He's just coming, Miss Green.' She emphasised the word *Miss* just to highlight the point. 'Is there anything else I can help you with?'

'No, no just a word with Ben,' I said curtly.

'Sure, well have a great day,' she purred. I could hear her passing the receiver over to Ben. His light laugh danced down the line, and she let out some cringy, girly giggle.

'Hey, Georgia! How are you?' I could hear the smile in his voice as he spoke but I couldn't place if it was because he was talking to me or because this sexy fembot was inches away from him.

I bit my tongue and plastered on a smile. 'Oh, fine, fine. Just calling up to see how everything is with…'

Ben cut me off as he started to laugh.

'What's so funny?' I lightened my tone as if I got the joke.

'Oh nothing. Just something Serena said earlier,' he said pulling himself together.

'Yeah, erm, who the hell is Serena?'

'Ah sorry! Serena is the new temp.'

What? It had only been a day!

'Oh, right. That was fast,' I said trying to hide the hurt in my voice, which was stupid as I was the one who'd told him to recruit someone. Serena DeVere. From that name and her butter-wouldn't-melt accent I instantly imagined a sex kitten. My stomach contracted. I hated her already. *She's going to marry him and have his babies all before you get your chubby ass out of your Delhi pit*, a voice sang in my tired mind.

'Yeah, I know, it was strange really; she walked in the moment I got off the phone to you with her CV. It was like fate or something, plus it saved me going through an agency.' He laughed. 'She's fitted in really well and already given us loads of great ideas to think about. You'll love her.'

I felt like I wanted to run to the bathroom to throw up.

'Great. Just great,' I said through gritted teeth.

Georgia – don't be jealous. Maybe she was really ugly and just has a sexy voice and exotic-sounding name. Maybe her parents felt sorry for her when she was born as she frightened all the nurses so they needed to give her something in order to survive this cruel world, I told myself. If things had been left better between Ben and me before I left, I probably wouldn't be feeling so paranoid that Little Miss New Ideas was going to come in and ruin everything. *What – like you actually telling him how much you freakin' love him?* My subconscious had her hand on her hip, giving me her best sassy face that would mirror Shelley and her *I told you so* look with her lips pursed, wagging a finger in my face for not admitting how much I liked Ben. Ooh but maybe I could send her down to spy on the shop for me?

'Georgia?' Ben's voice pulled me back to the moment. 'Did you hear what I was saying?'

'Yep, yeah. Great idea,' I lied.

There was a pause down the line. 'Great idea? Really? Wow, I wasn't sure you would be on board so early on, especially as you haven't met her yet but I do think it will be good for us, for the business as we keep getting busier.'

Wait, what was he going on about?

'Mmmm,' I added, too embarrassed to admit that I'd tuned out to what he was talking about before. Whatever it was he sounded really pumped up about it.

'Well OK then, I'll get the contract drafted up ASAP.'

Wait, contract? Contract for what?

'Oh right, erm, do I need to be there to sign it?' I asked, hoping his answer would shed some light on what I'd just agreed to.

I could imagine him shaking his head. 'No, you've got enough on your plate sorting out the Indian tour. Serena has so many excellent ideas on how to make the most of the Asian market. We're only just scratching the surface now, but I guess once she comes on full time then we can really start making our mark over there.' He sounded so animated; I hadn't heard him like this in a long time.

'Full time?' I parroted.

We were barely paying ourselves anything with each of us agreeing to take drastic pay cuts in order to get the business through its first year; I doubted we could afford someone else. She had only just started and was meant to be a temp until I got back. Why the hell did he want her sticking around? *Because he fancies her, because he needs a reason to see her every day,* the evil side of my subconscious piped up.

'Yeeeaaaah,' he said like he was speaking to a three-year-old. 'You know, her contract I said I would get sorted?'

'Well maybe we should wait till I get back so I can actually meet her and…'

'No, like I've said, you've got enough on and we've spoken before about trusting each other – fifty-fifty remember? Don't worry about it, Georgia. I've got everything under control from this end. You just focus on getting the Indian tour back on track,' he said sounding firm but friendly.

'Oh, OK.' I needed to show him that I trusted his business decisions, if only my heart and my brain thought the same.

'Speaking of which, how's it going over there?'

I thought back to the night spent cuddling the porcelain toilet seat and the way I'd flashed my breasts in the Indian restaurant. 'Fine, fine.'

'Ah, great. Well I hope you're having fun; you deserve it. So, any closer to finding out the deal with the terrible review?'

'Yeah, the review was a fake.'

'A fake? How do you know?'

'Nihal's ex-girlfriend wrote it as revenge when they split up. Oh yeah, the tour guide who is leading our tour of heartbroken guests is also heartbroken. Well he was. I think he is now more pissed off than pining.'

'Right,' Ben said slowly as if trying to keep up. I could hear someone giggling in the background and I knew it wouldn't be Kelli. 'Well that's good news, isn't it? Not the fact he's been dumped but the fact the review was just spiteful lies?'

'Yeah.' I rubbed my face trying to focus on this work conversation. 'I'm just nervous at what else this woman will do to get back at him for whatever he's done.'

The sound of laughter down the phone increased.

'Listen, I better go. We've been rearranging the brochure section.' *Let me guess, it was Serena's idea.* 'And the shop looks in a bit of a state so I need to get it sorted before we leave.'

'Oh OK,' I said quietly.

'Sounds like you've got everything under control over there. Take care and speak soon,' he said and hung up before I had the chance to reply or find out why he said 'we' leave and not 'I' leave.

As my room grew silent once more my mind was instantly filled with a stunning skinny blonde, her tanned arm draped over Ben, throwing back her head and giggling at everything he said, touching his muscles, leaving her manicured hand for a second longer each time until suddenly their eyes meet and before you know it he has her spreadeagled over my spreadsheets.

I raced towards the bathroom feeling like I was about to puke up.

Wiping my mouth on the soft white towel and avoiding my horrific reflection in the mirror I changed into a woman on a mission and did what any jealous lady does: operation cyber stalk. I finally managed to connect to the Wi-Fi by half hanging out of my bedroom window and hit Google. However, the only Serena DeVere listed was an Australian surfer who died seven years ago. I tapped open Facebook and looked for her on there but there wasn't a single person with that name and the same thing happened on Instagram and Twitter. Who lives in this century without being connected to social media? I wondered, before putting my hand in sticky bird poo on my windowsill by accident. I went to the bathroom to clean it off, telling myself stop to being so neurotic. I hoped that if I said it enough times I'd believe it.

CHAPTER 19

Unclubbable (adj.) Having or showing a disinclination for social activity; unsociable

The smells hit me first. Days-old body odour swirled around the packed station concourse mingling with scents of garlic, cow turds and heavy incense. I tried to breathe through my mouth to avoid the worst of it. It wasn't just the rancid smells turning my still-delicate stomach; we were so tightly packed in, as if it was rush hour on the London Underground, bodies touching other bodies, arms slicked with sweat and eyes darting around anywhere but making eye contact. Welcome to Delhi train station.

I tried to smile reassuringly at the group sandwiched behind me. Chris had his thin lips pressed into a constant frown, Bex was fanning her rosy-cheeked face and Ollie was thumbing through his dog-eared guide book as if the answer to this awful moment would be found within its yellowing pages. We were waiting for the next train to Mumbai. A journey that would take fifteen hours, roll past paddy fields and rocky views from the comfort of our private berth.

Looking at the swathe of people clamouring around the tiny windows of the ticket offices I was so grateful that Nihal was thankfully taking charge. Families carrying what looked like their entire homes shuffled past, plastic bags upon plastic bags clutched under their arms or on their heads. I was expecting to see people playing extreme sardines sat on the roof of trains, half leaning out of packed windows and overcrowded carriages but instead the only busy spot was the station concourse filled with people, bags and various animals and birds trapped in large cages. Children were skipping around us, seeing this as a game to dart through the static crowd, zipping under legs and through strangers' knees as their expressionless parents elbowed their way down the platform. Muffled announcements rang out through large speakers, their message incoherent above the buzz and noise of waiting passengers.

'OK, this way!' Nihal bellowed, waving a handful of tickets in his outstretched skinny arm whilst eyeballing three overweight men snarling at him for pushing in the queue.

'Thank the Lord, or should that be Allah?' Chris mumbled, stepping over a box of ripening mangoes that a gummy-mouthed old woman had plonked by his bright white trainers. The tart smell of the mangoes tickled my nose. The old woman's hand was outstretched, asking Chris for coins in return for a battered piece of fruit, but his face flushed with an equal mixture of disgust and fear and he ignored her.

I didn't have the chance to rummage out some change for her as Nihal was as quick as those children at finding gaps between the crowds, ducking and swerving like a boxer in a ring, managing to squeeze into spaces and then parting the way so we could trot behind him to catch up.

'Up here, guys, but hurry we don't have long!' The panic in Nihal's voice was only just perceptible but taking a look at the length of the train we had to file down to find our cabins, we started to jog in the sticky oven heat, backpacks bouncing on our shoulders and sweat dripping down our collarbones.

Middle-aged men carrying briefcases were running down empty tracks to move between platforms as people scrambled onto moving trains. The atmosphere was aggressive and very intimidating, as if there were some unwritten rules and invisible lines not to cross. I spotted two guys involved in a punch-up as they hung on to the large door handles of a commuter train where up to thirteen people squeezed into the space of a phone box. Fuck that for a way to start your working day.

Teenage lads were leaning out of the windows calling to other passengers in dialects I didn't understand, their eyes following us down the platform, some giving us hard stares and some with faces creased in mirth at the sight of us struggling in the suffocating heat.

'How much longer?' Bex gasped, her ample breasts jiggling about as she jogged along.

'Here we go! Come on now, hurry!' Nihal whipped open a door and hurriedly scanned down the platform, making sure we would all get on before the conductor blew his whistle. Piling in and tumbling up the steps we made it with just moments to spare as the train eased itself away from the station.

Next stop Mumbai!

The group were chatting excitedly about the journey as we found our beds and could finally take off our heavy backpacks. A narrow corridor lined the old, creaking carriage that had metal double decker bunks on either side. Chairs had been laid flat to make a sort of bed; you had to duck to avoid a stranger's foot in your face that hung over the bunk above your head. Indian men, women, teenagers and children each had their own space. In some cases couples or entire families were sharing, which only added to both the heat in here and the lively atmosphere too. There was no glass in the window frames; instead thick, bright blue iron slats had been welded on, acting as ventilation for the stuffy carriage along with noisy, huge metal fans stuck on the ceiling providing a warm but pointless breeze.

'OK, so this isn't exactly luxury but it's the best place to be to experience Indian train travel. Did you know that India's rail network is the third largest in the world?' Nihal stated proudly before muttering something under his breath as a fat Indian man with bushy black back hair tried to push past. 'It can be a little busy so please chain up your bags to the locks under your seats and don't drop food on the floor as the mice will be all over you.'

'Mice?' Liz shuddered and whipped her feet onto the seat, quickly scanning the dubiously stained floor for signs of vermin.

'Yep, but they're quite cute actually,' Nihal said. 'Get yourselves comfy as we have a long journey ahead – and enjoy!'

Trying to take my mind away from the fact I may be sharing my bed with the rodent chef from *Ratatouille*, I looked around at the other commuters on this journey with us. I smiled to myself seeing a young Indian couple in a bunk a little further down the carriage. The woman was sat upright with her slender legs outstretched as he lay with his head on her lap and his eyes closed, relaxed into a blissful sleep. She gently ran her fingers through his thick black hair and held a well-worn novel in her other hand. Back in the early days when I knew that Ben was going to be working with me running Lonely Hearts Travels, I'd daydreamed that we would get to travel through exotic countries, entwined around each other and sharing these precious moments together – just like them. I hadn't realised that although we worked in a travel agency and talked about travel all day every day, we were usually the ones staying firmly in one place. Literally and figuratively. The woman caught me staring at her and gave me a strange look, making me blush and dart my eyes away.

It was either gaze out of the window or stare at the soles of an older man lying opposite my bunk. They were almost grey due to the amount of dried dust caked to his rubber sandals. His gnarled and jaggedy toenails made my stomach turn. I focused my attention out on the tracks. Just inches away was a group of six or so children having a game of cricket using the dry patch of land between crumbling, half-painted derelict brick houses as their pitch. They shouted and laughed as the tallest one missed a shot again and stepped over piles of rubbish to retrieve his ball before waving to the train as we rumbled past.

To be fair, it was better than any of the views you get on the trains back in England. Here you could spend the whole journey gawping at the outside world tumbling past, and every few minutes there was something new to see. From school children playing games to families sat on brick walls waiting to cross the tracks to the other side, to herds of goats and white dirty cows with visible ribcages and bony haunches aimlessly wandering along, oblivious to anything but the dry tufts of grass they were munching on.

'Everything OK, Louise?' Ollie asked warmly, pulling my attention back to the noisy carriage. Since arriving in India freckles had covered his neat nose, and they made his green eyes sparkle even more.

'Yeah fine. How are you feeling?'

His broad grin broke over his face. 'Better than I was a few days ago, thank God. Been ages since I've felt that rough.'

'Ah, I guess it's a rite of passage over here.' I smiled.

There was something about him that made me happy. I didn't know if it was his easy-going personality, genuine smile, or that he seemed interested in how I was feeling rather than just making small talk. I listened to him tell a story about one of his mates, someone called Hard Sam who had wanted to impress a girl in their local pub by doing bench presses with bar stools that ended up in a trip to A and E.

I was half listening to him speaking with ease and confidence and half thinking about Ben. I had to finally admit that us as a couple was never going to work. If it hadn't happened by now then I guessed it never would. He had seemed desperate for me to come here, to 'take a break from each other' – my stomach clenched as I thought back to the sting of those words he had uttered. Plus the fact he had jumped at the chance to hire a glamazon replacement, moments after I left, spoke volumes about how he felt about me – we were work colleagues and nothing more. I needed to get over that spark that I was convinced we had both felt when we were in Thailand last year and pass it off as nothing more than a brief holiday romance, if you could even call it that. We hadn't even shared a kiss.

I looked fondly at Ollie laughing at his own story; he was cute and it had been so long since I'd had sex. Marie had told me once that if you didn't use it then it seals back up. I wasn't sure if she was joking or not. Ollie had this charming, cheeky-chappie persona, always wanting to make people smile; he was adorable. Ben could have Serena and I'd have Ollie. Simple.

'You OK, Louise?' Ollie said interrupting me from my thoughts. 'You've got a weird look on your face. Is it the smell from my feet? I sometimes suffer from athlete's foot and in this sticky heat it can flare up,' he said sheepishly before trying to sniff his battered trainers. And just like that, the spell was broken. I couldn't deceive my heart into trying to like someone else, especially not someone with rancid foot fungus, no matter how cute he was.

I laughed. 'No, sorry, I was miles away there.'

Ollie nodded and pulled out a tatty book to read before taking a final sniff of his feet.

'Chai, chai, garam chai.'

I'd dozed off thanks to the humid air and rocking motion of the train, but woke with a start when someone began non-stop hollering down our carriage. I rearranged myself and grumpily turned over to make eye contact with a lanky man selling tea, known as a chaiwallah, who'd stopped at my feet and put out his rough palm.

'Chai. You want chai?' he ordered.

I shook my head. Nihal had warned us about the toilets on the trains and I was trying to see how long I could last before finding out for myself how filthy they actually were.

'Only three rupees,' the tea man pushed.

'No thank you,' I said politely.

He muttered something in Hindi before continuing on his way, his foghorn voice echoing off the metal walls.

'You don't like chai tea?' a smartly dressed man with half-moon glasses and a bushy greying beard who was sat opposite me asked.

'Oh no, it's really nice. I just don't want one right now.'

'Well he'll be doing the rounds throughout the whole journey,' beard man said. 'So where are you from?'

'Manchester, England,' I replied.

'What do you do? Are you studying? It is very good for people to study and learn new things.'

'No, not studying. I…' I was about to say I run my own business but thankfully bit my tongue and remembered this alter-ego pretence I had to keep up. 'I work as a hairdresser.'

I understood that local people were curious about foreigners. I also quickly understood that being trapped on a long train journey with no form of escape meant the perfect time for them to chat to you. Although I hadn't realised that 'chatting' meant a nosy Indian man with a strange twitch asking you so many questions you could hardly keep up. After saying for the third time that 'no I don't have a husband' and that 'my father is retired' I was getting pretty sick of doing my bit for international relations.

'If you don't mind I really want to get some sleep,' I half apologised.

Beard man nodded and continued to stare at me to see if I was telling the truth or not. I smiled weakly, turned onto my side and closed my eyes as he continued to rabbit away about how it wasn't right I was single, not at my age. As I did I felt this sense of homesickness wash over me. I felt like I'd been consumed by India. I was sick of feeling so sticky and clammy all the freaking time, sick of trying to keep up this pretence of feeling positive, wanting to make sure the others were having a great time as *technically* I was a guest on this tour, not the boss in charge. I was sick of being stared at, constantly feeling like strangers' eyes were following me all the time. I tried to block out the noise of the rest of the carriage and just let myself be for a while. I felt dizzy with dehydration due to the relentless suffocating heat and constant sweating; I was even repulsed by my own reeking body odour.

I couldn't cope with the poverty that was right outside the window, the never-ending pushing and pulling from sellers and rickshaw drivers, the maddening way you couldn't get a solid answer out of anyone and the scabby, uncared-for street dogs just abandoned to roam through mounds of litter vying for scraps like the destitute street children. This country broke my heart. I felt completely wiped out, sick of eating curry, sick of using squat toilets and sick of being the one trying to keep everything together all of the time.

Not just here but back home too. A deep ache rattled through my chest as I allowed myself to cry, silent body-clenching sobs into the grubby pillow. I had returned home from Thailand fired up with this business idea, determined to help other travellers like me, but was I even helping anyone? I had pushed my family and friends away as I tried to conquer the world flying solo. I hadn't realised just how much Alex had destroyed my trust and faith in others. I'd clammed up my heart through fear; was that it, fear that Ben would get deep inside and hurt me the way Alex had done?

I realised I'd subconsciously forced myself to grow a hardened shell over my feelings. Trust no one. You can do it alone. I shook my head, laughing in silent mirth. What bullshit. I couldn't do it alone. I couldn't do anything alone. Look at how my business was blossoming but to the detriment of my social life, relationships and physical wellbeing. Burning the candle at both ends was only going to end up in literal burnout. Coming to this country famed for its extremes, and riding this emotional rollercoaster that it sends each of its plucky visitors on all by myself, was utter madness.

I dried my eyes roughly and tried to blot out a voice in my head, Trisha's voice, her words of warning about how India treats you like an elastic band, stretching you until the point where you think the only end result is for you to snap before she loosens her grip and you bounce back to the shape that you choose to be. Well I was at breaking point right now.

'Hello, how do you do?' A slim arm was poking me in the leg, willing me to wake up. Lost in my miserable thoughts I grumpily turned over to see a teenage boy with a bright smile and a tray of chai tea in his hands. 'Chai tea?'

I growled a guttural 'fuck off' through clenched teeth; the lad bobbed his head and went to wake up the person in the next bunk.

'It's like they can smell your exhaustion. A pack of vultures waiting to attack the weak,' a woman cradling a sleeping baby said in a soft lilt of an Indian accent before smiling.

I rolled my eyes. 'That's *exactly* what it feels like,' I said exasperatedly.

'They see the colour of your skin and think easy pickings,' she said, brushing her thick fringe from her warm face with a free hand. 'Well, it's like that but times a hundred when you get to Mumbai. You'll soon realise that everyone there is trying to get ahead. But you need to remember that they are just trying to make a living.'

I nodded, already feeling like such a bitch for the way I'd just spoken to that boy; he was only doing his job. I told myself that I'd buy a whole jug of tea the next time he came round.

'I know.' I sighed deeply. 'It's just hard to act polite, especially when you're feeling so hot and bothered and they've just woken you up. If they were selling ice cream then it might be another matter.' I smiled softly.

The new mum gently placed her baby next to her and rummaged in a large plastic bag before pulling out what looked like two strangely shaped white pears and handing me one. 'Here, it's not an ice cream but they are good for cooling you down.'

I shook my head. 'No, I mean, thank you but I'm OK.'

'Don't worry they're clean,' she said, flushing with embarrassment.

'Oh no, I didn't mean for that.' I felt my own cheeks redden. 'I meant because you have a baby to feed. I'll go and grab something from the snack bar soon.'

She pushed the weird-looking fruit into my hands. 'There isn't a snack shop on board and unless you want hot chai tea you won't be getting anything to eat or drink for the rest of the journey. I would like you to take it, really.'

I took it and bowed my head. 'Thank you.' Her hazelnut-coloured eyes crinkled in a smile. 'Err…what is it?'

'A little taste of heaven on a hot train.' Her short bob danced as she threw her head back and let out a tinkle of a laugh. 'It's called white jamun, also known as love apples. They aren't available all year round so enjoy it whilst you can.' She took a deep bite, breaking the waxy skin, and I followed her lead.

Crisp and crunchy like an apple with a snow-white pith that tasted cool and slightly sweet, it was exactly what I needed. And just like that I'd gone from wanting to punch someone to feeling humbled and overwhelmed by her generosity. This stranger, this friendly new mum, had nothing but offered everything. Something I could do well to learn. I smiled to myself thinking about what Trisha had said; maybe I was starting to shape my own rubber band after all.

CHAPTER 20

Candour (n.) The state or quality of being frank, open and sincere in speech or expression

Fifteen long hours later our train wheezed to a final stop and everyone around us started to collect their things and wearily stretch their legs. With our backpacks heavy on our shoulders we patiently filed off the creaking train and out into the bright streaming sunlight.

I waved goodbye to the man who I felt like I'd shared my life story with and the kind new mum and trotted to keep up with the others. Difficult to do as the station concourse was like a beating heart. Throngs of people poured past in the clammy oppressive heat, a tidal wave of commuters, a sea of faces all heading in the same direction sweeping myself and the tour group along with them.

Thankfully, a minibus was already waiting for us and the driver, an overweight man with a serious handlebar moustache and a limp fag between his rubbery lips, was soon hoisting our bags onto the roof and strapping them down.

'Is that safe?' Liz asked biting her thumbnail.

I looked up at the fraying straps and wondered the same thing.

'Well if it falls off then some poor sucker will just be getting a bag full of my dirty undies.' Bex laughed and roughly slapped Liz on the back. 'Don't worry so much.'

Liz nodded and took a last look at the roof rack before climbing in the minibus. I clambered on afterwards and noticed that she had taken the seat next to Ollie, both of their faces a lovely shade of crimson as their elbows banged together over the sticky armrest.

Nihal slammed the door shut and jumped into the front seat before turning round to face us all, his grubby shirt getting trapped in the gaps of the seventies-style beaded seat cover.

'OK, we made it. So we're going to head to the hotel and drop our things off and have a shower.' A cheer of applause erupted from the back of the van. 'Yeah, I can smell half of you from here.' He winked. 'Then we'll meet again in a couple of hours to head to the next stop on the tour. We're going to take another trip but this time by boat. Don't worry it's only a short journey to take us to Elephanta Island. A place that I can assure you will be worth the effort.'

I'd never felt so clean and fresh in my life after a long shower in the small hotel where the water had turned brown as dirt, sweat and the stresses of the train washed off me and settled down the rusty plughole. We were soon back in the minibus driving to the famous Gateway of India, down wide lanes of noisy, fast-flowing traffic against the backdrop of a buzzing metropolis of skyscrapers that reflected the sun's blinding rays. The non-stop beeping of horns wasn't just a Delhi issue; all the drivers were at it here too. The humidity was exhausting, my hair had frizzed up like some badly kept Afro and beads of salty sweat trickled down my arms. It felt like my heart never stopped hammering.

As we drove, Nihal explained how Mumbai is *the* place ambitious Indians come to make their fortune. Glancing up at the towering skyscrapers I imagined local billionaires toasting their successes in a cocktail bar overlooking the sprawling slums at their feet. In contrast to the sleek high-rises we drove past colonial buildings that were both decadent and shabby at the same time, offering a taste of faded glamour to this manic city. My head was spinning at the stark reminders of inequality everywhere, from children squatting in the street and defecating in the gutters to amputee beggars with nasty open sores that had been cast away alongside piles of rubbish.

Eventually we reached the Gateway of India, the iconic landmark of this chaotic city, a tall concrete arch plonked right on the edge of the busy waterways. Nihal effortlessly herded us from the minibus onto an old, small ferry. I think everyone was suffering from the exhaustion of that epic train journey, as well as just being in Mumbai, so we followed him without a word. Nihal's plan of moving on from his break-up with Ameera seemed to be working, meaning I could gratefully take a back seat as he revelled in being centre stage and explaining Mumbai's history. This was the guy I'd hired; he really was passionate about his job. At least one thing had gone right with me being here in that he'd forgotten about his ex.

As the city faded out behind us and we slowly made our way across the bobbing brown waves to get to the mysterious Elephanta Island, I noticed that Flic had gone a very pale shade of green as she gripped the edges of the red, shiny bench seats we were sat on.

'You OK?' I asked quietly as she squeezed her eyes shut.

'Are we there yet?' she gasped between deep breaths she was forcing herself to gulp down.

'Erm, I can see something in the distance. We must not be far,' I replied spotting a long stone pier jutting out from the deep green, hilly island where we were headed. 'Are you not very good on boats?'

Flic shook her dreadlocks; her knuckles had turned white she was gripping on so tightly. I half wanted to laugh; here was this apparently fearless world traveller freaking out over a leisurely boat trip. We were probably only going around five miles an hour. But instead of taking the piss I gently rubbed her clammy, slim arm making her collection of bangles jangle.

'Just try and concentrate on something else. Why don't you tell me about your family?' I suggested, hoping to take her mind off the journey.

She swallowed and nodded but continued to keep her focus on a crushed water bottle lolling by her feet. 'My mum is a psychologist and my dad is a surgeon.' She blew out her pursed lips slowly. 'I am the youngest daughter in a family of three girls. My older sisters both work in the "City": Harriet is an investor and Mimi is a trader.'

'Wow. You've got some clever genes in your family!' I smiled.

Flic scrunched up her face. 'Yeah, although my parents would say that my sisters took all of those genes and I picked up the scraps of what was left over.'

Oh. 'I'm sure they don't think that,' I said rubbing her back gently.

She turned to face me, her eyes red and watery and silver nose piercing shiny with snot. 'Louise, you don't know my parents. I'm just a huge disappointment to them. No matter what I do I'll never be as good as my sisters.'

'I'm sure they love you all the same. What did they say about you being out here? Pretty adventurous huh?'

'Adventure isn't something they understand. My mum thinks I'm going through a phase and Daddy couldn't care less. No matter how far across the world I go or the cool places I see, they never seem to notice I've even gone.'

A thought came to me; it wasn't just British politics she had become disillusioned with but rather family politics.

I was about to say something comforting when a large cargo ship went past, causing our vessel to sway dangerously. Flic grabbed her stomach and lurched over the side to throw up into the sludgy waters.

As we chugged closer I spotted a smartly dressed man waiting for us on the pier, waving at our boat. Peering at the welcoming guy I suddenly had this strange feeling in my belly, like when you take the stairs too quickly and miss the bottom step. Your stomach does this little funny flip at almost dying, and it was happening right now. We inched closer and closer to the rundown pier and I realised why I felt this foreboding sense of déjà vu. I'd met this guy before.

CHAPTER 21

Aficionado (n.) A person who likes, knows about and appreciates a usually fervently pursued interest or activity; devotee

Our boat chugged closer and the smiling man came into full view. He was grinning broadly as if meeting his family in the airport arrivals hall. I realised where I had seen that thick, black head of hair and those dazzling olive-green eyes before. He was the flash, know-it-all man at the Indian visa office in Manchester, Raj or Rahul or something. What the hell was he doing here and why was he waving at our boat? I glanced around trying to find Nihal to ask him but he was deep in conversation with some of the men working on board. I told myself to stop being stupid; even if we were meeting this guy it was unlikely he would remember and recognise me. But the thought that he knew my real name and could blow my cover darted into my mind, making my body break into more of a sweat than the suffocating heat had caused.

I reluctantly followed the others and traipsed off the boat, hoping to stay shielded behind Ollie's broad back. Flic almost kissed the dusty ground with joy and Chris once again had his camera phone out.

I kept my eyes to the ground hoping to make it look like I was concentrating really, really hard on watching my footing as I got off the deck onto the crumbling pier. The others were all chattering away about how stunning this place was.

I was so busy keeping my gaze fixed at my feet I didn't realise that I'd nearly walked slap bang into someone. Someone who wasn't looking where they were going either. Someone who grabbed my arms to stop me from tripping backwards into the murky waves lapping the rocks. My heart jumped into my throat and I let out a strange sounding yelp. I gripped on to this stranger's muscular arm to save myself from plummeting to my death. Well OK, plummeting into the dirty water and making a fool of myself.

'I've got you,' a deep male voice with a heavy Manchester accent said, tightening his grip and pulling me forward.

Of course it had to be him who saved me. I looked up feeling the eyes of the group staring at me with open mouths as I still had a tight hold on my knight. I mumbled an apology and jumped out of his firm but protective grip. I brushed myself down, thinking how slimy my arms must have felt with the smeared-on sun cream and sweat. Nice.

'Thanks,' I mumbled.

'Georgia?'

He remembered me.

I acted bashful, contorting my flaming face into a confused expression. The rest of the tour group were still staring at me and this admittedly very attractive, smiling stranger who put his hand out for me to shake as if we were long-lost friends.

'It's Georgia, isn't it?' he asked again. 'Rahul.'

'Sorry, I think you have me confused with someone else,' I muttered and ignored his palm, desperately hoping that my cheeks wouldn't give the game away and return to their normal blotchy pink colour.

'We met back in Manchester remember? At the visa office?' he said, although a little less confidently than before.

I shook my head. 'Nope, sorry, it wasn't me.' I then let out this stupid little shrill of a laugh that sounded like it hadn't even come from my dry mouth.

Rahul nodded slowly. 'Oh, right, sorry.' He shook his thick grabbable hair and smiled crookedly. 'You just really look like this woman I met.'

Eventually Nihal stepped forward, breaking up the awkwardness. 'This here is my friend Rahul.' He slapped smug-visa-man on the back and turned to face the group. 'We met a few years ago and he agreed to give you all a tour of this island, his childhood home. We're lucky he is here visiting as he knows all the nooks and crannies.'

Rahul gave me one last strange look and then turned and grinned at the group. 'I moved to England when I was a teenager, hence my accent, but I split my time working in Manchester and visiting my family here, helping out when I can to give tours to wonderful people like yourselves and sharing this island with you. So, we all here?' Rahul called out, avoiding looking at me again. I panicked that the group would think it was strange he had been so adamant that he knew me but everyone seemed too concerned with the hunky Indian man to notice. Liz was nodding her head manically, practically melting into a pool of lust at his feet. I felt Ollie bristle beside me. 'Great, well let's go.'

We followed Rahul as he strode off purposefully past rows of small stalls lining the pier walls. They were selling carved figurines made out of rock and bright, colourful saris.

'The temples were thought to have been created between AD 450 and 750; it is called Elephanta Island not because elephants live here but because the Portuguese discovered an elephant-shaped stone near the shore that collapsed as they were trying to move it,' he explained as we strolled on.

'What, no elephants? Well that's a bit of a con.' Bex crossed her arms and huffed.

'The name may be a little deceiving but trust me, this place is about more than mammals with trunks.'

Suddenly the canopy of trees above our heads swayed with movement. Small brown monkeys scampered through the branches, their long curly tails almost taking Ollie's eye out.

'I forgot to tell you that although we don't have elephants here we do have a lot of monkeys,' Rahul added, smiling.

'Aww, look at them in their natural habitat,' Flic said staring at the furry creatures. The colour had come back to her cheeks and I couldn't help but wonder if our current tasty tour guide had something to do with it.

'They may look innocent but please don't give them any food as they already live like kings,' Rahul warned. 'Oh, and be careful as they are the thieves of the island.'

'Oi!' Chris called out. He had one hand on his bare head and the other arm outstretched, trying to reach a monkey who had taken a shine to his hat. The monkey seemed to laugh at him and flew off with the hat in his teeth. 'Hey! I need that back!' Chris shouted.

Rahul tried to laugh. 'I think it's long gone, my friend.' He slapped Chris on the back. 'Don't worry you can buy another.'

Monkeys were sitting on iron railings, drinking out of cans of Coke they'd stolen from tourists, and looking as if they were smirking at us because they found the whole thing hilarious. Chris gave them a dirty look and stomped off, shaking his fist. We carried on past mango and tamarind trees, hearing Chris muttering to himself as his eyes darted around looking out for his hat thief. Eventually we reached the entrance that was carved out like some James Bond-style lair deep in the rocky hill. Four stone columns were equally spaced out as if holding up the entire island.

'Whoa. This is mint,' Ollie breathed, looking up at the hollowed-out mountain.

I took a step back drinking it in, feeling overwhelmed by the size of it. Rahul looked justifiably proud. The damp and cool temple was a relief to walk into, a small refuge from the scorching sunshine. Inside the dimly lit cave were colossal three-dimensional statues carved from stone looming out over the room, watching over us as we traipsed through.

'They are like bodyguards, keeping an eye on things for Lord Shiva.' Rahul nodded at them, before explaining the history behind the island and the rock art dating from the fifth century as we wandered down excavated tunnels chiselled out of rock. We walked into another cave that was much larger than the others with scenes from Indian mythology etched on every wall. I noticed Rahul had suddenly gone silent as he and Nihal bowed their heads in respect.

Just feet away from us and taped off by a single red rope was the largest carving I'd seen. A three-headed man's face emerged out from the high slate wall, his eyes closed and a sort of Mona Lisa smile dancing on his large plump lips. The attention to detail was insane.

'You can imagine just how many man hours it took to carefully tease the rock and stone into the intricate designs and patterns you see before you,' Rahul said, pointing to the light grey concrete.

'Wow, this is so serene. Look how his eyes are closed as if deep in some prayer or meditation,' Liz mused, tapping a slender finger to her lips.

'Wait, I know where we are and who this is!' Flic said excitedly. Everyone turned to face her. I spotted both Ollie and Bex roll their eyes that *of course she would know*. 'This is Shiva, one of the Hindu gods.'

Rahul's face lit up. 'Ah, you know.'

Flic looked proud and faux bashful. 'He is the patron god of yoga; we always bow to him before every class. I swear it totally works as I can nail the downward-facing dog.'

'Hmm, not quite, I don't think you truly understand the power of Shiva.' Rahul cleared his throat and leant forward as if he was about to bestow a great secret upon us all. I'd lost some of that panic that he was going to reveal who I really was to the group and instead found myself entranced by how passionate and knowledgeable he was. He also smelt really bloody good. 'Shiva is seen as limitless and transcendent but he is also one to fear.' He moved closer to the velvet rope and stretched his arm up.

'Look here; can you see the third eye right bang in the centre of his forehead?' We nodded. 'This is to show he is always watching. Also you will notice that his hair is not like yours or mine, instead the holy river Ganges flows from his scalp.'

'Bet that's a bugger to keep clean.' Bex laughed but stopped suddenly when Rahul threw her a look.

'Wrapped around his neck is the snake Vasuki, showing he is beyond the power of death and poison. He is thought by some to be a god of yogis due to his self-control and how he's often depicted as posing.' He glanced at Flic who was sulking that he'd dismissed her earlier. 'But he is more than this; Shiva is seen as the destroyer of the world.'

Liz let out a loud gasp.

'What? So you pray to some river-haired dude to destroy the world?' Ollie shook his head, confused.

'No,' Rahul said softly. 'You misunderstand. Shiva is seen as the destroyer as he has the power for change, to allow us to shed old habits and attachments that are no longer serving us.' He looked around the group slowly. 'He is also an excellent listener in matters of the heart, you know, old and toxic relationships that you need to kill before you can move on.'

'So that's why you've brought us here? So we can rid ourselves of the negative energy from our failed, broken relationships?' Bex said slowly.

Rahul nodded. 'Exactly. Destroy those ties and move on.' He cleared his throat. 'All that has a beginning also has an end. This is not something to be feared but instead something to savour. If you only have a short time then make the most of every second. Don't spend that precious time and energy reminiscing or beating yourself up over the past.'

Whoa. He was good. I noticed that during this passionate speech Nihal had wandered off, ignoring what Rahul was telling us.

Rahul saw me looking. 'Don't worry, for some it's hard to hear these truths. But they will get there.' He cleared his throat and stared right at me. 'Now it doesn't have to just mean relationships. This could also be applied to work situations; maybe you have a stressful job that overwhelms you, for example. Well Shiva will help you see your reality much more clearly than you can right now. You know the saying that sometimes you can't see the wood for the trees?' I nodded without realising; I had moments like that all the time. 'Well Shiva will be your forest guide.' Rahul laughed. 'Shiva stands for letting go of everything the world forms.'

'So you want us to talk to some dude made of rock?' Bex asked sceptically.

Rahul laughed. 'If you put it like that it does sound a bit crazy.'

'I think it's a wonderful idea,' Flic enthused.

'You bloody would.' Bex rolled her eyes. 'This is right up your street with all your flower-power, hippy bullshit.'

'At least I believe in things, use my voice and don't just waddle along with the flock of sheep,' Flic replied sharply before making sheep noises under her breath.

'OK, ladies, please remember where we are.' Rahul stepped between them with his arms outstretched, apologising to the other visitors in this temple. 'Let's take a time-out on this and head outside. I've organised a treat for you all.'

Flic grumbled that some people were too scared to think for themselves and try new things but quickly shut up when Bex almost growled at her. She would snap her like a twig if there was an actual fight, that non-dairy diet making her bones soft.

We stumbled our way down a crumbling path ahead, which led us back outside, making us squint in the bright sunlight. Rahul was leading the way through thick undergrowth, warning us to watch our step before we came to a stop. We were now faced with an enormous temple covered in complex latticework. Sat on the thick long steps were three half-naked old men staring at us.

'OK, guys, come gather round.' Rahul beckoned us all over. 'You may have noticed we are not alone.' He flicked his head to the three men who were sat cross-legged with flimsy pieces of saffron-coloured cloth protecting their modesty. Greying, long hair lay matted on their shoulders and vacant expressions were etched on their wrinkled, weather-beaten faces.

'These holy men are called sadhus. They have chosen to live away from the normal forms of society to focus on their spiritual journey, removed from the life we know with technology, McDonald's and iPhones. They live in caves, in forests and in temples like this all over India.'

'My friend Giles visited India on his gap yah; he worked in a leper home and everything,' Flic said brushing her hair from her face. 'Anyway he spent some time with a sadhu wanting to really understand this way of life but it's all a load of bullshit as these holy hermits just smoke weed and sleep all the time.'

'Thought you'd love a fella like that, smelling of eau de hash,' Bex teased Flic who stuck her tongue out.

Rahul winced slightly. 'I think they can sometimes be misunderstood. Sadhus are like clouds, forever moving.'

'Like wandering nomads.' Chris nodded slowly.

I glanced up at the men who were lost in some repetitive chant I couldn't work out the words to.

'They're saying their mantras. Everyone should have one,' Rahul explained. 'In fact now we are here I want each of us to think of a mantra for the person next to you.'

Flic turned to face me and bowed her hands together, 'Louise, yours should be *I will stop being so uptight all the time,*' she said in a hippy-dippy voice.

'I'm not uptight!'

Rahul put his hand up, ignoring my annoyed expression. 'Louise, this is the time to let others speak and listen to their words of wisdom. Sometimes others can see us better than we can see ourselves.'

I huffed and turned my back on Flic's innocent face. I was sat next to Chris. 'Erm, I think your mantra should be *let go of the hat*.'

I heard Ollie stifle a giggle.

Once again Rahul was looking at me. 'Please, something serious.'

'I am serious.' I began to protest but stopped when I realised the others were actually thinking of proper things to say. I took a deep breath. 'OK, Chris, your mantra is *I will get involved more.*'

Chris didn't say a word. He just nodded sharply and turned to offer a mantra to Liz who was sitting cross-legged next to him. After we had all shared our wisdom Rahul clapped his hands to get our attention.

'Excellent work, guys. Now we would like to invite you to go and see the sadhus and repeat the mantra you've been given three times.'

I got to my feet with trepidation but followed the others. Joining the end of the line I watched as Ollie knelt down before the half-naked wise men and said his mantra that Bex had given him, something about *being bold and brave*; the three gurus nodded regally and Ollie got to his feet before giving the rest of us a thumbs up and jogging to a waiting Rahul.

When it was finally my turn I slouched to my knees, feeling the gravel slicing my kneecaps, and repeated the mantra Flic had given me. Two of the sadhus nodded and I was about to get onto my feet thinking the third must have dozed off when the silent one grabbed my hand in his gnarled, calloused claw and traced a dirty finger down my palm. The long, brown, curved fingernail almost scratched my skin.

I let out a yelp in surprise.

His watery brown eyes met mine; I could feel the rest of the group waiting with bated breath for what this man would utter. The sadhu slowly nodded and then turned his face and spat on the floor next to my feet. Stringy, wet strands of chewed, red tobacco hung between his chapped lips and wiry beard. I pulled my hand away and raced to meet the others who were in fits of laughter.

'Well what the bloody hell is that supposed to signify?' I asked Flic.

Instead of explaining it was the symbol of some higher purpose, she just shrugged. 'I reckon he just needed to hack up some phlegm.'

Wow, well so much for enlightenment.

CHAPTER 22

Star (n.) A person who is celebrated or distinguished in some art, profession or other field

According to our itinerary we had a day at the beach, and the thought of lazing on pure white sand and trying to get my head together sounded blissful. However, Nihal hadn't explained that this Mumbai beach was one of the most polluted in the world. Moving cranes, piles of rubble and building sites in the middle of construction were the backdrop to the mucky shores. Mumbai life already feels like it's squashed and compressed into tiny spaces and the beach was no different. Shacks were propped up against the pier walls, next to stalls that appeared to have been assembled overnight on the coarse sand. Hawkers plodded along the enormous stretch of the tide, hoping to sell their wares. Looking around at the fug in the hazy sky, with engine fumes where there should have been the smell of coconut sunscreen, and the brown uninviting waters instead of crystal-clear ocean, I wanted to cry.

'Well paradise this ain't,' Bex huffed, slapping a mosquito away.

'Usually we get very nice blue skies here.' Nihal was blatantly bullshitting as he sensed the team spirit fall as flat as a chapatti. 'Isn't that right, Rahul?'

Handsome Rahul had joined us again today; I had to admit that I had found myself smiling at seeing his face as he waited for us in the hotel reception earlier.

'Yeah, I'm sure it will clear up later,' Rahul said brightly. He was one of the most positive people I had ever met; maybe he had been hanging around sadhus for too long.

'Follow me, there is a nicer section of sand just ahead where we can chill out.' He walked off purposefully as we dragged our feet behind him, trying to avoid crunching on chucked-out chicken bones and Coke cans.

'What's going on up there?' Ollie called out, pointing further down the beach.

A crowd of people had circled together by a cluster of drooping palm trees and were looking at something. Wondering what the commotion was, Nihal ran off to investigate, straining his neck to peer through the throng to see what was going on. His face broke out into the first real smile I'd seen since I'd met him. His eyes sparkled and he squeezed his hands together, clapping for the group's attention.

'Guys, come and look!' he called, bursting with excitement as he spoke. 'So many Hindi-language films are made in Mumbai; that's why it gets the name Bollywood. We make over nine hundred a year.' He started reeling off name after name of popular films that had been shot in the city that none of us had heard of, even though Flic pretended that she had. 'They are usually a mix of singing and dancing with handsome men and beautiful women who are deeply in love but kept apart for some reason.' His eyes dipped as he said this, and I knew he was thinking about Ameera. 'Today you are very lucky as one is being made right here in front of us!' He seemed like a kid at Christmas buzzing with excitement, the same sort of feeling I would have if Beyoncé herself was belting out one of her hits just feet away from me.

'Cool,' Bex shouted, almost elbowing Chris to get a sneaky look.

There were cameras, boom sticks and women dressed in beautiful saris in all the colours of a peacock feather, the sunlight glinting off the many gemstones adorning the soft billowing material that rustled in the sea breeze. As the sound of excited chatter bubbled away amongst the group, my mind wandered back to Marie and for a moment I felt a crushing sense of sadness for being a crap best friend. She would be in her element here. I hadn't heard from her since she'd walked out on me in the pub and I promised myself that making amends with her would be the top priority on my to-do list once I got back.

Nihal had been swallowed up in the crowd, desperate to spot the leading actor. Just a few feet from the shore of the Indian Ocean a harassed-looking director bellowed down a chipped megaphone, shouting things in fast Hindi and English. An even more harassed-looking runner raced up to our group.

'Hello!' the young skinny lad shouted, wiping his dark forehead as he caught up with us. 'We are very short on extras. Is there any chance you could help us out and take part?' he pleaded, looking nervously over at the gruff director.

'Hells yeah!' Bex half screamed in my ear. The young guy almost jumped back from the shock before smiling gratefully.

'OK. Fantastic.' He turned on his heel, about to sprint back to the director, before I stopped him.

'Wait, what do we need to do?' I glanced at him apprehensively.

'It's very simple; we need westerners to add class to the film. We just need you to dance like you're at a beach disco behind the main couple. They are in love and want to show each other what the other means to them through movement.' His words tumbled out. The director ranted something in Hindi down his megaphone, making the young assistant flinch. 'Please, you would be helping us out considerably. The other group of tourists we had previously selected haven't turned up.'

'Course we will. Won't we, guys?' Ollie answered for all of us, and everyone nodded fervently.

'Thank you. Now hurry and come with me.' The assistant padded down the sand to the crowd, shouting at them to stay back, before beckoning us over with his thin fingers. Half jogging to catch him up I noticed that Chris was the only one to stay behind.

'You not coming?' I asked as he shook his head.

'I'll, erm, get some photos shall I?' He seemed insistent that he didn't want any part of this. It was strange how he shied away from being in any photos but was happy to play photographer.

'Suit yourself,' I said, and ran to catch up with the others who had been led behind a white truck that had its doors flung open. Inside was an Indian woman with an enormous bun, rummaging through costumes that were spilling out of large, battered suitcases. I hoped Bex hadn't noticed the way she did a double take at her larger body and tutted to herself.

Bun-haired lady shooed us all into the van and thrust bright red and blue material in our hands and told us to get changed; it was nothing like how I'd imagined a trailer to be. Ollie was sent to a separate van for the men to get changed.

'Eurgh, it smells. I don't know if this dress has ever been cleaned,' Liz said holding out the stained fabric and wrinkling her neat nose.

A loud rapping sound on the truck door made us jump. 'Ladies, hurry hurry!'

Taking a quick look at one another I tried hard not laugh. Each of us was wearing an A-line knee-length dress. The fabric was scratchy and Liz was right, it did smell musty. However, it certainly wasn't a case of one size fits all. Every lump and bump was on show for Bex whereas Liz looked like she was dressed in some sort of queen-sized bed sheet as it bunched and gaped at her skinny armpits.

'I thought he said it had to look like we were some guests at a beach party. This looks like we've escaped from a mental asylum and raided the nearest charity shop with the lights out.' Bex sighed.

'Come on, let's go and see what they've got Ollie in,' I said shaking my head and giggling.

Turns out Ollie hadn't fared much better. His flame-red nylon polyester shirt was obscenely tight, naff gold buttons were straining over his chest – well the ones that were fastened – and a heavy-looking chain hung around his neck. He had squeezed into some Lycra flares that admittedly did make his bum look super peachy but left nothing to the imagination from the front. Not that I was complaining, I found myself thinking.

'Wit woo,' Bex cheered as Ollie's cheeks flamed the same colour as his shirt. 'The seventies called; it wants its style back.'

Ollie shook his head. 'What the hell have we signed up for?'

I couldn't hear what he said next as a noisy group of tourists were heading across the beach, all chatting excitedly and pointing at us.

'Oh God look. It's those chumps we met at the Taj Mahal.' Bex nodded her head to the group congregating behind us.

Turning round I was almost face to face with Ameera. *What the…?!* I was now certain that she had stolen my carefully crafted itinerary; India is too large a country for this many chance encounters.

'Oi. What you staring at?' Bex shouted to a short Chinese man in the group who was ogling her breasts.

Ameera swished back her petrol-coloured shiny hair, a sheepish look flashed upon her pretty face before she arranged her delicate features into a scowl. '*We* were booked to take part in this shoot. So if I were you I would go and get changed,' she said. Her perfect English accent had a sharp tone.

I realised they had to be the group of tourists the runner guy had said were meant to be here, wearing these itchy clothes instead of us.

'You're late. That's why they asked us to take part,' I said finding it hard for any confrontation in this ridiculous get-up. Nothing I said would sound right wearing this much flammable material.

'Well, we're here now. So run along and get changed.'

'No way. I'm not missing this opportunity.' Bex crossed her arms and glared at her.

'Well we're not either,' a lanky man from Ameera's group replied in a thick German accent.

Bex squared herself up to him, despite only coming up to his armpit. 'Back off; find your own Bollywood film to be in.' Liz quickly darted in front of her, to both protect Bex's modesty and to act as a barrier before she launched herself at him WWE style.

It was starting to look like some naff version of *West Side Story* with the two tribes coming face to face. As if drawn by a magnet, Nihal bounded over and judging by the dark look on his face I thought he might implode in anger.

'Ameera,' he growled, glaring at his ex, his tone full of unspoken words between them.

The harassed runner who first got us into this situation came running over. I thought he was going to say something about the clothes, the fact that Bex's large breasts were struggling to escape for freedom or our unplanned stand-off with the other group but instead he let out a deep sigh. 'I'm sorry, you need to get changed.'

'What? I can't try anything else on. It's their fault,' Bex said.

Lanky German man stared her out. 'We were officially here first.'

The runner put his hands in the air, separating the two of them. 'No, I am sorry but the shoot has been cancelled. No one is taking part in this film.'

'Cancelled? Why?' I asked.

The whole area was set up for filming and after all the tales Marie had told me about making a film, no matter how small or low-budget, there were a hell of a lot of costs involved.

The runner swatted a fly away; a swarm of pesky mozzies must have seen our lurid outfits as tropical flowers as they began dancing around our shoulders. 'The main actors have fallen ill.'

'Can no one else stand in?' Flic shouted out.

Runner man shook his head. 'This is the last scene to shoot, when they realise they still love each other. It is the pinnacle of the film so unless we can find their identical twins we just cannot film today.'

Grumbling, Bex, Liz and Ollie headed to the truck to get changed. Ameera's tour group padded off, moaning that it was all our fault and Nihal looked like he was about to cry. He was so excited to see his favourite Bollywood star in front of him. The runner was about to race off to join the rest of the clearly irritated crew who were dismantling equipment when I softly grabbed his arm.

'Wait. I have an idea.'

CHAPTER 23

Accord (v.) To be in agreement or harmony; agree

It hadn't taken much persuading. Both tour groups wanted to take part in the filming, the stressed-out runner looked like he just wanted the day over with, and the director wanted to finish his masterpiece. I really didn't want to let my tour group down, plus I knew from our warring exes' body language that both were desperate to be the main stars in a film. Shame they had to act out the love scene with the other. Once I'd suggested Ameera and Nihal standing in for the couple the runner had looked like he wanted to kiss me before excitedly racing off to sell the idea to the director. The fat, gruff man turned in his sunken chair and with one look at beautiful Ameera he gave the slightest of nods.

The film was back on.

'But we don't look anything like the main actors,' Ameera said, avoiding Nihal's reaction.

'Actually, you do look very similar to the main actress, especially when we get you in costume and hair and make-up,' Runner man said, making Ameera blush. 'And you.' He pointed to Nihal. 'You'll wear make-up to look like you've been very badly injured defending your love for her; this should help disguise you. Plus these shots will be filmed from a distance so we can edit in the close-ups of the real couple at a later date.'

'So, we're all good to go?' I asked him, crossing my fingers behind my back.

The assistant sighed. 'The only problem is we don't have enough outfits for all these extras as we didn't plan for double the number of people.'

Unable to bear with the thought of us missing out or starting another turf war with Ameera's group I quickly glanced round the beach hoping for some sort of inspiration.

'Scarfs!' Liz nudged me. Her pale, sun-cream-laden arm was pointing to a beach seller lugging around a heavy woven basket trying unsuccessfully to sell sarongs to scarce sun worshipers.

The runner shrugged. 'I guess…'

Flic was already jogging over to the woman, whose eyes shone with glee that she would sell out. Flic raced back, her arms laden with brightly coloured silky material that she handed out to both tour groups. 'Maybe you could wear this dress, as you would fit into it.' She nodded towards a quiet, frizzy-haired woman from Ameera's group who looked like she could actually pull off the look. 'And the rest can cover up in these. Fashion them like saris?'

The runner translated to the director and the crowd of people around him who nodded and gave us the thumbs up.

'Thank the Lord. I thought I was going to be sucked to death in this thing.' Bex sighed happily and grabbed a jade-coloured scarf.

We got changed out of the rough fabric of the naff dresses and wrapped the soft satiny scarfs around us. I breathed a sigh of relief and looked over to Nihal and Ameera who were sat in the shade of separate palm trees being tended to by make-up artists. I noticed their eyes meet for a moment before an excited passer-by took their photo. God knows how Nihal could even bear to be so close to his ex after her dirty, sabotaging tricks but at least the tour group would experience something totally unique.

'OK, everyone in position in five minutes,' the runner barked.

The two groups, including a more comfortable-looking Ollie who had fashioned a sort of toga out of his deep royal-blue sarong, headed into the marked-off area of the beach. It felt like hundreds of people had picked the best spots, lining up around the cordon excited to see what was going to happen. I felt my stomach do a slight flip with excitement at the randomness of this moment. Secretly crossing my fingers behind my back I said a silent prayer that everything would work out and there would be no more drama.

The crowd broke into applause as Nihal and Ameera strutted onto the sand. I did a double take at Ameera: she was now dressed in a pale lavender dress that seemed like it was designed just for her lithe limbs; her slim ankles were adorned in jangly gold anklets glistening in the sunlight; a beautiful, intricate headband was placed like a halo on her jet black hair and dramatic, bronze eye make-up made her emerald eyes even more striking.

Nihal looked dapper in a glitzy white suit. Jewels and gems shone from his lapels and the 'injuries' that had been painted on only added to a sort of rugged charm. He couldn't keep his eyes off his ex either. *Nihal, think with your brain not your member,* I telepathically willed him.

'OK, now you stand over there and when the music starts you need to dance over to her begging for forgiveness whilst the dancers on her side try to shield her away,' the runner explained.

'Nihal never apologises for anything,' Ameera said quietly enough for the runner to miss but loudly enough for Nihal to hear.

'Only because you would make me apologise for *everything* if I did! I can't ever win with you, Ameera,' Nihal answered back, adjusting his tight, black collar. 'I know it was you who wrote that nasty fake blog post too. Why on earth would you sink to such low depths to get back at me?'

Their eyes locked for a second before she dipped her long lashes to the sand. 'I am sorry about that. I will delete it. I just… I just…'

'Just what? Why are you doing this? Why are you following our tour?' Nihal hissed.

Ameera took a deep breath. 'If you hadn't spent so long away and forgotten about me then I wouldn't need to,' she replied, glancing over at her tour group who were practising the basic dance steps we'd been quickly taught.

'What?' Nihal stepped back in shock. 'I would never forget about you. I was working for *us*. I took this job so I could save up enough money to ask your father…' Nihal faded out, his cheeks flamed up, and he scuffed the sand. 'Doesn't matter.'

The director blared something through the megaphone, which the assistant translated. 'OK, guys, in three, two, one.'

'What did you say?' Ameera turned to Nihal, ignoring the director.

'Nothing.' Nihal shook his head and moved into position. Loud jazzy music started, a fast-paced Indian tune with an array of clanging instruments all rising to the crescendo. We started to practise the steps we had been taught, kicking our feet and shaking our hips to the strange rhythm. I couldn't take my eyes off Ameera.

'What did you say, Nihal?' she pushed.

'OK. And, Nihal, you go!' the assistant shouted as the dancers backed out of the way. Nihal gave Ameera a look that said the conversation was over and stepped forward, shimmying like a true professional.

'And now, Ameera, you move,' the director boomed.

She didn't have a choice but to delicately twirl over to Nihal trailing an almost see-through scarf behind her that floated in the sea breeze. The buzz surrounding them was electric; I almost stepped on the lanky German's foot, as I was too busy keeping a close eye on the two star-crossed lovers.

'Oi, watch it!' he growled.

I raised my hand in an apology and tried to dance my way closer to Ameera and Nihal to hear what was going on.

'What did you mean? Ask my father what?' Ameera asked through a plastered-on, fake smile when they were just inches apart. Nihal dipped his head and flexed his biceps to the beat, as if these moves had been rehearsed; maybe they had been practised and refined over the years in his bedroom. I was craning my neck to hear what Nihal said but Bex hip bumped past me, giving me the thumbs up.

'And cut!' the director called.

Nihal took that as his chance to stride back to his corner of the ring like a boxer would, fired up for his next fight. Ameera just looked on longingly behind him before the make-up artist trotted over and quickly touched up her flawless skin and sprayed hairspray on her locks. It seemed like Ameera's icy exterior was melting in this tropical heat. She had lost that steely look in her eyes and instead a childlike and vulnerable air clouded around her. I hoped to God it wasn't just an act.

The runner was over in an instant, calling the extras over to him. 'OK, we like your energy but we need more. You.' He pointed to the lanky German man. 'What's your name?'

'Stefan,' he replied firmly.

'OK. Well, Stefan, you need to move your hands and make them much more relaxed. Imagine you're using them to entice a fine lady.' At this Stefan blushed the same colour as his maroon sarong; judging by how uncomfortable he appeared I wasn't sure if he had ever seduced anyone before.

'You.' The runner pointed to Bex. 'Be more ladylike; think a goddess *not* a guy.'

Bex clenched her jaw; that had hit a nerve, but surprisingly she didn't fight back – instead she nodded and scuffed the sand with her bare foot. I saw a quick glance between her and Stefan as they both mumbled something under their breath.

'The rest of you, fantastic work. OK, and three, two, one.' He clapped his hands and the whole scene was repeated.

This time as Nihal danced closer and closer to Ameera she stared at him outright. 'What did you want money to ask my father for? For me?' she whispered, swishing her hair and gently swaying on the sand.

Nihal sighed and he nodded slowly. 'I knew he would not agree to me asking to marry you otherwise. I needed to prove I would always be there for you, to provide for you, to look after you,' he said, and then quickly shut his mouth, embarrassed by saying too much already.

Luckily scarfs were being wafted around the two of them so Ameera's blush was hidden from the view of the camera. They were edging closer to each other. The tension coming off them was incredible. I hoped the director realised just how much emotion was going into this ridiculous, random scene.

'I would have married you without any money,' Ameera admitted quietly.

Nihal's head snapped up as he focused his eyes on her.

'Great, keep going. Now, Nihal, you slide in and try to offer your hand to Ameera to dance but she turns you down,' the runner called over the music, interrupting this special moment.

Nihal followed his orders and as his palm was inches from Ameera's delicate wrists he leaned in and said, 'I wanted *you* to be proud of me.'

Ameera spun on her heel, leant her head towards Nihal and whispered, 'I am.' A coy smiled played on her bright painted lips.

'Fantastic, guys. Now this time, Ameera, you take his hand and together you dance through the line of extras.' The runner interrupted this moment of honesty as he flicked through the pieces of messy paper stuck to the clipboard in front of him.

I felt like I was watching this film play out rather than actually being part of it, and I pulled myself together, realising I was here to work not gawp at the real-life love scene before me.

'Extras get into twos – one man and one woman, quickly,' the runner shouted, tapping his wristwatch.

I glanced around to find an available man but the only one left was Rahul. 'Will you be my partner, Louise?' he asked offering me his hand and flashing an honest but bashful smile.

'Oh yep, sure,' I said, clearing my throat, suddenly feeling very warm.

'Great, well let's see your best moves.' He winked.

I don't know if it was the frisson of tension building between Nihal and Ameera, the exotic setting or the romantic music that had faded into a slower love song but

I had this inexplicable urge to kiss him. I turned to face him and his eyes creased into a smile. His hair had been slicked back with gel and sweat into a quiff that really suited him.

'More like my two left feet.' I laughed, or was that giggled? I couldn't tell. Rahul looked down at my bare feet, tanned against the pale sand, and shook his head confidently, pulling me in by the waist. I tried to both enjoy the moment and steer us over to Nihal and Ameera who were at the centre of a group of three other dancers. Their hands were clasped and their feet moved effortlessly in time to the beat.

'Now, in three you all share a kiss at the exact moment our main couple share their passionate moment,' the runner called out.

'What?!' Flic shouted looking horrified at the chunky Chinese man who had made an unsubtle beeline over to her. 'You never said that when we signed up!'

A couple of others grumbled too. Rahul had his arm slung casually around my waist; I realised that neither of us was complaining.

'Just a pretend kiss, a quick kiss on the lips like you do when you play as a child,' the runner explained, looking harassed. 'If not, then you can leave this scene now but we have to start all over again.'

This slight blackmail seemed to make everybody's mind up. As cool a story as this was going to be to tell friends back home, we had been prancing about in the heat for what felt like hours. We were all flagging and desperate for the director to cry cut.

Flic grumbled to herself and scowled at the Chinese man. 'Don't even think about slipping a tongue in,' she warned.

'OK, Nihal and Ameera, are you ready?' The husky voice of the director boomed through the microphone.

Their bodies were so close, heads tilted and besotted smiles on their faces. Right there and then I understood that all really is fair in love and war. I believed that Ameera didn't know how much harm she had done in writing that fake blog post; she had just been desperate to grab Nihal's attention. People do daft things all the time in the name of love. Staring at the two love birds I realised that maybe it was better to do something big, bold and stupid to make them remember you exist rather than stay mute and try to cover up your feelings, like I'd been doing with Ben.

'You don't have to really kiss me, if you don't want,' I heard Nihal say softly to Ameera, looking at her shyly; all the bravado was just an act.

Her eyes dipped to the sand and she gave him the slightest of nods that shook her cascading sheet of hair. 'I want to,' she replied – just audible over the romantic rift of music that was blaring down the beach.

Nihal's lips twitched into a smile. Soon they were both trying hard to hide grins that were desperate to fill their faces.

Rahul still had his arm slung around my waist and was now effortlessly swaying me to the beat. 'You OK with this, Louise? You haven't got some secret boyfriend who's going to jump out of the bushes and kick my ass, have you?'

I smiled at his faux terrified expression, although I wouldn't know who to put my money on in a fight between him and Ben. Both were tall, had muscles in all the right places, toned but not with over-the-top, vein-popping guns, and very hot.

'No, no boyfriend.'

He dramatically let out a breath he had been holding and wiped his forehead. 'Phew.' He grinned.

Ben wasn't my boyfriend and apart from the odd flirtatious comment or lingering glance I sometimes clocked from him, there was no suggestion he actually liked me. I then thought back to Serena – no doubt they would be working overtime, locked in our beautiful little shop and laughing over something before one thing led to another. My stomach turned at the thought.

'You know, I'm sorry about the mistaken identity yesterday. You are just so similar to this woman I met a few weeks ago who was with her mate getting a visa for here,' he said quietly.

'Oh.' I let out a weird laugh. 'Strange.'

'Mmm.' He looked past me over the busy beach as if about to say something else then decided against it. 'So, what is it you do then?'

'For work?'

He nodded and confidently flicked off a fly that had landed on my scarf.

'I'm a hairdresser.' I was so grateful that none of the other guests had interrogated me too much about this white lie. I could barely use a pair of GHDs without burning my ear. 'What do you do, when you're not starring in a Bollywood film in Mumbai?'

Rahul laughed gently. 'This certainly isn't the norm, although I am used to being near cameras.'

Please don't say you're a part-time porn star.

'I work in TV, behind the scenes mostly. It's great as I can be on a job shooting anywhere, then when I'm not working I can head over here to see my family and get a bit of extra cash giving tours of my island.'

'OK, on three, two…' The runner cut me off from asking any more questions.

As if rehearsed, everyone including Ameera, Nihal and all the extras moved their heads closer and locked lips on the count of one.

Rahul gently cupped my jaw and tilted my head to the sun as I closed my eyes. His warm lips grazed mine for what felt like a millisecond before the music stopped and the director boomed down his microphone again.

'Great work. We've got the shot. OK, thanks everyone.'

People started clapping, pulling away from their unplanned love interests. Flic was roughly wiping at her lips, looking as if she wanted to cough up phlegm into the sand. The Chinese man was grinning non-stop. Rahul winked at me as soon as the director told us the scene was finished and walked up the beach. I was left gazing after him. For some reason I wanted more; I knew the kiss was just for show and it wasn't like a full-on snog, but the feel of his lips, the salty taste they left on mine and the way he certainly acted like he knew what he was doing made my stomach flip.

'Thank God that's over!' Flic had stomped over to me. 'I could have thumped that turd. I swear he tried to slip his snake tongue in,' she said shuddering at the memory. 'You OK, Louise?'

I glanced from Rahul who was laughing with one of the crew members to Flic. 'Yeah, yeah fine. Come on, let's go and get changed.'

It really had been ages since I'd been kissed; I shook my head, pulling myself together. If I was thinking silly thoughts about the smug Indian visa man, then I definitely needed to get my life sorted out. As we walked up the sand to the applause of the audience I realised that Ameera and Nihal were still full-on snogging. I didn't know if they realised the director had called cut but after what felt like years of trying to get them back together, for them to finally see sense and stop with the bitchy break-up, I wasn't going to be the person to tell them to stop.

The runner had seen them too. 'This never happens. Usually the lead actors hate each other's guts, desperate for the filming to end to get away from them,' he said, nodding his head at the newly reformed couple. 'The director wants to speak to them after they, you know, break for air; apparently he has never been so impressed with the acting skills of a pair of extras before.'

'Oh, I don't think they were acting.' I smiled. He didn't know the half of it.

CHAPTER 24

Xanadu (n.) An idyllic, exotic or luxurious place

We were all on a high as we left the beach and found a small restaurant where we could rest our weary legs, have a drink and replenish our energy. I nipped to the toilet but was stopped from going back to my chair by Nihal who was waiting for me in the dimly lit corridor.

'Oh hey, you – the star of the show!' I smiled at him.

'Hey, erm, I just wondered if we could have a chat,' he said blushing. He seemed to have this glow, this aura around him, ever since we had started filming.

'Sure, everything OK?' I asked nervously.

He nodded. 'More than OK! I wanted to thank you without the rest of the group hearing for bringing my love back to me. I guess you're wondering what happened between me and Ameera?'

I shook my head. 'Nihal, I get it. You messed up, she messed up, but you realised that you'd rather mess up together than mess up apart.'

Nihal smiled shyly. 'She is *really* sorry about that blog post. So, I have a proposal to make. I wondered if it might be possible for the two tour groups to become one?' He winced slightly waiting for my reaction. 'Ameera has promised to delete the whole blog post tonight and can make a formal apology to the group if you like?'

'No don't do that. I don't want them to know what has gone on in case they work out who I am. Maybe instead of deleting the post she could write another one saying she made it all up?'

'OK, consider it done. She really does feel very embarrassed about it all.' *I bet she bloody does*. 'So, erm, about the two groups?'

I thought for a moment; technically I wasn't responsible for the guests in Ameera's group, but it seemed like she was probably going to follow us anyway and it was nice to have more people in the mix. 'Fine by me.'

That evening was one of my favourite since arriving in India. Both tour groups were huddled around low tables in a busy restaurant, the buzz from the day's filming, the taste of being a celebrity and the new romances that had sparked because of it were all everyone could talk about. The smells of coriander, aromatic spices and sounds of a sitar player became background noise to our excitable, rowdy bunch.

'I'm defo putting that on my CV,' Bex said talking with her mouth full.

'I can't wait for it to come on Netflix to make all my mates watch it, although I know they won't let me live it down.' Ollie winced then laughed.

'I reckon I've got a new career as a Bollywood film star ahead of me,' I said before giggling.

We laughed and chatted and laughed some more after the most random day. The only one who didn't take part in the fun debrief was Chris. His tight, dour expression had barely broken all night. I couldn't tell if he was kicking himself for not taking part or relieved that he hadn't had to dress up like an idiot.

He cleared his throat and changed the subject. 'What time is our flight tomorrow then?'

'We've got another early start,' Nihal said. We would be catching a morning flight to Goa as the Holi festival was starting soon. 'And, we will be continuing the rest of the tour as one larger group.'

'Fine by me,' the chubby Chinese man said, practically licking his lips as he gawped at Flic who clenched her jaw and turned to face Rahul.

'Are you coming too?'

He shook his head, 'Nope, 'fraid not. But I hope you all find what it is you're searching for.' I could have sworn he was directing that at me.

Even though I felt ready to go to Goa tomorrow my stomach lurched at the thought that it was the last leg of this trip. I'd been so focused on playing referee between Nihal and Ameera I hadn't given much thought to how I was in the most spiritual country in the world. I hadn't managed to focus on myself or my self-improvement – bar a half-naked holy man spitting at my feet. I didn't feel like I had finished on my journey through India. All that faced me at home was being a raspberry to Ben and Serena's loved-up coupledom. I knew I had to call him soon but truthfully I didn't want to hear about how wonderful this woman was, and weirdly I was actually enjoying not thinking about work all the time. Maybe I was on the path to enlightenment after all.

It was quite amazing that Nihal had managed to herd everyone up, the two groups that had now merged into one, as we boarded our flight to Goa without any major incidents. The transformation in Nihal from the guy I had met just a few weeks ago was really astonishing: gone were the deep bags under his dull eyes; the spark was back in his voice; he seemed full of beans. The Nihal who I'd hired all those months ago, based on recommendations for his fun personality, was appearing right before my eyes.

I was relieved to be flying and not reliving the, ahem, joys of Indian train travel. Once was most certainly enough. We had just a few days left on the tour, and then I would be on my flight back to Manchester, jetting away from this group of mismatched but lovable personalities. A week ago I would have happily jumped on the plane home but actually, since Nihal and Ameera had patched things up and we were leaving the mayhem of Mumbai for the blissful beaches of Goa, I really didn't want to leave. Not yet. Of course I missed Ben so much, and missed my business, but truthfully I was starting to feel more like myself.

More like the Georgia I'd become when I'd travelled solo around Thailand last year. The harassed version of me who'd boarded her flight to come to Delhi had softened, relaxed, left the stresses of running a new business behind, and instead of feeling flustered over finances or burnt out over bookings I could take this time to just be me. It was a feeling inside, like a tight knot that had somehow loosened. Strange really, as I hadn't even known it was there. Maybe this was what I needed to get the confidence back that travel had given me in the first place. I sunk back into my seat and closed my eyes.

'What are you smiling about?' Bex asked, putting down the inflight magazine.

'Nothing. Just thinking how much I love to be on the move. I can't wait to see what Goa's going to be like.'

'Me either.' She smiled.

I couldn't help but notice that for nearly all of the flight Stefan had been casting glances at Bex. I nudged her. 'I think you're well in there.'

Bex shifted in her seat and cleared her throat. 'Nah, you need to get a trip to the optician's sorted, mate.' She started fiddling around with her iPod, brushing off the idea that she had a not-so-secret admirer.

'Err, Bex, I swear he's into you. I mean, he can't stop gazing gooey-eyed at you for one thing,' I said quietly.

'Shush.' She wafted her hand at me, her cheeks growing red.

'What's wrong? You don't think he likes you?' I questioned, tilting my head, wondering why she was so dismissive.

Bex let out a deep sigh and turned to face me. 'Louise, when you're a big girl like me you expect people to stare. I get that. But you don't get cute, strapping German men staring in *that* sort of way. It's fine; I know what I'm talking about.'

I went to protest, to tell her that size had nothing to do with it, when she raised a hand gently to stop me.

'I've always been the curvy girl, the big-boned, bonny lass, or however you wanna call it. I'm Fat Bex and I know it. And I don't want to change. I'm happy being this size; when I did try dieting – and trust me I've tried them all – I'd never been so bloody miserable. Being big suits me; it just doesn't suit a lot of men out there.'

'What do you mean?'

'Well I had an ex who told me that I'd actually be quite pretty if I lost weight, another got too sick of his mates ribbing him for going out with a whale, and so many have given up on me when their "get Bex skinny" project has failed.'

'Whoa. I never realised it would be such a problem,' I said softly.

She placed a warm hand on my arm. 'It's fine; there are just a lot of very sizeist people out there. I'm comfortable with knowing that only James Blunt will ever think I'm beautiful.' She laughed.

I looked back at Stefan's seat; he had his headphones in and was gently nodding in time to the music.

'I still think he fancies you. Maybe he is the one who will love you for you?' I suggested.

Bex shrugged. 'I don't think that man exists and that's OK. I've got a wicked family, awesome mates and if I'm meant to be the funny, chubby, single one for the rest of my life then so be it. I'm not giving up chocolate for anyone.' She laughed.

I smiled back but I could read her like a book: under her confident demeanour she was as vulnerable as everyone else.

The short flight passed by quickly. Soon we were crammed into a stuffy minibus and trundling away from the airport, heading for our new beach home. With the windows flung open and the warm breeze carrying salty sea air tinged with exotic, perfumed flowers it felt like I could finally breathe here. It smelt like paradise. There wasn't any of that frenzied chaos there had been in Delhi or Mumbai; here the roads were practically empty. Everyone seemed to have adjusted their speed settings to chill. Street dogs were snoozing under the shade of luscious palm trees, cows ambled down the quieter roads, twitching their tails and swatting flies, and unusual birdsong filled my ears. Shabby-chic, pastel-coloured houses, bright white churches and sunflower-yellow shops jumped out against the dusty red soil. The Portuguese influence here was evident in the detailed architecture and laid-back, siesta-time atmosphere.

The sun was beating down on us and everyone appeared to be in very high spirits. It felt like we'd reached a turning point on this tour. Even Chris seemed to have relaxed; his shoulders less bunched up around his bony neck. He snapped away with his very fancy-looking camera as the roads broke into bumpy, dried-mud paths. I was slowly learning to give up control, letting Nihal take the lead, even if I did have to keep craning my neck to see where the driver was taking us. He bobbed his head to the beat of the energetic Indian music on his tinny radio, treating this as a Sunday drive.

'OK, so just a little further and we'll be at our accommodation.' Nihal turned round in his seat and grinned at the group. He looked like he was desperate to tell some secret he knew, but when I glanced at him quizzically he just turned back round to face the front and quickly started up a conversation with the driver.

According to the itinerary we had booked a simple but pleasant hotel for the guests to stay in not far from the small town centre of this village, but judging by the way Nihal jiggled his knees and tapped his fingers along to the beat of the radio something else was being planned. *Oh, please don't screw this up, Nihal*, I thought to myself. I could feel the familiar clench in my stomach I got when I didn't have the faintest idea of what was coming next.

'Wow, look!' Flic shouted, flinging her arm right out of the window, almost touching a cow that was stood on the edge of the kerb and looking at us through deep brown eyes.

The group turned to look where she was pointing. We'd now left the tarmacked road and were struggling to get over a small hump on a winding dirt track.

'What is it?' Ollie asked leaning over me. 'Is that where we're staying?'

Nihal turned back round. This time his face had broken into a wide, excited smile. 'It sure is!'

'Cool!' Bex cheered.

I tucked my head to look round Ollie, straining to see what everyone was looking at. Then I saw them. Rickety beach huts lined the shore of the sandy beach with small verandas looking out to the lashing waves in the ocean, near mismatched reclaimed barrels that doubled up as seats and an open air restaurant in the centre of it all. It was an Indian version of the Blue Butterfly huts, a place I'd stayed in Thailand on the island of Koh Lanta, where I'd not only completed my travel wish list, met Shelley and the gang of original Lonely Hearts backpackers, but also where I'd met Ben.

'You OK, Louise?' Nihal asked, his brown eyes wide and nervous at my mute reaction.

I nodded and cleared my throat that had inexplicably become clouded with tears and emotion. 'Yep. Yes, it looks great. Thank you.'

Nihal kept his worried gaze on me for a few seconds longer before telling the driver to stop a couple of metres ahead to let us out. The tour group clamoured out of the bus, stretching their sweaty limbs, exclaiming to one another how we had arrived in paradise. They weren't wrong. The beautiful little cove of golden sand with rugged hills merging into the sea at either end was practically empty, bar a few upturned wooden fishing boats and a couple of smaller restaurants further on. Quickly counting the huts I realised that we had the whole place to ourselves.

'You sure you're OK?' Nihal was back by my side as Ameera busied herself with getting everyone to grab their bags.

'I'm great,' I said genuinely.

I *was* great. Of course, who wouldn't be, stood under the shade of an enormous swaying palm tree with their feet sunk in the soft-as-cashmere sand, looking out onto an unspoilt Indian beach? However, I knew I wasn't showing the same level of enthusiasm as those around me, purely because it felt strange to be here when Ben wasn't by my side. How long would it be until I didn't automatically think of him? I blinked back tears, happy tears definitely, I think, and squeezed Nihal's arm softly.

'You've done well. Look how excited everyone is.' It was true. The tour group appeared wired with their constant chatter, laughter and posing for photos.

'Thank you,' Nihal said, and then turned to address the excited rabble of the group. 'OK, guys!' He clapped his hands and grinned. 'So this is where we'll be staying for the next few nights. After the noise and craziness of the cities we've visited, I figured you all deserve some relaxation time!' People cheered. 'The huts are for two people, have an en-suite bathroom *and* even have air conditioning.' Another cheer. 'So, please choose who you want to share a room with and go find a hut.'

I did a quick count in my head. With Ameera's tour group we were now up to twelve people meaning I'd be sharing with someone. I quickly looked over to Bex who had buddied up with Liz, Ollie was with Lanky Stefan and Flic was with the quiet, frizzy-haired woman, whose name I think was Sarah. The Chinese man, Bo, had partnered up with another guy from Ameera's tour leaving just Chris, Ameera, Nihal and me.

'Erm, so I guess the women should go together,' I said lightly, not wanting to hurt Chris's feelings but *really* not wanting to share a room with him.

Ameera and Nihal scuffed their feet into the sand. 'Well, yeah, I guess…'

I knew that look. They wanted to share a hut. Of course they did. They had a lot of, ahem, making up to do. I glanced at Chris who looked like he wanted to be anywhere than in this awkward dilemma.

'Or…maybe we could…'

Before the words had left my mouth Nihal's and Ameera's faces lit up.

'If you don't mind, of course,' Nihal said, before taking Ameera's hand and half jogging to find their hut, not giving us the choice to take the offer back.

'So, I guess that leaves us then,' I said, as brightly as I could muster.

Chris just nodded, as sour-faced as always. Great. I was bursting for a wee, so I quickly took charge and led us to our hut.

CHAPTER 25

Squad (n.) Any small group or party of persons engaged in a common enterprise

'I hope you don't snore,' I teased Chris, wanting to make conversation as we began walking over to the last available hut, the one right on the edge of the semi-circle.

The silence between us was suffocating. He was one of the rudest men I'd ever met and now I was lumped with sharing a room with him.

'I wouldn't know. I'm usually asleep if that happens,' he said wryly.

'Yep, of course.' I let out an odd laugh.

No wonder he was single. He probably bored all his ex-girlfriends to sleep and when they woke up they realised what a huge mistake they'd made.

'Right, here we are.'

I climbed the wooden steps to the door and pushed it open. Its loud creak gave me a start. Even though the huts may have looked similar to the ones in the Blue Butterfly on the outside, the inside was a complete contrast. Basic was an understatement. The room held two narrow beds on either side of the thin wooden walls with just a small gap in between. I would be able to stretch my arm out in the night and touch Chris's face they were so close together. I continued to the back of the hut where a plywood door opened onto a bathroom no bigger than my parents' dining table. A spout came out of the roughly tiled wall for the shower, which also doubled up as a wash basin, and on the opposite side was a hole-in-the-ground toilet.

I hadn't even thought about the fact I'd be sharing the bathroom facilities with Chris. A man. Going to the toilet is the most natural thing in the world, so why is it so rife with stress and problems? When I'd lived with my ex, Alex, going to the bathroom was one of the things I'd gotten so worked up about at the beginning. I'd been terrified that my womanly allure would be threatened by a pongy fart, loud wee or even a floater that wouldn't flush. Everyone on this planet has to shit but when you're in a new relationship you wish that wasn't true. Obviously, as time wore on I didn't care as much with Alex, even letting him walk in whilst I was having a wee. But number twos stayed firmly behind locked doors with a can of air freshener to hand and loud music playing to hide the plops and splatter in the toilet bowl.

I wondered if it was too late to see if anyone else wanted to share; I would feel so much more comfortable with one of the other girls. Then I realised that Chris was probably just as uncomfortable with this situation as I was.

Well we won't be in here for long, I told myself.

'Just nipping to the loo,' I said, not able to keep this wee in for much longer, and walked the three steps to the bathroom.

I shut the door behind me and cringed that I could hear not only Ollie talking to Stefan outside our hut but that I was also certain I could hear Ameera and Nihal chattering in the hut next door. Awkward. My bladder wouldn't let me find an alternative solution so I got into an uncomfortable squat position and held onto the exposed stone wall for balance. I could hear Chris pottering about just outside the bathroom door, the sound of the zip on his backpack opening and clothes rustling. I could even hear his breathing; the walls were so thin.

Come on just have a wee. My bladder refused to co-operate.

'You OK in there, Louise?' Chris rapped at the door.

'Yes. Just having a nosy around,' I called out loudly. My hands were clammy, my face red and my thighs were shaking in pain from this stupid position.

Just ignore him and have a wee.

'Right, well I'm heading off to this yoga class that's about to start.'

Yoga class?! I'd forgotten that was on the agenda for today.

'Right, yep. I'll meet you there,' I said squeezing my Kegel muscles tight waiting for his heavy footsteps to walk away. Once I heard the door to the hut squeak shut I emptied my bladder. God that felt good. I quickly washed my face, sprayed some deodorant and went to join the others on the beach.

A supple older woman wearing a shiny, purple leotard over electric blue leggings smiled at me as I trotted up the sand to join the others who were already sat on pale blue yoga mats near the shore.

'Hello! Namaste.' Lycra lady clapped her palms together and bowed at me. 'Please take a mat.' Her skin was as brown as a tree trunk but delicate like crêpe paper, especially against her bright silver hair that had been woven into a long plait down her skeletal body. I guess she must have been in her late sixties but had the body of a twenty-something.

I nodded and stepped over the group to the last remaining mat right at the front. Great. I was so un-supple, I'd given up trying to touch my toes back in primary school PE classes. This was going to be fun.

'OK, so welcome everyone. My name's Yvonne and I'll be your teacher this evening. For those of you who are yoga virgins I'll be taking it slow but for some of you who have already benefited from the power of this wonderful activity –' she nodded at Flic who beamed back '– you can up the level and feel the strength from the sun, which is about to set.' Her voice floated across the air; she spoke as if she was stoned – maybe she was. 'Erm yes?'

Bo had his hand in the air. 'I think we should all put on some Vaseline to stop any chafing. The mix of sand, stretching and sun can cause bad rashes.'

'I'm not slathering myself in oil,' Bex said aghast at the idea.

'Thank you for that helpful suggestion but I think we will all be fine,' Yvonne said diplomatically. 'OK, great. So let's lie back on our mats and concentrate on our breathing.'

Whilst trying to get comfy I glanced around at our group and realised that Nihal and Ameera were missing. Hmm… wonder what yoga moves they were trying out in private. Flic was chomping at the bit to get started, looking irritated with Ollie, Stefan and Bo who were more focused on a game of beach cricket taking place further up the shore than on their chakras. Liz and Sarah were wafting away pesky mosquitos as Bex yawned loudly; clearly she was feeling Zen already.

'OK, and take a deep breath in, then exhale,' Yvonne said, letting out a loud heavy whoosh as she exhaled. 'And again.' She continued to sound like a steam train, making me want to giggle.

'Excellent! Now onto all fours as we do the cat pose.' She effortlessly changed position as the rest of us pushed ourselves onto our hands. I dug my knees into my mat and tilted my head back, gazing into the hazy sunset that was starting to peek through silhouetted palm trees. 'Now keep in that position as I come round and check your lines.'

The sky above our open-air yoga session was changing with every second. The daylight was slowly dimming as a fiery flame of sun licked the top of the waves crashing opposite us. Streaks of raspberry red danced with soft blood-orange hues that skittered around the hazy glow of the sunset. It was magical.

Yvonne jumped to her feet and padded around us on the sand. 'A little higher, that's it. Excellent core work there. Now just move your hands slightly more under your shoulders,' she softly told the group before coming over to me.

Her tanned face peered down at me. 'Now, you need to push your bottom higher into the air.' I did as she said feeling like a right numpty. 'Lovely.' She went back to her mat and resumed the ridiculous pose all of us were doing. 'Now inhale, and when you exhale I want you to dip your back, but keep that core tight. And exhale.' Another whoosh from Yvonne's mouth, we all dropped our stomachs to the mat. With this simple movement I suddenly realised that it wasn't just a wee that I'd needed earlier.

I let out an enormous squelchy fart.

Crap bags.

I squeezed my eyes shut, dying inside and pretended that it wasn't me who'd just set a world record for the fart that was so noisy even my parents back home could have heard it. For a never-ending second afterwards, I swear all I could hear was the sound of waves and the rustle of palm tree leaves.

Amazingly Yvonne took no notice and started telling everyone to stop giggling and repeat the move. The flame in my cheeks subsided but I kept my focus on my mat for fear of giving the game away.

OMG I've got away with it. No one knew it was me!

And that's when it hit me.

I gagged and coughed at the pungent smell that followed. Sulphuric, propane gas wafted through the air, warming in the heat, making it even more potent. People behind began coughing loudly too; the sound of giggling turned up a notch.

'Who the friggin' hell let that rip?' Bex shouted out. 'Jeeezus!'

'Now now, it's only natural that we let our bodies relax in every way possible,' Yvonne piped up; I could feel her narrowed and slightly amused eyes trained on me.

Stare at the mat, stare at the mat.

'There ain't nothing natural about that gas explosion!' Bex continued, followed by others chuckling. 'Who was it? Come on, own up!'

Stare at the mat, stare at the mat.

'Please, miss, we are here to relax and centre ourselves. Now if you will all follow me into the child's pose.' Yvonne was desperately trying to continue with the class that had now erupted into schoolgirl giggles.

I joined in and laughed along too, peering round at everyone as if trying to find the culprit. Until I met Chris's eye. He was on the mat just behind me where he literally would have just experienced a full face of my flatulence. Bugger. He looked at me sceptically as if daring me to own up and admit that it was I with the mistimed bowels. I stayed mute.

'Well, whoever it is needs to lay off the curries.' Bex continued to dramatically waft her nose.

'That's enough, miss. Now please everyone come back on your mat and tuck your legs underneath yourself.' Yvonne gave Bex a look far removed from her normal hippy, yoga-teacher demeanour. Bex muttered something under her breath and soon the class was back on track. I didn't dare look at Chris again and tried my hardest to keep my bum cheeks firmly together for the rest of the lesson.

Once we'd finished with a final over-the-top, exhaling flourish I rolled up my mat and left it in the pile near Yvonne's feet. She smiled at me – *she knows*. Then I half trotted back up the sand to my hut to quickly check that I hadn't followed through on that fart and stained my pants.

There is a God after all. Covering my still red face with my hands I climbed into my bed and cursed this stupid country, the stupid thin walls, stupid sharing a room, stupid curries and stupid yoga. Chris wandered in not long after and nodded at me before continuing to unpack his bag. All his shirts looked like they'd been pressed as pristinely as you'd find in a posh clothes shop.

'You know, lentils are one of the key ingredients in causing stomach upsets,' he said without a hint of sarcasm before continuing to sort through his impeccably ordered clothes.

'Thanks, I'll, erm, bear that in mind,' I answered quietly, then turned over and pulled the thin sheet above my head, wishing I was anywhere but here.

CHAPTER 26

Ebullient (adj.) Having or showing liveliness and enthusiasm; exuberant

A few hours later I emerged from the empty hut; Chris had decided to go off on a walk according to the neatly written note he'd left me. I'd taken a cold shower, freshened up and padded out in the dim evening light to find the others. The cheerful voices of the tour group travelled on the air making my heart leap for a moment. I was so pleased everyone was getting along; no one seemed to mind the additional travellers and fairly chaotic tour up to this point. Nihal's voice boomed over the empty beach as he told a joke, making everyone crease up with laughter. I thought back to the trip I'd taken in Thailand, with sketchy tour guide Kit and the people I had been lumped with when I'd experienced my first taste of backpacking. That awful tour was one of the reasons I'd created the Lonely Hearts Travel Club. I never wanted anyone who'd found themselves suddenly single to have to experience that nightmare.

Seeing the outlines of this tour group, sat on oversized cushions and paisley, padded mats that were scattered around an open fire, reminded me that this was why I was here. Helping these people through their problems whilst seeing another side of the world was what this was all about. I waved at them as I found an empty space in the circle and sat down on the sand.

'Hey, so what did I miss?'

'Well we're just about to eat. I've arranged with the chef to bring us out a traditional Goan dinner,' Nihal said proudly.

'Sounds great.' I thought back to Chris's comment about the lentils. I decided I'd pass on the dal.

'And tonight is also a special evening as it's the night before Holi. It's tradition to have a Holika bonfire to get us all ready for the festival tomorrow. So as we wait for dinner I thought we could play a game? To get to know each other a little better.'

Ameera nodded then added, 'I know it may have felt a little disjointed but now we're here in Goa and especially with two groups coming together it would be nice to find out about each other.' Murmurs of agreement came from around me. 'So, maybe…Louise, you might like to begin? Tell us why you're here?'

I tried to hide the way I was gawping at her; Nihal knew why I was here but must not have explained to Ameera who the hell I was.

'Erm, yep sure,' I stuttered as the group turned to face me.

'You don't have to go first it you don't want,' Nihal jumped in before Ameera patted his arm gently.

'You don't mind, do you?' The question was innocent but I had no idea what to say; did I make up a fake heartbreak story to go with my fake persona or just tell the truth.

I shook my head and took a deep breath. 'So, erm, this time last year I was planning on getting married.' I paused; it still felt unbelievable when I thought back to that girl. The one obsessed with preparing the perfect wedding day, the one drowning in table settings, flower arrangements and cake tastings, the one who didn't realise just how unhappy she was to be in that situation until she lost control and ended up boarding a flight to Thailand and never looked back. Liz smiled sympathetically, encouraging me to continue.

'Erm, so just a few months later my fiancé came home from work one night and broke it off. He didn't want to marry me and couldn't go through with it. Now, this wasn't just a case of cold feet and pre-wedding jitters, he'd actually been cheating on me for a good few months before that.'

'Bastard!' Bex cried out, making me smile.

'Yeah that's what I thought,' I said, letting grains of sand run through my fingertips.

'You don't think that now?' Liz piped up.

I shook my head. 'No. What I think now is, yeah, that was pretty shitty, he was a complete coward in leaving it till two weeks before the expensive and stupidly over-the-top big white wedding but actually he gave me a wakeup call. I had got so consumed in being this perfect version of myself, changing and moulding into what he and his family wanted me to be, that I'd lost all sight of who I really was. I was no longer Geor – I mean Louise – sorry, just Louise and Alex.'

'I can't believe how calm you seem about it all,' frizzy-haired Sarah said, nodding her head sagely.

'I guess in every break-up there's always a silver lining and every ending has a new beginning,' I said, thinking back to what Rahul had told us in the Mumbai temple. 'It's so frustrating but all those thrown-about, well-worn clichés are true. Time is a healer, you do deserve better, and things *will* get easier. You just have to know your self-worth and trust that it will all be OK, eventually.'

Staring at the faces looking back at me etched with worry, lack of confidence and a grief-like loss at their failed relationships, I felt buoyed to continue. 'You are all here half a world away from your routine and the places that feel comfortable and familiar to you. You've gone through what has been an, erm, challenging start on this tour but I hope you can look back and grow in confidence at the experiences you've had so far. Hell, I know being part of a Bollywood film is a once-in-a-lifetime opportunity that has to give you a little pick me up!'

'So how did you, you know, get over him?' Liz asked twiddling the rough frayed edge of the mat through her fingers.

'I went travelling. I changed my perspective, both literally and figuratively. I hung out with some awesome, positive strangers and I let myself cry over what I'd lost. But even though I know I'll never share those times with him again, I feel so much happier because of the things I've learnt to do by myself, of the friends I've met and the places I've been because of what he did to me. So, in answer to your question, and in the words of Kelly Clarkson, I didn't let this kill me, instead it made me stronger.'

A small round of applause broke out that had me blushing and wafting my hands in front of my tearful eyes.

'So why did you come on this trip then? If you had already gone travelling to get over it?' Chris said, bringing me back down to the ground with a bump.

'Well, I, erm…' I stuttered. 'There's no timeline on when you will start to feel better and more like yourself again. I'd always wanted to visit India but even with the confidence I found when I travelled last time I was still apprehensive about seeing this country by myself so I booked on this tour. Erm, so anyone want to go next?' I smiled at the others, hoping my quickly made-up answer was suitable enough.

Just as Flic waved her arm in the air to begin, Chris interrupted. 'So, you could say you were the original member of the Lonely Hearts Travel Club?'

I laughed awkwardly. 'Erm, yeah I guess you could.' I really didn't want to tell people that I was the bloody CEO of the company, especially not when they were about to open up to each other. 'Right so Flic as you were about to say…'

'Well yes. I'm –'

'So, I'm guessing you're not heartbroken any more then. If, you know, travel helped fix you.' Chris interrupted again, receiving a lot of pissed-off looks from the others. He really wasn't doing himself any favours or making friends here.

I turned to face him and plastered on a big smile, hiding the growing sigh that was building in my chest. I wasn't heartbroken like the last time I jetted away but I still wasn't in the loved-up state with Ben I'd dreamt about.

'Well, erm, I guess I'm not where I thought I'd be,' I stuttered.

'I reckon Ollie will help take your mind off your ex,' Bex called out, making the others laugh.

'Shut up, Bex,' Ollie replied. I caught him glancing under his long lashes over to Liz who was sat upright, looking very uncomfortable.

'OK, so as you were saying, Flic.' I turned to Flic, half blocking out Chris and that smirk he wore so well, indicating that interrogate Louise/Georgia time was over.

'Doesn't matter,' she said looking bored.

'I'll go next then.' The Chinese guy raised his arm. 'My name is Bo.'

As Bo told us all about his messy break-up with his high school sweetheart who'd left him for a guy she'd met in the gym, I tuned out. What *was* going on between me and Ben? I felt like I was on this rollercoaster ride of emotions alternating between forcing myself to have the courage to tell him how I felt, and brushing whatever we had off as a silly nothing, destined to stay in the past. Would he ever be part of my future or were we just friendly colleagues? Did I need to finally move on?

Bo was obviously still in the angry fuck-you phase of his break-up as he finished telling us his story by muttering under his breath that his ex was an absolute bitch. I was about to jump in and explain that those feelings of wanting to find a voodoo doll with Kiko's face on it would pass, when I spotted Liz raise her pale arm that was almost translucent against the glowing embers of the fire.

'Yes, Liz.' Ameera smiled at her warmly.

As she cleared her throat, Ollie's head jerked up. 'I understand what Bo is saying.' Her voice was barely audible over the thrashing waves. 'I…I was in a similar situation.'

It was almost painful watching her open up. Her bony shoulders were hunched up to her jaw as she fiddled with a loose thread on her harem trousers.

'OK, do you want to tell the group? It might help others,' Ameera gently encouraged her.

Liz nodded. 'I know what Bo means because I was that girl. I cheated on my ex.'

Her grey watery eyes were filled with even more tears shimmering in this light. I braced myself for the group, well namely Bex, to chuck her in the fire, chanting *burn the cheating whore* as she did so, but everyone remained silent. They were probably shocked that Liz was speaking out loud for the first time, like, ever.

'I was with this wonderful man for four years. He never did a thing wrong to me. We had a very vanilla relationship, if you know what I mean. Which was fine at times but… but, somehow it wasn't enough.' Tears now streaked down her drawn face and plopped onto her trousers. Ollie looked torn between wanting to hug this vulnerable woman he so obviously liked and waiting to hear her explanation. 'I got really drunk one evening in a bar by myself when he was working away. I went home with a man, a stranger; I didn't even know his name. Afterwards I was consumed with this guilt, regret and disgust at what I'd done.' She sniffed loudly. The whole group was entranced. Who knew Liz was such a dark horse.

'But I carried on doing it. I was excited by the thrill of being caught; of showing him that he'd underestimated me. I wasn't this weak, quiet, boring woman. One night he found some messages on my phone and quite rightly went ballistic, screaming at me that I was a slut, a whore and had broken his heart. I'll never forget the look of absolute revulsion on his face as he packed and left. He never came back. After that I decided to go and see a therapist to talk about what I'd done, how my urges had led me to hurt someone I cared about so much.' Liz took a deep breath before continuing. 'She explained that it was natural to want to feel fulfilled in every aspect of a relationship and how the way I had gone about it had been wrong, but it had shown me what I valued most in a partner. Sadly, my ex and I just weren't meant to be.'

Ollie's eyes were as wide as Liz's; I could almost see his brain ticking from here, thinking how this girl he blatantly fancied was actually a sex nymph. Result!

'I've never told anyone that before – apart from my therapist.' She wiped her eyes with the base of her hand and glanced up at everyone. 'I'm so sorry to have cheated on my ex. I know a lot of you are here because of your partners doing that to you and you probably all hate me right now. But I couldn't carry on with the pretence that I was the one who'd been the victim when I wasn't.'

'Come here you!' Bex said, roughly pulling Liz into a hug. Ollie looked like he was itching to do the exact same thing. 'Course we won't think any less of you. It's brave what you've just admitted and we –' she eyed the group as if daring anyone to disagree '– we are all here for you.'

'Thank you! You don't know how good that feels,' Liz said through gulps of tears.

Man, she was really cut up about what she'd done. I wondered briefly if Alex had ever felt similar feelings of regret over how he'd treated me. I shook myself not wanting to revisit my past and quickly brushed his face out of my mind.

'I wanted to come on this tour for so long but once I'd heard everyone talking about being cheated on I just felt I couldn't say a thing. I know I'm not officially heartbroken but I am still adjusting to being single, to working out what I want in a relationship and how I can be more confident in myself, rather than feeling ashamed.'

'I think step one of the new Liz has already happened.' I smiled at her. 'Bex is right; that was brave to open up to us all and I am sure that you'll find exactly what you're looking for very very soon.' I couldn't bring myself to make eye contact with Ollie but I could feel his excitable energy from here.

'Guys,' Stefan piped up.

'Do you want to go next?' Nihal asked. 'As I think dinner is nearly ready.'

'No, well yeah, I can wait till after dinner but look.' Stefan had his arm outstretched pointing at the ocean. Dancing and diving out of the waves was a huge shoal of flying fish shimmering in the moonlight.

'Cool!' Ollie said, sitting back on his elbows watching nature's show.

Suddenly the tide drew in and the fish were left stranded, flailing and glistening on the wet sand.

'We've got to get them back in the sea!' Ollie shouted, getting to his feet.

We all raced to the shore and began scooping up wet, slimy fish and throwing them back into the water before it was too late. It was a real team effort to make sure the tiny fishes were all on their way back to their families, safe from harm.

After dinner we traipsed back to our huts feeling stuffed, content and closer as a group. The night sky had clouded around us so all I could hear was shrieks of laughter as people stumbled to their huts with the light from their iPhones guiding their way. Chris was already fast asleep as I tiptoed inside. He'd left hours earlier than everyone else as apparently all these cathartic chats weren't for him, which was a shame really as I was itching to find out why he was here and who had hurt him; maybe I could go and shake their hand. *No, Georgia, be nice.*

Strangely, sharing a room with a man I barely knew didn't feel that odd. I guess because the only way I could feel in danger at being in such close proximity with him was death by awkward silence. I brushed my teeth and got into bed, which was actually a lot comfier than it looked, and turned out the small night light.

'Louise… Mnnnnnmm.'

'What, Chris?' I whispered before realising that he was sleep talking. Great. Next he'd be snoring.

'Business. OK, I'll write it. OK.'

Sounds like someone needed to lay off the cheese before bed. I popped in a pair of ear plugs and promptly fell asleep.

CHAPTER 27

Delectation (n.) Delight; enjoyment

'Happy Holi!!'

Nihal and Ameera were running down the beach clutching carrier bags under their arms and laughing together. After the last few days everyone had needed to catch up on some proper undisturbed sleep so we had had a lazy morning doing absolutely nothing. Most of the group had assembled in the restaurant, enjoying a late brunch, playing cards and lying on the multi-coloured hammocks reading.

'Guys! Happy Holi!' Ameera gushed, laughing at Nihal dancing around the table before sitting down to join us. 'Today is the festival of colours and of love, so you need to change into white clothes. We picked up a few T-shirts that you can wear if you didn't bring anything and then let the celebrations begin!'

'This is Holi paint.' Nihal held up sandwich bags filled with bright electric-coloured reds, blues, oranges, neon yellows and acid pink powders.

'Powder?' Bex asked. 'Thought this was a paint festival? You're not going to decorate your walls with that.'

'Ah ha! We mix these powders with water to create a paste which is then splattered and thrown over everyone!' Ameera was giddy with excitement and passed out bags to everyone.

Soon it was a carnival of colour. The streets filled with people who looked like they'd been gunged on Nickelodeon. Small, giggling, skinny boys raced around with water pistols aiming at anyone and anything that stood in their path, including street dogs that barked and chased the spurts of brightly coloured water streaking the hot ground.

'Water bombs!!' Bex cried, dashing around and chucking what looked more like condoms filled with colour than small balloons.

A noisy but melodic banging of drums grew louder as a street procession of men and boys proudly chanted a lively song whilst marching through the small village. Their eyelashes were covered in a fine dusting of green paint, their hair was matted to their heads under the dye and their arms were splodged with Monet-style coloured blotches.

'As the full moon approaches, spring arrives and the air is filled with possibility. It is a time to heal broken relationships and forget and forgive the past,' Nihal explained as seriously as he could, even though he looked like he had emerged from a chemical explosion under the riot of dust, chalk and colours. 'This is why we were very keen to be here in time to celebrate Holi with you guys. Perfect for the Lonely Hearts Travel Club as you can move into the new phase feeling lighter, happier and ready to find love again! There is power in the powder.'

I felt so carefree, forgetting that I was meant to be this professional businesswoman undercover as a backpacker as I dabbed, smeared and threw handfuls of the soft powdery paint over anyone and everyone. These Hindus were onto something with this festival. Out with the old and in with the new; it was like a good spring clean but, you know, messier and a load more fun. The whole village was in high spirits acting like big kids for the day; no one was exempt, even the huddle of grandmas who sat with their swollen feet on wooden stools were soon raising their varicose-veined arms in the air and getting covered in colour as they chuckled.

Once all our paint had been used up we traipsed back to the huts, taking selfies of how ridiculous we looked.

'Oi, Chris, take our photo! Smile, Louise!' Bex shouted as Chris nodded and brandished his prized camera towards us. I scrunched my messy face into a big smile and put my thumbs up. 'Right now let's get a group shot.' She placed her chubby arm over Nihal's shoulders, pulled the big clan of us into the mix and made Chris pass his phone to a kind stranger wandering past to take the photo. 'Say Happy Holi!'

'Happy Holi!' we all cheered.

A few hours later, as the sun had said goodnight and the bright full moon watched over us, we commanded yellow and green three-wheeled auto rickshaws to get us out of the village and into the hills. We were on our way to Leopard Valley, a big Holi party in the jungle that was set to carry on all night long. I'd skilfully avoided sharing a taxi with Chris, who had somehow managed to stay impeccably clean compared to the rest of us who were still in our paint-splattered clothes. Instead Ollie called me over to ride with him to the party. The smiling driver was pleased to have business and not in the least bit bothered that we would be smearing his seats with paint.

'You don't want to sit with Liz?' I asked, ducking my head to get into the back of the tuk-tuk and sinking onto springy, ripped leather seats.

Ollie got in, his knees almost touching his chin. 'So, you've worked out that I like her then?' He looked bashfully at the string of beads dangling from the rear-view mirror that began clicking as we careered forward.

'Ollie.' I turned to face him. 'Everyone knows you like Liz. Well, everyone apart from Liz, and maybe Bex,' I added.

He placed his head in his hands. 'Right, well… But you don't think Liz knows?'

I shook my head. 'I think Liz has been too caught up worrying that the tour group might turn on her because of that secret she shared yesterday.'

'I still can't believe that!' Ollie blurted out in shock. 'Obviously I don't condone cheating but I would never in a million years have said that she would be the one to do…that.'

'Yeah well, they do say it's always the quiet ones.' I smiled and grabbed hold of the seat in front as we practically zoomed around a tight bend on one wheel. 'But if you don't have a problem with that, with, erm, her needs…' I trailed off feeling quite uncomfortable discussing Liz and Ollie's potential sex life. It suddenly felt very hot in the tuk-tuk.

Ollie looked as embarrassed as I was as he gazed out of his dusty window, seemingly transfixed by what was going on outside. 'Yeah. Well, you know. I like a challenge.'

'Great!' I said way too overexcitedly. 'Erm, great. So just talk to her; ask her to spend the day just you two. I'm sure Nihal wouldn't mind if you snuck off – in fact I bet he'd be happy to give you some tips on romantic places you could go.'

'Mmm,' Ollie mumbled, flicking some paint from his thumbnail. 'But Louise…'

'Yeah?'

'What if I can't, you know…perform.' He looked so distraught and vulnerable I tried to supress a laugh. Instead I placed a hand on his shoulder and gave it a little squeeze.

'Ollie, she would be mad to miss out on going out with you. Don't overthink it, all right?'

He nodded and then unexpectedly gave me a quick hug. I felt the eyes of the tuk-tuk driver focus on us through the rear-view mirror.

'Thanks, Louise; I mean it. I'm so pleased you're on this tour.' He let me go and grinned that cheeky wide smile of his. Liz would be insane to resist that.

'Thanks, me too,' I said genuinely. 'What have you got to lose? You don't know what tomorrow will bring.'

'OK, Leopard Valley!' the tuk-tuk driver exclaimed breaking up our heart to heart, as we pulled into a busy car park.

The rest of the group were waiting by a large sign for us. The banging baseline of the DJ set was pounding through the stillness of the lush, green palm leaves surrounding us.

'Usually in Goa there are strict noise pollution laws that mean any outdoor entertainment has a ten p.m. curfew,' Nihal was explaining to the others as Ollie and I made our way over after paying the driver. 'But as it's Holi all the rules go out of the window!' He laughed.

'For those who can't handle the pace then tuk-tuks will be running all night from here if you want to leave early to get your beauty sleep.' Ameera flashed a quick and unsubtle look at Chris. 'For the rest of you party animals the fun won't stop until late. We've got you some more paint packs so go wild and enjoy this wonderful festival.' She passed out more sandwich bags filled with multi-coloured powder and headed down the winding path marked with flaming torches to get deeper into the jungle rave.

Outrageously dressed performers energetically moved their lithe bodies to the beat on raised, glittering podiums. One man was breathing fire as we wandered past and two girls were axle grinding and smiling serenely, as if grating sparks from their vaginas was totally normal. Hundreds of clubbers, made up of locals, backpackers and expats danced to the electro music, their colourful marbled bodies lit up under the bright strobe lights. This was unlike any party I'd ever been to before.

I'd never got into the raving scene when I was younger as I was much too paranoid that I'd get my drink spiked, jittery that a fight would break out, and not to mention the mind-numbing boredom of spending half your night waiting in the queue to the ladies' loos. Marie and I used to prefer spending our Saturday nights going on bar crawls or having pre-drinks at home, which usually never amounted to us actually going out as I'd be holding back Marie's flaming red locks as she made out with the toilet bowl.

It was like walking through a cloud of smoke, *Stars in Their Eyes*-style, trying to get to the bar. Colourful puffs of powder came at you from every direction.

'Hey, what we drinking?' a smiling barman wearing a bandana and neon dots peppering his wide eyes asked.

'I'll get these,' Ollie shouted over the baseline to me.

'Ah cheers! I'll have a beer, please.'

'Coming right up!' The barman sprinkled some powder onto his open palm and leant down to blow it away as if he was sprinkling fairy dust.

With some Dutch courage inside him Ollie turned to face me. 'Right. I'm going to talk to Liz. To tell her that I like her.' He tensed his arms looking ready to go into battle. 'As Nihal said, today is about new beginnings. I can do this.'

I patted him on the shoulder getting my palm covered in apple-green powder. 'Go for it. You've got this.'

He nodded and sniffed his pits before stomping off to find his fair maiden; I just hoped he'd be able to recognise her under all this paint.

'So, you having fun?' Nihal half danced, half jumped over to me and leant his arm on the bar.

'Yeah! This is wild!' I laughed, pointing at the energetic crowd of ravers who were bowing down, tooting whistles and waving glow sticks at the guy spinning the decks. 'After Mumbai and Delhi this was *just* what I needed.'

'It's the least I can do to thank you for bringing my love back to me.' He paused to wave at Ameera who was swaying gracefully in the corner with Flic. She was wearing a full-length skirt, the colour-splattered fabric seemingly dancing all on its own. 'We are so grateful, Georgia.' He quickly checked no one was nearby to hear him slipping up. 'I mean Louise,' he said louder.

'I didn't do anything.' I blushed.

'OK, now less talking and more dancing, Miss Green!' Nihal laughed and pulled me by the hand away from the safety of the bar to join him and Ameera.

As the DJ blasted out 'Shake it off' remixed with a bhangra beat, which was a lot better than it sounds, the whole place erupted. If there had been a roof it surely would have blown off. It was one of those moments when I needed to take a minute to let it all sink in. That I was sweaty, covered in paint, dancing like no one was watching in the middle of an Indian jungle during Holi festival, on a tour that my own business had organised. Wow.

'Just going to find the ladies'!' I shouted over to Ameera who nodded.

Moving away from the sticky heat of the packed dance floor I wandered through the trees to find the bathroom. A chill-out area under a vine-covered veranda had been set up nearby. Blissed-out backpackers sat on enormous beanbags, lazily smoking shisha pipes and chinking their bottles of beer, acting as if they weren't sat metres away from an Indian full-moon party.

'Happy Holi!' a girl with a blonde pixie haircut cheerfully said to me as I washed my hands at the sink.

I did a double take; she could have been Shelley's twin with her smattering of freckles on her neat nose and playful green eyes. She frowned at me for staring at her in what must have been a very odd way. Seeing Shelley's doppelgänger, I was reminded that I had survived this far without my dear friend; those anxieties I'd felt racing through Manchester airport so I wouldn't miss my flight sans Shelley had all but vanished. I had done it; I had lasted this long and everything was absolutely fine.

'Err, yeah, sorry! Happy Holi!' I grinned at the girl who nodded and quickly made her exit.

I swerved my way round three Indian men who were wobbling up the path and went to find the others, laughing as I ducked past a young girl, no older than seven, who was covered in colourful paint. Her shiny, almost-black eyes were creased in enjoyment as she mischievously sprinkled powder on anyone who walked past her before shrieking when they clocked her.

'Hey, guys, anyone fancy a drink?' I asked half dancing up to Ollie, Bex and Liz who were crowded around Chris and his mobile phone screen.

They all ignored me.

'Guys?!' I said louder.

Slowly they looked up at me with a mix of disgust, annoyance and sadness on their colourful faces.

'What's wrong?'

Glancing down at Chris's phone I felt like someone had chucked an ice cube down my T-shirt. The cold sobering realisation of what I'd tried to keep hidden was being played out right before my eyes.

CHAPTER 28

Verisimilitude (n.) The appearance or semblance of truth; likelihood; probability

Taking centre stage on Chris's iPhone screen was a clip of Ben and me in our shop. It was a short video that he'd encouraged me to do so we could use it in publicity for the business, even though I hated being in front of the camera. I'd worried that my voice had sounded manly, that my under-eye bags were very prominent, and that I should have gone to the hairdresser's before filming.

God, I looked different.

That had been only a few weeks ago and still, seeing my tired eyes, wiry hair and hearing my hoarse, exhausted voice, I felt like I didn't recognise myself. Although, right now hearing my shrill laughter and even a silly jingle that one of Ben's mates had created competing with the booming bhangra beat, my appearance online was the least of my worries.

'Where did you find that?' I asked Chris boldly, feeling my bottom lip wobbling and heat coursing through me.

'So, Georgia Green: heartbroken backpacker, aka businesswoman and founder of this whole tour group,' Chris said sharply. The rest of them just gawped at me, waiting for me to say something.

'Is this really you, Louise?' Liz asked, her eyes filling with tears. 'You're the boss of this whole company? You're not here as a backpacker like us?'

I felt sick. Words just weren't coming out so I simply nodded my head, wishing Chris would turn the bloody footage off. Other members of the group had come over to see what was going on, peering over Chris's shoulders to watch the clip and then snapping their heads up at me, a confused look on their faces. Chris looked like he was lapping this up, finally being centre of attention; you could see the power this was giving his ego and it made me want to vomit.

'Louise? You're Georgia?' Bex stuttered. For once she seemed lost for words.

I could feel their eyes boring into me, the music was making my head spin, the paint was making me feel itchy and uncomfortable, and the merriment I'd been feeling just ten minutes earlier had evaporated into a puddle of sweat at my feet.

'Wait, so what…you lied to us?' Ollie was standing just inches away from me, his whole body tense as if he wanted to punch me.

I lamely nodded once more.

'I can't believe this. I thought you were one of us,' he seethed. I noticed that he had his arm around Liz's shoulders that were juddering in the disco-ball lights.

'I am!' I pleaded.

The only people missing from this *coup d'état* were Nihal and Ameera; I glanced around desperate to find them, knowing that they'd stick up for me. But in the sea of painted faces I couldn't spot them.

'Oh yeah right, so this hasn't been some sort of weird experiment, some undercover boss challenge just to feed back to head office on how you can improve sales or some crap like that,' Ollie spat.

I hadn't realised he could get this mad. Bex just shook her head in disappointment before she stalked off.

'Bex, wait! Ollie, listen! You really are making this out to be worse than it seems. Yes, I created the tours, yes, I own the business, but I was also heartbroken, I understand how much this pain fucking hurts. But also how it can get better.'

He rolled his eyes. 'You really expect me to be sympathetic when you're over here spying on us before you return home to your mansion, using our break-up stories to sell more tours? Getting us to open up to you, not because you care, but because it was just a box-ticking exercise. I can't believe you lied to us, Louise…Georgia, or whatever your fucking name is! I trusted you.' His whole face was shaking, his voice breaking slightly as it was forced out through his clenched jaw.

'I wish I had a bloody mansion!' I scoffed, then realised that wasn't the point. I softened my tone. 'Ollie, please. I did tell a few white lies: I do own the business but I have also been heartbroken. I wasn't planning on coming on this tour to spy on you; it was only because I thought Nihal had been having a rough time that I dropped everything back home – in my tiny flat, can I add – to make sure all of you experienced the tour of India that you deserved.' I was crying now; frustrated tears streaked with the mess of paint on my face.

'Well you sure made it one we won't forget,' he said, dryly.

'I know and I'm sorry. It wasn't meant to be like this. All I wanted was to help you get through your break-up. All of you.' I looked around for one friendly, understanding face in the tinted tribe before me.

'Yeah, well, if you're such a relationship expert then you'll know just how difficult it is to trust again.' With that he stormed off past me, kicking up a cloud of dust as he went and taking Liz with him. 'Ollie, wait, please!' I turned to face the others who had also stomped off, leaving just me and Chris standing face to face.

'You didn't have to do that!' I said.

'I didn't do anything.' He placed his hand on his chest smugly. Bastard. 'I simply thought the others should know that they were unwittingly involved in some naff undercover boss experiment.'

I gritted my teeth. 'It wasn't an experiment.'

Chris sighed and finally put his bloody phone away, before nodding slowly as if listening to a small child explaining the theories of life. 'Mmm. OK. Well, Miss Green, I mean, Boss, will you please excuse me?' He too then sauntered off, leaving me stood alone, humiliated and upset on the dance floor.

I'd fled the jungle rave, taken a tuk-tuk back to the huts by myself and gone for a long walk down the empty beach. Kicking up sand between my feet, I chucked any random pebbles I could find into the dark waves and watched their ripples illuminated by the bright stars popping from the cloak of darkness. I had to stop myself jumping in and swimming far away from here. I'd fucked this up. I should never have come here. These people had trusted me, opened up to me and expected me to be just like them, not a fraud, a fake, a pathetic businesswoman who had just been burning herself out trying to make a success of the Lonely Hearts Travel Club.

But things had been looking up. The last two days were the happiest I'd felt in a long time, probably since I was last in Thailand hanging out with the original Lonely Hearts Travel Club crew and Ben and Jimmy. We'd spent so many evenings on a secluded perfect beach just like this one, larking about, putting the world to rights and letting off Chinese lanterns with handwritten wishes tacked on. Well, none of those wishes had come true.

I closed my eyes and let out a deep sigh. Marie wasn't talking to me, Ben seemed to be coping fine without me and the guests here – some of whom had become friends – wanted me to fuck the fuck off. Watching the woman I had been in that short video, it was no wonder Ben hadn't shown the slightest bit of interest in me. I had looked a mess.

I had been a mess. I still was a mess. And I didn't have the faintest idea of how I was going to fix this.

CHAPTER 29

Flee (v.) To run away, as from danger or pursuers; take flight

Nihal had arranged for the tour group to visit an animal sanctuary, which looked after the many stray dogs around, followed by a spice plantation. I was still huddled under the thin sheet of my bed, not wanting to leave my own sanctuary. I'd ignored Chris as he got up and ready an hour earlier, sticking my fingers in my ears as he whistled to himself in the shower – although now I couldn't get the bloody theme tune to *Star Wars* out of my head.

I'd hardly slept a wink all night; I still hadn't worked out why Chris had done that. OK, fair enough if he'd found the clip, but he could have asked me rather than turn everyone against me. Oh God, just think of the reviews this tour was going to receive now.

'Morning, Boss,' Chris said, smirking. I half expected him to whip out a white fluffy cat to stroke as he gave me a dirty, venomous look, James Bond-baddie style. I could so see him in a satin housecoat. 'You not up and ready to snoop on us some more this morning?'

'You know, you didn't have to do that, Chris,' I said, my hands balled into fists at my sides. I wasn't going to let this strange, arrogant man beat me. I had too much to lose.

'Do what? Tell the truth?' He laughed bitterly, flashing a row of fillings as he did. 'These people trusted you, Georgia. They trusted you and opened up to you and all along you deceived them.'

I was almost shaking with both anger and guilt. 'OK, so maybe it looked like that but I swear it wasn't my plan.'

He tipped his beaky nose in the air and sighed loudly. 'Whatever. Right, if you'll excuse me, Boss, I'm off to meet the others. You can write that down in your sales notes too, if you want. I take it you're not coming.' With that he turned his back to me and got his day pack ready. I suddenly wondered whether his bony spine would hurt against my knuckles if I gave him a good thump…but decided against it, you know, being the boss and all.

'I'll catch you all up,' I mumbled, and turned over until I heard the creak of the front door closing.

What was I going to do? I knew the mature thing would have been to jump out of bed, plaster on a fake smile that wouldn't meet my tired eyes and act like nothing had happened last night. I knew I should try and pull myself together and stop being such a whiny mare. Yeah, I had messed up, yeah, I needed to inject some fun back into my life and find that elusive work-life balance, and yeah, I need to invest in some eye-bag cream. But still, I'd managed to co-create a business at a time when eight out of ten weren't surviving past their first birthday.

OK, so things with Ben hadn't taken off like I'd hoped, but that was because I'd become a business bore, worse than mums bragging about everything their newborn baby does on Facebook. Marie would come round if I actually treated her like a friend and not just someone who would always be there in the background. I knew I should get up and call a meeting to explain to everyone just what the truth was, with the help of Ameera and Nihal backing me up. Simple.

The thing was, I knew I couldn't do that. I was crap at acting for one – Marie was the talented one in that area; and two, I still felt so guilty for not telling the truth. Visions of Ollie's outraged face, Liz's trembling bottom lip and Bex storming off in disgust played on repeat in my mind like some sick, screensaver slide show.

Trying to get back to sleep was fruitless so I made my decision.

I wasn't going to go and meet the others; instead I was going to try and get the hell out of here. I couldn't face them. I wouldn't know where to start or what to say so it was for the best that I went home and prepared for the awful reviews to come pouring in.

Amazingly, I managed to connect to the dodgy Wi-Fi from my hut and quickly booked the next flight back to Manchester, leaving tomorrow lunchtime. After pressing confirm and hoping the connection wouldn't cut out, I breathed a sigh of relief. I was going home. I then reserved a cheap hostel near the airport where I could stay tonight until my flight. I would leave them a letter explaining how sorry I was, but that it was for the best that they finish the tour without me.

After closing down my open apps I lay back on my bed and pressed my fingers to my pulsating temples. Leaving was the right thing. I'd finished what I'd come here to do, I'd sorted out the tour, and once this one was over, I had no doubt we would start to receive rave reviews, just as we had in the beginning. Plus, I'd managed to match-make Nihal and Ameera back together, as well as Liz and Ollie, which was just the icing on the cake. With a deep sigh I flung back my bed covers and clicked off the air conditioning. Chris had kept it on all night, and I felt like even my bogeys had frozen in my nose. With a relaxing whirr the small room became silent again. The sound of the waves outside and birds singing filtered in, along with beams of hazy sunlight. I began packing my bag, looking sadly at the paint-splattered outfit I'd worn for Holi. So much for new beginnings. The past clearly wasn't finished with me yet.

Once my clothes were rolled up and stuffed into any available space, I neatly made my bed and lugged my bag onto my shoulders. I decided not to leave a note for Chris after all – he'd probably only criticise my grammar skills. I trudged outside, blinking in the bright sunlight. My body sighed as my skin warmed under the late morning heat. Like some cat stretching out in a sun-dappled spot I turned my face to the sky and shut my eyes. God, I was going to miss this feeling. Maybe I would buy a sun lamp or repaint the office bright yellow to get the same effect.

'Louise!' Someone had called my name; I flicked my head back and clasped my hand over my eyes to see who it was. I thought the tour group had all left? Shit, I really didn't want to be shouted at again right now.

'Louise!' the voice continued. Peering down the beach, which was empty apart from three skinny children dancing in the surf, I couldn't see anyone, then I realised the voice was coming from my right. From Ameera and Nihal's hut.

'Oh, hi,' I said waving lamely; Ameera was sat on the small terrace with her bare feet tucked under her petite body. She was wearing a hot-pink, floaty beach dress and had intricately braided her hair. She looked a lot perkier than I felt.

'You OK? Come and have some tea with me.' She beckoned me over.

OK, tea first and then I'd find a tuk-tuk to take me to the airport hotel. I quickly stepped over the sand; even in flip-flops the heat radiating through was scalding.

'Hey, how come you're not at the animal sanctuary?' I asked, creaking on the wooden steps of her hut.

'Well, I needed to be apart from Nihal for a bit.'

My stomach dropped. 'Has something happened?'

She flicked her braids back and laughed lightly. 'No! Don't worry. Come on, sit down.' She brought out a large flask of tea and two small cups and poured the spiced liquid in; swirls of steam tickled my nose. 'It's Nihal's birthday, so I needed to send him off whilst I sorted out his present.' She pointed to the material on the table in front of her that I hadn't spotted before.

'His birthday!?'

'Yeah, I'm making him something as I didn't have the chance to go shopping when we were in the big cities and all the places here are just full of beach stuff; he's not really a sun worshipper.' She laughed. 'So did you enjoy last night then? How come you didn't go off with the group this morning?' she asked, fiddling with the small needle, sticking her tongue out to the side of her mouth.

'You didn't hear?'

'Hear what?' She stopped faffing with the needle and looked at me.

'That everyone hates me.' I sipped my tea, which burnt the back of my throat.

'What? What are you talking about?'

'Last night, the tour group found out that my name isn't Louise, and I'm not a hairdresser from Manchester. I'm Georgia Green, CEO of the Lonely Hearts Travel Club.' I paused to blow on my cup, watching Ameera wince. 'And now they all hate me for lying to them, believing that I led them on just for some strange business experiment or to increase sales.'

'Ah.'

'Yep.'

Ameera didn't say a thing, just nodded and carried on with her bloody needlepoint. I stared out to the calming froth of the sea. Usually the greeny-brown water churned around with constant waves coming from the Arabian Sea but today it just gently lapped the shore. I had a sudden urge to strip down to my bikini and race in for a swim.

'I don't understand why you weren't honest with them at the start,' she said quietly, not looking at me.

'How could I have been? Oh hey, welcome to India. I'm the boss of the company. Come on; please tell me all your sordid secrets.' I pressed a hand to my face. 'I get why they're mad at me. I would be too.'

'Maybe you're not giving them enough credit. These people have gone through some tough times back at home, probably because of people they loved lying to them. They're desperate for honesty and would have adapted to that.' She paused and stared me straight in the eye. 'But you building this whole persona wasn't just about them, was it?' I nearly spilt my tea.

'What do you mean?' I asked slowly.

'Well, Nihal told me about you. About the rushed emails he'd received, the late night phone calls with you stressing about how things were going, needing him to account for every minute of his time so you could input it into some big plan.' I winced. Yep that was me. 'To be honest, Georgia, I'd built you up in my head to be this power-hungry, workaholic bitch,' she said shrugging her shoulders. This wasn't helping my fragile state of emotions.

'Thanks,' I mumbled.

She laughed softly and patted me on my hand. 'But then I met you, saw how desperate you were for this tour to go well, how hard you worked to get me and Nihal back together and that's when I realised: you weren't just desperate for control because you had sales targets to meet, but because you couldn't let this business fail.' I nodded, wanting her to continue.

'When we arrived here and you could let go of the grip you had on your business baby, you started to soften around the edges. Everyone could see it. You laughed more, chilled out and went with the flow.'

'Only because India forced me to be like that!' I interrupted. Why was I fighting this still?

'Yes. India does that to people. She is a wonderful, complex beast that even the strongest of men cannot tame. But she also gives you what you need at the times when you need it, even if you think you don't.' She folded the material gently on her knee. 'You're doing a good job. Your business will be fine but you need to let some of this manic control go and trust others to support you.'

I thought back to Ben, how he was always telling me to trust him, to work as a team and that he was there to support me if I let him. She was right; I'd been wanting to control every aspect of the business to make sure it didn't fail. Because this was the only job I'd ever had where I'd given it one hundred per cent, because I wanted to make my parents proud, because I wanted to have something that I felt proud of.

'I guess.'

'You can be Louise *and* you can be Georgia. Just find a way to balance the two.' She smiled sagely. 'Now top up my cup will you? I'm dying of thirst over here.'

I poured the thick tea, thinking about what she'd said. I did need to get fun Georgia back.

'So, do you think he'll like it?' she asked, proudly holding up the pale apricot coloured fabric onto which she'd intricately beaded and threaded different scenes. It was incredible.

A large heart made from bright red silk took centre stage with the words 'You're in my heart' sewn on in swirly print, and around it was a detailed replica of the Taj Mahal on white lace. Golden satin jumped out against a bluey-green piece of cloth as if she'd expertly found the exact colour of the sea it represented. A small, neat cross-stitched train was in the bottom corner, and glittering swathes of colour wrapped around the rough edges. She'd created the Lonely Hearts Travel Club.

'That's for the Holi festival, and this is for the filming on the beach in Mumbai.' She pointed at it, beaming at her masterpiece.

'Wow, Ameera. He's going to love it!' I grinned.

'Looks OK, doesn't it?' she asked, as I ran my fingers over the material. It must have taken her hours.

'Exactly like the tour I'd imagined.'

It was like she'd stumbled across my Pinterest boards where I'd pinned hundreds of images, trying to picture what India would be like so I could sell it to customers. But this was better.

'Here. It's for you.' She pressed it into my hands.

'What? No! It's Nihal's birthday present,' I protested.

'Erm, well I may have made that up.' She smiled shyly from under her long, dark lashes. 'His birthday was three months ago.'

'What?' I sat back confused.

'I knew what happened last night. It was all anyone could talk about. I came to try to find you but you'd raced off back to your hut. I also knew you how you'd be feeling, not wanting to see anybody, probably about to silently disappear and fly home without saying goodbye.'

She nodded to the bag at my feet that she had previously acted like she hadn't seen. I stared at her.

'So, I decided to take the morning off and let Nihal take charge, knowing that I would be able to speak to you alone. I started making this as a thank-you gift to you, after we were in Mumbai, but I didn't know when it would be finished to give it to you. I also wanted to say how sorry I was about that blog post.' She looked guiltily at the sandy deck of her hut. 'I truly didn't know how much damage it would do.' She pushed her masterpiece back into my hands. 'You created this, Georgia. Nihal and I are back together, Liz and Ollie are loved up, Bex has found the strength to be true to herself, and everyone else is healing from their past, all because you created this tour. But you've gone on this journey too.'

'Erm…' I was lost for words. Her wide loving eyes made me want to cry.

'Please, don't go without saying goodbye. You need to leave on a high, proud of what you've done, not making a speedy exit with your tail between your legs.'

She was a wily minx. I nodded and took the material, never feeling so overwhelmed and emotional over a piece of handicraft before.

'OK.'

'Thank you. So when's your flight booked for?'

'Tomorrow lunchtime.'

She nodded. 'Plenty of time to make things right. So, you fancy a quick dip then?' I nodded and grinned before hugging her.

The water was colder than I'd imagined. In Thailand, the piercing blue sea was as warm as a bath; here the waves slapped your thighs, forcing you to jump right in and swim around to heat yourself up. It was fast-moving and powerful, just what I needed to kick myself back into action. Ameera was like a water baby, powerfully slicing through the surf with strong butterfly strokes. I only knew how to swim breast stroke so kicked my feet out and raised my neck like some grandma in the local swimming pool not wanting to get their blue-rinse curls wet.

'If we swim over there, we can rest on the rocks!' Ameera shouted from ahead of me, pointing to the hilly cove dunked in the water, where waves were thrashing the sides.

Yeah, looks like a lovely place to rest, I thought sarcastically. 'I don't know if I can make it!' I called back, awkwardly treading water. It seemed like a bloody long way off. The beach was so much closer. Couldn't we just head back there and sunbathe?

'Come on, Georgia! Of course you can! Louise would do it.' She laughed and effortlessly increased her speed, heading to the rocks.

I took a deep breath and thrust myself forward, coughing up salty water that was slapping my face. She was much further in the distance now and the beach was slowly slipping further behind us.

Suddenly a burning pain jolted through my right leg.

'Argh!' I screamed but Ameera was too far ahead to hear.

I jolted my head around but couldn't see any grey shiny fins bobbing in the waves. Do they even have sharks in India? I expected a pool of deep crimson blood to emerge around me but there was nothing, just the throbbing pain as I kicked harder. What the hell? I winced and rubbed my leg; my fingers didn't sink into any open raw wound; they just brushed against my stubble. Oh, not a shark attack, just leg cramp. But still it bloody hurt. I needed to make a decision: I could turn back to the beach, or carry on.

Ameera was almost to the rocks now, her black hair bobbing on the surface ahead. I couldn't see or touch the bottom. What was I doing? I hated being this far out at sea. When I was in Thailand I'd almost died going scuba diving and here I was having willingly put myself at risk again.

Come on. You can do this. You can do anything! I screamed at myself, forcing my tired brain to ignore the cramp and keep going. *Don't give up. Don't be a failure.*

I splashed and moaned, gritted my teeth, and swam. The breast stroke move was long gone as I flailed about, putting one aching arm in front of the other, thrashing one exhausted leg behind the other, pushing myself forward. I'd thought we were going for a leisurely dip not a bloody sea marathon. Was that even a thing? Well, it was now.

'Come on! You're almost there!' Ameera cheered as she found her footing on some rocks away from the scary, enormous waves and effortlessly slid herself up to her feet. 'You can do this!'

'*Just keep swimming, just keep swimming*,' the blue fish from *Finding Nemo* chanted in my head. The rocks didn't seem to be getting any closer. I was about to protest that she was going to have to come back in and pull me to safety when she started to jump up and down.

'Shark!' Ameera screamed and pointed to somewhere behind me. 'Come on!' Her eyes were wide and her finger was jabbing in my direction.

Fuck! I gave it everything I could, swimming like my life depended on it, which apparently now it did. I reached the rocks and followed her lead, placing my shaking feet on rough granite and scraping my hands on sharp, jagged stones to heave myself out of the shark-infested waters.

'Where? Where's the shark?'

I was shaking and anxiously darting my eyes at the frothy sea for a telltale dorsal fin. I felt like I might collapse, my breathing was erratic, my head pounded with blood, and my chest was contracting stupidly fast.

'Ha ha ha!' Ameera was doubled up laughing, holding her tiny waist as she bent over. 'There aren't any sharks. I just wanted you to get a move on.'

I could have hit her.

'Sorry! I'm sorry. But look, you did it!'

I half growled at her, not remotely seeing the funny side of her joke, and looked back at the non-shark-infested waters. The beach was a small dot of golden yellow, our beach huts tiny brown specks.

'Oh my God! I did it. I hate the sea but I did it.'

Ameera high-fived me. 'Yeah you did! Now, let's grab some lunch. I'm starving.'

I stared at her like she'd lost the plot. 'Lunch? What, we going to catch some fish?'

Ameera laughed again. 'You didn't think I'd make you swim all this way just so we could get back in and swim home did you?' Err yeah, that was exactly what I thought she was doing. 'There's a hidden little café through the trees that only locals know about. Our table's waiting.'

'But I haven't got any cash; we're in our bikinis!' I wobbled up the rocks wincing at the stones slicing my bare feet.

'Pfft. Don't worry! Come on, everyone is waiting.' She bounded off like an Indian Lara Croft down the rocks and through the trees.

I gulped. *Everyone?*

CHAPTER 30

Confront (v.) To face in hostility or defiance; oppose

I picked up my pace to catch up with her, my burning thighs and leaden arms acting as victory wounds. Pushing back palm leaves and stepping onto soft, spongy moss I saw there were a few tables clustered around a hut made of corrugated iron. Smells from a barbecue rushed up my nose and the sound of applause rang through the air. Everyone from the tour group was here, sat at a long table partially hidden by bushes, and clapping their hands as Ameera and I stumbled up to them. What was going on?

'You made it!' Nihal jumped to his feet to give Ameera a kiss and shake my soaking wet hand.

'What's happening?' I asked, still trying to get my breath back, feeling very underdressed and exposed in my bikini. As if reading my mind, Ollie chucked me a warm dry towel. I took it gratefully and wrapped it around myself, looking at him nervously in case he was going to start shouting at me again.

He smiled softly. 'Nice entrance. We were all watching you and even had bets on whether you'd make it or not.' He quickly glanced over to Chris who was suddenly very interested in the salt and pepper shakers.

I felt like Leo in *The Beach* after he'd swum to the secret tropical island. Only for him he was welcomed into paradise; I was faced with a group of people who yesterday had hated my guts. I nervously chewed my bottom lip and glanced over to Ameera who smiled innocently.

'Thanks. I wasn't even sure if I would make it.' I sat down at the only remaining chair, which was at the head of the table, and cleared my throat. I needed to make amends. 'Listen, everyone. I am really sorry for not telling you the whole truth about why I'm here. I really didn't mean to hurt you.' I looked over to Liz who was holding Ollie's hand and nodding at me to continue. 'I am going home tomorrow. But I couldn't leave without saying goodbye and thanks. To all of you, for showing me how lost I'd become without realising it.'

'You're going?' Bex asked, her mouth wide open.

I nodded.

'Because of us?' Ollie said, biting his thumb.

'Because…it's time for me to leave. I wasn't meant to stay for this long and as you all know I do have a business that I've been neglecting.' A few people laughed lightly. 'I know you're all going to be just fine. Nihal and Ameera have totally got the rest of the tour covered,' I said confidently.

It was true; they did. If he could take charge of herding the group around and Ameera could trick me into admitting my true feelings, then the Lonely Hearts Travel Club was going to be absolutely fine.

'We're going to miss you, Louise, I mean Georgia,' Liz said, as the others nodded their heads in agreement.

Slowly I felt the pressure of the group subside. Ameera grinned at me and Flic blinked back the tears, acting like she had just swallowed a strong chilli in her mild curry. The only one who kept looking at me was Chris; he seemed reluctant to let this go, as if desperate to understand if there was something more to it than we were letting on.

'It won't be the same without you,' Bex said before raising her glass.

Everyone clinked their bottles of Kingfisher beer in unison; the dappled sunlight through the palm trees made the soft ruby glass glow.

'Thank you,' I whispered, gulping back the emotion clouding my throat.

'Right. Enough of that. Is no one going to comment on the fact that Flic is eating meat?' Bex boomed across the table. We all darted our eyes to our boho beach babe who was in fact gnawing on a stick of barbecued chicken and looking like she was loving every bite of the succulent, oily meat.

'What?' she asked nonchalantly with her mouth full.

'Err… You forgotten about all this weird food crap you preach about? How the government controls what we eat and everything that goes into *your* mouth is pure?' Ollie asked.

'Unlike the stuff that comes out of it,' Bex grumbled quietly.

Flic put down the empty wooden stick and wiped her greasy fingers on a paper napkin. Ignoring Bex, she looked like she was stalling for time as she concocted some hippy theory or something. But then as she slowly took a sip of her mineral water she began to laugh. 'I just really, really missed meat! Screw morals when it tastes *so* good and this stuff is flipping fantastic.'

We burst into laughter as she caught the waiter's attention for another order.

Bex put a chubby, pink arm around Flic's shoulders and squeezed her tight. 'Lose the dreadlocks and you and I could become friends!'

'Speaking of friends…' I trailed off, leaning my head close to Bex and whispered, 'You *have* to do something about that Stefan. I can't go without knowing that one of you had the courage to make the first move.'

The smile dropped from Bex's rosy cheeks as she seemed to withdraw into herself. She cast a furtive glance up the table at the strapping German man who was deep in an animated conversation with Chris.

'He's actually asked me out…'

'See! I told you he liked you!'

'Yeah, but Louise, I mean Georgia, I've never been on a date before,' she admitted before slurping Coke loudly through her straw and trying to keep down a belch.

Ah.

'OK, well maybe don't do that.' Flic winced through another mouthful of freshly cooked chicken.

'See. I'm such a fanny. I ain't got the foggiest how to act like anything other than how I am,' Bex half whined before checking Stefan hadn't heard.

Watching how this usually confident woman had suddenly slipped into the role of a lost and petrified teenager was heartbreaking. Trying to get someone you like to like you back was a minefield that could turn even the most sassy, self-assured person into an overanalysing neurotic puddle of self-doubt. The hours I had spent panicking whether the tone of my messages to Ben were full of witty, flirty banter or that I had covered up my blemishes with enough foundation… It was exhausting. I now realised that I had to believe that I was good enough just the way I was, and if he was looking for a Serena-type then he was better off with her as I couldn't change to be anyone else other than who I was. I was more than OK with that.

'Exactly,' I said firmly.

'You what?'

'You should never change yourself to make others happy. He obviously has taken a mahoosive shine to you as you are, so don't overthink it. If it comes naturally to you, then just say or do it.'

Bex raised an eyebrow and wiped her nose on the back of her hand. 'Cheers. That does sound a lot simpler. God I'm going to miss you!' She pulled me into a warm hug and whispered in my ear, 'Thank you. For being here, for creating this whole business, and for making me feel like I'm going to be just fine.'

I pulled back and dabbed at my wet eyes. 'I *know* you are.'

'Right, someone pass me some of this amazing chicken. I'm starvin' over here.' She winked at me and called out to the others. It wasn't long before we had all tucked into buttery-soft naan bread, stuffed paratha and freshly grilled fish curry served on giant banana leaves with extra servings of barbecued chicken. The last supper had never tasted so good.

After many goodbyes, swapping contact details and hugs, I caught a tuk-tuk and headed to the airport. Sinking back in the bouncy leather seats I glanced out of the window and watched the lush green jungle whoosh past. I'd made it through India. I'd survived food poisoning, farting during silent yoga, starred in a Bollywood film, and now it was time to go back and face whatever was waiting for me at home. It wasn't just work that I had to get my head prepared for but also seeing Ben, my Ben, loved up with Supermodel Serena, *and* make amends with my justifiably pissed-off best friend.

I'd checked my WhatsApp messages just after I'd woken up but still not a peep from Ben. I tried to put it out of my mind telling myself that I would soon be back in gloomy Manchester, in our shop, and able to see what had been happening since I'd been away. I'd smoothed things over with the group, yes I felt them looking at me a little differently after what I'd done, which stung, but I wasn't running away any more. I just hoped I'd done enough that the reviews wouldn't be completely scathing. I still needed to warn Ben that we might not get five out of five because of this.

I sailed through security and wasn't interested in buying anything from the bright duty free shop so I rushed into a small café, ordered my last cup of chai tea and eventually managed to connect to the Wi-Fi. I messaged Shelley and my parents telling them I would be coming back earlier than planned. I decided not to call Ben; I wanted to see his face when I walked into the office. A part of me wanted to keep my return secret so I could see exactly what was going on between him and Serena, just so I knew where I stood. I slurped my tea, but the strong flavours just made me feel sick. I felt like I had a wave of cinnamon and saffron burning my chest. It was like the onset of indigestion but worse.

'Flight 10KV to Manchester now boarding through Gate 3,' a tinny voice boomed through the speaker above my head. Sighing, I left my tea half drunk and plodded to join the queue to board my flight. Standing in the stuffy heat of the airport, fanning my face with my passport and surrounded by tanned holidaymakers and smartly dressed businessmen, I suddenly had a sinking feeling of dread at what I was about to go back to.

CHAPTER 31

Discombobulate (v.) To confuse or disconcert; upset; frustrate

'Hi! God, it feels good to be back,' I said, breezily walking into our shop and dumping my jacket on my chair. My desk looked like it had been taken over by a Barbie princess, judging by the pink fluffy pens and diamanté-framed photos of pug dogs.

'Hey!' Kelli said, rushing over to give me a hug. 'You're back early!' She was like a puppy wagging its tail as its owner walked through the front door after a day of work.

'Good to see you too, Kel!' I smiled. 'Where is everyone?' I glanced around the empty room; it was after nine but there was no sign of Ben or this mysterious Serena.

Kellie shrugged. 'Dunno.'

I picked up my mobile to call Ben when suddenly the door to the shop swung open and in walked the pair of them, laughing like long-lost friends. Ben stopped and did a double take as he saw me.

'Georgia?' His face broke into a genuine, bright smile. He walked over and hugged me, filling my nose with his spicy aftershave. 'What are you doing back?'

Before I could answer, an attractive blonde stepped out from behind him.

'Oh hi! You must be Georgia. It's so nice to finally meet you. I'm Serena. I've heard *so* much about you,' she sang, putting a tray of coffees down on my desk and shaking my hand, limply.

'Yeah sorry – Georgia, Serena. Serena, Georgia.' Ben did the introductions and smiled at us both.

'Hi, nice to meet you too,' I said, trying not to cough at her sickly sweet perfume clogging the back of my throat.

She was wearing a tight-fitting charcoal-coloured dress that seemed to be moulded to her toned but curvy frame with patent, red, killer heels that I would never be able to walk in. It looked as if her shimmering, highlighted hair had been professionally blow-dried and her teeth professionally whitened. I self-consciously rearranged the New Look blouse I'd owned for years, kicking myself for not making more of an effort this morning. I'd been exhausted after my flight so had gone to bed as soon as I'd got back to my cold and quiet flat last night, and I'd also accidently turned off my early alarm meaning I had overslept. Waking with a start and with no chance to iron anything, I'd hurriedly applied some make-up and pinned my greasy hair back after dousing it in dry shampoo so that I'd be in the office on time. God damn you, jet lag.

'So, wait, what are you doing back? Is everything OK?' Ben's smile turned into a worried frown.

'Yeah fine, I just decided to come back a little earlier,' I said wafting my hand in the air. 'Can I get anyone a cup of tea?' I offered, not knowing where to start and why I felt so uncomfortable. 'You know, I couldn't drink another glass of chai tea if you paid me.' I laughed lightly and awkwardly.

'All sorted, thanks.' Ben nodded at the cups of coffee Serena had brought in with her.

'OK, just tea for one then,' I mumbled to myself, plodding to the kitchen and plopping a teabag in the new sparkling mugs hanging neatly from the rack. The old, mismatched mugs had been replaced with colour-coded ones bearing our logo. Not a scummy stain to be seen.

'Nice mugs!' I said, in a weird sing-song voice.

Kelli flicked her head up for a millisecond. 'Yeah. Serena sorted that.'

I nodded, even though she wasn't looking at me. Was this how cats felt when someone pissed on their territory? I wondered about accidently dropping a mug to the floor but decided against it. I had other much bigger things I needed to sort out…and come clean to Ben about.

'So, are you free for a quick catch-up meeting today?' I asked Ben, who was deeply engrossed in his laptop.

He sighed and ran his hands through his hair; he'd had it cut since I'd been away. It suited him. ''Fraid not. I wasn't expecting you so I've got a jam-packed day. Maybe tomorrow?'

I felt this weird, disappointed sinking in my stomach. Of course he had to work; he hadn't known I would be back. I'd just foolishly thought he might have dropped everything he was doing to go for lunch, or even a quick coffee, so I could fill him in. I thought he might have missed me.

I nodded. 'Yeah, fine. What have you got planned?' I asked lightly.

Ben was already putting his coat on. 'I've got a dentist appointment.' He groaned, making Serena let out this girlish giggle that made me bristle.

'Hey, I take no blame for all those cakes you've been eating,' Serena teased; they looked lost in some private joke then caught my blank expression. 'You should have seen him with the red velvet cakes I made the other day, like a kid in a candy shop.'

'No, it was those little white ones with the thick frosting; they were unbelievable,' Kelli piped up and practically licked her lips.

'So, you bake?' I asked Serena.

'Georgia, you will not believe the things Serena makes. I swear I've put on, like, a stone since she started.' Ben patted his still trim stomach.

'Oh shush, you look great,' Serena said touching his arm, leaving her slender hand on his biceps for longer than normal. I gritted my teeth at the sight of it.

Ben shook his head in mirth then turned to face me. 'We need to watch out. She'll be leaving us to join the *Great British Bake Off* soon.' He laughed.

Yeah, I bet she'd love to show off her buns to the nation.

Serena fake blushed and patted her flawless cheeks. 'Oh stop it!'

I burped down vom. I couldn't even bake fairy cakes. What was it they said about the way to a man's heart? Well she seemed to have this worked out.

'What else are you up to?' I asked, hoping to turn the conversation away from this cringe fest.

'Oh yeah, sorry. After that I've got a networking lunch over at Media City. I'll be a while; you know how long these things can take. But let's get some time together tomorrow?' He smiled briefly.

'Sure, well good luck,' I said.

'Break a leg, or should that be tooth?' Serena called out, as Ben walked out the door, laughing at her crap joke.

'So, how was India?' Serena breathed, pulling me back from gazing behind Ben and his peachy bum. God, I'd missed that.

'Erm yeah. It was great.' I plastered on a fake smile.

'Excellent. Well I've got so much to update you on. Ben and I have been working really hard on the Travel Trade Convention.'

'Oh, fab,' I mustered.

I wanted to rush off to the kitchen and whip up a batch of cookies or something to prove that whatever she could do I could do better, but instead I listened to perky Serena chat away about exhibition space and merchandise. Of course Ben wanted Serena here rather than me. Who wouldn't want to stare at her blemish-free skin, perfectly applied eyeliner and toned upper arms. In my charity-shop suit that bagged around my knees and with my sun-scorched hair that didn't want to obey orders to stay flat, I felt like a bloody leper next to her.

'What do you think?' She turned to face me expectantly with her French manicured hands on her hips.

'Yeah, yeah. Sounds great,' I mumbled, acting like I'd been paying attention. 'You know, I'm just going to try and make a start on all these emails waiting for me.'

I sidestepped over to what used to be my desk. Before it had got Serena'd.

'Did Ben not tell you? After he spoke to you when you were away he passed your emails over to me to deal with. I implemented this new sys –'

'– system.' I finished her sentence and nodded. Of course she had.

'Yep.' She blushed faintly. God I bet she was the type of woman who knew how to contour her make-up, made a fresh green juice every morning and exercised just for fun. 'I hope you don't mind but I've suggested a few changes to help with the efficiency levels in here.' She must have caught my scowl as she quickly added, 'Just to improve things a little.'

I nodded.

'Sorry, is this too weird?' She tilted her head, a look of mock concern on her doll-like face.

'No. No, it's fine.' I smiled tightly. 'So, my emails then…'

'Yes! OK, so I've replied to the most important ones, checking with Ben first of course. The rest I have sorted into folders for you to work through.' She pointed to my computer, clicking on the mouse that had been dunked in diamantés since I'd left. A bright screen popped up; there were all my emails but they had been sorted into colour-coded files in order of urgency. Fuck, it looked good.

'If you have any problems just let me know. I'm sure Ben won't mind if I use his desk whilst he is out today.' She smiled and sat on Ben's chair. 'So, I'll be right here if you need me.'

'Right, thanks.'

I slunked onto my seat but the height was all wrong. I leant under my desk to alter it, quickly wiping the tears from my eyes and taking a deep breath without her or Kelli seeing. Annoyingly her system was super-efficient with everything neatly filed and recorded, and she'd signed off my emails as *Serena DeVere, On Behalf of Miss Georgia Green,* replying to clients in a very professional manner. I did think it was strange that I didn't have any personal emails in my inbox. I clicked on my junk folder and saw a couple of messages from my parents that had been flagged up to go in there.

'Erm, Serena?' I asked.

She bobbed her head up. 'Yes?'

I cleared my throat. 'I just wondered where you put any personal emails, as I've found a few in junk but wondered if there were any more?'

A flush coloured her cheeks. 'Oh, sorry, Georgia. I really don't know. Anything that looked like spam I put in there or in the trash.'

I went to look in the trash section.

'But I clear that out at the end of every day, sorry.'

I smiled tightly. 'Not to worry. I'm sure they'll be back in touch if they were that important.'

I was seething inside, but not wanting to make a scene in front of Kelli, I just took a deep breath and carried on reading through my messages, trying to catch up. My head spun, after just twenty-four hours since India I felt like I'd been pushed out of a gang I'd created.

It was only four p.m. but I'd had enough. Ben hadn't come back that afternoon; he'd called Serena's phone as she played with her hair and giggled at something he'd said to her and told us that he would see us tomorrow morning instead. I couldn't concentrate any more on watching my bright screen that played an irritating jingle every time a message dinged in my inbox, most of them addressed to Serena.

I stood up and pulled my coat on. 'I'm going to head off.' I felt like I needed to make up some excuse before leaving. Kelli had left an hour before, having arranged it with Serena yesterday.

'Oh OK. I've got a set of keys so will lock up,' Serena said sweetly as she looked up from her screen. Course she bloody did. I hoped to God that Ben had vetted her before leaving her in such a position of power. 'So, I'll see you tomorrow bright and early! Have a great night,' Serena chirped.

I mumbled goodbye and sloped off out into the high street, feeling like an alien in the place I'd once called home. I took my time wandering through the streets of Manchester, looking in shop windows and feeling utterly dejected. I didn't really want to head back to my cold and lonely flat where all that lay waiting for me was unpacking, washing and an empty fridge, but I couldn't stand being at work any longer either.

I decided to try and see my friends but Shelley had already messaged me that she was going away with Jimmy on a spur-of-the-moment couples trip. I thought about calling Marie to finally put our fight in the past and see if she wanted to crack open a bottle of wine with me. But I hadn't heard a peep out of her since our fight and stubbornly I couldn't be the one to back down first. I called my parents and thankfully my dad answered the phone immediately, perking me up, as he sounded thrilled to hear from me. I trudged to the train station to head over to their house where the promise of a cooked meal and some family love would be the perfect way to end a shitty day.

CHAPTER 32

Retrocede (v.) To go back; recede; retire

'Shall I open the fizz, Len?' my mum called out from the kitchen where smells of corned beef and mashed potato wafted into the cosy lounge. 'We are celebrating after all!'

'Fizz? You don't have to go to this trouble just for me being back.' I laughed.

'Yeah that would be great, Sheila,' my dad called back then turned to me, patting the seat cushion next to him. 'Oh sorry, Georgie, it's…erm…it's not just because of you being back. We've actually got some news to share with you.' He blushed and fiddled with the remote control. 'It's only the cheap stuff, cava I think. You know I prefer my bitter but your mum got carried away; you know how she is. I'll let her tell you.' He tapped the side of his nose. 'Don't want to spoil the surprise.'

'You haven't told her, have you?' My mum blustered in holding a tray with three champagne flutes filled to the brim.

'Tell me what?' I looked at her quizzically and carefully took a glass.

My mum beamed and beckoned for my dad to stand up next to her. 'Well, as well as celebrating you being back in one piece –' she looked up to the heavens as if saying a prayer that I'd survived India '– we also wanted to let you know about something very exciting.'

She could hardly contain herself, her tiny size four feet tapping the carpet excitedly. 'You tell her.' She nodded to my dad. 'No, wait I will! OK, so, me and your dad have decided that we're going to sell the house.'

She paused dramatically scrutinising my face for a reaction.

The sweet bubbles caught at the back of my throat. 'No! I mean, you can't! This is your family home, my childhood home. You can't sell! What about all the memories, the stories in each room? Wait, why are you selling?' This wasn't something to celebrate; this was the end of an era!

'Georgia Louise Green.' My mum chastised me and huffed.

'Sorry. I'm just in shock. I never thought you guys would sell this place,' I apologised, still letting the news sink in. I couldn't face any more change today.

'Well, after what happened last year, both with my accident and you and the wedding, then seeing you go off travelling, having the courage to follow your heart to return and open your own successful business, well…we've been talking about having our own fun too,' my dad explained, putting his untouched flute of fizz on the cluttered mantelpiece.

'Are you in money trouble?' I asked quietly.

My dad laughed. 'No, we've just realised that we aren't getting any younger and this place was paid off years ago, so it's time to spend some of our savings on us. All three of us. Now you're living in Manchester, and who knows where your business will take you; you could expand to London, Paris, New York…' He chortled. 'Well we want to have the freedom to come and see you wherever you go.'

'But why not take a holiday? I've got some great trips for older people,' I offered as my dad ruffled my hair.

'We might. But first we want to sell this place, buy something smaller and more manageable, maybe in the city centre, that we could rent out if we did want to go away from home for longer.'

I guessed it made sense. Since my dad had retired and my mum had cut down her hours as a dinner lady, they were free to do as they liked. Still, it was going to sting to think of new people living here, redecorating and putting their mark on the place that all three of us had built together. I had thought they would live here for ever. I had imagined bringing my children here and showing them the height chart my dad had etched on the wall in my bedroom when I was a child. But children were so far from where I was right now that it would be mad to expect them to wait, holding on for something that may never happen.

'God, sorry, well congratulations. It's just a shock I guess.' I raised my glass half-heartedly, realising it was almost empty.

'Thanks, love; it's a good thing. We get to be closer to you for one.' My dad smiled.

'We've seen some lovely two-bed flats not far from you,' my mum chipped in, pulling out the iPad they'd bought before I went travelling last year just to be able to Skype me. She was quickly pulling up Rightmove and clicking onto her list of saved properties to show me. They looked so happy and excited; it was like being squidged in the middle of two newlyweds planning on buying their first pad together.

'I'll carry on with dinner if you want to have a look.' She thrust the iPad at me and topped up my glass. 'You look like you could do with a proper meal.'

With my mum in the kitchen humming to herself and my dad popping open a can of bitter and swiping his thick finger over the tablet screen, pointing out the square metres and value they could add, I suddenly wanted to cry.

'You all right, pet? Sorry if we've just landed this on you.' He gently squeezed my arm and moved the iPad away.

'No, no, it's not that.' I wiped my eyes. 'I'm happy for you. You deserve to be happy. It's just that out of the three of us, you two are the only Greens with everything mapped out.'

My dad sat back and tilted his head. 'What do you mean? Everything going OK at work?'

I sniffed. 'Yeah, busy as always. It's just, coming back from India, everything feels different – weird somehow. Like I'm chasing my tail and that real life is on hold. I only moved into Marie's flat as a short-term thing, but now five months on I'm still there with no plans of moving out. I never see you, or my friends, Ben has fallen in love with Serena and I don't have a speck of a social life, let alone a love life.' He shifted in his seat uncomfortably. 'Sorry, Dad, I don't mean to bring you down – not today.'

'Hey, you never bring me down. I've noticed you've not seemed yourself the last few times we've seen each other, but I always thought you liked being super busy. However, if it's making you unhappy then you need to change something.'

'I am happy. I can't believe how successful the business is. I mean for such a new business, we should be living hand-to-mouth, but for some reason people love what we offer. I guess I'm just trying to keep up with demand, making sure everyone goes away happy.'

'Including the boss,' he said nodding his head slowly.

'Yeah, including her.'

'Well, you know, Georgia, in times like this you need to be brave. Even if you're not, just pretend to be. I promise you that no one will know the difference. Listen, why don't you stay over tonight? I'm sure your mum can lend you some pyjamas and I'll drive you in to work tomorrow morning,' he suggested softly.

I nodded. 'That sounds perfect.'

After stuffing myself at dinner and watching some naff film that had my dad snoring in his armchair the moment the opening credits started, I did feel a little better. I padded up to my childhood room and slumped onto my single bed, still with its pale pink duvet and Robbie the sheep teddy that I used to sleep with every night in homage to Robbie Williams. I wiped off my make-up, put on the PJs that my mum had given me and tucked my legs under myself, trying to drown out my parents' concerned voices just behind my closed door.

'I didn't think she'd be this upset about it,' my mum said.

'Well, no one likes change.'

'Still, she is nearly thirty years old. It's not right she's this bothered by it all.'

I shoved my pillow over my ears and tried to drown out their worried tones. Everything was changing and I couldn't do a thing to stop it.

I slept better than I had in ages, and then woke to the smell of coffee and bacon that gently eased me out of my pit. It took a moment or two to work out where I was when I opened a bleary eye to be met with Take That and Boyzone grinning down at me. I remembered I'd stayed at my parents' house last night, *probably for the last time ever*. The thought swirled in my mind. I couldn't find my clothes that I'd left crumpled next to my bed last night so padded downstairs in my mum's dressing gown that she'd left in the bathroom.

'Morning, pet!' My dad grinned. He was wearing an apron with a naked woman on it and pouring milk into two mugs of steaming coffee. 'How did you sleep?'

I yawned and pecked him on the cheek. 'Great thanks, you?'

'I think that bitter knocked me out; I slept like a log. Anyway, I knew you'd be an early riser so I've made breakfast. Your mum's just in the lounge ironing your clothes and I've checked the traffic so we can leave in thirty minutes. Here, take this.' He passed a full plate of buttered, thick, white toast and rashers of crispy bacon to me. I suddenly felt choked up. When was the last time I'd been cooked breakfast – no actually, when was the last time I'd eaten breakfast?

'Wow. Thanks, Dad; you didn't need to go to all this trouble.'

'No trouble for you, Georgia. Right, go and make a start on that and tell your mum hers is on its way.'

I walked out of the kitchen into the lounge where my mum was hunched over the ironing board, half watching morning television. It made my heart swell in a way that being looked after by your parents and home comforts can do. She'd washed and ironed the clothes I was wearing yesterday, and they smelt so fresh and clean. She'd even left out her make-up bag that I could rummage in – luckily this time less gothic rocker and more M&S neutrals. I wolfed down my breakfast and got ready. With my stomach full and a face of war paint, I was ready to start taking back control – Louise style.

CHAPTER 33

Paroxysm (n.) A sudden violent emotion or action; outburst

'Morning!' Serena said in a sing-song voice as I walked into the office.

I was used to rushing down the street to get to my desk but today for some reason each step was taken in trepidation, even with the pep talk I'd given myself in my dad's car that I could do this.

'Morning.'

'I'll pop the kettle on, shall I? You look like you could do with a strong coffee.'

'Thanks,' I said, trying to bite my tongue at the way she'd looked me up and down before she'd made that offer. Ben was already at his desk and on the phone so I waved brightly. 'Is Kelli not here?'

'No, not yet. I gave her the morning off,' Serena said, busying with the kettle.

I nodded and tried to hide the bristling feeling inside. 'Great, well I'll just get started then.' I looked at my desk, too nervous to touch it in case I messed up the pristine order of things on there.

'Morning, Georgia. I thought maybe you could use Kelli's desk,' Ben said ending his call.

I swung my head to face him. 'Oh.'

'Just for this morning,' he hurriedly added. 'Just to give Serena time to get her things sorted and moved across. Then we'll need to sort out somewhere for her to sit permanently.'

'Yeah, fine.' I smiled tightly and went to sit further down the office at Kelli's messy wooden desk next to the fireplace. The room would be way too cramped if we tried to shoehorn another desk in. I couldn't face having Kelli sitting cross-legged on the floor but I didn't know where else she could possibly go.

Luckily the morning passed quickly. We'd had a slow but steady stream of customers coming in. I'd decided to focus on working through my emails, paperwork and other dull admin whilst Ben and Serena took centre stage. It pained me to admit it, but Serena did have a good bedside manner, subtly pushing a box of tissues near the tearful ones before making them a cup of tea, and buoying up the more nervous ones with an infectious excitement. I'd tried to get Ben alone, without bloody Serena sticking her neat nose in, so I could tell him about India but just hadn't had the chance. Strangely, he hadn't asked me a thing about what I'd been up to over there. It was as if he thought I'd been on some relaxing holiday or something.

Just after midday Kelli arrived in a frenzied whirlwind, clutching a pair of tickets in her small hands. 'I got them! I got them!'

Serena did a little jump. 'No way! You didn't?' Kelli nodded. 'Oh my God, excellent!'

Kelli beamed at her. 'Couldn't get the front row but near enough. I can't believe it! I never thought I'd get to see Battlestar Death Wing live!'

'Who?' I asked, my nerves frayed from seeing Serena so bubbly.

Kelli rolled her heavy kohl-lined eyes. 'God, Georgia, Battlestar Death Wing. They're like *the* band of the nineties.'

'Oh, right. Them.' I spotted Ben trying to contain a small laugh as if he didn't have a bloody clue what they were on about either.

'You don't remember them?' Serena asked, finally stopping dancing around with Kelli. I shook my head. 'I had ALL their hits. Was a bit of an emo in my youth,' she whispered loudly behind her hands.

'So, you're going together?' I asked.

'Yeah, we were chatting one day about music and it was Serena who found out they were making a special one-off comeback gig. Here in Manchester!' Kelli told me looking at Serena adoringly. 'Thanks so much for giving me the morning off to queue for them.'

'Oh, no. Thank *you* for getting them. I'll sort the money out later, OK?' Serena blushed and swatted Kelli's compliment away.

Ben just shrugged and smiled to himself. I turned back to my screen feeling very left out, very uncool and very irritated.

'I was going to grab us some sushi for lunch. I know you said you liked it, but I didn't want to be late,' Kelli said to Serena.

'Ah that's so sweet. But don't worry as I've made some healthy curry, in honour of Georgia coming back,' Serena jumped up. 'I've got enough for everyone, though I forgot to bring some rice,' she apologised. Probably the batch she'd handmade didn't puff up to the preferred height, I thought grumpily.

'Is it lunchtime already?' Ben glanced at his phone.

'Yeah, doesn't time fly when you're having fun!' Serena giggled. 'So, is curry OK for you, Ben? I remember you saying you liked it spicy so I've made you a separate hotter version.' Oh God, she was like some robotic Stepford wife.

Ben's eyes lit up. 'Ace. Could get used to this; beats a soggy sarnie any day.' He laughed. 'I need to head to the bank anyway, so how about I buy us some rice that we can chuck in the microwave. You want anything, Georgia?' Ben asked as an afterthought as he got up to leave.

'Oh, I'll come with you. Think I'll just stick with a Boots meal deal,' I said.

Serena looked dejected that I wasn't as excited about her curry as the rest of the office.

'Sorry, Serena, it's just that I've had enough curry to last me the rest of the year, thanks.'

'Oh, OK. Well some other time,' Serena said sadly.

I knew I was being a bitch throwing my toys out of the pram, but I was glad to finally get Ben to myself for a moment. I grabbed my jacket as the phone rang, and with Serena heating up her curry, I called over to Kelli to pick it up and take a message.

'You know you might be curried out but she has gone to a lot of effort to make lunch for everyone, in your honour,' Ben whispered nodding his head over to the small kitchen.

'I just really fancy an egg mayo sandwich,' I muttered.

'No one ever fancies an egg mayo sandwich,' Ben said, raising an eyebrow. 'I know it might feel weird for you coming back with her being here but trust me, she is a real asset.'

'A real ass more like,' I whispered more loudly than I'd planned as Ben gave me a look. 'Sorry. I just think it's going to take a bit of time to get used to her perky ways. We hardly know her, you know?'

Ben sighed. 'You don't trust her?'

I was spared from replying when Kelli called out. 'Georgia! Wait!'

She hurriedly put the phone down, a strange look on her pale face. 'That was a journalist.' I stared at her patiently, feeling my stomach grumbling. 'He works for the *Daily Times* and is running an exposure on us.'

'Do you mean exposé?' Ben asked, stepping back into the shop. 'What did he say, Kelli? Exactly.' He was biting his bottom lip and had his arms crossed.

Kelli rolled her eyes to the sky and started tapping her chin trying to remember this information as if we'd just asked her what she'd eaten for dinner two weeks ago. 'He said, he wanted to let us know that an article would be published in a few days, out of curtsy.'

'Courtesy,' Ben interrupted, for once looking irritated at how long she was taking to spit out a phone message.

'Yep that.' She pointed her finger at him.

'An exposé?' Ben repeated shaking his head. 'Why would the *Daily Times* be running an exposé on us?'

'Erm, he said he went on the Indian tour and is writing a piece about our business. About our unusual methods of management or something.'

My stomach lurched. 'Kelli, did he say what his name was?' I asked slowly, feeling the ground rise up to meet me.

She nodded and looked down at her hand where she'd scrawled the details. 'Erm, yep. Kennings, Christopher Kennings.' She glanced up at us.

Ben spun his head to face me, waiting for a reaction.

'Fuck.'

'What do you mean fuck?' His tone of voice and the smell of Serena's curry wafting through the already crowded room was making me feel sick. 'Everything went OK on the tour, didn't it? Didn't it, Georgia?'

I gave a nod that was half a shake and half a shrug.

'Georgia?'

Damn! I'd been planning on telling him what had happened when we went to the shops, finally getting him on his own, so I could explain properly.

'I've found him!' Kelli shouted from Ben's laptop. She'd immediately started cyber stalking Christopher Kennings. I ignored Ben's scowl and raced up to his screen that Kelli was jabbing her finger at. 'Was this dude on your tour?' she asked me. 'Wait…I remember this guy. He was a weirdo who came in here aaaaaages ago asking about the finances; do you remember, Georgia?'

Chris's smirking face filled the screen; Kelli started reading out loud from the text under his large, grey face, oblivious to my aghast expression. 'Says here, he's a renowned and scathing – whatever that means – investigative journalist in the world of business.'

Chris was a journalist. No wonder it was him who'd found out about my real identity and had wanted to stir things up with the group, why he'd never really opened up or got involved, and had always been writing stuff down in that notepad of his, or snapping away with his camera. Not for some travel journal or holiday memory book at all.

'Whoa.' Kelli stopped.

'What?' Ben demanded, flicking his narrowed eyes between me and the laptop. Serena had heard the commotion and tottered over to Ben's desk that we were all huddled around, still wearing a pink frilly apron that she must have brought in from home.

'Everything OK?' she asked nervously.

No one answered her.

'You remember that bread business, Grains and Barley? The one that went bankrupt because of some undercover report of their dodgy management style or something?' We nodded. 'Well our Mr Kennings here was the guy who wrote it.'

I was going to be sick.

'Georgia.' Ben turned to me, a heavy darkness clouding his features. 'What happened with this Chris guy on the tour?'

The steely look Ben was giving me gnawed at my insides. 'I, erm, he…' I trailed off feeling a strange heat pulsate through my body. 'OK, I'm sure it's not as bad as it seems.' I let out a high-pitched, fake laugh. No one else did. 'Ben, can I have a word with you? Alone.' I jabbed my head to the front door.

He clenched his jaw before nodding curtly. I grabbed my handbag and my jacket and shuffled after him, ignoring Serena's wounded look that she wasn't privy to what I was about to tell him, and hearing Kelli grumble that she never got to hear the juicy stuff.

Once outside I began to stride over to the café opposite before Ben grabbed my arm. 'Will you just tell me what's gone on?'

'I screwed up, OK? I screwed up,' I replied, my arms outstretched almost knocking over a passing pensioner, who tutted loudly. 'Please, let me just get us a drink and I can explain.'

'Explain what? You tell me you're going to India to fix some dodgy reviews and now we're going to be bent over and fucked royally by some big-shot journalist doing some exposé on the business?' he half shouted. The old woman I'd nearly whacked had stopped tutting and was now staring at us, as if watching some live episode of *Coronation Street*. 'Why would they be running a piece on us? What went on?' I could see the anger and confusion swell in his chest.

I was desperate to lead him off the street and into the calm of the coffee shop. Over a mug of cappuccino we could talk about this like adults, not have some slanging match in the middle of town. My eyes were already on the brink of tearing up. I took a deep breath and glared at the old woman to bugger off, but she ignored me.

'I went to see what was going on with all these bad reviews and find Nihal to work out what was happening.' Ben nodded along, already knowing this part. 'He was in such a state after splitting up with his ex, Ameera, that I had to step in from time to time to keep the fun atmosphere going. It was going well. We eventually found Ameera, who was running her own tour group. We were in this silly Bollywood film and it got Nihal and Ameera back together, and our two groups became one.' I paused.

'Okaaaaaay.' He sighed loudly. 'But what's that got to do with this journalist?'

I winced. This second part would be harder to hear. Old grandma had the cheek to start sucking on a Werther's Original, popping the golden sweet into her wrinkled mouth without taking her eyes off us. The rustle of her shiny wrapper set my teeth on edge.

'Well, Chris was on the tour but he was really strange, always separate from the rest of the group.' Ben's eyes grew wider but he stayed mute, waiting for me to continue. I could have kicked myself that I hadn't listened to my suspicions that things weren't right with Chris. 'Anyway, the tour group started to open up to each other, sharing their secrets and so on. They trusted me and confided in me and everything was going well until…until Chris found this clip of us.' I motioned my hand to Ben. 'The one filmed in the office.'

'So he knew you weren't Louise the hairdresser…' Ben said slowly, following along.

'Yep. The rest of the tour group were so angry with me for deceiving them.'

'Shit, Georgia.' He slapped his hand to his head. Old grandma sucked louder. 'Anything else I should be aware of?'

I scuffed my shoes against the ground not able to look at Ben in the eye. 'I may have farted on him during a yoga class…'

Ben stared at me aghast. Well there goes that womanly allure – nice one, Georgia, nice one.

'I know! But I thought I'd cleared the air. I swam in the sea to apologise to them all.' Ben looked confused; saying it out loud it didn't sound like much of an achievement. 'I left the next day feeling like they understood why I'd not been completely honest with them from the beginning.'

'But apparently not Chris,' Ben said, rubbing his face and letting it all sink in.

'Apparently not.' I wiped the tears from my eyes and swallowed this Kinder-egg sized bubble of emotion clogging my throat. 'Ben, I'm really sorry. I thought I'd fixed this. That it was just a silly mix-up.'

'A silly mix-up?!' His eyes grew wider. 'Georgia, we've got a national journalist crawling all over us probably going to write about how we lie to our customers, how we trick them into sharing their inner secrets just to improve our profits. Do you know how much damage a piece like this can do to a new business?'

I half nodded, half shrugged. 'I'm sorry. I was only trying to help.' My voice sounded distorted and childlike.

He let out a deep breath and looked heavenwards, taking a long pause. 'I think it would be better if you took the rest of the week off.'

'What?'

'I think it's best if you took some time away from Lonely Hearts Travels. From me. And I'll sort this out the best that I can.' His eyes were cold; his voice was flat. He looked exhausted.

'Ben, please. I really didn't mean to mess this up. I thought I was doing what was best.'

He nodded. 'I know. Listen, I'd better get back and try and figure out a way to put a positive spin on this. I'll see you on Monday.'

With a sad smile he left me and walked back into our shop. My legs became leaden as I watched him go, convinced I could see Kelli pressed up against the window watching us. Old grandma rolled her glassy eyes and shook her head, dropping her sweet wrappers on the pavement as she shuffled off.

I stumbled down the street, rubbing my face, letting this day sink in. Chris was Chris Kennings, capable of bringing our business to its knees, all because of what I'd done. My heart urged me to race back into the shop, to show Ben that I was capable of sorting my own mess out and to call Chris demanding he retract his article. But my head told me to leave him to cool down, that if I went all guns blazing with a national journalist I could end up doing more damage than good. It was probably a good thing that I hadn't saved Chris's number onto my phone so I couldn't call him, not in the state I was in.

I remembered reading the bread exposé; the papers had gone mad for it, calling it a real bun fight. Back then I'd agreed with many others, that it was a good thing that such a shambolic business had got their comeuppance. Now it was happening to my baby I'd never felt so sympathetic to another person's cause. If the business went bust because of my mistakes I wouldn't just be unemployed having lost a load of cash, I'd also lose Ben. That was much, much worse.

Idle chit-chat, kids blaring rap songs from their mobile phones and trams honking their horns all washed over me, numbing how utterly low I felt. I knew who I needed to speak to. Who would give me solid advice about what I was meant to do now. My best friend. I pulled out my phone and tried calling Marie. This stupid fight had gone on long enough; I needed to grow up and apologise to her. But her phone just clicked onto voicemail. I left a garbled message asking her to call me back, saying that we needed to talk. God, I'd missed her voice. I couldn't bear the thought of telling my parents what was going on and Shelley wasn't back from wherever she'd gone with Jimmy.

I found myself in Tesco and, in a daze, stumbled my way round the packed store full of workers on their lunch breaks. I picked up a bottle of white wine, Marie's favourite, and a huge bag of Monster Munch and decided that I was going to go and see her. If we were going to sort this tiff, then we were going to do it properly.

I walked out of the store and tried to give her another ring but as I had my face glued to my phone screen and my arms full of snacks I didn't see the man walking directly in front of me stop suddenly. I caught his heel with my foot and tripped into him narrowly avoiding dropping the bottle of Sauv Blanc down his camel-coloured, wool coat.

'Ow,' he seethed and turned to face me.

'Watch it!' I replied before breaking into a strange smile. 'Rahul?'

'Louise!'

'What the…? What are you doing here?' I asked with my mouth wide open at the shock of seeing his handsome, chiselled face again. What was it with us two always bumping into each other?

'I've got the go-ahead for a new TV show so I had to rush back to sort the planning for it. Going to be headed to the dizzy heights of Rotherham to film it.' He laughed, revealing those perfect white teeth that lit up his tanned face. 'Hey, I'm glad I saw you, actually as I could do with a quick trim.'

I gawped at him like a true idiot.

'You know, a haircut?'

'Oh. Right. Yep.' I rolled my eyes at how slow I was, remembering what I supposedly did as a career. Then, all of a sudden, I was hit with a wave of wobbly emotion. I had my dream career, but probably not for much longer.

'You OK? You don't have to cut it if you don't want to,' he said, as I began bawling my eyes out, gripping my phone, a bottle of rapidly warming wine and a crushed family-sized bag of crisps under my sweaty armpit in the middle of the busy street.

'It's not that…it's just…' I couldn't find my breath to get my words out.

'Here, pass me those, will you?' He took my shopping off me and gingerly led me to a nearby graffiti-covered bench. I slumped down gratefully next to *Dave Luvs Shaz 4evs* and took some deep breaths.

'Thank you. I…I'm not Louise. And I'm not a hairdresser.' He nodded along slowly, not showing an ounce of shock at what I was saying, but probably recoiling at the glistening snot I could feel on the tip of my wet nose.

'Here.' He passed me a tissue and gently rubbed my upper arm as I honked into it loudly. 'I was right all along, wasn't I? Georgia.'

I nodded and scrunched up the tissue into my pocket.

'I'm sorry I couldn't tell you who I was; I had to keep it a secret from the other guests. I am, or should I say was, the co-owner of the tour company, you see.'

Rahul frowned, knitting his heavy dark brows together. 'Was?'

Taking a slow and long deep breath I nodded. 'Because of being in India, my real identity has been discovered, and now we have the press running a story about how I lied to my customers. A story that is going to ruin us.'

'Ah.' He rubbed at his temples; he seemed genuinely concerned. 'I now understand the bottle of wine. But listen, from the little I know about you, you seem to have this resilient streak.'

'Is this what Lord Shiva would say?' I teased wanting some light relief as well as hoping that I could get the Indian gods on board to help my plight.

'I reckon he would say that you have to trust your instincts. You obviously have this fire in your belly to have created your own business in the first place. Now you just need to make sure that no one is going to put it out.'

I frowned, thinking about what he was saying. 'It feels like that flame has dimmed to a pathetic tea light right now.'

Rahul threw his head back and laughed. 'But it is still burning.' I nodded slowly, actually feeling slightly better and – pardon the pun – fired up. Oh God, if Flic were here now she'd be in her element hearing these hippy-dippy words of wisdom, but somehow coming from him, out of his admittedly kissable mouth, it didn't seem that cheesy.

'If there's anything I can do to help then let me know, but it sounds like you just need to prepare yourself for one hell of a battle and trust that you're going to succeed.' He glanced at his expensive-looking silver watch peeking under his sleeve. 'I'm so sorry but I need to be making a move.' He winced. 'It was honestly so great bumping into you again, although we have to stop meeting like that!'

I sniffed and pulled myself together, preparing to head off as well. 'Thank you, Rahul. It was great to see you too. Good luck with your show and cross your fingers for me.'

He stood up and shook his head. 'You won't need any luck. You can do this, Georgia.'

I caught the bus from town and walked up to the small terraced house that Marie and Mike were renting. Clutching the bottle of wine I rang the doorbell. A few seconds later Mike opened the door, his hair tufted, and a harassed expression on his usually chilled-out face.

'Oh, hi.' He seemed as surprised to see me as I was to see him.

'Hi, Mike, you not at work?'

'No, erm, got the afternoon off so I can pick up Cole.' He stared down at the bottle of wine, still not inviting me in. This wasn't like the Mike I knew.

'Oh right. Is everything OK? I just thought I'd pop in to see Marie as I've not heard from her in a while.' I looked down at the tufts of grass poking their heads through the cracks in the paving slabs. 'I wanted to offer a white flag, an olive branch after, well, you know.'

He nodded and pressed his arm to the door. 'Yeah. It's not like you two to go so long without speaking.'

'So is she in?'

He glanced behind him into the hall. 'Erm, the thing is, Marie's not feeling so great. That's why I'm back early.' He nodded to the bottle of wine. I knew I should have got flowers. 'She won't be up for drinking that with you – isn't it a bit early for wine o'clock anyway?'

I flushed. 'Yeah, I guess. I've just had a really shitty morning at work.'

He nodded as if he understood. 'Right, well…'

'So can I just come in and say hello? I won't stay long.' God, this was really awkward. Marie never got sick and when she did she hated playing the invalid card. It was unlike her to get Mike running around doing errands. Usually I had to physically plonk her in bed and threaten her not to move as I prepared vats of Lemsip and *Gavin & Stacey* box sets as a distraction.

He scrunched up his nose. 'I don't think so, Georgia. Maybe in a few days when she's feeling up to company. Sorry.' He stared at me for a few moments and then shrugged sadly before going to close the door.

'Oh, right, well…'

'I'll let her know you stopped by. I'd really better be off; can't be late for Cole. You know what those nursery Nazis are like with timings.'

I nodded. No, I didn't bloody know. 'OK, thanks.' I smiled weakly and clomped back up the overgrown path as Mike retreated into his house. Weird.

CHAPTER 34

Valour (n.) Boldness or determination in facing great danger, especially in battle

I was waiting at the bus stop to head home, resigning myself to a solo drinking sesh when my mobile chirruped to life. Marie! I struggled to pull it out of my handbag, accidentally flattening the mega pack of Monster Munch when I saw Kelli's name on the screen.

I pressed the green button. 'Hello?'

'Georgia!' Kelli said breathlessly, as if she was cupping her mouth right up to the mouthpiece. 'You have to come back.'

'What? Kelli? Are you OK?' I felt a strange prickly feeling crawl up my neck.

'No, I…Ben…'

'Kelli, I can't hear you very well. The signal's shit.' I peered at the pathetic bars on my phone going up and down, realising that my battery was running dangerously low too. 'What's going on?'

'Georg… Come back…'

'Kelli! I can't hear you. Can you call me off the landline?' I shouted.

'No…' It was like she was under water. 'Serena…Ben… Lies…'

'Kelli. Kelli. Are you there?' The phone cut off. I tried to call her back but instantly got her moody voicemail.

What was she talking about? I hailed down a taxi and jumped in, giving the driver the directions back to our shop.

The journey through town took ages. The school kids had just left for the day and the roads were blocked with harassed parents on their way to pick up their little darlings. My phone had officially died. I'd tried taking my phone battery out, shaking it, blowing it and putting it back in but it was useless. The many variations of what I'd heard Kelli say raced through my mind as I fiddled with the stupid telephone.

'You want me to take the Mancunian way, love?' the driver asked, rolling his eyes at the queue of stationary cars in front of us.

'Erm, yeah, whatever you think's best,' I said distractedly. What had Kelli meant and why hadn't Ben been the one to call me?

'Well, you see at this time of day you get the kids from Saint Mary's down by the estate but if we try and cut through Elderware Street then we may miss the school buses from Green Oaks; however, it's never a guarantee, not since they've built that Tesco megastore down there.' He chattered away as if I was the least bit interested.

'Mmm. Fine by me.' *Just get me to the shop!* I wanted to scream but didn't. I didn't even have a phone to preoccupy myself with, just my messed-up thoughts.

'Why we need a supermarket that big is beyond me; you know it's three floors! Three floors filled with crap we don't need. It's like going to IKEA; my wife's always dragging me there. You walk about as if in some bloody TARDIS. You always get stressed, get lost and end up leaving without the thing you came in for in the first place. Madness if you ask me. I don't understand why people like to over-complicate things. What's wrong with the nice simple approach? That way you always know where you stand.'

We eventually pulled into a tight side street and I flung notes at him, leaving the now warm bottle of wine on the back seat and him chattering about the farce of this country's road networks, before racing to my shop. Flinging the door open I tried to catch my breath. Kelli stared up wide-eyed at me, looking like she was about to cry. Ben was slumped over his laptop, his phone pressed to his ear. Serena was nowhere to be seen.

'What's gone on? Are you OK?' I asked Kelli breathlessly, wiping the sweat off my forehead and dumping my bag at my desk.

'No,' she said quietly, pointing her finger to Ben. He held up his hand to tell me he'd be with me in a minute. Kelli scuttled off to the bathroom before I could ask her another question, leaving us alone.

'Great. OK. Well thanks for your help,' Ben said, angrily slamming his phone down and turning to face me, looking as if someone had died.

'What's happening?' Oh my God, had something happened to Trisha? I'd meant to go and see her but had been too preoccupied with things here since I'd been back. My heart was hammering against my chest before I remembered that Kelli had definitely mentioned Serena, Ben and lies on the dodgy phone line.

'Sit down,' Ben said, firmly. I kept my eyes on him as I sat upright on my chair.

'It's Trisha, isn't it? Is she OK? I thought she looked peaky the last time I saw her. It wasn't just a fall she had, was it?' Words rushed out of me as I gulped back the lump building in my throat.

Ben sighed. 'It's not about Trisha, although I have forgotten to tell you that she is back in hospital.'

'Oh God! Why?'

'She's fine; she's just gone back for some more tests on her ankle as it hasn't healed properly, but they've said it's nothing serious. They just want to keep her in to monitor it because of her age, that's all.'

I exhaled heavily, so relieved she was OK. 'So, what is it then?'

He cleared his throat. 'Serena's gone.'

'Gone where?' I jerked my head back.

'She's done a runner.'

'What? What do you mean?'

'You know I told you I was off to the bank?' I nodded. 'Well I asked Serena to go for me as I needed to concentrate on trying to get in touch with this Chris bloke.' I nodded, feeling a sharp pain in the pit of my stomach. Ben rubbed his face and let out a deep sigh. 'Well, she never came back.'

I stared at him trying to piece this together.

'You were right, Georgia – not to trust her. She's done a runner with the cash, never made it to the bank.'

'No!'

'Yep.' He nodded dejectedly.

'But we only keep a couple of hundred quid here.' I looked over at the opened safe. I was always so paranoid about being broken into that I made sure we did the bank run regularly so we didn't keep much cash on-site.

Ben shook his head. 'Before you came back we'd had this huge tour booking, about five thousand pounds. I'd been too busy to get it banked away.'

'What!' Most people paid by credit card or cheque. 'Who pays that sort of money in cash?'

'Kelli overheard Serena telling the customers that our card machines were broken. She figured that she was telling the truth, as you know how dodgy they are sometimes. Anyway, when Serena had been out for ages and still hadn't come back I called her mobile, which went straight to a robotic voicemail. I thought it was strange that she'd taken her coat and bag with her when the bank's just two minutes away. That's when Kelli realised that she'd emptied her desk drawers.' He sighed. 'That's not all, as part of this new email system Serena had put in place she'd secretly been contacting loads of our suppliers telling them we hadn't received payments, that all their cheques had bounced and it was a matter of urgency that they needed to resend their payments via her.'

Fucking bitch! My breathing was still erratic, but not from having raced here. I was fuming. Delirious with anger that this woman had come in here and stolen from us.

'I called the bank who hadn't any record of cash being deposited today and I asked Kelli to call you whilst I was onto the police,' Ben finished, looking like he might cry himself.

So not only did we have Chris Kennings breathing down our necks with his article that could threaten our business but now we also had pissed-off clients, had lost a huge wad of cash and one rogue member of staff. Great, just great.

'I took my eye off the ball. I fucked up,' Ben said quietly, biting his bottom lip.

I sighed and walked over to his desk, gingerly placing my hand on his hunched-up shoulders. 'That makes two of us.'

He looked up at me, visibly crushed. 'This could ruin us.'

'I know.' I blinked back tears.

I didn't know what else to say. We'd both made mistakes, and our decisions had resulted in very unwise business actions. The phone rang, its shrill tone interrupting my thoughts of hiring a hitman to track this bitch down.

'I'll get it!' Kelli shouted. I'd forgotten that she was here, sitting in the corner shaking her head and wiping her eyes at the realisation that Miss Serena-perfect-knickers was a figment of our imaginations and that she'd taken the Battlestar Death Wing gig tickets with her too.

'I've been onto the police and the bank. As she didn't have a formal contract here – another thing I'd meant to get around to sorting out – and the address on her CV was made up. We have no idea how to track her down. Even her name was fake. Serena DeVere doesn't exist.' No wonder I couldn't find any record of her online. That skank, she fooled us all! 'And as we were dealing in cash, I don't think we're going to get a penny back.'

Kelli put down the phone and shouted over, her voice sounded distorted. 'That was the *Daily Times*; the article will be out tomorrow.'

'Well that's it then. We're fucked,' Ben said, banging his fist on the table.

I winced, feeling Kelli's large eyes well with tears.

'Really?' she asked, wringing her pale hands together. I tried to give Ben a look, hoping to telepathically tell him to calm down and stop frightening our young assistant, no matter how furious he was.

It seemed to work as Ben's shoulders dropped and his voice softened, 'I'm sorry, Kel, but it looks that way. I just don't know how we're going to come out of this financially positive, let alone after all the negative PR we'll no doubt receive.'

'But you two will work out a way, won't you? You always do!' Kelli stuttered, flicking her head between us both. 'There can't be no more Lonely Hearts Travels, no more Georgia and Ben. You two will fix this, won't you?'

It felt like he'd just told her Father Christmas didn't exist by the way she was willing us to be making all of this up.

'I don't think we can, Kel,' I said quietly. My head was banging, my legs felt like jelly and I just wanted to lie down and sleep for a thousand years. 'Maybe it's best if we close up early today – all go and get some rest. By the looks of things, tomorrow is going to be a busy day,' I suggested sadly.

Ben coughed and nodded. 'Good idea.'

We all turned off our laptops, the fight inside us gone, and flicked off the lights.

'Well, I'll see you tomorrow then?' Kelli said, rubbing her nose with a tissue before fixing a steely look on me. 'Please, Georgia; I know you and Ben can save this. You are the best partners I've ever seen.'

I smiled sadly. 'We'll try our best,' I said, not knowing what to add, and closed the door behind her before facing Ben who was tapping his pen on his desk absentmindedly. He looked like he had the weight of the world on his shoulders.

'Poor girl, she seems terrified. This was her first proper job you know,' I said, watching Kelli wander down the street feeling a pang of emotion for our emo geek. 'She seems adamant that we will fix this. I only wish I was that confident.' I shook my head. 'You ready to go too?'

He let out a deep sigh. 'Kelli's right.'

'What?'

Ben turned to face me, the anger had left his face and in its place a sad sort of realisation. 'She's right, about us.' He paused. 'About us being good partners.'

He arched his fingers before pressing them up to the corners of his closed eyes. 'When you suggested the idea of the Lonely Hearts Travel Club I was so excited to see what we could achieve, together. But as time's gone on, the business has just moved too fast compared to what I was expecting, and I guess I wasn't prepared enough for that. I've never stayed in a place as long as this, never had a nine-to-five job before, and to be honest, at times I find it tough. Why would I want to swap travelling the world to watch other people do it instead? Office jobs have never suited me, let alone having to schmooze clients and play along with the corporate crap.'

I stared at the floor in shock; he'd never been this honest with me about the business before. 'But you know every new business has to fight for the first few years?' I said, my voice sounding high-pitched and wobbly.

'Yes, and don't get me wrong, I do think the business and the brand, what you're trying to achieve, is incredible.'

I wasn't sure I liked where this was going. 'What *we're* trying to achieve.'

Ben sighed and nodded sadly. 'Yes, what we're trying to achieve, all three of us.' He paused, fixing his deep eyes on me. 'But even though I sometimes feel like my wings have been clipped I wouldn't want to be anywhere else. Even today.' He laughed. 'The reason this whole Lonely Hearts Club works is because of you.' He cleared his throat before continuing. 'It's you. It's always been you.'

I felt the room tilt. I couldn't breathe. Those memories of us, the ones that had softened around the edges over time, suddenly came back in super sharp focus. I felt like no one else existed in this city, in this world, apart from the two of us right here, right now.

'But we were just friendly colleagues. I thought you liked Serena,' I said.

I saw his jaw clench at the sound of her name. He took a deep breath. 'Georgia, you don't realise how special you are. When we were in Thailand, Shelley told me about your past, about being engaged to a guy who just tossed out this beautiful girl, an idiot who didn't realise just how lucky he was to have you.'

I stared at him, willing him to continue, shocked that he had never mentioned my past to me before. I'd never wanted him to see me as damaged goods.

'I tried to pluck up the courage to ask you for more than just coffee so many times, but I was scared. I was scared that you would think of me as just another guy desperate to get into your knickers, or that I would be the rebound. You deserve more than that.'

A big fat tear rolled down my cheek. Ohmyfreakinggod Ben actually liked me. It was too much to take.

'But…but you hardly know me.'

'I know what I can see. This strong, fearless woman who has had a heap of shit piled on her, but has handled it with grace, dignity and the courage to make changes. You don't know how inspirational and amazing you are.' He boldly moved his hand to take a loose strand of my hair and tucked it behind my ears whilst looking directly into my eyes. 'I know more about you than you think. Like how you make this adorable sound when you're eating something you really enjoy.' I blushed. 'Like how you practise your speeches in the bathroom when you think no one can hear. Like how your nostrils flare when you're reading important emails. It's you, Georgia.' Ben smiled at me. 'Wherever you are, that's where I want to be.'

My mouth was dry; I was so confused, happy, tired and scared all at the same time. 'But what about the business? As much as Kelli hopes we will fix it, it's fucked, like you said,' I whispered, not wanting him to move his beautiful eyes from mine. God, he smelt so good. I probably smelt like a festival portaloo.

'I know; don't get me wrong. We will be fighting like hell tomorrow with whatever comes our way, but in case it really is all over then I wanted you to know how I felt. I should have told you a long, long time ago. I just had this sudden realisation that if it has gone tits up, I might not get the chance to say this to you. It might be the cheesiest, lamest thing on the planet to be stood here declaring my feelings for you but I knew I had to try.'

I shook my head. 'No, it's not cheesy at all.'

Suddenly I wanted to find Serena more than ever – not to throttle her, but to kiss her for what she'd done in getting Ben to profess his feelings for me. I felt like I was floating, my senses were heightened, and my irises had turned into hearts. I was sure he could see my heart fluttering under my blouse.

'I think I'm falling for you, Georgia,' he said, so quietly I was convinced I'd misheard him.

He glanced up through his long thick eyelashes at me, staring at me so intensely I gripped on to the desk behind me for support. Tears were freely spilling from my eyes.

'What? R- r-really?' I sniffed and shook my head lightly. 'Ben, I fell for you a long time ago.'

I wiped my eyes on the back of my hand as he cautiously stepped towards me and curled his arm around my waist. A simple movement that felt clumsy at first but then wildly amazing as we both grew bolder. I tiptoed to meet him. He dipped his head lower as we just gazed at each other for a moment. I'd never been so close to his face before. I'd never noticed the faint silvery line of a scar above his lip or the flecks of moss green in his dark eyes. I felt my legs weakening as he teased me, letting my body fizz with anticipation.

'You are wonderful,' he breathed and with that he tipped my jaw up to his and softly placed his lips on mine.

My breathing was all over the place; my head was filled with nothing but sheer joy, happiness and lust. He was an even better kisser than I'd ever fantasised about. His arm pulled me closer, completely up against his broad, warm frame and softly ran a hand through my hair. I felt my whole body melt and react to his touch. My heart was racing, our tongues exploring, our breathing heavy. I had never been kissed like this. Gentle *and* passionate. Full of unspoken words and lost time to make up for.

We eventually broke for air. Our chests rising and falling, the room coming back into focus. The silence around us suddenly sounded really loud as we tried to control our panting, all the while never losing eye contact. Was it always this quiet in here? I wondered. I suddenly got the giggles.

'What?' he asked, nervously pulling back and running a hand awkwardly through his hair.

I shook my head. 'Ben Stevens kissed me.'

'About bloody time too.' He grinned before cupping my jaw and dipping his lips to mine once more.

CHAPTER 35

Reparation (n.) The making amends for wrong or injury done

I walked down the clean antiseptic-smelling corridors of the hospital where my dad had been critically ill just last year. Every corridor looked the same with disorientating but identical minty green walls, meaning I'd been wandering around in circles looking for Honey Oak ward where Trisha was for bloody ages. I felt like I was floating not walking after Ben professed his true feelings for me. I couldn't stop grinning, which was strange considering my business was on the brink of collapse. I guess after surviving India and hearing Ben whisper the words I'd longed for him to say since I'd met him, it put things into perspective. I felt stronger and ready to fight what tomorrow would bring, knowing that he was firmly by my side.

After forcing our lips away from each other we'd locked up the shop and I'd headed here to see how Trisha was doing. Although Ben had told me she was fine, just bored stiff due to being cooped up on bed rest, I still felt like I should make the effort to see her. Plus, I needed some time to compute everything that had happened in the last twenty-four hours, both good and bad, and try to come up with a plan for how we were going to save our shop.

Not seeing any hospital staff wandering around I sighed and decided to head into the small café that I must have passed at least twice to ask for directions. A plump lady with an ample chest smiled at me as I entered.

'All right, lovey? What can I get for you?'

'Oh, sorry, I'm just looking to find out how to get to…' I paused, feeling my stomach do that strange flippy thing as I realised who was sat at one of the few tables laid out behind the counter. What was she doing here?

'Doesn't matter,' I said distractedly to the busty woman who tutted. I edged over to her table, feeling another wave of anxiety wash over me.

'Oh my God! So you really are sick? Oh no, what is it? What's the matter? I knew I should have tried harder to see you more, to be a better friend,' I blurted out a hundred miles an hour at Mike and a pale-looking Marie through tearful eyes. 'I am so sorry.'

Marie looked at me strangely. 'Georgia? What are you on about?'

'You're sick, aren't you?' I looked between the two of them and realised that Mike actually seemed to be really cheerful for someone with a dying girlfriend.

Marie shook her head and laughed before pulling out a chair for me to sit on. 'I'm not sick –'

'Oh, thank the Lord,' I said.

'Well I was for a few days, but it turns out I wasn't sick sick.' She looked at me as if I should have the faintest idea at what she was trying to get at.

'What?'

'Georgia. I'm pregnant.' She let out a quiet scream and gripped my hands.

I flicked my gaze between her and Mike and suddenly saw that on the table in between their empty cups and empty crisp packets was a grainy black and white photo of an ultrasound scan.

'No! Wow, oh my God, this is amazing news!' I hugged them both.

'Thank you, and it's me who should be offering you an apology for being a crap friend,' Marie said, fiddling with a sachet of sugar as Mike went to get me a drink.

'No, it's me.'

'No. I have a confession to make.' She took a deep breath. 'You know they say being pregnant makes you a little crackers sometimes?'

'Oh yeah.' I rolled my eyes and let out a little laugh. 'I remember before you found out you were having Cole you suddenly became almost stalker-like for Shane Richie.'

She blushed and checked Mike wasn't around to hear that. 'Yep, so this time those hormones happened again although instead of Mr Richie…it was passport stealing.'

It took a moment for this to sink in. 'You took Shelley's passport?'

'I am so, so sorry. I've been in touch with Shelley to apologise and asked her not to tell you until I'd had the chance to, but then I had really bad morning sickness, well, all-day sickness, and there was no way I was going to tell you this over the phone. I was actually planning on coming to see you this weekend with the news. Please say you forgive me.'

No wonder I hadn't heard much from Shelley.

I pulled her into a hug. 'Of course.'

'Anyway, aren't you meant to be at work?' She glanced at the clock.

'Well, let's just say that you're not the only one with news.' I sighed and told her everything.

CHAPTER 36

Aftermath (n.) Consequence; result

The following morning after barely a couple of hours' sleep I raced to the local newsagent who was just pulling up his shutters. I was still wearing my onesie and had scraped my hair up in a pineapple on my head; it couldn't be worse than the images Chris had slyly taken when we were away and probably published. I'd planned my route to tackle all the nearby newsagents; I was going to buy every single copy before anyone else could. As helpful as Marie had been yesterday I was still no further on with a solution to our business problem, and this was the best plan we'd come up with. I stacked all the copies I could onto the counter, nearly knocking over the pick and mix sweet bags.

'Anything else, love?' the guy behind the counter asked through a loud yawn.

'You don't have any other copies do you?' He shook his head. 'Just these then, thanks.'

He took my cash, barely raising a pierced eyebrow at the scruffy woman with a voracious reading appetite.

'Thanks, come again,' he said as I raced out of the shop.

I sat on a bench outside and closed my eyes before taking a deep breath and flicking through the crisp pages. News, news, news. Ah, business. Oh fuck. My gurning face, splattered in paint at the infamous night of the Holi party, took up half the page with the headline 'UNDERCOVER BOSS UNMASKED ON TRAVEL TOUR=' in intimidating block capital letters. I took a deep breath and read…

The Lonely Hearts Travel Club, a travel tour agency designed to get sad singletons back on their feet, has been a rising star in the tourism market since it launched last November. But, in the wake of damning online criticism, has this new Manchester-based business got what it takes to survive? Chris Kennings reports.

THE boss of tour agency The Lonely Hearts Travel Club risked her reputation by posing as a hairdresser to get the inside scoop on her own business — but did she dupe her own customers? Georgia Green, who set up the tour agency for newly-singles after suffering her own heartache, secretly travelled to India for the low-down on trips organised by her company in the wake of scathing criticism on a popular travel blog.

In a particularly damning post, Lonely Hearts Travels were blasted for sending clients on a substandard, disorganised and shambolic trip, hosted by a 'lazy' and 'rude' tour guide. The *Daily Times* signed up to the two-week India trip to investigate the allegations — since retracted by the author — only to discover Ms Green among the tour group, posing as Louise, a jilted hairdresser from Manchester.

Unbeknown to five other travellers on the trip, she masked her true identity, presumably to investigate the blog's damaging claims for herself.

But was it right that she faked who she really was in front of her very own customers? On the tour, which took in the sights of the Taj Mahal, the madness of Mumbai and the beaches of Goa, Ms Green may have fooled the other guests, but not I.

Uh-oh, I thought. Here it comes…

Before booking my trip I made a quick visit to the firm's base in Manchester, I had been impressed by the professionalism and attitude of her small band of employees.

So, I was curious to know why she felt the need to lie — was this an easy excuse for a getaway of her own or an extraordinary step to ensure her company was up to scratch?

At the start it was difficult to tell.

On the first evening in New Delhi, Ms Green hid little as she indecently exposed herself, while singing awful karaoke in a busy Indian restaurant. I shared a small and extremely basic beach hut on the sandy shores of Goa with her and was even flatulated upon during a yoga class.

As time went on, Ms Green took no notes, as far as I could tell. There were no reports back to her sales team and she asked no questions of the group about how things could be improved or if we thought the trip represented value-for-money. Had I been asked after the first few days, I would have argued that it didn't.

But it soon transpired that Ms Green had been making improvements in a far more subliminal way.

Behind the scenes, she had been working her magic on our tour guide, Nihal. This flaky, lazy man who we met on our first evening evolved into a competent and passionate tour guide. He was no doubt helped by the surprise recruitment of a female tour guide, Ameera. Together, they created the perfect double act.

The dynamics, relationships and professionalism of the tour increased ten-fold by the end, which was in no doubt due to Ms Green's coaching and mentoring - and her willingness to get her hands dirty.

She risked her reputation in order to ensure her guests had the time of their lives and put their troubles to bed.

As part of the tour we starred in a Bollywood movie, filmed on a beach in Mumbai, and opened up to Hindu holy men in an awe-inspiring temple. The packed itinerary of activities meant that guests who arrived as strangers left as friends. They confided in one another about their relationship woes and returned home stronger.

One backpacker described her trip as 'priceless' — while another said he would 'never forget' his two weeks in India.

Her lack of transparency by going undercover was a risky move, and she could easily have been caught out.

But her passion, attention to detail and focus on service shone through. I thought this could have been a trip I'd remember for all the wrong reasons — but I was wrong.

The Lonely Hearts Travel Club will make you glad you've just been dumped.

Oh my God! Oh my God! I scrambled to get my mobile out of my fluffy pocket to call Ben.

He answered in one ring. 'Georgia!'

'Ben! Have you seen – ?' I asked breathlessly.

'Yeah. What a bloody blinding article. I don't know how we pulled this off,' he said, with the croak still in his morning voice.

I shook my head and re-read the text, pulling bits of it to say out loud.

'The photo though…' I winced.

'The photo looks like Georgia. The one I met in Thailand, the one I know and fancy,' Ben said.

'Oh.' I blushed.

'You look great; don't worry. Also, I realised that you never actually told me what it was you got up to in India, something about naked karaoke…?'

I smiled. 'Err yeah, it wasn't *quite* as bad as that.'

Ben laughed. 'Well I'd love to know more. You fancy an early coffee? I'll meet you in our shop.'

'Sounds perfect.'

We had only just opened up when Kelli arrived in a complete daze, her kohled eyes wide and disbelieving as she stumbled through the door clutching a copy of the paper.

'I knew you could do it!' she shouted before racing over for an awkward hug.

'Ha ha, morning,' I laughed, squeezing her bony frame and getting a strong whiff of hair dye in my face.

'I've already shared it on my Facebook and Twitter. You should see how many people have commented and retweeted. It's got even more likes than when I posted a gif of a pug dancing to Marilyn Manson.'

'Cheers, Kel.' I smiled at her fondly as she picked up Serena's diamanté-framed picture of roses that was still lingering on my desk and unceremoniously dumped it into the bin.

'Take that, you stupid skank.'

My laughter faded as I realised that we still had this problem to fix. The article had been a huge and unexpected success but we still had lost a significant amount of cash and needed to make amends with a lot of suppliers. Ben must have read my worried expression as he handed me a cup of coffee and placed a warm hand on mine.

'I'll call the police again and see if they have any new leads. We just need to stay positive that she will be caught and that this great write-up will lead to more business. Maybe the police can track her through the gig tickets, catch her red-handed when she rocks up?'

I smiled gratefully at him and nodded. 'Fingers crossed.'

The rest of the day was a complete whirlwind. I'd had a call from my parents telling me that they'd sent clippings of the article to everyone they knew, although my dad had to restrain my mum from Tipp-Exing out the part where I farted on a national journalist. Shelley called me telling me she'd read it online and had already commented on it twice, although she was gutted she'd missed what sounded like an epic trip.

The phones didn't stop ringing with people who had read Chris's article and wanted to book themselves on one of our tours. The shop was full of excited, wannabe travellers flicking through our brochures, handing over deposits and at one point our website actually crashed due to the increase in traffic. All the signs were there for us to claw back some, if not all, of the cash that Serena had stolen from us.

'Georgia?' Ben had his palm covering the mouthpiece on his phone and a sombre look on his face. 'It's the police. They want to speak to you.'

I finished with a very excited woman who left clinging on to the brochure for the Indian tour and took the call.

'Hello?'

'Miss Green? This is Detective Wilkinson. I have been speaking with your partner Mr Stevens.' I could hear the rustle of papers as the policeman with the nasally voice checked his details before continuing. 'We will likely be concluding our investigation, as unfortunately we have very little to go on. Without your business going through the official protocol of verifying references and past employment, not to mention a very lax approach to the hiring process, we have no good leads in tracking down this Miss DeVere. We will continue to monitor the possibility of those gig tickets that Mr Stevens mentioned, but I wouldn't get your hopes up.'

My stomach dropped. I knew it had been a long shot and Ben had already apologised at how rubbish he'd been when he'd offered Serena the job. He'd never got round to sorting out her full-time contract either, meaning we had no concrete details for her or her history. I would still keep a small flame of hope that karma would deliver her what she deserved.

'I understand.'

'However, we have been able to check our records and even with these scarce details of this missing employee, it did ring a bell of a previous case my colleague was working on a few years ago in Hull. The circumstances are very similar and the woman matches the exact description you have given us.'

So she'd done this before.

'I know this is little consolation but you are not the first, and most probably won't be the last, to fall for a scam like this. In the future, I suggest you tighten your recruitment policy.'

I glanced round at the busy shop and smiled at Kelli who was in her element, comfortably and confidently dealing with the customer in front of her.

'Don't worry. It will never happen again. I already have the perfect employees.'

Once the last customer had filed out I literally fell onto the sofa exhausted and very overwhelmed. We had survived. I could have cried with happiness.

'Thought we should pop this open,' Ben said grinning as he brandished a bottle of champagne.

'Nice thought, but champers tastes like cat piss,' Kelli grumbled.

'Cheers, Kel, well luckily for you I got you a couple of bottles of fluorescent green alcopops.' Ben laughed as Kelli's eyes lit up.

I sat up, shook my head to wake myself up and accepted the cool, crisp bubbles Ben had poured into my favourite mug. Thankfully he had saved it from Serena when she chucked all the others out. 'Thank you. I've ordered us a takeaway too.'

'We should nearly go bust every day.' Kelli laughed. 'What did you go for?'

'An Indian, of course.' I smiled.

'Brilliant choice, so raise your glasses or mugs everyone,' Ben said. 'I want to say a huge well done to all of us today; we definitely deserve a drink. Kel – you have been a complete superstar and I know you're gutted at missing out on going to see Battlestar Death Wing.' Kel shrugged, trying to hide how disappointed she felt. 'So, I've made a few calls and have managed to bag you a pair of tickets for when they play Liverpool. I couldn't quite get you front row but at least you'll be there.'

'What! For reals?' Kel jumped to her feet, sloshing lurid green liquid as she did, and hugged Ben.

'All right, calm down.' He laughed. 'Just don't even think about asking me or Georgia to go with you.'

I smiled at how excited Kelli was, and she promised Ben she would take this guy she had her eye on instead of us, and was straight on her phone tweeting all her followers with the news.

'Georgia – I also have something for you.'

I wanted to say that I hoped it was his hot naked body but bit my lip and stared at him expectantly. 'Oh really?'

He came and sat on the sofa with me, and I felt this shiver of excitement as he put his arm around me. It felt so natural, but also filled me with this strange new bloody fantastic feeling.

'I've been thinking about what you told me about those street children you saw in Delhi.'

My stomach clenched. Immediately the vulnerable, ghostly eyes of that little girl begging on a busy street swam into my mind. 'Yeah.' I suddenly felt extremely guilty that we were sat here in the warm drinking champagne and toasting our success when she was God knows where, with God knows who.

'I was going to bring it up at our next staff meeting.' His eyes creased with a slow smile. 'But I wanted to propose a new initiative for the business, especially now that we seem to be far from closing.' He paused as I tilted my head. 'I haven't yet figured out all the details, but I want us to launch the Lonely Hearts Foundation, a not-for-profit fund that will go directly to the charities we choose. It means I get to use my knowledge of the charity world and we get to help others. A chance for us and our customers to give back to the places that they've travelled to.'

I smiled, looking up at the handmade craft that Ameera had given me in Goa, which took pride of place above my desk. 'That's an incredible idea,' I breathed. 'Seriously, you're amazing, you know?' I leant over and kissed him softly on the lips. The thrill of being able to do this and not waking up from it being all a dream was insane.

'Get a room already!' Kelli shouted out as she covered her eyes.

'Right, I say we finish our curry then close up the shop and all head on to the pub.' I laughed and rose to my feet.

Kelli stared at me and seemed to nod her head in admiration. 'I never thought I'd hear you say that.'

'Well, we've got a lot to celebrate.' I glanced at Ben who winked at me. I raised my mug of champagne. 'Here's to new adventures.'

'I'll certainly drink to that!'

Loved *Destination India*? Then don't miss the first book in The Lonely Hearts Travel Club series:

Destination Thailand

CHAPTER 1

Wanderlust (n.) A strong desire or urge to wander or travel and explore the world

It was my wedding day. A day I'd been fantasising about since I was a little girl, a day I had spent the last twelve months planning and organising. It was going to be a rustic English country wedding, complete with homemade bunting strung from the beams of an outrageously expensive manor house and a billowing marquee set up in the perfectly manicured grounds. The harpist would pluck a simple but charming set as we glided into the grand reception room with our nearest and dearest cheering and clapping our arrival as Mr and Mrs Doherty. That was the part I was cacking myself about the most; all those people staring at me, expecting a radiant blushing bride, when really I was terrified I would go arse over tit on my train. Being the centre of attention made my stomach churn and my sweat glands go into overdrive, but I'd limited the numbers as much as I could and *technically* I was only half of the centre of attention.

I should be in my creamy, laced, fishtail gown by now. As I glanced at my watch, I realised the hand-tied bouquets of soft powder blue forget-me-nots, complemented by the sweet scent of freesias, should have been delivered ten minutes ago. I should be preparing to sink into the plush chair at the pricy hairdresser's as they transformed my limp locks into a work of art.

Except that I was sat on an uncomfortable plastic sun lounger trying to hide the big fat tears falling down my slightly sunburnt face, as my best friend Marie passed me yet another dodgy watered-down sex on the beach punch from the all-inclusive pool bar.

In one hour's time I would have married my fiancé, Alex, but this had all changed fifteen days earlier when I was half-watching a re-run of *Don't Tell the Bride* whilst triple-checking the seating plan matched up to the 3D replica Alex's sister-in-law Francesca had loaned me. She was the one who'd been to school with Kate Middleton, and managed to bring it up into *every* conversation I'd ever had with her. Waiting for him to arrive home after yet *another* late shift at work, I had become so engrossed in this episode in which the henpecked husband-to-be had got it oh-so-wrong by choosing a size eight dress for his blatantly curvy size sixteen bride, that I hadn't realised Alex was standing in the doorframe chewing his fingernails and loosening his tie.

'We need to talk.' His voice sounded strangled and distant. His tie had an ink stain that no doubt I'd get chastised by his mother for not being able to scrub off. She'd pursed her lips many a time at my lack of domestic goddesstry. Alex had rebelled against it at the beginning, being the last single man in a family of smug married older brothers. I had been the breath of fresh air next to his Martha Stewart sisters-in-law. Five years later that sweet scent had soured into country air.

We'd met at a dodgy Indie nightclub in Manchester, having been dragged there by our respective best friends one wet Saturday night. Bonding over cheap lager in plastic pint pots, chatting like long-lost friends to the strains of the Smiths and the Kaiser Chiefs, as our two 'besties' got off with each other. After sharing a deep appreciation of cholesterol-clogging cheesy chips in the taxi ride back home, and a mutual love for garlic mayo, I knew this was something special.

The years passed, the clubbing stopped as focusing on climbing the career ladder became a priority. After years of renting mould-filled hovels with dodgy landlords, we had saved up enough to buy our own home. Alex had proudly turned down his parents' offer of financial support, so we couldn't live in Millionaires' Row rubbing shoulders with WAGs like the rest of his family, but he'd revelled in our bohemian charm even if it meant our neighbours were often more likely to be guests on *Jeremy Kyle*. I'd loved how steadfast he was to his morals, even if at times we could have done with a helping hand.

So it was inevitable when one wet June night Alex asked me to marry him. OK, so it wasn't the engagement of my dreams. He hadn't even got down on one knee, just passed the ring box over as we shared an Indian takeaway, both of us on our iPhones half-watching *Coronation Street*. He did leave me the last poppadum, so that was something, I guess. Of course that wasn't the engagement story we told people. No, in that one he'd whisked me away unexpectedly, showered me with unconditional adorations of love and asked a nearby elderly couple to take our photo; me blubbing and him bursting with pride, shame that they couldn't use the camera properly, meaning we had no evidence of this. But real life isn't like a Disney film, is it?

However, with both a mortgage to pay and a wedding to save for we'd gone out less and less. So yeah, maybe life had got a little stale; routine ruled our world and

I could recite the TV guide off by heart, but we were building a future together, that's what we both wanted, wasn't it?

Looking up at his tired face in the doorway, I didn't recognise the man that had bounded into the basement club years earlier asking me to dance. Then looking down at myself in stained oversized pyjamas, I didn't recognise the fresh-faced girl who'd said yes.

'It's not working…I, I, can't marry you,' he stuttered, his thin fingers nervously twitching down his stained tie.

He'd met someone else, a girl from his work who he'd started to develop '*feelings*' for. He didn't want it to be like this but he had changed, we had changed. He didn't need to spell it out but his mother was right, I just wasn't marriage material. As with the voluptuous bride on the TV in the too-tiny dress, I felt like I couldn't breathe. He packed his bag that night and left, as I sobbed, drank an old bottle of peach schnapps, spilling half onto Francesca's seating plan, and curled up in a ball not believing my world was falling down around me.

'Come on, let it all out.' Marie rubbed my sun-heated back as tears plopped into my now warm glass. She had decided that we had to get away for what would have been the big day, so hastily booked us a week's last-minute holiday to the Aegean coast, dubbed the St Tropez of Turkey. This accolade had obviously come from someone who had never visited Southern France, as the once-sleepy Turkish fishing village was now a prime party spot full of neon-lit bars, kebab shops and tattoo parlours. Not that we had hit the town – the past few nights had been spent playing cards on the balcony, downing a bottle or two of cheap white wine, Marie slagging Alex off, as I fluctuated between brutal put-downs and scared sob-fests that I wasn't strong enough to be alone.

'Thank you. It's just… Well, that's it…done.' I wiped sweaty strands of hair from my blotchy face, fixing my red-rimmed eyes on Marie's. She winced, not just at my appearance but because her idea of guaranteed sun, hot men and an all-inclusive bar being the perfect solution to my pain wasn't exactly going to plan.

She paused for a moment rearranging her small bum on the hard seat. 'Think about it, Georgia, you're exactly right.' She paused. 'It is all in the past and now it's time to look to your future. And as we're both single ladies, the best way to get through today is to show Alex a big fat two fingers and have a wicked time together. So I'm taking charge and I rule we're going to the beach.' Marie jumped up, stuffed our things into an oversized Primark beach bag and put her extremely large floppy sun hat on.

'I guess,' I pathetically murmured, gulping the dregs of my drink.

'Come on! You can do this, I know you can. Let's work on our tans and then tonight we'll find a really cool place to go and have fun, just the two of us, like the old days.'

I nodded and scraped my chlorine-soaked hair up into a messy top knot and jogged to catch up with her, my cheap flip-flops loudly slapping against the wet tiles. Strolling down the small rocky path connecting the hotel to the busy beach, our eyes took in row upon row of full sun loungers.

'Bugger, it's a bit crowded isn't it?' Marie chewed her lips, clasping a hand over her eyes to see further, even though they were covered in oversized Jackie O sunglasses.

'Yeah, you could say that,' I sighed, my resolve slipping as I thought longingly of an afternoon snooze back in our room between crisp white sheets. The sound of laughter, cars tooting and music wafting out from the competing beach bars was making my head spin. *Why couldn't Marie just let me sleep today and wake me up once the church, the cake cutting and even the first dance had passed?*

'Come on, hun. Let's wander along a bit, I'm sure I overheard there's a little cove not too far away,' Marie said chirpily, acting like a Girl Guide off on an adventure, which belied the fact she had been expelled from Brownies for giving Tawny Owl food poisoning trying to get her cook badge.

Snaking down the sandy beach, past thick fragrant bushes, and successfully navigating rocky steps we eventually arrived at a pristine horseshoe bay, which had just a smattering of sun loungers. I felt my bunched-up shoulders relax a little. We had found a small oasis of calm from the chaos of the Turkish town. With the quiet and unspoilt topaz blue bay glistening ahead of us I let my toes spread out on the sand, inhaling the balmy air which carried familiar smells of coconut sun cream and greasy chips.

We settled on two loungers and stripped off to reveal reddening skin. If she wasn't my best friend, I could really hate Marie. Her toned figure hid the fact that she had a son, Cole, who was the unexpected result of a jaeger-bombed night of passion with Mike, a guy whom she'd met down at her local. With long, fiery-red hair that she only admitted to 'touching up', plus the dirtiest mind and most caring personality, she commanded the attention of any room she entered. I wished I were more like her; secretly I had always hoped that by hanging out together some of Marie's sparkle would rub off on me.

'Hello there, ladies. I'm Ali. Just the two beds is it?' A local man in his early thirties with a smiling tanned face bounded over. He was topless, wearing just a necklace holding an animal tooth which pointed to his six pack, and his sculpted chest was adorned with faded tattoo script which crept down into the waistband of his battered denim cut-offs.

'Yes please.' Marie smiled up at him.

'It's suddenly got very hot around here.' He winked, taking our money.

Marie's eyes followed his admittedly nice arse back to his beach cabin before turning to me grinning. 'Phwoarsome or what?'

I made a noise between a huff and a sigh. Members of the opposite sex were so far off my radar right now I needed to wear binoculars just to see them.

'Oh come on, Georgia. You can't pretend that a bit of eye candy doesn't stir something deep in those closed-off loins of yours?' Marie laughed as I rolled my eyes. 'You know what, I'm suddenly really thirsty, want a beer?'

'Strange that the bar is right next to his hut.'

'Maybe.' Marie ignored my raised eyebrow and delved into her bag bringing out a pen and unscrunching a flyer that we'd been handed for a ladies-drink-free night. 'Anyway, while I'm gone I have a plan for you. I think it's time to make a list. I know how much you love them, plus my mum's always said, "if in doubt, write it out."' She paused with the pen lid pressed to her lips. 'I want you to make a list of everything you want to do and see in your life. Kind of like a bucket list, but with no terminal cancer spurring you on.' She passed me the pen, moist at the top, and the flyer, blank side up.

'I don't know what I want any more. I thought I knew. I had everything planned and sorted, but now I feel like I'm in some horrible limbo,' I whined. But I took the soggy pen as it was true, I did love a good list. There was something about the control you get from emptying your head by simply jotting your thoughts down, then the satisfaction when slicing through them with a big fat tick once completed.

'No. You've moped enough and now it's time to make changes and take action,' Marie said firmly, looking as if she was scoping out a nearby rock as a makeshift naughty step if I didn't play along. 'What's happened has been shit. Really shit. But think of it like this, at least you never have to see his demon mother again, never have to worry about fitting in on their ridiculous family getaways. No more putting up with their la-di-dah ways.' She pursed her lips and cupped her hand like the Queen waving – not a bad impression of Alex's mum Ruth, to be honest. 'I wouldn't be surprised if all this time he's been taking that trust fund they offered him, but then playing the *I'm one of the common people* card. Bastard.'

I sniffed loudly.

'I know it's hard. But please try and think of the positives, hun. If you don't know what you do want then maybe think about what you don't want.' She paused, adjusting her sunglasses as Ali waved to her from his beach cabin, tearing his eyes away from a nearby game of beach volleyball. 'You don't want to be with he-who-shall-not-be-named. You don't want to be living in my spare room for the rest of your life. You don't want to be some lonely boring cat-lady –'

'– Only because of my allergies,' I returned.

'No. You don't just want to be someone's other half. You need to be a whole and we're going to get you back on track with a plan that's going to do that.' She smiled gently. 'Just give it a go, please.' She pecked me on the top of my head, tied on her sarong and headed off to buy us both a drink, sashaying effortlessly across the sand.

I glanced down at the blank paper so creamy and fresh, scared to write anything down, as it felt like committing to achieving it. The problem was, I had always had a plan. But now? Now, all that lay ahead was an empty space like this paper in my sweaty hands.

A family had taken the sun loungers next to ours and were chatting animatedly to one another in what sounded like fast Spanish, their foreign tones seeming so exotic compared to my broad Northern accent. I'd never learned another language, apart from my French GCSE thirteen years ago, but I could barely remember any of it. Maybe that's something I could do?

In fact, apart from this trip with Marie, I hadn't been abroad in years. What with saving for the wedding and the house, all of my summer leave was spent doing DIY or visiting Alex's family's second home in Edinburgh. When I was younger I had always dreamt that my salary would be spent on exotic trips, but my pitiful wage never seemed to stretch far enough. Even when I'd found a last-minute billy-bargain to Benidorm, Alex had scoffed that it would be like going on holiday with our neighbours, that only *those* types of people would go book a package deal then spend all week drinking English beer in an Irish bar. When I'd protested that by those sorts of people he could have been describing my family he'd pulled me close and nibbled my neck. 'Oh Gigi, you know what I mean. I love your family but maybe we need to think about the finances. My mum said Ed and Francesca are looking for someone to housesit their place in Devon for the week?'

To be fair, Alex had seen a lot of the world when he was growing up, so I had sacrificed my wanderlust dreams for him and his happiness, telling myself that one day I'd get some much longed-for stamps in my passport. I could cringe at how lame that sounded.

The nearby family pulled out a picnic blanket and opened a cooler box full of things I hadn't seen before.

Foods I didn't know the name of, had never tasted but which looked and smelled amazing. This is what I wanted to do. I wanted to be the girl who would *parlez* a new lingo effortlessly, who would cook up exotic recipes with ingredients I couldn't currently pronounce, who would have stories to share at dinner parties, '…oh, that reminds me of a time when I was doing a silent retreat in an Indian ashram', sharing facts and tales from far-flung locations, rather than grumbling about the rising property market or council tax brackets.

OK, I can do this. I started to write…

I want to eat the world. I want to explore, travel, learn and push my limits. I want to find myself. Mountains and oceans will be my best friends, the stars will guide me home at night and my tongue will be desperate to speak and share all I have seen. I want to travel.

Yikes. My pen kind of ran away with me there. I looked at the paper in my hand and tucked my legs underneath me. Apparently I wanted to become Michael Palin. OK, so how was I going to achieve all this? Just like before, the pen seemed to have a mind of its own.

Quit and go.

That simple, hey biro?

What's holding you back? No man, no children, soon to be no home. Just a crappy job where you constantly moan about feeling undervalued but stick it out as they have good maternity packages. Packages that you won't need now. Sell everything, buy a backpack and go.

OK, maybe the pen did have a point. My job as a PA at Fresh Air PR, a small but growing firm near Topshop on the high street, was where I'd stayed for the past five years working my way up from post-room assistant to personal assistant to the Director of Marketing; same office, same faces, same printer problems. The thought of not having to worry if I'd chosen the right mug to brew up in, not to be forced to drink through the mundanity of the Christmas parties, to avoid listening to petty arguments over who had the best parking space and what Boots meal-deals were the best value for money sounded pretty good. I'd got too comfortable; like everything else in my life, agreeing to things I didn't want to please others and not pursuing my own dreams for fear of failure or embarrassment. The routine of cohabitation had come naturally with Alex, even if there were times when I looked at my chore list, my shopping list and our practically empty social calendar and despised the domestic drudgery.

But where would I go and what would I do? *Pen, don't let me down.* I closed my eyes, breathing in the salty sun lotion-filled air and started to write.

Go skinny dipping in the moonlit ocean
Dance all night under the stars
Taste incredible exotic food
Ride an elephant
Visit historic temples
Explore new beliefs
Climb a mountain
Make friends with different nationalities
Listen to the advice of a wise soul
Do something wild

My hand was aching but my head was whirring. Then I caught myself, as a mix of doubts and reality sliced into my thoughts. *How can you do this? It'll take months of planning, saving, and organising. Where do you even start with a trip like this?! You'd never be brave enough to touch an elephant, let alone ride one. The last time you did any exercise you nearly passed out, so trekking up Everest is out of the equation, and you cried when you had your blood taken, so how are you going to manage something wild like getting a tattoo?* The wildest thing I'd done recently was sleep with my make-up on.

I much preferred the dreamy freedom of my pen than my stupid conscience.

Today is meant to be your wedding day, or have you forgotten that? It's absurd that you're sat here writing about a whole new life you intend to start when you know you're not strong enough to change anything, I scolded myself.

We'll see about that, said my pen.

ACKNOWLEDGEMENTS

Ah . . . That awkward second book in a series . . . I hope I did you proud.

Thanks to my best friend Jen Brown who never ceases to amaze and inspire me. Speaking of inspiring women, I want to say a mahoosive shout out to the fantastic females in my family who push me to be the best version of me that I can be. The Taylor women are to be both feared and revered especially when we're 'doing a grandma'. Watch out world, is all I can say!

I wrote *Destination India* when I was living in France which wouldn't have been half the fun without the support from Manu, Laura, Anthony, Alexia, Edouard and especially Gill Lethuillier who has been so much more than an aunty. *Merci pour tous.* Thanks to my incredible parents and siblings Charlotte, Isobel, Jack and James for keeping me grounded during a time when I felt like I'd never come back down to earth.

I am so lucky that I get to work with such brilliant ladies including Victoria Oundjian, Lydia Mason, Jennifer Krebs, Hannah McMillan and blooming ace agent Juliet Mushens. Serious #squadgoals going on here. I have been blown away by the fantastic and never-ending support from everyone at Carina and HarperCollins, who knew I would be breaking records?! To my writing gang aka tireless cheerleaders, you know who you are. I ruddy love you.

To my friends old and new from all over the world, your messages of support have made me laugh, cry and burst with pride. Thanks to Anna Lloyd for letting me literally bounce ideas around during a game of ping pong and for making spaghetti bolognese the ultimate break up food. Thanks to a bunch of ace newshounds including Alice McKeegan, Nina Warhurst and Mel Dawkes for sharing both mine and Georgia's story with the world. Super special thanks goes to John Siddle:

I feel so lucky being able to share this with you. One day you'll get that drink/Greggs chicken bake that I owe you.

I am constantly amazed by the hardworking book bloggers whose passion for reading is seriously infectious including Laura Lovelock, Maryline VP, Simona Elena Schuler, Kelly and Lucy aka The Blossom Twins, Sophie Hedley, Kirsty Maclennan, Rachel Gilbey, This Chick Reads, Alba Forbe, Ellen Faith, Rebecca Pugh and Sharon Wilden.

Thanks to everyone who has bought, read, shared and enjoyed my debut novel *Destination Thailand*, I really hope you love this next stage in Georgia's journey even more! A huge hello and virtual squishy hugs to all followers and friends on NotWedOrDead's Twitter, Facebook and Instagram. Thank you for all the comments, RT's, messages and likes – you're the ones that inspire me and I'm thrilled to bits that we're on this adventure together. So, where to next?!